CLEVER AS THE DEVIL

A DARK ROMANCE MAFIA SERIES

AGOSTINO CRIME FAMILY
BOOK TWO

DAHLIA REIGN

Dear readers,

Dark romance is my specialty. Therefore, triggers lie within this book. You have been warned. Xoxo, DR.

About the Book

My name is Apollo, but to the men that make my list… Well, they call me il mietitore because I am the Italian fucking grim reaper.

He'd spent his youth fighting to survive, a kid forced to strip down to the most innate and basic of instincts. The doctors were quick to label him a psychopath, a diagnosis as damning as his cold, dead heart. Manifesting amoral and antisocial behaviors, he grew into a man incapable of expressing love. Instead, he fed on vengeance, bloodshed and the pleas of weaker men.

Apollo Deluca wasn't born into the Agostino Crime Family, but his salvation soon turned into theirs. He became the right-hand man to the Devil himself—just as clever and twice as twisted.

When a new adversary threatens the Family, and more specifically the eldest daughter to the New York City crime boss, will Apollo be able to overcome his inner demons in enough time to save her body and her heart? Or will Sienna Agostino fall victim to his dark past, destroyed by his sins and left in the shadow of a man who can never return her affections?

DEDICATION

TO MY READERS, OLD AND NEW. WELCOME TO THE FUCKERY I CALL HOME. I HOPE YOU ENJOY YOUR STAY.

PROLOGUE
APOLLO DELUCA-PAST

"You of all people know what it feels like to be raised without a family," Mario whispered from the back seat.

The car was idling at the curb outside an opulent restaurant that catered to the wealthiest and elitist members of New York Society. Their self-proclaimed aristocracy made them feel entitled to receive such luxuries as this establishment. From the car, I could see their diamond jewelry, expensive ensembles and their noses permanently raised in the air. The restaurant was glamorous with sparkling chandeliers and fine crystal stemware.

They made me sick.

They flashed their wealth like a coat of armor, as if their affluence allowed them to treat the less fortunate like peasants with no repercussions for their own demoralizing actions. But every action had a reaction. Every decision they made had a reverberation that I planned to execute with an efficiency karma lacked.

"He has two small sons who will no longer have a father. They won't even have a body to mourn." Mario paused to further drive home his point. "They will be left with an empty coffin in the ground and a tombstone naming him as their father. They will continue to pray that one day he will suddenly appear as if it was all a mistake."

"He won't," I growled, staring at the dead man walking before me.

"No, he won't. And all because of a decision he made on a whim, one that will forever torture innocent souls. And that will send him to his eternal damnation. His children are innocent, they'd…" Mario stalled.

"They'd be me," I clipped, my tone direct.

"They'd be who you *were*. But you're not that person anymore." Mario's phone rang but he ignored it. "Am I wrong, Apollo? Are you still that scared little boy who was living on the streets?"

"No. I'm not weak anymore." My breathing increased as my mind fought to stay in the present. To avoid the ever-present indignation that was threatening to overtake my consciousness.

"You're not weak. You protect the weak. You destroy the guilty to save the innocent and protect the *family*… your *family*. You may not have been born an Agostino, but you are a son to me." Mario's volume rose, his voice becoming sterner and more aggressive.

I straightened my spine and pulled my shoulders back as I honed in on my target. Mario was giving me the guidance and discipline to harness what he called *il demoni* within my soul. I didn't believe I possessed a soul, but he did. Often people said that the Devil was dancing on their shoulder, whispering evil thoughts in their ear. But the Italian version, *il diavolo*, was my brother and Mario's eldest son Lucifer.

You reap what you sow and, in my world… I destroyed those that have trespassed against the innocent and more importantly, against my family.

"He is the first on your list, Apollo. You will deliver the punishments and ensure justice is exacted for our family. And once a name has been added…"

"The only way they're removed is by their blood coating my hands." *You were as good as dead, the moment the ink dried.* As I reached for the door handle, my target rose from his table and headed towards the front entrance.

He smiled and waved at the other affluent patrons, his head held high with no remorse for his actions. And all of them returned his pleasantries—their good manners interred in their brains from a young age and as a result of a fine education. If they only knew what he did behind closed doors, they'd shun him from their group. Once word got out after his *disappearance,* I'd ensure the entire world knew exactly what he was—*rivoltante.*

"Go." I exited the car and moved silently into the shadows.

Several other dinner guests waited at the valet stand, muttering their impatience with the valet's speed. My prey stood among them, mocking the young kid for his speech impediment. As the cars returned for the other patrons and the crowd diminished, I stepped out from the shadows.

My expensive suit hid the tattoos coating my skin and allowed me the ability to present myself with the same allure of wealth and refined attributes. I didn't stand out—the exception, of course, being my towering height and considerable frame.

A bright red sports car pulled to the curb. I stepped forward, blocking the valet. I thrusted a hundred-dollar bill into the kid's hand and he happily flocked to his friend at the stand. I called my target to his car and he muttered rude comments, a pestering lack of patience due to misguided self-importance.

The annoyed and clipped tone spurned my embittered rage to boil over the surface. The steam blowing into the air was crackling with electricity, fueling my adrenaline to spike to dangerous levels.

I cracked my knuckles in anticipation of doing so many terrible, terrible things to this vile coward. He was a waste of human flesh and I knew this moment alone was going to be so satisfying. The promised high was igniting my affirmation that all of this felt so right, and akin to my true nature.

I loosened my tie and unbuttoned the top of my shirt, freeing my neck from the hindering ensemble I wasn't accustomed to wearing just yet.

He tucked his phone into his pocket and approached me in the street. With a quick glance to the valets—their attention focused on the large tip I'd given—I held open the door to his sports car, motioning him inside.

He wanted to ignore me, clearly an affliction of his wealth, until my large shadow entered his personal space. His eyes took me in from head to toe—suddenly alerted to the threat before him—his pupils dilating as he inspected the tattoos on my chest, now peeking out from under my open shirt.

Before he could open his mouth to speak, a solid punch to his kidneys made him collapse. In one swift movement, I shoved him into the car and forced his agony-riddled body into the passenger seat. His tortured moans and murmured pleas were a cacophony of static which, unfortunately for him, didn't register any empathetic feelings within me. I was a man on a mission and *nothing* got in my way—*I'd make sure of it.*

It was why Mario had chosen me. It was the value that I could bring to the Agostino Crime Family. Mario Agostino was a man of imminent power, the indisputable King of New York City. He empowered a large "family" of meticulous and savage individuals that ensured he stayed on his throne. And I was his *newest creation.* It all came so naturally to me.

The bedlam and bloodied chaos. The thrill and the chase—the sweetest high any drug could give—at his beck and call for the very specific messages he wanted to send to his foes.

I was *il mietitore,* the Italian-*fucking*-Grim Reaper. My mere presence alone affirmed that your end was near at the hands of my chosen scythe—whether it be knives or my bare hands. Whatever invigorated me as I ended your dismal and pathetic existence.

"How did it feel?" I directed my question to the slumped and barely conscious man. He was tied to the metal table and stripped bare.

"Huh, wh-what?" he mumbled, his eyes opening wide and taking in his surroundings. "What the fuck? Who are you? What the fuck are you doing?" he stammered, echoing the same questions screamed by my previous tortured souls.

"Answer me." My pointer and middle finger pressed into the center of his forehead, slamming his head back down onto the table. "How did it feel? Did you enjoy his cries of pain? Did he call out for his mommy or daddy?"

"Do you know who the fuck I am? You *can't* do this to me. I have money… connections." He was a blubbering mess, shaking the metal frame and roaring with all his *terrible* might.

"I know *exactly* who you are. Eugenio Affanad, once a member of Mario Agostino's trusted counsel. Husband to Mary and father to two sons, Carlo and Fausto. Owner of a dummy corporation that Mario started for you... when your first two restaurants failed. A wealth created at the hands of Mario, and his introduction into the society you so desired to belong to. And a fucking philanderer with a grotesque affinity for little boys." I snarled the last sentence.

His fear was dripping out through his pores and the smell permeated the air like an alluring perfume. My hands shook with the need to start my fun, but I also knew that he deserved to be punished—both mentally and physically—first and foremost.

I'd promise to let him free, if he repented his sins and promised to cleanse his evil ways. Though, in reality, I'd make him beg and plead as I peeled his skin from his body—one limb at a time.

"Tell me. Have you touched your sons too?" His eyes popped open and a look of disgust marred his face as he hurled some creative words my way. "No, that's right. They're too old for you. Fausto is fourteen and Carlo is twelve. Your victims were younger."

I nodded to myself as I wandered over to my table of toys. It was a simple metal tray of common devices you may find in a home, but when used in the appropriate manner, they could exact an immense amount of pain. Pruning shears, a stapler, a lighter, a kitchen knife and other odds and ends littered the oxidized receptacle as I debated where to begin.

My hands shook with anticipation as I tried to control my need to start unceremoniously stabbing away at his body. I needed to pace myself.

"As if those perversions weren't atrocious enough, you spit in the face of the man who saved you. And then, just for good measure, you had to do the ultimate betrayal and steal from him. You of all people should know that Mario doesn't miss a single detail in *any* of his businesses." I chose the rusted steak knife. "He wanted you dead for the theft. He sent *me* in regards to the kids you hurt."

There is nothing wrong with enjoying the high you get from the cries of pain and the smell of blood. But be sure to breathe deep and make precise, conscious thoughts as you savor the pain you inflict. Slow and steady are the promises of true retribution and ecstasy.

Mario's words during my first kill assaulted my memory. He tried to teach me that it was okay to find gratification in it. He was my puppet master as he attempted to control my erratic movements. To give me the confidence to hone in on the man I was truly capable of being.

Mario had taken me to the best doctors in the city when he first took me under his wing. They all gave me the same diagnosis—*antisocial personality disorder. Or in layman's terms—I was a certifiable psychopath.*

Apparently, it was one of the hardest disorders to diagnose but these doctors didn't hesitate to deliver—with confidence—their assessment. Mario tried to teach me how to harness my lack of empathy and sense of detachment. The only true thing I felt was loyalty to Mario and his equivocation to make me part of the family.

"You are my first kill... unassisted. I guess you should feel pleased at that fact. Previous to you, Mario has attempted to teach me all the best ways to inflict pain." I held the steak knife in front of his face. "I am still learning and growing, but I must admit, I feel confident in my abilities to make you suffer."

No hesitation. No faltered movements. I began my arduous task of slicing my knife in a circle just under his knee. Skin was the largest organ in the human body but it was also the most complex—the three layers all had very specific jobs.

As I sliced, I started with the epidermis. This controlled the immune system and skin pigment. Less knowledgeable individuals didn't realize simple scratches could often be the deadliest.

The top layer of skin was directly connected to the immune system and if not properly cleaned, infection could manifest and rapidly metastasize.

I pressed down harder on the blade and sought out the dermis—the nerve endings and sweat glands. His screams heightened as his brain began registering the pain and in consequence, his blood pooled more freely against my knife.

The metallic smell permeated the air and it was pungent, but in the most strangely satisfying way possible. My hand, which had held a death grip on his knee, began smearing the blood across his leg on its own accord—as if it had a mind of its own.

Then finally I reached the subcutaneous tissue of fat and larger blood vessels. This was, by far, my favorite because the flow of blood damn near tripled and poured from the wound like a river of angst. It flowed down his leg, onto the flat of the table, and began dripping on the concrete floor of the abandoned warehouse. Once the incision was made, and encompassing his entire leg, I placed the blood-soaked knife back onto the tray.

Eugenio was covered in perspiration and nasal mucosa, mixed with a thick translucent stream of saliva dripping down his cheek. His body rattled the table and his chest wracked with erratic undulations of agony.

The straps on the table kept him in place as I dug my fingers into the now gaping wound. I felt around for the exact layer of tissue I needed and pulled downwards. The blood made my grip slip a few times as I pulled the skin down, revealing a small patch of muscle.

"Stay with me! We've only just begun," I roared, leaving a bloody handprint across his cheek and laughing at his tortured whimpers. "Did those little boys beg for you to stop? I bet they did. And I'd bet my life that you ignored their pleas. So, why should I listen to yours?"

"They… they were mine. J-Just part of a d-deal." His eyes held truth and bolstered the sincerity of his words.

He actually believed he was entitled to do what he wanted with them because they were merely a transaction to him. Rage like nothing I'd felt before tore a hole through my chest cavity and threatened to destroy my vascular system.

I, too, was once part of a transaction. A pawn in the sinister game of disturbed men just like Eugenio. But that would end tonight. He would end tonight.

"They were kids!" I screamed in his face.

His consciousness was fading quickly as his brain fought to shut down his nervous system, in order to escape the traumatic shockwave, sending blazing red impulses of pain throughout his body.

My mind faded, rational thinking dissipated, and my knife lifted in the air with no preamble to my inner discussions of drawing out his pain.

Over and over again, I lifted it into the air and buried it into different parts of his flesh. The table, Eugenio and I were all covered in his blood as I lost myself to my insatiable need to eliminate this depravity.

Once I came back down from my high, I surveyed the mess I'd made. Dozens and dozens of holes dotted his torso as his eyes stared lifelessly at the ceiling.

"Fuck," I grunted.

It was supposed to last longer. This was the exact warning that Mario had given to me. Control. I needed to harness my control.

I chastised myself as I gathered his carcass and wrapped it in plastic. The car ride to the funeral home Mario owned was short, and the director made quick work of sending Eugenio to the fiery pits of hell.

Once he was in the incinerator, I headed back out to my victim's car to take it to the junkyard and have it stripped. I was almost at my destination, when I saw the red flashing lights behind me. I cursed under my breath, knowing I was fucked, and grabbed my cell phone as I kept driving.

"You lost control, didn't you?" Mario questioned.

"I did. But I have bigger problems." The cop turned on his siren and it echoed in the car. "His body is gone but I am in his car and covered in his blood."

"Pull over and comply. I'll have you out no later than tomorrow night," he said, muttering to someone else in the background. "I just finished meeting with Anthony Moretti and Lucky is none too pleased with some facts that were delivered. I'll call the lawyer. Just hang in there, son."

Son. I fucked up and he wasn't mad. He still held enough concern and pride in me that he sought to maintain our relationship.

I began to edge to the side of the road when my cell phone started ringing. "This isn't a good time, Lucky."

"I need you to reach out to your contacts for information. I want a full report on Mirabella Moretti, Anthony's daughter." The sirens continued to blare in the background.

"Any particular reason you aren't asking your sister to do the work for you?" I pulled over and shut the car off. From behind his open door, the cop started shouting his commands, ordering me to exit the vehicle.

"Sienna's too fucking nosey, that's why," he ground out. His sister Sienna was indeed obtrusive, but she was quickly becoming a successful hacker and could acquire information on anyone. "Why're you being ordered around?"

"Mario already knows. I'll be getting arrested and charged with murder," I stated.

"Fuck. Me. Apollo."

"Depending on what my sentence is I just might take you up on that offer. I usually like a warm and submissive woman after a kill, but you'd probably be the prettiest thing in prison," I chuckled, earning me an amused cussed response.

"Pops is on it. Hold strong." He ended the call.

I rolled down the window and opened the car door from the outside like the officer had instructed. However, the moment he registered my tall, wide and blood-soaked appearance, the rookie panicked. He started calling in backup as I raised my hands in the air and dropped to my knees.

I wasn't concerned with what lay ahead. I had been locked up before, not just in jail, but as a child in a precarious situation. I knew Mario would pull strings to get me out, and until then, they'd keep me in solitary confinement as I waited for my release.

Anyone else would be apprehensive in regards to their fate, covered in the blood of a man who would soon be declared missing. Not me. A body was needed in order to declare a crime and a motive was required to establish one. Neither of which the New York City Police Department would be able to uncover. Not to mention, I had a fail-safe.

Mario Agostino was making calls to get me released and no one… And I mean no one, fucked with the King of New York City.

CHAPTER 1
APOLLO DELUCA-PAST

"Who would be stupid enough to steal from Lucifer Agostino?" asked Al, one of the loyal *soldati* to the *famiglia*.

Lucifer "Lucky" Agostino was the future King of New York in the mafia world. He was Mario's eldest son, and I was raised alongside him as an enforcer and his number two. Over the years, I had learned to harness my embittered soul as well as contain my compulsory rage to wreak havoc. Now when someone muttered *il mietitore*, there was no mistaking the pain and terror that would be inflicted on those unfortunate enough to find themselves on my list. That was me, *The Reaper.*

Mario had grown to be like a father to me, an idea I couldn't fathom previous to meeting him all those years ago. I was merely a broken and battered migrant that had fled certain death and trauma while living on the streets with my foster sister Cara. One fateful day, I just so happened to come across a particular corner store; one in which I thought to rob. I took note of all the usual vulnerabilities—*the place was practically asking for it.* However, I had no clue that it was a storefront protected by Mario Agostino—fuck, I didn't even know who he was back then—an oversight that could have gotten me killed. But he saw my potential and offered me mercy.

Mario Agostino was the kind of authority figure you didn't fuck with, not if it could be avoided and not if you valued your oxygen intake. Nowadays, he focused on his legitimate dealings, opting to let Lucky and I take over the relationships he'd built over the years. Guns, drugs, loan sharks and enforcers made up the majority of the income in our entrepreneurship. Lucky was creating an empire for himself out from under the name of his father—earning his own following and respect. And as his enforcer, I acted as his muscle and reassurance that his dealings were handled.

"I have my assumptions, but I am confident I will find answers shortly." The clicking of the phone filled the silence after my verbal confirmation.

The Agostino namesake controlled the docks on the Hudson River. Anyone who wanted to import or export through the docks had to pay homage to the Agostino's—top dollar homage.

Our base of operations, a warehouse on the waterfront, acted as a convenient place to conduct business away from prying eyes. As we waited for our security to unlock the gates, commotion across the street at the abandoned building caught my attention. A male realtor, a blonde woman and Dominic Moretti were standing outside talking.

"The fuck is he doing here?" Al muttered, rolling down the driver's side window.

"No fucking clue." Picking up my cell phone, I snapped a couple of pictures.

Dominic Moretti was the middle child of Anthony and Serafina Moretti. When it came to hierarchy in the mob-controlled city, that family was the closest competition against the Agostino's. Furthermore, Dominic's older brother, Gio Moretti, was who I assumed was fucking with our shipment. Lucky garnered his power and success from hard work and perseverance. Whereas Gio lied, stole and cheated his way to mediocrity.

My assiduity with which I used to monitor that family added this observation to our list of potential complications. When one parasite was able to make its way into your home, many more would try to follow through the cracks, which were inevitably left in its wake. And I planned to exterminate the stragglers long before there was an all-out infestation.

"Bad location for a titty bar." Al pulled through the gates, laughing, before parking the car outside our warehouse.

I rose from my seat, and standing to my full height, I watched the trio wander the sidewalk. Dominic Moretti owned a couple of restaurants and strip clubs around the city, crossing into New Jersey. There'd been rumors that his club was the front for a lucrative trafficking operation. That was a depravity *we* didn't mess with and wouldn't harbor in our city.

The realtor stood next to Dominic, and animatedly talking with his hands, he pointed to the building. The blonde at his side was tall and extremely thin with a sensuous sway to her slight hips. Her clothing was tight and revealing and she shifted on the high stilettos, as if she was forcing herself to stand still. The girl appeared lost in her own world as she stared up at the sky.

The portly realtor would send her appreciative glances—bordering on inappropriate—each time Dominic turned his back. As the men wandered further down the premises, I followed along our fence line in clandestine form. I visually examined the blonde and took note from the tense hunch of her shoulders that the constraint Dominic held on her arm was likely not affable; he was practically dragging her down the sidewalk behind him.

The more I watched, the more my internal nervous system was flashing red with warning. Dominic and I had graced the same social circles for years, and usually he was the portrait of platitude and impassivity. However, in this moment, he seemed to be losing patience and was vehemently angered by the small girl. I trailed further down the sidewalk, maintaining my obscurity from the assessment of their glares.

"Let me think about it and I will be in touch tomorrow." Dominic shook his hand and they went their separate ways.

The couple walked to the waiting car, his grip still wrapped around her slim arm. He continued to aggressively drag her in his wake, his contentious tone echoing in his stead. As they drew near, I could see that the girl was holding a fist at her side—her jaw closed tight—as she stared at the concrete in front of her. He pulled her onto the sidewalk, and closer to the fence, when his anger got the better of him.

"What the fuck did I tell you?" he yelled. "I took you out of your cage to test your training. And you, my little pet, you failed… pathetically."

The fuck? Dominic's words grated my skin; it was like an ice bucket of water was dumped over me. I knew what cages were like, cramped and demeaning. And meant to break you. My knuckles cracked as I continuously flexed my hands—in an attempt to absorb my natural reaction for *fucking* violence.

"I didn't do anything wrong." The girl's voice was strong with an undertone of annoyance. But each word was like a slap to Dominic's face. He growled in displeasure before throwing her against the car. Her svelte frame bounced off the unrelenting metal, flying forward. Dominic grabbed her by the neck and pinned her to the car.

"Nothing wrong?" he snarled in her face. "Try, you didn't do a-fucking-thing right." He slapped her across her profile with enough force to snap her hyoid bone and potentially cause irreparable damage to her retromandibular vein. To my surprise, the girl didn't make a single sound, instead merely holding her cheek and looking away from him.

"I'm sorry," she muttered. However, from my position, I could tell there was no sincerity in her voice.

"Get in the fucking car," Dominic growled, shoving her away from him as he straightened his tie in the vehicle's reflection. The girl stood extremely close to the fence—so close, I could hear her labored breath.

"Did you enjoy the show, lover?" She stared in my general direction, somehow attuned to my presence. "Come to the club, and I'll give you a real show." Her blue eyes lit up in amusement.

There was a depth, showcasing what lurked beneath the surface—a woman full of fire and a rancorous soul. There was no life or spark of sanity left in them, just a captivating shade of blue that wrapped up her stereotypical blonde hair supermodel appearance. Her mention of the club didn't surprise me. She was, no doubt, one of the best dancers Dominic employed.

"Now, Perse," Dominic ordered from inside the car.

My thoughts were rattled, inundated by the savage rage threatening to release the beast inside me. As far back as I could remember, there was a part of me that was detached from other human beings. Their actions were peculiar and unfamiliar to me, their emotions consuming them and hindering their ability to think rationally.

I'd learned to harness my rage and confusion over normal social interactions in order to perform methodical decision-making; while others appeared hell-bent on self-sabotage, allowing themselves to become collateral damage in the games played out by their betters.

As I stood in the shadows and watched the car drive away, I was unnerved by my unanswered questions. I didn't get as far as I had as a *made man* by being unprepared for potential attacks. I was inclined to decipher the threat, untangling whatever intricate web that sought to threaten the family, *before* it caused an impairment to our business. I assumed that a large warehouse with access to the water—free of the Agostino's fees—would be extremely lucrative for Dominic.

I stepped out from the darkness and headed back towards the warehouse, murderous thoughts exhausting my mind. Inside, there was a rat; one whose untimely torture at my hands would reduce some of my pent-up frustration. He would be my catalyst, telling me all I needed to know about the *stronzo* messing with our shipments. A few steps from the entrance, I pulled my phone from my pocket.

It rang twice before *she* picked up.

"Oh my, Apollo. To what do I owe the pleasure of you calling me in the middle of a workday? Something the *Almighty* wants from little ole me?" Sienna Agostino was as cavalier as she was intelligent. She was one of Lucky's younger sisters and also the biggest pain in my ass.

Previously, when I was trying to work my way up the ranks, I was tasked with watching Lucky's sisters, Sienna and Octavia. It seemed an easy stint to show my value, but the two girls couldn't have been more opposite from each other. For as quiet and demure as Octavia was—her nose forever stuck in a book while she was locked away in her room—

Sienna was a fucking lunatic. She loved to challenge my patience and add to my confusion; the perplexing emotions in women seeming to only further befuddle my already limited grasp on humanity.

She was just as calculated and savage as her father and older brother. She sat back with a silent intensity as she watched and acquired knowledge from those around her, much akin to myself. She could smell weakness, detect lies and plot your death—all from one meeting. She learned your likes and dislikes, watched your social cues to uncover all your secrets and didn't hesitate to use them against you. She was also one of the most impassioned women I'd ever met.

And she practically drowned in her own overconsuming emotions.

She was a cunning little bitch with soft brown hair, intense blue eyes and a tight body wrapped in tailored designer wear. People on the outside, looking in, saw a vivacious and gorgeous woman whose intellectual prowess was intimidating. She put on a sweet and endearing facade until she had the ammunition that she needed to take your legs out from under you. She learned all the grating mannerisms and quirks she could; the kind meant just to piss me off. And she fucking used them often.

She was too smart for her own good and just as cutthroat in her own business dealings. Her aspirations had been to get out from under the Agostino limelight, and to create a name for herself. She graduated at the top of her class in college and was now running a technological super company specializing in surveillance, creating apps and building supercomputers. The type of intricate and borderline ingenious industrial science that she would patent then sell to the highest bidder. She was a technological prodigy doing the dirty work for the family's background checks and pertinent Intel.

"I need information," I clipped.

"Of course you do, or else, why would you be calling?" she asked; the sound of her hands flying across keys echoed in the background.

Grinding my teeth, my voice dripped with agitation. "Fucking Christ, Sienna." I took a deep breath and counted to five, opting to ignore her loathsome giggle. "You're undeniably the most abhorrent female on the planet."

"I highly doubt that. We both know Tatianna takes that cake." She practically snarled the name of her high school nemesis.

"Dominic Moretti was just meeting a realtor across the street from the warehouse," I deadpanned.

"What in the world would possess him to buy such a large, dilapidated building near the wharf?" I could practically envision her tapping her lip as her mouth contorted into a snarl.

"It's why. The fuck. I am calling you," I grunted; the stones under my feet scraped across the broken concrete.

"Calm down, you crazy bastard," she muttered, the clicks on her keyboard resuming. "I'll sniff around his finances and see what I find."

Before she hung up, I halted her. "I need another favor," I said, breathing out my agitation as she chuckled once more. "He was with a girl." Her sharp intake of breath stalled my line of speech.

"And?" Sienna's voice was clipped, an undertone of anger boiling beneath the surface.

"My intuition is telling me she's a possible connection to the trafficking rumors in his club," I ground out; my jaw popped from the harsh movement. "Ten minutes ago, east side camera, aerial view two."

Silence stretched between us; the only indication that she hadn't disconnected was the sound of her rapid breathing. Sienna excelled in many things but her poker face—and often, the misguided actions that followed—was the poorest I had ever seen. She was intuitive, and could eloquently assess situations for risk. She operated her business with ruthless tactics in order to destroy all her competition, and she could drop a powerful shield to mask the crazy lurking inside her head.

But... when Sienna's feelings were hurt, she screamed it from the rooftops.

"Sienna." I waited a beat before hearing her huff, and then continued. "She showed signs of abuse and trauma. The probability of her being an asset and confirming our suspicions is extremely high," I added, softening my voice a degree.

"Right..." She gnarled into the phone before hanging up.

"Fucking little bitch." I looked to the sky, taking a deep breath before turning to Al. "What the fuck are you looking at?"

Al threw me a knowing grin. Sienna was one of his best friends and they both reveled in their shared ability to piss me off. The games each liked to play were sheer asinine. But put the two of them together, and they became a fucking nuisance, nothing more than pests tromping about—their sole intent to irritate me. It was hard to adhere to a code, that focused on concealing your weaknesses from your foes, when it was those closest to you that sought to make you suffer.

"Nothing, man. Nothing." He chuckled, holding the door open for me.

We had two prime locations where we conducted business, depending on the exact type of *business* we were handling. Lucky's penthouse sat above a secured basement that was an enforcer's heaven —a dungeon of torturous delight. The Agostino family compound outside the city was for more legitimate dealings. But this warehouse was used for all of the above and just so happened to be housing a conspirator I planned to dismantle—piece by piece—until I got a resolution. Subsequently, I'd make it known—a reminder, if you will—that we didn't tolerate operatives working in our midst; foes would not go unpunished.

I opened the locked room and Rocco, another of Lucky's men, stepped aside to allow me entrance. The rat—fuck, he was practically a kid—was chained to the chair in the center of the room; it was bolted to the floor to keep our victims in place. His fear permeated the air, like a thick repugnant cologne, and mixed with the odor of his soiled pants.

It sent a chill of excitement down my spine.

I walked towards the closet, ignoring the kid's pleas for mercy. I took off my suit jacket, neatly placing it on the hanger with my tie, and unbuttoned my shirt. Rolling my sleeves up, I turned back towards the *deficiente* in the chair; eyes wide with fear, he regarded my tattoo-covered body. I could practically outline the confusion on his face as he took in my biblical tattoos.

I wasn't religious nor did I believe in God. There was no way a God could exist if he created a creature such as me. I was born to rule as the gatekeeper for Lucifer, to punish those deemed guilty and sent to the fiery pits of hell. Not a single emotion or wave of remorse—for any of the turmoil I had inflicted—had presented itself to me in my entire life. God didn't prevail, but the Devil… he was my savior.

"Were you, or were you not, previously warned to stay away from Agostino property?" I motioned towards his missing fifth digit. "And yet, here you are, caught with a team of perpetual schmucks, armed to the gills as if they are about to start a war. Waiting for a shipment perhaps? One that never came?" I paced around him in a circle; his whimpering cries were music to my ears.

Once again, the Devil was dancing on my shoulder, urging me to douse my soul in blood.

Lucky and I avoided pilfering by switching schedules and locations frequently. This could mean only one thing—there was no other cogent argument—we were dealing with a traitor. I had too many open-ended questions and I refused to accept surprises. I'd get my answers from him… just like all the rest. One way or another, he'd fold. They all did.

"From past meetings, you know who I am and what I do for Lucky. Make this easy for yourself and answer my questions," I chortled, watching the front of his jeans soak with urine from a mere utterance of words.

"Wh-what do you mean? I didn't do *nothing*!" the jackass cried, his lies echoing off the concrete walls.

"That's a double negative." I frowned at him, his brows pinching in uncertainty. "Never mind."

There were no windows in the room, the only light from the small bulb above our heads—which flickered on occasion. Being locked inside a dark confined space, trapped with only your thoughts as you awaited your death, was a very fine form of torture. And one I'd learned to endure from an early age. My interesting childhood never dulled my mental predicaments; although, it was partly at fault for who I became.

"Cut the bullshit. You were there to steal a shipment. Who told you where to go?" I asked, leaning into his face so he could see the menace swirling behind my irises. "Two words, that's it. The name of the mole and the man you're working for."

When he didn't immediately respond, my barely-composed

patience shattered. Putting my dress shoe between his legs, I pulled the knife from my ankle holster. I engaged the switchblade in one motion, and in the next, it was embedded into his thigh. My eyes were wide with excitement—I watched as his internal nervous system tried to comprehend what I'd just done.

The human body was an interesting thing. The brain had many key components that controlled one's anatomy; it tried to protect all of its organs as best it could. The injury I'd administered to his thigh took several seconds to register, before sending unpleasant impulses throughout the rest of his body. His screams were heightened as his automatic distress signals recognized the pain, eliciting a satisfied smile from me.

"Tell me!" I roared, leaning further into his face. I removed the knife from one thigh and sliced through the flesh of the other—all in the same seasoned motion.

The unsolicited ring of my cell phone forced *il demoni,* lurking in the recesses of my brain, back to its cage. Stepping away from the pained cries, I wiped my blood-soaked hands down the front of his shirt. Once they met some semblance of clean, I grabbed my phone from my suit jacket.

It was Lucky.

"Boss." I spoke over the *cagna's* whimpers.

"Did you get an answer?" Lucky's voice was tranquil, and yet, it bore a vibration of anger.

"Just started." I affixed my prey with a stare of malevolence.

"Pops called a meeting. I want you there," Lucky commanded.

"Would you like me to leave him on ice until I get back?" My mind flashed with the prospect of a painful, and quite literal, ice bath.

"Al can take over. I'll be there in fifteen." Lucky hung up.

I put the phone back into my pocket before turning to my victim. "Sadly, my time is almost up. Bigger things to do and all. Do you want to save me from missing the fun and just tell me what I want to know?" I asked, watching the kid mutely stare at his bloody thighs.

"Am I taking over?" Al asked, cracking his knuckles and motioning forward.

"Indeed. I do, however, have fifteen minutes." I grabbed a rusted pair of pruning shears from the wall of decaying devices. "Last chance." He continued to ignore me as I stepped closer.

Without a word, I tugged his remaining fifth digit into the shears and squeezed. His agony was like a classical melody strumming softly in my head—I could visualize each and every note as it danced along with the blood-curdling screams. The chaos was a soothing symphony that overtook my senses. Clipping the ring finger on the opposite hand, I was lost to the torment I was inflicting. The room around me disappeared as I closed my eyes and listened to his misery. I was no longer capable of calming myself, of drawing out his suffering, instead opting to revel in the grotesque imagery I had just created.

"Boss is at the gate," Al announced, bringing me back to reality.

"Fuck. Last chance to please me." I pushed his foot with mine, only to be ignored, as he once again whimpered.

I washed my hands at the metal sink in the corner of the room, inspecting my appearance in the reflection of the rusted mirror above it. Buttoning the collar of my shirt, I unrolled my sleeves and retrieved my tie. Tightening it in place, I left the room with a nod to Al as I threw my jacket on and headed for the door.

Mario Agostino instilled many things since he took me under his wing; one of which was my attire. I dressed to paint the image of a wealthy and controlled man. Not a single one of my suits cost less than five grand and they were in constant pristine condition or I required a change of apparel. Though ink marred my skin, winding up my neck and almost to my face, my hair was cut weekly and my face neatly shaved or my beard cleanly trimmed. On the outside, I had smooth flawless lines. On the inside, I was a combination of chaos and unethical thoughts—attempting to navigate a world that was overrun with what I saw as melodramatic absurdities.

"Update," Lucky clipped as I climbed into the car.

"Nothing," I said, raising a brow at his mocking smile. "What?"

"You're losing your touch," he snickered, while texting on his phone.

"Hardly, I had just started. Your interruption was intrusive and ill-placed," I huffed, anger seeping back into my system.

"To *Vino*," Lucky ordered his driver. "*Had* just started… then I gave you an additional twenty minutes." Lucky put his phone down, his smirk growing into a large contemptuous grin.

"Fuck you," I murmured, the urge to beat the shit out of him encroaching upon my sanity; switching tactics, I focused on the meeting. "Why are we needed at *Vino*?"

"You know Mario Agostino. A command without any explanation," he muttered, turning back to his phone.

It was true. Mario was a man who didn't explain himself, the sort of man who demanded respect. If he was calling us for a meeting, something was going on. *Vino* was a restaurant in the center of New York City. It was prestigious, expensive and known to host mafia-linked families. In fact, it was owned and operated by the Agostino's themselves.

"Go," I answered my cell phone.

"Little bitch only took one more finger before he cracked." Al snickered as the rat begged to have his missing appendages put on ice. "Gio Moretti orchestrated the attack. He wanted the shipment. The kid doesn't know who the mole is. I'm starting to clean up now."

I hung up; my grin directed towards Lucky.

"You were right," I said, watching Lucky grimace; though he did not falter, as his attention remained on his cellular device.

Lucifer Agostino and Gio Moretti had been rivals from an early age. Gio wanted what Lucky had, and everyone knew that conniving little shit would stoop to the bottom of the barrel to try to take what wasn't rightfully his. He loathed the fact that Lucky was always one step ahead, a million bucks richer, and in turn, had that much more control in the city. This time when thwarting his plan, and for good measure, Lucky made sure he was *two* steps ahead. Lesson learned.

If you were going to come after a man, take what didn't belong to you and earn respect in doing so—you'd better succeed. And as always, Gio hadn't.

"I thought as much. It's always him. I'm officially fucking pissed.

He must be dealt with." Putting his phone back into his pocket, Lucky grinned at me.

"Ultimate punishment?" I asked, cracking my knuckles in anticipation.

"No. Not yet anyway... Besides, if anyone is going to empty a clip in him, it's going to be me. Because when that son of a bitch finally goes in the ground, he'll have no doubt who put him there. Truce be damned. My father may head the family on paper, but he knows better than to get in my way on this..." He paused. "No... Let the man sweat. I want it known, *I know.* We'll wait him out... give him just enough rope to hang himself. After all, idle hands are the Devil's playground. Let's see what he does." Lucky laughed as I sneered, a formidable union of power.

We pulled up to the front of *Vino* in well synchronized succession. Hopping out of our respective vehicles, I followed Lucky and another four of his men inside. As we entered the building, the hostess flashed a hungry smile in acknowledgement. I attempted to hide my physical quiver of disgust at this salivating *puttana*. She was the type of woman with little self-respect. She happily gave herself to the bottom of the food chain, assuming that made her *something*.

But she was nothing.

Without looking in her direction, we stormed past and headed straight for the private lounge. I had no idea what awaited us on the other side of that door, and still we entered unburdened by any further thoughts or hesitation. I peered around the room, the Moretti boys appearing in my direct line of sight. Though I was snarling internally, my usual shielded mask of indifference dropped over my face.

With the confirmation of Gio's attack, the tension was palpable; and the metallic sting of vengeance lingered on my tongue. I was surprised that Gio was not only back from Italy, but that he willingly dined in an Agostino establishment so soon after his failed attempt at thievery. At the thought of immediate confrontation, cowards like him ran with their tails between their legs, especially when cornered.

"Lucky, please join us." Mario gestured to the seat beside him as I motioned for Lucky's men to spread throughout the room. "Anthony, you remember my son Lucky, don't you?"

Blood was in the air—thick and fervent—and I could fucking taste it. Mario Agostino was a puppeteer and the Moretti men were his puppets... And I couldn't wait to see how he made them dance.

CHAPTER 2
SIENNA AGOSTINO

I couldn't help the devious smile that pulled tight on my face as I hung up the phone. It tickled me with delight to do everything within my power to rattle *il mietitore*. For all of his self-proclaimed control, in no capacity was he able to stay true to himself when I decided to play with him.

"Let me guess!" Octavia whispered from the other side of my desk. "That call must've been Apollo."

"Correct, per usual." I smiled at her.

My little sister was gorgeous both inside and out. She held the same Agostino steel-blue eyes as myself, and all the other Agostino children in fact, thanks to our father. We each had our own niche within the family and we played our parts well. Octavia just hadn't figured out exactly what hers was yet.

She was the third child and the sweetest human being you'd ever meet, though a bit of a recluse, often opting for a book rather than choosing to participate in family events. She came with a softness that the rest of the family vowed to keep intact.

Marco was the baby and the most useless member of our entire organization… and family. He was more akin to a gutter whore than resembling anything close to a viable Agostino male. He enjoyed women, women and more women—*but never the same woman*. One day, his world would come crashing down around him; and it would be the same day his actions had repercussions which his namesake couldn't save him from.

Lucky was the oldest and the future leader of the family, much to my dismay. Had I been born first—and, well, born a man—I'd have conquered the city by now, but whatever. He was in preparations to take over after our father stepped down; and at one point, that fact had filled me with such animosity, I was practically drowning in disdain for him. Like most things, I'd overcame that *phase* in my life.

After all, I was an Italian woman raised within this powerful patriarchy. I was to stand tall and proud of the men's accomplishments. A woman's worth was the shape of her body and the beauty of her face— not the brain in her head or the fire in her heart. I was fortunate that unlike most other girls in our circle, my father didn't allow us to feel inferior. Lucky had to take over by birthright as eldest son. But the Agostino's had a saying they held firm and true.

We are only as strong as our weakest family member.

A motto that bothered Octavia—she assumed she was the weakest —and that was of no concern to Marco. Whereas, Lucky and I took it to heart and demanded we prepared ourselves for war. I trained with renowned coaches in the boxing ring and graduated at the top of my class in college. It wasn't within me to bow down to the masses and accept anything other than perfection in all aspects of my achievements. And much to Apollo's disdain, I regarded him with shrewd psychological savagery.

For fun.

"What did he want?" Octavia asked, pulling her messenger bag onto the seat beside her.

"Four." She stopped, regarding me with suspicious eyes as I pointed to the bag. "Four books in there today, aren't there?" Her cheeks burning bright in embarrassment gave me my answer.

"Five." She chuckled, flicking her long brown curls over her shoulder and adjusting her glasses. "I couldn't decide! Now spill!"

"Book nerd." I smirked, rising to my feet and standing in front of the floor-to-ceiling windows in my office. "Dominic Moretti is shopping for water access."

It had taken me months to get my office styled just the way I had envisioned. I was going for powerful and sophisticated with the hint of femininity. When you walked into the room, you felt warm and fuzzy, but there was an undertone of the cutthroat businesswoman I truly was. There were a lot of white and soft cream colors, the elongated windows keeping things bright. Then I added splashes of *blood-red* accents —*perhaps a subconscious forewarning...*

I explained to Octavia what Apollo had observed and needed me to research. None of us would sit idly by and allow the Moretti's any attempt to gain a stronger foothold. I crossed my arms over my chest and stared at the cityscape below, the sun slowly setting. The symbolism was not lost on me. Just as the moon began to take over the sky and eclipse the pink hues, it was understood that this advantage was momentary—the sun would always rise again the next morning.

No matter what they pulled, we'd always burn brighter.

"What girl?" Octavia asked, shattering my silent contemplations.

"Some Moretti whore, no doubt," I muttered, walking back to my computer and accessing the cameras around the warehouse. A few clicks of a button and we watched together as Apollo stalked around in the shadows to follow the little blonde tramp.

"She's pretty," Octavia noted, much to my disagreement.

"What's your story?" I questioned, staring at the blonde on the screen; though this was directed more to myself than Octavia.

Everyone had a story. Everyone had a weakness. And I loved extorting all of the above from those in my way. Whatever interest Apollo was showing in the little bitch, I'd stomp on her like she was goddamn on fire. A few more clicks and I uploaded a clear image of her face into my software, allowing my system to do the job I built it for.

The program could learn anything about a person with but one simple image. Birth records, family information, crime jackets—hell, even your dental records if I wanted them. Then it was able to take medical records, fingerprint database information, and anything else possible to link potential genetic matches. Everyone was one click away from their entire life flashing before my eyes.

"Miss Agostino." My secretary's voice came from the intercom. "Your appointment is in the conference room when you're ready."

"Thank you." I disconnected the call. "I just need to set up a few more schematics into the software to advance my search and then I get to deal with the men of Alias Marks Corp." I muttered.

"What is the meeting about?" Octavia started packing her things onto her shoulder.

"They want me to sell the patent for the criminal genealogy software." I laughed, as if my pride and joy had a price tag on it. "Alias Marks assumes his pompous son offering me a date would be the nail in the coffin." I shuddered at the thought of the gross man-child.

I rose from the desk and locked everything up as my computer continued its analysis. Alias Marks had built his technology company by muscling computer software engineers into working for him. He also had very little dignity when he strong-armed those opposed to selling their patents, such as myself. I did very little for other businesses like his. I only worked with individuals who needed the leg up in life or those whose practices were above reproach.

I opened my closet door and checked my reflection in the full-length mirror. My chestnut brown hair was wrapped in a sophisticated bun that added to my polished attire. My cream *Chanel* pantsuit was fitted perfectly, accented by the fine silk shirt underneath. The only real glimpse into the true me was my red-soled stilettos with a modest diamond design on the buckle.

"I'll walk you out?" I motioned for Octavia to follow. "Peiro is here today, correct?"

She rolled her eyes at me but I ignored it. Though I often opted—or rather, demanded—that I be left alone when it came to security measures, the entire family required Octavia to be monitored at all times. Usually, I was either in my security-coded office or at home, so only the time between required extra attention. Octavia was the light to the dark of our family and needed the added protection, much to her dismay.

"I love you." I pulled her in for a hug before she left with Peiro in the elevator. "Ready?" My secretary and Chief of Operations both nodded, following me to the conference room.

It was a ploy, a female show of force, against two simple-minded men who assumed women were incapable of running a man's corporate world. Little did they know, I was in the process of buying out their three largest engineers and two of the companies they *thought* they were under negotiations with. I had little time and patience for men such as these and planned to leave a very strong message in my wake as I ushered towards total corporate domination.

"Hello, Alias. Thomas." I nodded, ignoring their extended hands. I took a seat at the head of the opposite end of the table with both women, one on each side. Another power play… it made them uncomfortable.

"Sienna." Thomas nodded in return, stopping when I interrupted him.

"Miss Agostino. Please," I corrected dryly.

I would have to replay this tape for myself later to further enjoy his shocked expression. His brows shot to his hairline, before morphing into uncontrolled rage. I, on the other hand, wore my poker face as I queued up their presentation on the large flat screen behind them.

"Continue," I stated, glancing at my watch.

"We've come prepared to make you an offer. One, we doubt you'd want to refuse," Alias started with a confident smirk, motioning for his son to begin.

"Miss Agostino." He practically snarled my name. I half-expected him to be frothing at the mouth. "As my father said, our offer is well above the standard rate for the genealogy software, and we've prepared a presentation to show you how we can drive it to the next level."

"Yes, so you've said. Your contract is under attorney review with Engineer Farewell, correct?" I lifted my head, waiting for a response, and I was met by their stunned silence. "No need to answer. It was rhetorical."

I rose from my seat, approaching their end of the long conference table. Marissa, my Chief of Operations, followed behind me and handed each of them several papers. Both men refused to acknowledge what she had placed before them, staring me down instead. Alias was giving me a look of agitation mixed with intrigue. But his son, Thomas, was openly glaring at me and his expression was that of pure loathing.

"You see, I had absolutely no intention of selling this patent or any of my other patents to your organization." I clasped my hands in front of me as I stared back at them. "I do not conduct business with men who will steal someone else's hard work and claim it as their own."

"Purchasing a patent is hardly stealing," Alias commented, his forehead scowling.

"Of course not. But underbidding its worth and using the threat of violence to get what you want is indeed... stealing." I motioned for them to sit in their seats and open their packets. "As you can tell by my extensive research, there is no stone that has gone unturned. Note the examples, showing the depravity of your negotiations throughout the years."

"This is bullshit," Thomas barked, shoving the documents aside. A further display of incompetence as he couldn't even understand the data before him. "Enough." Alias grunted at his son.

"Engineer Farewell is now with *Energia* Holdings." I smiled at Alias' scowl. "As are Telepark, Roam USA and West Coast Telecom. *Energia* is my baby and I won't allow you to touch what is rightfully mine." *No Agostino would.*

"You... you, can't. They weren't up for sale," Alias stated in disbelief, flipping through the packet with a sudden renewed enthusiasm.

"Money talks." I wandered back down the table, my fingers trailing along the veneer, and sat with my ladies.

"You're just a fucking whore! You can't do this! I won't allow it!" Thomas shouted, rising so quickly his chair rolled into the wall and rattled the TV behind him.

"It's already done. And I suggest you mind your tongue before I completely destroy you." My tone was clipped and direct—it was a challenge.

"Thomas..." Alias warned, knowing he'd met his match and didn't stand a chance against the fucking *whore*.

"No! It's all empty threats. I won't allow some dumb bitch to come and take what *we've* worked so hard for," Thomas sputtered; clearly now grasping at straws, he started ripping up the packets.

"You've built nothing. You're no more significant than an ant under my *Louboutin's*, Thomas. Your father built the company. Although it was off the backs of individuals who didn't know any better or couldn't fight back, I respected that he did it by his own hand, at least." I sat back in my seat.

"You *fucking* bitch." Thomas growled as his father slapped his arm. "Thomas, shut up."

"This is your last warning, Thomas. Heed your father's advice," I commanded, but he'd already lost his control and began aiming some creative slurs in my direction.

I'd heard it all before; he wasn't original in the slightest. *Agostino whore. Dirty money. Stupid bitch using her daddy*—pot, meet kettle. It didn't matter that I built this company from the ground up, first selling a video game before expanding into a large corporation. Those initial funds enabled me to start *Energia* Holdings without a single thing from my father. Well, except his unending support and love.

"That's it." As I stood again, Farrah, my secretary, handed me a manila folder. "Just remember I did warn you."

Instead of walking towards them this time, I slid the folder to the end of the table. Alias pulled it from Thomas' grasp; his face blanched as he began flipping through the photos. When it came to something I wanted, I was nothing short of thorough and methodical. And Thomas had plenty to be worried about; especially if it were to come to the light of day.

"June first, two years ago. Thomas went to a frat party at his old brotherhood and got himself into some trouble. Evelyn Campbell was a freshman from a small country town in the Midwest. She was drinking soda and preparing to leave when Thomas approached her." I clicked the TV on, and it paused on a close-up image of Thomas.

"Thomas… you said." Alias stopped, his mouth agape, silently begging his son to spew more lies.

"He said she was a liar that was looking for a payout. There were no charges because there was no proof. For having access to some pretty powerful computer geniuses, you'd think you would've protected your little secret better." I hit play.

Marissa and Farrah averted their gazes and I turned my back, not needing to see the depravity once more. It would show Alias that his son was a sick son of a bitch. He carried an unconscious Evelyn into the room and dropped her on the bed. He repeatedly raped her over and over, before electing to save the video for later. He then forced her into a shower to clean the evidence and abandoned her—naked—in a frat house bedroom.

"Shut it off!" Thomas roared. I spun on my heels, preparing myself, in case he charged forward. When I made no move to do as he commanded, he smashed his chair into the screen. "Lies! Sh-she photoshopped this, dad!"

"Enough!" Alias warned, remorse filling his face.

"Fucking whore." *Apparently, his vocabulary was as limited as his intellect.* He started around the table towards Farrah, who hit the alarm before hopping out of his reach.

When he turned to charge at me, I smiled, waiting for his next move. He was sloppy and sluggish—evidently, the man required sedatives to try to elicit any real authority. I stepped away from his punch and answered with two fingers jammed into his throat. His gasps and sputtering were audibly gratifying. I caught his arm, twisting it behind his back and slamming him face first into the table. He was larger than me, but I was more able-bodied. My hold was painful and his incapacitated breaths worked in my favor.

"I fucking warned you. I have more gifts for you when you get to prison. *Sei morta, cagna.*" The door to the conference room opened and three police officers entered. They began shouting, citing their warrant for Thomas' arrest for the rape of Evelyn Campbell.

The NYPD made quick work of escorting him out, while Alias remained rooted to his seat. He stared at the door for several minutes after it closed before speaking. I had a feeling underneath the lies and manipulations, he had always suspected that his son was full of shit.

What father wants to believe their children are capable of being monsters?

Oh, mine. Ha!

"I paid an investigator to look into that story. Thomas has always been a little off, but I couldn't find anything. I only allowed him to join the company so that I could keep an eye on him, but apparently that wasn't enough." A light knock landed on the door and Farrah moved to open it.

Evelyn Campbell was a frail, tear-soaked little girl; one who would be haunted by the actions of that piece of shit for the rest of her life. Her father and Amy, my attorney, stood beside her in silent strength. Alias' eyes went large as he recognized her.

"Not only will we be seeking to have your son charged to the full extent of the law, we are also requesting that you pay punitive damages to Miss Campbell," Amy stated.

"I-I." Alias stopped, his head hanging low. "I thought I had monitored him close enough to avoid something like this. My dear, I will give you the apology that will never come from my son."

"Your son is a monster," Evelyn said, her voice strong and loud.

"I am sorry for what he has done to you." His face and words held nothing but regret and sincerity. "Send me a proposal. I won't fight you." And then he was gone, the door shutting briskly behind him.

"Miss Agostino, I can't thank..." I raised my hand to halt her.

"You do not need to thank me. I am happy I could help you and I will continue to do so. Now, and any way possible in the future," I said with a slight smile, wiping a tear drop from her cheek. "You're back in school, right? Getting your degree?"

"Yes. You were right. He tried to ruin my life and it was up to me to fight him. My parents moved into the city to help me." Evelyn smiled at her father.

"Farrah." I extended my hand, gesturing for the next file I needed. "Take as much time as you need to go over these numbers, Mr. Campbell. I am sure you will find it adequate enough, should you choose to join us as an accountant at *Energia* Holdings."

Her father's eyes went round in surprise, as he took in the very hefty number I'd offered for his salary. I'd done my research on her father, Jacob Campbell, who was an esteemed accountant in their small town in Idaho. No doubt moving here to support his daughter hurt their finances and I wanted to make amends. The money that came from Alias would just be a bonus, so they could live comfortably.

"Why?" her father asked, unshed tears filling his eyes.

"I need a solid accountant and you came considerably recommended. Now, as for you." I turned my attention to Evelyn. "I expect nothing but the highest mentions from your professors, and as long as that stays consistent, you will be allowed to intern with my law department."

Evelyn burst into tears, the loud sobs wracking her small frame. I squeezed her shoulder, silently instructing Farrah to take care of them, and slipped from the room. I waited until I was in my office—the door locked and secured—before I broke down. This world was cruel, fucked up at best; but to women, it had a propensity to be far more vicious.

Evelyn came from a low to middle income family, working her ass off to get a partial ride to NYU Law School. I refused to allow an insignificant prick like Thomas Marks to destroy something she'd worked so hard for. When I found the information that I needed on him, I learned she'd left school after the incident and moved back home, losing her scholarship. I worked it out with the school, ensuring that she would be back and the tuition would be paid in full by the Alias Marks Corporation.

I sat at my desk and took a deep breath, wiping the tears away with a tissue. I was many things but being overly emotional was my least favorite attribute. I could go toe-to-toe with the best in the ring or at a conference table, during negotiations. But even I had my moments of weakness, moments my heart couldn't take the travesties against the innocent. I wanted to be a resource for people like Evelyn.

"Let's see what we've got," I muttered to myself as I unlocked my computer screen. The software had continued its search and had already come up with a huge arsenal of information for me to scour through.

The building in question, the one that Dominic Moretti was looking to purchase, was more expensive than I thought. There were several dummy corporations registered under his name and they were funneling different funds from one to the other—out then back again—in an attempt to keep up the appearance of legitimacy. But my program was smarter than that. Most of his funding seemed to come from a man named John Hardwicke.

With two clicks of a button, the file my software created came up with a plethora of unanswered questions. I read the findings from top to bottom before switching to the *Moretti whore,* the blonde that Apollo had asked about. She was caught on several street-angled cameras and I'd already uploaded several different images of her.

"A ghost?" I asked myself, flopping back into my seat with disbelief. This software had a ninety-nine percent accuracy rating, and as of today, I had uncovered over ten thousand identities using it. It has only been unsuccessful in five ID's... now six. "Who the fuck are you?" I asked, staring down at my screen.

I tapped away for a few more minutes, pissed off that her identity remained ambiguous. I picked up my glass paperweight and chucked it across the room; the fine crystal burst into hundreds of shards on impact. I was *always* able to get answers. And Apollo's interest in this *ghost* only made me angrier.

I took a breath and grabbed my cell phone, prepared to tell Apollo to go fuck himself. He thought she could be helpful in uncovering Dom's alleged trafficking ring, but I had strong doubts. As shown on this video feed, she was clearly not that imperative to the deal, considering he toted her around like his own personal ragdoll.

Instead of dialing out, the phone started ringing in my hand, a picture of Apollo and me flashing across the screen. I couldn't help but take a deep breath and laugh at it. It was a still shot from a random trip to New Jersey I'd tagged along on with him and Lucky. They had business with a motorcycle club in the country and I played the tourist. I was smiling like an idiot in a cowboy hat, and he was scowling trying to take his off.

Ah! Memories!

CHAPTER 3
APOLLO DELUCA

I was on high alert, taking in all the individuals in the room who weren't on the Agostino payroll. Anthony Moretti sat at the opposite end of the table from Mario with Gio on one side. I glanced at Dom on the other but faltered when I noticed the figure at his right. She was tiny compared to her brothers, soft with slight feminine curves. A demure little thing, as she stared at her lap as if she were trying to disappear, her raven locks shrouding her in a dark cloud of attempted anonymity. But she couldn't hide from me.

Mirabella Moretti had returned.

The family started digging into their meals, but Lucky was practically salivating… biting at his chance to make Gio suffer. I could tell he wanted to provoke an argument. My hand itched to grab my Glock —to make an example out of him—in front of his *famiglia*. I craved the feeling of the kickback, the sulfurous smell as it fired and the damage it would inflict.

"Lucky, son. This is Mirabella Moretti, daughter of Anthony and Serafina." Mario motioned to the girl at the other end of the table.

My gaze snapped back to her, sitting so poised and elegant in the corner. Though I yearned to punish all of the Moretti men—gouging their eyes from their sockets, inflicting permanent disfigurement and tearing the glands and cranial nerves when I broke past the orbital cavity—she seemed so innocent that a part of me didn't want to tarnish her.

Lucky came into my peripheral, a simple nod of his head forbade me from acting upon my instincts. We would have our recompense, and I would ensure that it would be nothing less than pure poetic expression, doused in blood. Of course, that would be when Mirabella was out of sight.

Ever since an impromptu meeting with the girl, Lucky had been hooked. She had mesmerized him with her bi-colored eyes and sweet disposition. The moment he left the house that day, he enacted a plan to have her watched while she was in Italy. He claimed it was because Gio was following as her chaperon, but his lies couldn't hide the fact that *il diavolo* had fallen for his *angelo celeste*.

You see, five years ago, Lucky ran into Mirabella in his family compound when she visited with her father, who was seeking to barter some sort of a deal with the Agostino's. Mario presented us with limited details, however, he told us that the girl's future had been sealed during negotiations for the use of our docks. And I knew that her return from Italy wasn't by accident; Anthony had plans in motion.

"Hello. Pleasure to meet you." She was assertive and boisterous with her greeting.

She didn't waiver nor did she look away, which was more than I could say for her brother. The imbecile was anxious. He held himself as if he wasn't accustomed to this life, inadequate and unable to converse with any sort of logical thought. There was no way he was *that* incompetent; something was amiss, and my intuition told me as much.

I looked back and forth between the two—Lucky and Mirabella—knowingly, Lucky catching my subtle smirk. Yeah, the bastard was practically swooning in his seat for the Moretti girl. It wouldn't be long now before Mario would start to step back from the business and Lucky would take the reins… the new King of New York.

And, of course, every king needed a queen.

He needed a capable woman at his side, one with a potent veracity to stand tall against shared enemies. A family would bolster the Agostino stronghold and heirs kept the namesake relevant. A feeble-minded whore—like those that normally flocked in droves around Lucky—wouldn't do. But Bella, she was an ideal match. Something unspoken and peculiar was whispering in the back of my mind—she was the start to his own *revolution*.

"Whispers of your beauty traveled all the way from Italy. While I see the rumors are true, the details haven't done you nearly enough justice. It's a pleasure to meet you, Mirabella," Lucky cooed at the girl, a red blush creeping up her neck.

I would have laughed if we were alone, but I wouldn't dare a public display of disrespect. Gio seethed as Lucky openly flirted with his sister, while Dominic stopped eating to stare at Gio in amusement. The Moretti brothers were similar in looks but their personalities couldn't be more disproportionate.

Dominic was stronger and a bit wider with a calm, even mind. Gio was smaller—though he still bore a large frame—but the boy was an unhinged jackass. His immoral behavior was a direct insult to all that our life demanded. We weren't good men by any means... but we did have sordid codes we lived by. And when you tampered with those, you were signing your death warrant.

Gio hadn't worked for a single thing in his life, choosing to be a permanent leech on daddy's tit. He hid behind his name and acted as if that alone held power. He made rash decisions; decisions that caused him to act out violently when things didn't go his way. In fact, he was so inept, his father sent him to babysit his sister in Italy. Although, his angered expression at Bella made me question the dismal protection he actually afforded the girl.

"Bella. Please," Gio scoffed, drawing her attention back. Noting the threatening undertone, she looked to her lap in submission.

"How was your day, son?" Mario's attempt at levity sparked Lucky's ulterior motive.

"Ah. Now that you mention it, it was quite productive actually. I got wind of a little rat problem at the docks, but it didn't matter. You see, the thing with rats is they always leave tracks and I just so happen to have an exterminator on the books. Drove the vermin out before they even reached the merchandise." Lucky stared at Gio with pure malice; and now the boy was sweltering under the heat of *il diavolo's* stare.

"My son, always the strategist. Always one step ahead. Did you find the source of the… infestation?" The sound of utensils cutting across ceramic echoed in the room. Gio twitched in his seat. Good. Lucky had him right where we wanted him.

"Trailed 'um right back to the nest. And the rat did what rats do best. He squealed. Next step is to eradicate the whole colony… starting with the leader of the pack." Lucky stopped chewing; instead, he leaned forward in his seat, his penetrating gaze glued to the eldest Moretti offspring.

"Lessons must be taught. Actions must reap repercussions," Anthony added over a sip of scotch. Gio's face soured at his father's inadvertent condemnation.

"Truer words have never been spoken, Mr. Moretti. And I am a man who believes that if someone wants to tempt their fate and throw down with the Devil, they must be prepared to go through hell. And I do love the heat." Lucky was growling with menace, his tone dripping with sincerity as *il diavolo* thrashed against his metaphorical bindings.

I took a single step, heightening my proximity, while my eyes searched for any indication that Gio thought to strike. I focused on the psoas major muscle. Its primary function was to flex the hip—though it also played a role in side-bending the spine. The slightest contraction served as a telltale sign that someone was ready to move forward with an assault. If there was any hint that the kid had suddenly grown a pair, I'd destroy him, my knife slicing neck to navel.

"Sometimes men forget their place or have ambitions for more beyond it. Healthy competition can't always end in blood. There is no progress if you are never challenged to begin with. After all, a champion cannot be called a champion without those he's bettered." Bella's sudden admission stalled my errant thoughts.

"Well said, Bella," Mario applauded her.

"Now, onto the docks. You've been using them for the last five years at our agreed upon price. Our five-year contract is up and a rene-gotiation must be had. Increase of twenty-five percent." Mario dropped that bomb onto their laps without a care in the world.

Shouting insults at nearly every direction in the room, Gio appeared ready to leap out of his seat. Anthony lost his composure, standing so quickly that his chair tumbled backwards. All the guards jumped to alert, weapons cocked in unison. Sitting back in his seat, ankle to knee, Lucky sipped his scotch watching the show. I stepped closer to Lucky's side and honed in on the potential threats.

"That's not what we discussed, Mario." Anthony breathed fire; while Mario, unsympathetic and impassive, continued his meal as though the blaze couldn't touch him.

Raising a hand, Mario interrupted Anthony. "We discussed this five years ago. I was to get a gift for allowing you the use of my docks. The waiting period for said gift and contract is up."

The rest of their conversation disappeared into background noise; my mind was focused on the room. Dominic had his hand on his sister's arm, attempting to shield her. Anthony remained enraged, but his self-preservation won out, knowing better than to throw down the gauntlet. But Gio didn't seem to understand that.

The *asino* sat on the edge of his seat, his leg bouncing and his hands shaking in anger. He stared at Lucky with such disdain you could practically taste it. He was close to snapping and his fingers itched to take out his gun and pull the trigger. But intent was a far cry from action. He didn't have the balls. He was in way over his head.

Though vigilant, I waited, a mental checklist taking up residency in my frontal lobe, recording what needed to be done—to whom and why—with perfect precision. The dark recesses of my mind were plagued with images of bright blue eyes and tight pencil skirts. Long blonde locks whipping in the wind and a bearing of savage electricity doused in pandemonium. As I stood there, I added Dominic and his girl to my to-do list.

I'd happily set her free at a simple cost. The only tender I'd accept would be her riding my dick, a mutually beneficial payment.

Lucky's voice pulled me back to the conversation. "Would you like to tell daddy, or should I?" Lucky asked Gio, baring his teeth in triumph.

"Fuck you." Gio grunted, looking around the room for an ally he didn't have.

"No. Fuck you. You insignificant son of a bitch." Lucky stormed to his feet, rounding the table and meeting the man-child at eye-level. The quick action spurned me into motion, and I positioned myself at his side.

"Little Gio Moretti. Nothing more than a pup begging for table scraps and hoping to snatch 'um off the counter when he thinks no one's looking. Pay attention to how the big dogs... how the alpha... conducts his business and maybe next time your rat will get the shipment schedule right." Lucky was playing with his food now and I was a hellhound thrashing against my leash.

Anthony *seemed* shocked at his son's disobedience—*seemed* being the relative word. The coerced contract—forcing Anthony to heel to Mario—as well as the former man's limited resistance on the matter clearly said the Agostino patriarch had an ace up his sleeve. There was no way a proud man, like Anthony Moretti, was so willing to take it up the ass from his rival.

As Anthony attempted to drag his son from the room, all hell broke loose. Time slowed as Gio brandished his weapon. Assessing the situation, I moved to a more favorable vantage point, at the Moretti boy's back. And just like I thought, the *fanculo* couldn't take aim at Lucky; instead, he waved his firearm around the room, like a kid with a cap-gun, spouting accusations and insults while cursing the Agostino name.

If truth be told, I wasn't paying a bit of attention to his ramblings. I was too focused on Lucky, waiting for permission to rip the mother-fucker apart with my own firearm, now solely fixated. Graphic images invaded my thoughts. A bullet embedded in his thoracic cavity. A knife sliced across the carotid artery. Anything to bathe in his traitorous blood. My creativity beckoned forth, conjuring up numerous ways to end the Moretti boy's life. I wanted bedlam... this room to be drowning in the carnage I'd leave in my wake.

It took me a moment to register the small, feminine presence that stepped to the barrel of my gun. Mirabella was doing her best to thwart her brother's self-injurious actions. Normally, I would have considered it valiant of her. But not at a time when I was ready to throw my proverbial moral inhibitions to the wind and do what I do best. I fucking maimed… I destroyed… I reveled in tormenting…

And I didn't like to wait.

Instead, the modest girl was able to lighten the tension and force her brother from the room, much to the disappointment of my inner *demoni.* Lucky and I held a silent conversation, concerned over the repercussions her actions would ensue. She'd made a huge mistake in involving herself; her brother wasn't the type to hesitate enacting his revenge—sister or not. I sent out a text, confirming additional security for Bella, unbeknownst to the Moretti's.

Lucky finished a few things, including swapping intel with his father, before our entourage exited. I grabbed my cell phone, wanting an update from Sienna, when movement at the curb caught my attention. Lucky's growl filled the foyer, forcing everyone to turn towards the commotion outside.

Gio, ever the tactician, slapped his sister across the face, mere feet from the front door. It took me and two others to hold Lucky back, giving Gio just enough time to run into his awaiting limo. I wasn't attuned to a moral compass or a conscience, but things needed to happen at the right time. And now… wasn't that fucking time.

I picked up my phone and dialed Sienna. "What do you have?" I asked her.

"Yes, hello. I am doing well, Apollo. You're such an incredible gentleman for asking," Sienna chirped, never one to miss a moment to insert her proclivity for sarcasm.

"Cut the shit, Sienna. I have an overwhelming number of things to decipher, so give me what I need… *now.*" I growled into the phone, right before the little shit hung up. "Fucking bitch!" I hollered, slamming my fist into the dashboard.

"This ain't Lucky's, you fuck! It's my car. Knock that shit off," Al yelled, punching me in the arm. "Christ! Take it out on Sienna's belongings, not mine."

I took a deep breath and dialed out my phone again; this time she answered on the fifth ring. "Sienna Agostino... spy extraordinaire. How may I serve you?" She sang happily into the phone.

"Hello, Sienna." I all but growled, trying to calm my rage in order to keep my temper from exploding. Al unsuccessfully covered his laughter with a cough. "How're *you*?" I asked the unnerving *dolore nel culo*.

"Oh! Apollo, it's darling to hear from you. I am well, you?" She spoke with the softest voice.

"Good." I released another deep breath. Thankfully, she finally cut the crap before my anger got the best of me.

"Anywho, I am sure you are calling for the information you requested earlier. Dominic Moretti is looking for a warehouse to conduct his import-export business. He has the excessive cash to purchase that building, which happens to be the only one with water access that *we* don't own," Sienna rattled off.

"What's the asking price for that place, and how does he have that much cash?" I prompted, curious over Dom's financial aspect.

"Without spending my entire day trying to help you, I'd say illegal activities, considering these various deposits from random corporations. But the building is going for... nineteen mil," Sienna said dismissively, while the incessant typing on her keyboard continued to echo through the receiver. "He owns several corporations outside of the strip clubs and restaurants."

"What could he be importing that would have him wanting to remain off the Agostino radar... *and* requires that much space?" I asked, more to myself than anyone else.

"He has a partner, it appears. The paperwork they signed today with the down payment states Dominic and John... Hardwicke. Please hold." Sienna started humming to herself, aggressively clicking away. "Interesting," was her only response.

"Sienna..." I growled, my patience quickly dwindling.

"Oops. Sorry, forgot we weren't on skype." More clicks on the keyboard. "I am emailing you what I have. As of a couple of years ago, John Hardwicke didn't exist. Suddenly, he is this popular architect and importer of... fine arts. Dude is loaded, too."

"Something isn't right," I said, tapping my top lip in thought.

"No website, no auctions, no information on whatever he is dealing in. I smell... a rat. Oh, wow. He is worth billions... literal billions. Oh my, and he's handsome." I growled at her unnecessary tangents.

"Sienna! Any ties with known traffickers?" I muttered the question; the obvious answer to me would be yes. But she didn't have anything concrete, promising she'd get me more. "And... the girl?"

She huffed into the phone, mumbling to herself in the background. "Nothing."

"Sienna. Don't fuck with me because you have some petty ass..." I started yelling, but she cut me off.

"Fuck, Apollo! Finish that sentence and I will never help you again. I have literally nothing on her. I pulled her images from the cameras and she didn't come up on any databases. She's never been arrested, paid taxes, had a driver's license... nothing. She's a fucking ghost on all systems," Sienna growled; I could tell by her tone that she wasn't lying.

Sienna was meticulous and her accuracy above reproach. Her software and her work ethic were unparalleled; unanswered questions would unnerve her to no end. She'd be strapped to her computer for days as she continued to sniff out leads.

"So, let me get this straight..." I replayed the information for Al to hear and to ensure I missed nothing. His grip on the steering wheel tightened.

"And he's buying a warehouse across the street?" Al asked, staring at me out of the corner of his eye.

"Yup! Let me work! I don't put up with this bullshit." Sienna hung up before I could respond.

I returned my phone to my pocket and glared out the window—the buildings passing, a blur. We pulled up to the warehouse where I would spend the night reorganizing our delivery patterns to avoid further issues. Once everything was in place, Lucky arrived to review schematics and give his final sign off.

"I need a meeting scheduled," Lucky commanded; grabbing my phone, I waited for him to continue. His face pinched with discomfort as he shifted in his seat; for the first time in all of the years I'd known him, he seemed uncomfortable. "With Bella."

I couldn't help but laugh at his pained expression and the forced words. I knew five years ago when he requested a full jacket of information on her that this was... *something else*. He had always had a predilection for superficial women who knew the score—he wasn't the marrying type.

Except for Tatianna—Sienna's high school rival and a leech he couldn't shake. Her daddy was rich and she circled our crew as we grew up... well, circled Lucky to be more accurate. Ultimately, she wanted him to propose but he'd made himself clear that he'd *never* marry her. She wasn't made to be at his side.

To this day, she assumed she had a right to take the power he had created. She was so pathetically wrong with this ill-conceived notion.

"I suppose, logically, the best way to go about that... is her mother," I offered. Serafina Moretti was as kind as she was beautiful and would be a strong ally. "Though, I must admit I am curious as to why?" While my tone was nonchalant, the smirk I imparted was not.

Acknowledging my statement with a wave, he simultaneously ignored my newfound humor and left me alone to work. He shook his head, barking out the words "never mind" before exiting.

Things were falling into place. And I had no doubt that in the next few years, Lucky would cement himself as head of the family, and in turn, command authority over the city. That being said, I'd handle our current predicament with Gio and end the Russian delivery concerns that had recently arisen.

I hadn't forgotten that I'd missed out on my chance for bloodshed, and my thirst wouldn't settle until satiated. It wouldn't, until I coated my hands in blood or buried myself deep into a willing, malleable woman. I enjoyed the control... the dangerous thrill submission elicited. Her pleasure, her pain and her deep-seated need to satisfy me fed my dark side; a side that challenged my restraint.

Rising to my feet, I took a shower and changed into a new, fresh suit. The ironed and perfectly creased edges allowed me to feel whole again—like I could breathe past the savage beast that threatened to break loose. That's what an immaculate facade created, a chance for normalcy amongst those around me.

I locked the offices and headed downstairs to the enclosed garage. I grabbed my keys to my customized, matte-black Rolls Royce Phantom. I didn't own much real estate, but I cornered the market in expensive cars. A couple million in worth, all stowed away in a temperature-controlled garage under the warehouse—a wide selection of limited release and customized luxury vehicles.

I sat in the plush leather seat, inhaling the ever-present brand-new car smell—with less than three thousand miles on it. Idling in the garage, it purred off the concrete walls with a smooth vibrato. Pulling up the ramp, I headed out of the locked gates and into the city. My body was vibrating along with the powerful engine as I imagined what I planned for my evening, my thoughts on autopilot as I headed towards my destination.

"Sir." The valet greeted me as I pulled up and outside the cordoned-off establishment.

Hush was a venue for individuals such as myself who liked to indulge in fine whiskey, Cuban cigars and submissive women. It offered a safe environment for all involved to fulfill their fantasies with both anonymity and the finest of participants.

I knocked on the heavy steel door, waiting for the slot to open and the bouncer to appear. I passed my card into the slot; the bright green light permitting my entrance was a sight for sore eyes. I could feel my blood collecting in the upper chambers of my heart, sending out an electrical current and causing the atria to contract rapidly as the hinged locks disengaged with loud clicks. Opening the door, I inhaled, the warm scent of leather and cigar smoke overwhelming my senses.

It was like a calming breeze that settled over the passing storm.

I stepped to the counter allowing the desk girl—wearing head to toe latex—to scan my card again as the system swept over my information. She picked up the phone and a moment later, a waitress arrived.

The girl carried a tray with a rocks glass, ice bucket, and a bottle of *Lagavulin 16-Year Single Malt Scotch Whisky.*

My mouth was practically watering from the sight, add in the delectable waitress, and I was damn near panting. She was a tiny thing against my six-four height and solid frame. Her long blonde hair and piercing blues peeked out from her black-sequined mask. Her body was thin, but athletically toned and she stalked with a natural rhythm to her gait.

We stepped into a private suite; she beckoned me forward and ahead of her. The room was dark with earthy tones, housing an elevated stripper pole in the center and a large four-post bed—equipped with restraints and covered in black silk sheets—in the back corner. I didn't need whips and chains, no hanging cross or any of that nonsense. Someone with my talents and desires merely needed compliance; even that wasn't a necessity, though it certainly aided in the legality of it all.

It was a natural endowment of mine... to control with a simple stare, a hand to the throat, a calloused palm to your reddening ass. My ability to dominate was intrinsic and shrouded you in a cloud of confusion, before you fell to your knees and at my feet with a simple snap of my fingers. That was the alpha within me—the caveman who proudly beat his chest—as I conquered your desires, while appeasing my own.

"Sir." The waitress offered me a glass; and taking my first sip, I savored the slow burn.

She raised her tray, presenting the cigar and seeking my approval. *Belicoso finos*—the perfect Cuban selection for my taste. I ran the expertly-wrapped tobacco under my nose, enjoying the scent, before handing it back to the waitress. She made quick work of snipping the end, placing it in my mouth and lighting it.

I took several fast puffs of the fine cigar and watched her through the smoke. She was a new girl; one I'd yet to taste. There was a current radiating between us, crackling in the air with an electricity that threatened to overload the system. When she went to turn on her heel, I grabbed her wrist, holding her close for a moment. She was an innocent doe, trapped in the hunter's game; one she had no chance of surviving.

"Cassandra is here tonight, sir." Her voice was small and timid, the perfect submissive tone. It made my dick hard, begging me to bend her to my will. "I only dance, sir."

I reached into my wallet and took out a couple of hundred-dollar bills. Laying them on her tray, I motioned towards the pole. She was wearing a tiny, black silk bra and panty set; but an overlay with leather straps covered her chest, torso and waist. It was like a bondage present you wanted to unwrap. She walked to the wall with the sway of a sensual seductress. Dimming the lights, she turned on a slow melody; one I hadn't heard before but it was entrancing. She hypnotized as she danced a slow waltz but methodically hit each beat with a strike of a salsa.

She continued towards the stage, her hands roaming her body in perfect tempo. My dick grew harder, feeling each move she made and threatening to burst through the zipper of my pants. She climbed onto the elevated platform, walking circles around the pole and acting as though she were unsure of what to do, while her natural captivating movements proved it to be a lie.

The song ended just as she climbed to the very top of the pole. Dropping upside down, she looped around the cylindrical, polished metal. Her grasp remained firmly in place as her arms constricted and flexed—aiding in the complexity of her movements—before she extended the entirety of her petite figure from the pole. She held her form, now horizontal to the stage, spreading her legs wide and open.

The beat picked up and the song went into a crescendo. Descending headfirst, she gave the illusion that she had plummeted out of control. Instead, she landed on her hands, kicking her long legs out from the pole. Her silhouette gleamed in the dimmed lighting. She dropped to her knees and crawled towards me. Sliding to her stomach, she leaned off the stage. Her head disappeared between my thighs and flipping her body onto mine, she straddled my waist before giving me a lap dance.

My hands roamed while her muscles shook beneath my touch. My initial evaluation had been correct. She had a dancer's body, slight but toned from a lot of training—practicing the art of persuasion. As the sexy little minx flipped her hair over her shoulder, my fingertips darted towards her mask, seeking to remove it. She grounded herself harder against my erection. Slapping my hands away, her intense blue eyes dared me to push her.

I was intrigued to see just how much bite she had.

"I'll have Cassandra come in to finish you, sir." The way her tongue rolled around the direct address, flaunted the defiance bursting through her bright eyes and soft tone. She was a siren, her words and demeanor calling the beast forward. Threatening to break free from his chains, he'd destroy her.

Body and soul.

I grabbed her arm again when she tried to leave. "What's your name?" I asked, holding tight as she stared down at me.

"Persephone," she said, shrugging herself loose before fleeing.

When the door opened again, Cassandra stood at the threshold wearing a red silk robe with the hood up. Her eyes cast to the ground as she approached, awaiting my orders. She wore nothing underneath the covering, knowing that I preferred her naked.

"Down," I ordered, enjoying how quickly she dropped to her knees. Her thighs were spread wide enough that I could see her glistening pussy.

I came here with several dark intentions, of which I thought to enact on Cassandra, but suddenly I was exhausted from the past few days. Rising to her feet, she came to kneel before me at the snap of my fingers. She calmly removed my belt and slid down my zipper. I stood to my full height as she took my hard cock out of my pants.

Opening wide for me, she watched as I slid languidly into her awaiting mouth. At first her movements were slow and practiced. But once she was warmed up, I took over—sliding further into her throat until I hit the back of her esophagus. Her mewls and gasps were a welcomed cadence as I lost control, chasing my high with a penchant for rough strokes.

She had no hard limits when it came to *playing* and was satisfied with how I liked to fuck. She was a smart girl, almost too sweet, to have caught the attention of a man such as myself. Like a moth to the flame, she couldn't stay away and I loved seeing just how brightly she could burn.

I finished with a deep growl, and my mind stuck on a blonde-haired and blue-eyed vixen. Persephone lurked in the recesses of my brain, serving as a challenge I hadn't had as of late. The need to find her and teach her who held the power consumed me. My palms itched to scar her round ass… and to show her just who she was fucking with.

I opened the door to my suite and ventured into the club, unsure of what exactly it was that I was looking for. The blonde siren's fall from grace sounded appeasing but I wasn't certain if even *that* would satiate the beast. I stepped into the main lobby and peered around the room, watching the voyeurs with curiosity; some patrons hid behind masks, unlike myself.

I didn't give a fuck who saw me here. No one would have the balls to come up and say anything to me. I didn't do pleasantries or bestow anyone with a polite embrace. They wanted to cozy up to Lucky—the future boss and the man you wanted on your side—in hopes of garnering his favor. But I was the man that you prayed didn't visit in the dark of the night, not the one you welcomed to your table.

One moment, the club was up to its usual antics; the next, a fight erupted. Men and women started screaming as a gunshot rang out from across the room. My instincts took over and I searched for the shooter. The corner that served as its origin point was overloaded with bodies, and I couldn't tell which was the offender. Flipping over a cocktail table, I threw myself behind it, my Glock cocked and ready at my side.

"*Figlio di Troia.* Of course, it'd be my fucking luck to die next to a prick like you." A deep intonation with an Italian accent came from my right. His features were hidden in the shadows, but I'd know that voice anywhere.

"*Fongool.* Go fuck off in another corner and die alone then," I barked, my eyes glancing at the man beside me.

Carmine Ragetti was a fucking terror, clothed in an expensive suit and designer cologne. His family resided in California and controlled the entire west coast. The Ragetti's didn't venture to this side of the country much since Carmine's uncle, Sal Junior, died.

Almost two decades ago, Carmine's grandfather—Sal Senior—ruled California with a torrent of influential power and an affinity for bloodlust. He wanted a part of New York, so he brokered his son—Sal Junior—to wed Mirabella's mother, Serafina. The engagement ended quickly when Sal Junior was murdered in the city, and a few days later Serafina was engaged to Anthony Moretti.

Senior believed the death was at Anthony's command, his subsequent actions a clear indication. Mario Agostino promised answers in an attempt to maintain peace, but he never found any. It was a thin line that we constantly threatened to cross with each interaction. With this in mind, Carmine's entrance to the city was disconcerting.

The commotion across the way escalated into sheer anarchy as security struggled to get a handle on the situation. A sudden surge of bodies in riot gear charged into the chaos. It was a blur of black suits, tactical vests, and frightened screams. The only color I could see was the vibrancy of *her* blonde hair. She seemed to be caught in the center of the melee. But she was no damsel... she was laying down fire on those around her.

Noticing that my assistance was no longer needed, I lowered my weapon but I kept it at the ready. My switchblade was also under my jacket as a stoic back-up if the ordeal turned sideways. The club's security was losing control to this presumptive tactical unit, which was no doubt attacking a wealthy benefactor, who had been dabbling in expensive and illegal goods.

"That's a big motherfucker," Carmine noted, his eyes glued to the heavyset man in question.

"And you're a little bitch," I mumbled, observing his laughter at my side.

I would never, in any circle, call Carmine and myself friends. However, we both did share an affinity for fighting, adrenaline boosting activities and feeding our insatiable appetites for carnage. The gore in the room around me called forth *il mietitore*, the reaper on my shoulder begging for his chance to play.

Me, they labeled a *psychopath.*

Carmine, he was deemed a *troubled soul.*

And in no world was any of that okay, but mental health wasn't easily diagnosed.

And *fuck,* if I wasn't the poster boy for mental health issues.

CHAPTER 4
APOLLO DELUCA

"**S**ecurities got it," Carmine said; rising to his feet, he straightened his jacket.

"Do they though?" I asked mockingly. The large man attempted to shove our table out of his way before making an abrupt exit.

While the cloud of smoke settled, errant thoughts broke free as I envisioned the satisfaction I could feel at his demise. When our eyes locked, he startled at the realization, as though he himself could see exactly what I had been thinking. My blade glinted in the light as I pulled it from under my suit. I dropped low, swiping at his calf. The man stumbled and shouted. Seeing his opening, Carmine attacked and swung his own knife into the patron's carotid and the pulsing artery erupted—a geyser of blood raining down and coating us.

Carmine was a mean motherfucker. And that was coming from me, who was undisputedly certifiable to be making such an assessment. The Ragetti heir was a silent threat. He attacked ruthlessly and with a laudable stealth. The man was six-seven, covered in ink and wore enough hair gel he could oil a tanker. His tattoos were a mix of biblical verses and images—some mocking, others in prayer. He was wider in frame than I was, and his heavily built muscles threatened to shred his suit.

"Is that?" Carmine paused, pointing the tip of his blade across the room.

"Raffaele Rifiuto," I confirmed. We stared at the rat—the fucking traitor to another family—with pure loathing.

"This night just got even-fucking-better." Carmine rose to his full height, nonchalantly stepping over the carcass of the man that now lay at our feet.

Raffaele Rifiuto was from a mid-level family in Philadelphia; though not much could be said for his bloodline's accomplishments. He was given one chance—singular—to show the boss of Philly that he was worth more than mediocrity. Instead of putting in the work, he opted to lie, steal and cheat. He had been dealing drugs and refusing to report to the appropriate hierarchy in the *famiglia*. Once he had been found out, he fled with a considerable price tag on his head.

If he would've come forward with his crimes and paid his dues, he would've lost a finger—or several—not his life. Instead, the fucking *topo* pulled a runner, seeking police protection by turning in key members of the Philadelphia syndicate. However, his low-level status turned up little information of worth to the investigative team, and as a result, he lost his government protection.

"I've got right," Carmine muttered, suddenly camouflaged by the crowd.

His ability to conceal himself was fascinating, especially for a man of his size and caliber. Brutish appearance or not, he moved among them with ease. To the untrained eye, he went unnoticed until he was already upon them.

I—on the other hand—well, I had no interest in hiding. I wanted Raffaele to see me coming. I wanted to watch his fear takeover. I wanted his mouth to quiver as I stalked towards him. And true to form, recognition filled the space between us before the coward attempted to dart towards the exit.

Raffaele peered at the door behind him. As he sought an escape and to turn towards it, Carmine slapped his back in greeting. I stepped in front of him—a sinister smile across my lips—as Carmine squeezed his shoulder, eliciting a pathetic whimper. Though before I could even speak, Raffaele mewled in bewilderment and a dark pool formed on the front of his pants.

"There is a rather high bounty on your head, Raffaele," I said, grabbing his chin and forcing him to look at me. "See, Carmine and I are smart businessmen and have a deal to broker with you. You pay us from those missing drug funds you swindled from Philly and we'll *help* you get out of this city."

Carmine smirked behind Raffaele, knowing damn-well neither of us planned to let the man live. But the boss of Philly wanted his funds allocated and in turn, planned to use the cash to pay whoever handled his little rat problem. It was a win-win. Consequently, it would be a strong alliance for Lucky in his future business endeavors.

"Yeah, yeah. I have it. I will give it to you both. Just... Just get me out of this city." Raffaele shook in trepidation, disdain trilling his lips. "Follow me to an address and I'll get it for you."

"Do you smell that?" Carmine leaned forward, sniffing the air in our captive's proximity. "Because I smell bullshit," he sneered.

"No, no. I'm not... Here." He turned into a sniveling mess as he reached into his pocket. "I'm just getting my phone."

I took hold of Raffaele's throat. Then, stepping into his space, I relished in how his pulse quickened beneath my grip—his hands shaking as he dug deeper into his pocket. Carmine was practically drooling behind him—his fingertips clenching tighter into the meat of Raffaele's shoulders and holding him in place.

"Here." He thrust his phone at my chest, but I held my grip for another beat.

"Well, well. Look here." I turned the screen to Carmine, showing him the extra zeros in the account balance. The deal was around a million but his account showed upwards of three, a little added incentive.

"Th-that's a bonus for you to get me out of this city before the Agostino's find me." Raffaele's entire demeanor pleaded with me, as if

I were his savior. But I wasn't that man. And Carmine sure as fuck wasn't either.

"Deal," I said, entering the information needed to transfer the funds from his account into mine. Once my cell phone pinged with a resounding alert, indicating my financial gain, my calm facade turned more sinister.

"I want half," Carmine said, planting his chin on Raffaele's shoulder.

"We-we had a deal!" Raffaele cried, his eyebrows reaching his hairline at the sight of my serrated knife, brandished from beneath my suit jacket.

"And we are men of our word. Once we slice your fucking throat, we'll send your body back to Philly. All before the Agostino's know your presence has tainted *their* city," Carmine laughed.

I lifted my blade, my insides growing animated, as I sunk it into his thoracic cavity. The sharpened tip entered between his third and fourth rib, slicing into his flesh like a hot knife through butter. I plunged my implement directly through the notch of his left lung. In the same motion, Carmine—who couldn't be outdone—jammed his own knife into Raffaele's back. From his angle, he more than likely entered through the pectoralis minor muscle and ended in the inferior lobe of the man's right lung.

To his credit, Raffaele didn't make a sound. Granted, the penetrating wounds would've impaired his ventilation, creating a reduction of cardiac output and stunting his ability to do so. I glanced up. The room was still galvanized with movement as the police tried to handle the chaos, and thus, our actions remained entirely unseen.

"Send me my half now," Carmine demanded, typing on his phone. "I've got the delivery handled." He pocketed his cellular device and two of his men came out of the shadows. Grabbing the decedent, they disappeared once again.

"Come on." I gestured towards my suite before turning on heel and heading towards the locked room. I swiped my key and opened the door. Cassandra startled at the noise. She was sitting in a chair in front of a laptop, textbooks piled at her side. Her frightened eyes took note of our bloodied appearance. Quickly she rose to her feet, anticipating an attack.

"Cassandra, calm down. We won't be needing your assistance." I motioned for Carmine to sit. He disregarded my offer, venturing towards the trembling girl and inquisitively peering over at her work.

"A doctor?" he asked her, though her eyes only grew larger at his sudden proximity. "Beauty and brains," he stated appreciatively.

"Carmine, back off," I ordered. He laughed, sauntering towards me and all but flopping into the chair at my side. Taking out my phone, I dialed.

"Lucky's right hand? To what do I owe the pleasure?" Romano Bianchi—the head of the Philly syndicate—answered on the third ring. Before speaking, however, I fired off a picture message to him.

"A gift," I said, listening as his phone shuffled around. "He'll be delivered shortly. I will wire you the funds as proof before payment is expected."

"Not needed. His body is proof enough. My thanks to New York," Romano clipped, his voice both reserved and deadly. "Tell Lucky I'd love to... *catch up*. And send my thanks, if you will." I agreed and disconnected the call.

"Does Lucky know you're here? I've heard no mention of your visit to the city." While my voice was flat, my intuition was telling me that Carmine was hiding something.

"Mario knows I am handling some things for Pops," Carmine said, not offering anything more. "After all, Lucky isn't the boss of *his father's* city, now is he?"

I ignored his question and asked one of my own. "What things?" The calligraphed tattoo above his eye—a singular word that read *Possessed*— raised at my prodding.

"Things for Pops. Not Agostino business. I cleared my visit with Mario. He's fine so that's all you should care about, lap dog." He attempted to pat my head, but I slapped his hand away, his glass plummeting to the floor in the process.

"What a waste," he muttered towards the spilt liquid.

In the underground hierarchy, Carmine was above me, as I stood merely a soldier myself. He was a blood-born heir to a high-level family, and although the Agostino's considered me a son, I wasn't one. I was Lucky's right hand, his *soldato,* and a recently promoted enforcer. Cassandra's abrupt exit from the room, and the sudden lack of an audience, presented me with an opening. I stormed at Carmine's face before slamming the son of a bitch against the wall.

"Don't play fucking games with me, Carmine. What the fuck are you doing in the city?" I growled, slamming his body once more for good measure.

Our deranged and bloodthirsty expressions mirrored one another as we exchanged glares in silence, neither of us moving in our wordless pissing match. Carmine was here for a very specific reason—one he was being awfully cavalier about. I was curious if Mario knew he was still in the city. Afterall, *Hush* was the perfect place to hide if you wanted a drink and entertainment while remaining unseen.

Not many people in the family visited establishments such as these —they considered it beneath them. As if their closed-door activities weren't just as demeaning. And if they did choose to partake, they hid behind their masks and cloaked ensembles, using cash to further ensure their anonymity.

The perfect place for Carmine to hide in the open light of day without being noticed by the famiglia.

"All you need to know, errand boy, is that Mario cleared me. Now. Fuck. Off." He growled each word. Gripping my knuckles on his shirt, he stared into my dead eyes with a matching set of his own.

"If you fuck with them, you're fucking *dead.*" I snarled, not caring that the man had me by several inches in height and even more in weight.

"Sure, puppy dog." He shoved me back and we both realigned our suits.

He stormed from my suite, disappearing into the club as I exited before locking the doors behind me. Commotion from across the room alerted me to a few people still lingering after the mess. A man in a black suit with short white hair was fighting with the blonde waitress, practically dragging her out of the club.

Fanculo. A better man would have run after her… ensured she was okay. But I was the furthest thing from a good man. I had also just murdered two men in open view, and I had no desire to spend any more time in a cage. Thankfully the club operated under an agreement of discretion. There were no recordings and no one would *dare* speak out in turn against me. Bearing witness meant admitting one's membership to the club while simultaneously painting an Agostino target on your back.

I was also hard as fuck and needed to find Cassandra. Something about the metallic scent that lingered on my skin—even as their blood peeled off in clumps—turned me on like a mood-enhancing drug. The kill, and the resulting adrenaline spike, spurned me forward. I needed a different type of relief, the kind that Cassandra could provide. She was standing off to the side, watching the cleanup with two other girls. I snapped my fingers to get her attention and motioned for her to follow me.

The moment she stepped inside, I latched my hand around her throat. I closed the doors behind her, slamming her back against them. Her mouth opened but no noise escaped as she stared at me with large eyes—very similar to those she had worn earlier. I didn't have the want or need to play any games with her. I pulled her closer, one hand still encompassing her trachea and the other positioning her head in place. I kissed, bit and devoured her whole as she tried to gasp around my tightening grip.

"Sir." She wheezed under my impenetrable embrace, her face reddening as she fought to take in more air.

I released her neck, shredding her robe into unrecognizable scraps of material. I twisted her around and pushed her face into the wall beside the door, her shocked breath further exacerbating my arousal. There was a deep unsatisfied need reverberating within my bones; it created an ache that was now impossible to ignore. All that was real in this moment was watching her fall apart under my control, and chasing the high of coming while buried deep inside her tight pussy.

I was barely free of my pants when I wrenched her ass closer, rooting myself to the hilt inside her. Her resulting moan was guttural and pleasure induced. Giving her a minute to adjust to my width, her pussy enshrined my cock perfectly, holding onto it with a savage ferocity that almost forced me to come with one thrust.

I pulled out quickly only to bury myself back inside—rough and fast. I set a relentless pace as I sought my own pleasure—the *demoni* quieting as release drew near.

I pushed down on her lower back, her spine arching and taking me deeper. I leaned forward and pulled her shoulders back, lacing my fingers together as I held her neck hostage once again. Her ragged moans grew startled as I increased my pace and tightened my grip. Her walls closed in around me, thrumming with her own orgasm on the horizon. The doors rattled as I picked up momentum, thrusting into her even harder and pushing her over the edge.

Sweat coated my skin as I threatened to lose control and ordered her to come. She shattered into a million pieces—one hand let go of her neck as I caught her around her middle before she collapsed. She was utterly spent as her languid form gasped and convulsed beneath me, my own orgasm threatening to destroy my resolve. The *demoni* had been silenced—at least for now—as I went about my usual business of cleaning first Cassandra and then myself.

"Head home for the night," I ordered her, grabbing my wallet and handing her a decent tip for the extra bruises. "Fuck."

As I waited at the curb for the valet, I typed out a quick text to Lucky. I needed his attention on several matters and would stay at the penthouse for the night. The bus stop to the right had a single silhouette sitting on the ground—a large hoodie did little to obscure her small frame. I noticed she wasn't on the bench. She wasn't waiting for the next bus; instead, she was huddled in the corner.

"Cassandra," I clipped from the car, my unspoken question hanging in the air. When I saw her mouth open and close a few times, I sent her a warning. "Do not lie to me."

"Uhm, I'm crashing here for the night," she shouted from where she sat. Startling herself, she looked around to ensure she was still alone. This neighborhood in the middle of the night wasn't safe for anyone, let alone a young woman.

Fucking hell.

"Get in the car," I growled after a few moments of hesitation and a brief internal debate.

It didn't take an idiot—or an unemotional lunatic—to know nothing good would come of her staying here. Cassandra had a direct connection to me, and that attachment came with the propensity to be used as leverage. When she didn't immediately move, I hummed in annoyance and unclipped my seatbelt. I stepped out of the car, walking around the hood to open the passenger-side door. Once she was tucked inside, I returned to the driver's seat. "What happened?"

"Mom's illness is progressing. I can't afford the apartment, the best facility for her and school. My residency starts soon so I'll be able to sleep at the hospital," she said, staring out the window in silence until we pulled into the underground hotel parking.

I stood from my car, and repeating my previous actions, I walked around the front of the hood. Cassandra's eyes went wide as she stared at me. Looking down at myself, I realized the parking garage lighting allowed her an unobstructed view of the carnage soaking my clothes. She stepped closer, looking for any sign that it was my own blood—the naturally inquisitive doctor had come to the surface.

"Your dry-cleaning bill must be expensive," she said.

I didn't say anything in response as I led her to the elevator and entered my code. My apartment was a two-bedroom and two-bath layout; it was modern style with an open concept. Sienna had designed and decorated the space. Sleek with sharp edges and neutral colors, it was comfortable and offered me the solace I needed. Anything was a step up from the streets I grew up on. Sienna and Lucky had apartments above mine, keeping us close together for efficiency in business and personal matters.

"Here." I flicked the light on in the spare bedroom and dropped her tattered bag onto the bed. The room had light grey walls and dark-colored carpets; a king-size bed sat in the center of the room. "Bathroom is there, everything you need is inside. Housekeeper comes in the morning. Leave any clothes you need washed on the floor, and she'll handle it. Kitchen is stocked. Help yourself to whatever you'd like. And here is a spare key to come and go."

"Apollo… sir." She stuttered as she took in her surroundings. She turned back to face me, her eyes filled with a warmth I didn't much appreciate.

"Do. Not. Take this for anything other than me assisting you in a time of need," I gnarled. Understanding, she locked down her features.

I didn't have love in my heart for anyone, but I was a shrewd businessman—you took care of me, I took care of you. However, Cassandra suffered from frequent neural impulses that spurred her into action. Her automatic receptive behavior had adapted throughout the stages of her life, a natural survival mechanism. She often took our *relationship* for more than what it was, forcing me to remind her—and remind her again—of the cruel reality of it.

I abruptly turned on my heel and exited, allowing her the chance to break down after my refusal. I looked over at my ringing phone, sighing when I saw it was Sienna. This had been the longest fucking day and depending on her news, tomorrow planned to be just as incorrigible.

Sitting on the edge of my bed, I answered with a grunt.

"Charming. Want the new details or not?" she questioned with an exasperated breath. My phone beeped, alerting me to Lucky's presence on the other line.

"Hang on, your brother is beeping through. He's upstairs… probably wants a meeting." I was about to hang up when she interrupted me.

"Cool. I'm in my lobby. I'll meet you in yours." She hung up and I switched lines.

"Boss," I answered, exhaustion evident in my tone.

"What do you have?" he asked, shuffling the phone around.

"Dominic Moretti. Sienna is downstairs with additional information," I said, scratching the back of my suddenly stiff neck.

"I'm coming down," he clipped, grinding his teeth.

A moment later, a squall of turmoil resounded in the foyer just outside my apartment. Sienna's elevated tone was agitated while Lucky's was booming with fury. I dropped my jacket onto the bed and headed towards the commotion. Opening the door, I growled at the sight before me. Lucky was holding Sienna back as she tried attacking Tatianna—Lucky's whore.

"You want to get fucked up, Tatianna?" Sienna roared, struggling in Lucky's grip. "Run your fucking mouth to me again, *pezzo di merda con la faccia da cazzo!*" Sienna's Italian was always interesting, especially when she was angry. This time, her choice to call Tatianna what loosely translated to a "dick-faced piece of shit" had me laughing—much to Lucky's annoyance.

"Enough!" I shouted.

Tatianna jumped as a result, having just registered my presence, and her eyes practically bulged out of her head as she took in my blood-soaked appearance. Now startled to the core, she paled. This display of obvious discomfort pleased me as my lips curled into something resembling a grin.

"B-b-bye, Lucky." She struggled to find her words as she began aggressively punching the elevator button.

"I'm assuming you'll explain." Lucky pointed to my destroyed suit.

I nodded, relaying the favor I'd garnered with Philadelphia. I could see Lucky's mind twisting—no doubt realizing the benefits an alliance with Philadelphia would give him. When Lucky took over New York there would be a power struggle; one I'd ensure we'd win effortlessly. But having those surrounding alliances, it was certainly to our advantage.

"Come in, Sienna." She smiled sweetly as she entered. I shook my head at what was likely to be another one of our verbal sparring matches.

"Jesus Christ. Like today wasn't fucked enough, Sienna." Lucky walked into my apartment and went right for my bar, pouring each of us a scotch.

"I heard all about Mirabella Moretti." She taunted her brother. Sipping her drink, she flopped onto the couch.

It was late in the evening and yet Sienna was dressed to kill. Her *Chanel* business suit hugged her sculpted body in all the right places. She was taller in height, even more so in designer heels, and her body was tight and shapely. Her long chestnut-brown, almost black hair trailed down her back and her darkened eye shadow made her blue-steel eyes pop.

"Don't run your mouth about fucking rumors, Sienna," Lucky growled in a low voice. "Now who wants to start so I can sleep off this fucking day."

"Ladies first!" Sienna popped to the edge of her seat, opening a manila folder filled with pictures.

"Funny, I don't see a lady," Lucky muttered, narrowly avoiding a closed-fisted punch from his sister.

"Anywho, Dominic Moretti is in business with a billionaire and just purchased the building across from your warehouse," she said, catching Lucky up to speed on Dominic and his business partner, John Hardwicke.

"How do you suddenly appear?" Lucky gestured towards the pictures of the man in question.

"Assuming a new name, police protection… police officer…" She trailed off, looking between the two of us.

"Are you insinuating undercover?" I asked, sitting across the coffee table from her.

"Could be. Dom's corporations started a short time before Hard-wicke suddenly appeared. Now, with all of these details, it could point to that," Sienna responded, staring at me from under her lashes. "A small fish with access to a big pond—they'd put a noose around his neck to get what they wanted."

"His contacts, and to shut him and his associates down. Makes sense. The question is, does he know who Hardwicke is?" Lucky asked, his gaze focused on me.

"Based on his openly depraved interactions and his mention of locking the girl in a cage, I suspect he does not," I said, dismissively.

"A cage? Christ." Lucky sat back with a heavy sigh.

"What're the chances his father, Anthony, is involved?" Sienna asked the question which served as an unwavering threat to our entire organization.

"I can't imagine he is, but doesn't hurt for you to check, Sienna," Lucky ordered.

"Okay. I'll get on it tomorrow and let you know," she agreed. Lucky nodded before turning to me.

"What do we know about the girl?" he asked.

"Nothing. I have her picture in all of my systems and she is nowhere to be found," Sienna admitted, handing him a stilled frame of the blonde from the docks.

"A ghost," I said as Lucky nodded, staring down at the image.

"Pretty girl." At her brother's words, Sienna turned to look at me—gauging for my reaction—though I only huffed in agreement. Lucky continued, "Why did you need to meet?"

"Did you know Carmine Ragetti is in town?" I asked, as Sienna's head snapped back in my direction.

"What do you mean he *is*?" Lucky attempted to clarify, a scowl on his face. "Pops said he was here a few weeks ago… and only supposed to be around for a few days."

"I assure you, he's still here. When questioned, he told me your dad knew and to fuck off." I ground my teeth, a new wave of anger coursing through my veins.

"Does anyone know exactly what the beef is with the Ragetti's?" Sienna interjected, running her index finger over her plump, pursed mouth.

Sienna was an enigma—and a gorgeous one at that. As I watched her stroke her bottom lip, my mind went to places it shouldn't. I could feel my thoughts drifting off, and mingling with the bloodshed from earlier in the evening, they bordered on inappropriate.

She was an Agostino. She was Lucky's—my best friend's—little sister. Yet, I found myself wondering what she tasted like. What she looked like when she came. Things I knew I shouldn't question… shouldn't dare think about. I was loyal to Mario… to the family. I wasn't allowed to taste something so untouchable and remain above reproach. Though, knowing that did little to squelch her sex appeal.

"I'll reach out to some contacts and see what I can find. Maybe you should speak with your father," I suggested, taking another sip from my glass.

"First, I want to hear all about what happened at *Vino*," Sienna insisted, leaning forward as she raised a brow at her brother.

Lucky's face immediately locked down; his disinterested mask told Sienna he wouldn't bite. I was unsure if he was even aware of his affections for the girl, and yet, his quiet and distant approach with Sienna hinted that he was starting to figure it out. He attempted to say his protection of her was out of necessity, stemming from his hatred for Gio. But it was a lie. There was much more brewing under the surface between the two of them—this was just the starting line.

"I'm going to call Pops." Lucky rose to his feet, depositing his cup on the coffee table.

"Lunch tomorrow? To discuss when I get to meet my future sister-in-law?" Sienna hollered after him, finishing her scotch when my front door slammed closed.

"You truly cannot help yourself, can you?" I asked, shaking my head at her resounding shrug.

"I'm not wrong, am I?" Sienna affirmed. "I heard all about him at *Vino*… and the added security hired for her."

"I don't think you're wrong, no," I agreed, pointing to her empty glass. She nodded before handing it to me. "I just don't think he realizes it yet. You know he's always said he'd marry out of obligation and nothing more." I replenished her with two fingers of scotch.

"Which I believed… until today," Sienna noted, taking the glass from me.

"I agree. He already asked me to set up a private… meeting with Mirabella." I told her about my ploy with the girl's mother in order to arrange everything.

Serafina gave me a few insights about her daughter—evidently the girl enjoyed reading a book and relaxing in coffee shops. And it just so happened that Lucky owned one. I set up the arrangement and changed his schedule to aid in his impromptu happenstance with the Moretti girl. At least this was my suspicion—he had yet to verbalize his intentions.

"The next few weeks will be interesting. You know she's back from Italy to announce an engagement. How do you think he'll take that?" Sienna asked, kicking her heels off as she relaxed into the sofa.

That was the thing about Sienna and me, we'd known each other for so many years that we had an easy, comfortable time together. When she wasn't bothersome and intentionally pushing my buttons for her own amusement, anyway. She was down to earth, intelligent and had a good sense of humor. However, the underlying sexual tension we seemed to both suffer from was as debilitating as it was intoxicating—since I was forced to fight off her advances.

"Earth to Apollo!" Sienna waved her hand in my direction, an amused expression on her face.

"Sorry. When it comes to the engagement announcement… I wouldn't be surprised if Lucky had your father get involved," I offered, walking into the kitchen to grab something to eat.

Sienna followed and sat on a stool at the counter. "There is one good thing about this." When she didn't immediately answer, I rolled my eyes. She was enjoying my impatience. "It'll get rid of Tatianna once and for all." She glowered at the mere mention of the glorified blowup doll.

"Ah, yes, no one will miss that *pezzo di merda con la faccia da cazzo*," I laughed, repeating Sienna's words. "Your originality never ceases to amaze me." I laughed harder at the innocent expression she gave me. Then her face softened and she chuckled as well.

"It was fitting though," she announced between labored breaths.

Sienna grabbed a piece of *Godiva Gold Collection Chocolates* from the box on the counter just as I was reaching to do the same. Our hands touched for the briefest of seconds—a brush so slight yet startling. Sienna gasped at the connection, while I was confused over exactly what had transpired between us, and the mood shifted.

It was stifling, dealing with her innate sexual prowess. Her beauty was effortless and compelling, any idiot would be able to see that. As much as I told myself she was off limits, it was during moments like these that immoral thoughts about her plagued my mind. I was a red-blooded male—an alpha—attracted to her scent. Our eyes locked and the silence of the room filled the space between us with static. It was almost deafening, as neither of us spoke.

Natural defiance, the kind that was ingrained in Sienna, was an attribute I normally rejected. I liked women who willingly bowed to my demands… and she was quite the opposite. Often outspoken and unruly, Sienna liked to do things her own way and against my better judgement. Thoughts had crossed my mind, about all the ways I'd break her, but the weight of Lucky's disapproval burdened me. Even if I enjoyed how she looked at me—as if she was dying of starvation—I couldn't fall into my own temptation.

Or feed into hers.

She swallowed roughly—her breathing pitched and increased. She was sin wrapped in a designer label with an aura of confidence that made her even more surmountable. But… I *couldn't* do this with her. Not to mention, I'd just come from fucking another woman. Sienna deserved the world; she deserved far better things than I could ever provide.

"I-I'm sorry." Cassandra's voice snapped us both out of our locked gazes.

Sienna turned to the sound, shock marring her beautiful face. Cassandra stood at the entrance of the kitchen wearing one of my shirts. Sienna stared reticently, though a myriad of pained emotions flashed across her face. Quickly catching herself, she shifted to indifference. But her mind churned, the realization smacking her in the face. I wouldn't admit it to her, but her assumptions were accurate.

"I'll leave you to your guest. Once I know more about what we discussed, I'll call you," she said, walking into the living room and offering Cassandra a forced smile as she passed.

Within seconds, Sienna had slipped into her shoes and headed for the exit. Any other woman would've slammed the door behind her—but not Sienna. In fact, the quiet click of the knob seemed louder than if she *had* slammed it closed. Love was merely a blend of neurological chemicals—none of which I understood outside of lust—and Sienna was drowning in them. Her indifference was merely a ploy; one I had no doubt I'd pay for later.

"Apollo, go after her," Cassandra choked out. While her words told me to go, her face was conflicted. "I didn't mean to disturb you. I thought you were in the living room and I could sneak down."

I waved off her concern. "Mind your own business, Cassandra." I dismissed her as I stared at the front door; the same door that Sienna had escaped through.

"Be a good man and go to her, explain yourself." Cassandra tried to push me again.

"I'm not a good man," I muttered more to myself than to her.

"*'Anger is an acid that can do more harm to the vessel in which it is stored than to anything on which it is poured.'* You're hurting everyone with your lies," Cassandra said, while my eyebrow raised in challenge at her choice of quote from Mark Twain.

"Oh, yeah? *'A man cannot be comfortable without his own approval.'* And neither Lucky nor I approve of his sister pairing with me. End of story." I dropped my glass in the sink, determined to end this conversation. "And I *do not* believe in happily-ever-fucking-after."

Cassandra padded out of the room as quietly as she'd entered. I wasn't lying when I said I wasn't a good guy. Bloodshed aside, Sienna needed someone that could provide things I could not. She was strong-willed and could take care of herself, but she was a woman and women needed comforting and displays of affection. I couldn't give any of that to her, so it made no sense to chase her down nor to try to rectify the situation.

Instead, I shut off the kitchen light and headed to my room to turn in for the night. The blood was dry and irritating my skin. It peeled off in clumps as I walked towards my bathroom. Lost in thought, I wished I could've been what she needed. But I was only capable of offering her a mere piece of myself when she deserved the whole package.

She was on the hunt for a pristine designer label, whereas I was damaged goods.

I needed to sleep and not dwell on the emotional impact tonight would have on Sienna. I had a list of names that needed to meet with *il mietitore,* and the *demoni* within me were clawing at my skin, demanding their reprisal.

CHAPTER 5
SIENNA AGOSTINO

"D on't. Don't do it." I chastised myself as I waited for the elevator to arrive outside Apollo's apartment. *"Stupida donna."*

I bit the inside of my cheek to focus on that pain instead of the pain inside my heart. My embarrassment threatened to drown me—I was incapable of staying above the surface any longer. I didn't know exactly what I was thinking or why I was allowing myself to be upset over something so trivial. He was an Italian man, a *made man* for that matter. Of course, he had women on the ready.

"Come on, Christ!" I growled, stabbing the elevator call button more insistently. "Move fucking faster."

The only good thing was that Apollo was too stubborn to actually charge after me. He'd give me my time to burn off the embarrassment and to overthink my actions before talking to me again and as if nothing happened. This wasn't our first song and dance. No, it wasn't the first time I had allowed my mind to take me places it shouldn't. To feel things… I shouldn't. Things I had hoped—maybe even assumed deep within myself—were mutual.

I was born in July, and I was a goddamned emotional crab. Any article you'd ever read on Zodiac signs, all the personality traits and behaviors of a Cancer, I personified them times ten. But we didn't share the same feelings. *Fuck!* The man was incapable of it… of offering me what I wanted. Time and again, I chased him, seeking the one drug that I knew could kill me—all that mattered was the high it would offer.

Unbridled tears threatened to spring loose. Finally, the elevator was a floor away. I could've stayed in my place here at the penthouse but I needed to leave the city and clear my head. And the family compound was the solace I needed from this hell of a week. Thomas Marks was officially in custody and the police were reviewing more evidence I had supplied for them. Evelyn was back in school and her father had signed on to work for me.

I'd continue to work on answers for Apollo and Lucky with the Moretti's. I also needed to add Carmine Ragetti to my list of inquiries —*now that I thought about it.* I didn't like to feel broadsided by anything. It was why I was so successful in my business. I didn't miss a single detail. I worked endlessly to ensure the outcome was one I had coordinated.

"What a sight for sore eyes!" Big Al chirped as the elevator doors opened. I swallowed my tears and smirked at him.

"Alvin." I laughed as he wrapped me up in his big arms, lifting me off my feet.

"What's up, chipmunk?" he asked, shaking me twice, before putting me back down.

He was affectionately named Big Al because… well, I'd give you one guess. He was *big*. No, I wouldn't know a particular appendage's size. Though, if rumors were to be true, it was as large as the rest of him. He was six and a half feet tall and damn near as wide with a naturally burly, stocky build. He was the type that was by no means fat— he'd just never have a six pack with the frame he was given. His dark brown hair and light brown eyes were often filled with mischievous laughter.

He also happened to be my best friend.

"Just heading out." I had to give myself credit, my voice sounded much stronger than it felt. Of course, it didn't matter though—because as any best friend would—he saw right through me.

"What happened?" He pushed for answers. Looking over my head at Apollo's door, he stared in silent rage.

"Nothing, just exhausted." I stepped into the elevator in an attempt to end the exchange, but he followed me inside. "I handled the Marks' situation."

"Cut the shit, Sienna. Of course, you did… you're a badass boss-lady. Now, what's really bothering you?" he asked. His lack of patience for my lies filled the limited air of the elevator around his hulking stature.

"Just being dumb." I clamped my lips shut, showing him that I wouldn't budge—no matter how persuasive he tried to be. My phone alerted me to a text. "Octavia is going to murder Peiro if he touches her books one more time," I laughed, reading the message aloud.

The bodyguard was working his way up the ranks and was person-ally charged with protecting Octavia. His position was the easiest and yet especially hard. Octavia didn't go many places or do many things, so the safety aspect was relatively simple. But she also loved to disap-pear in a library for hours and cart around a ton of books—a task that could be as daunting as it was boring.

"Okay. I am heading to the compound." I stepped out of the elevator as Al trailed behind me, before leaning up and kissing him on the cheek. "Have a lovely night, Alvin."

"Not so fast, chipmunk." He latched his meaty, calloused hand around my wrist and pulled me along, his cell phone already to his ear. "Bring Octavia to the hotel bar." He ended the call and proceeded to drag me through the lobby.

"Alvin!" I hmphed as he threw me into a leather chair. "What the fuck?"

"Such crass words from such a *lady!*" The bastard had the balls to act appalled before trekking to the bar.

It was late enough that it didn't boast a large crowd, but there was still a decent number of patrons for such a small space. Most of them seemed to be businessmen, dressed in wrinkled suits, their ties undone and sleeves rolled up. Frank Sinatra was crooning in the background and the dark cherrywood walls settled the room into a nice, placating atmosphere.

"Sienna!" Al called me over to two barstools that had just been vacated. Well, more likely, the previous occupants had run for their lives when Big Al stood between them to order drinks.

"*Saluti!*" I cheered, throwing back the peculiarly-pink shot before sputtering with a series of coughs in an attempt to avoid choking. "What in the world..." I trailed off, scowling as Al roared with laughter.

"Do you not like my bartending skills? It's called a *tight snatch*." He chuckled, seemingly beyond proud of himself.

"A what? What the hell is in that?" I tried wiping my tongue on a napkin to remove the residual taste.

"Vodka, rum, more vodka, *Bacardi 151*." The bartender trailed off as my face turned sour. "Oh, and a splash of cranberry!" he boasted proudly.

"You two spend too much time together down here." I pointed between the bartender and Al. "And how'd you come up with the name, besides the fact that it's pink?" I asked curiously.

"First taste, did it not..." The bartender paused to look at Al, who was turning red from holding in his laughter. "Make you, uh, tense your muscles?" He finished his statement uncomfortably.

"Why are you concerned with how tight I am, Al?" I teased. Turning to my friend, I enjoyed how the tint from his face dissipated as he blanched.

"Uh, uh. No. That's disgusting. You're my best friend. Basically a sister," he stuttered, looking to the bartender for help; but the other man was already backing up, his hands held high in surrender.

"Cheers." The bartender gestured towards the four additional shots lined up along the counter.

"Come on. How often can you say you drowned in some tight snatch?" Al chuckled, urging me to take another one.

"Fine. But back-to-back so I can burn my tongue off after." We raised each shot in the air and slammed them down, one after the other.

I had to close my nose and breathe heavily through my mouth to avoid the taste—and potentially vomiting. "So gross," I muttered, enjoying the silence between us for a few moments.

"Now, spill," Al ordered, his face set in stone.

"There's nothing to spill. I'm just dumb." I stopped myself before the alcohol warmed my cheeks.

Once it settled into my system, I verbally upheaved the last several weeks to him. Everything from forcing myself to watch the videos of Evelyn's rape, to the confrontation, all the way to whatever the hell happened upstairs with Apollo. Another shot and a martini later, and all my dirty laundry had air-dried and I felt lighter.

"Sienna. You…" He hesitated, looking for the right words. "You know, he isn't capable of… what you deserve," Al said. His eyes softened but each word was like a slap to the face.

"I don't even want him." I waved the idea off, trying to believe my own lies. "I just have a lot on my plate and then my dad…" I cutoff my words. I didn't want to go there.

"Don't throw them!" Octavia yelled from the entryway into the bar. Al and I turned just in time to see Peiro dump her bag onto the floor by an empty table. "Asshole," she muttered, blowing her tousled hair from her face.

"Hey, baby sis!" I waved from my stool, too concerned I'd bust my ass if I stood to greet her. Al walked over and grabbed her bag from the floor, scowling at Peiro.

"Hey. You know I *can* stay in my own apartment and be left the hell alone once in a while." Octavia growled—in a cute way—like a little mouse growling at a lion.

"I missed you!" I raised both of my arms above my head in excitement, allowing the stool to spin me. Al grabbed me when I turned sideways—clearly, I had not been ready for the sudden *turn* of events. Ha!

"You're drunk." Octavia shook her head in annoyance, but I saw her smile. "Shall we?" she asked Al, heaving her bag onto her shoulders.

"You carry your library and I'll get this one." Al chuckled, helping me off the stool.

My ankles burned from the exertion of holding my drunk ass up in these expensive stilettos. I wiggled my fingers in an exaggerated, condescending goodbye to Peiro before lifting my middle finger. When he scowled in return, I laughed harder. Kissing the end of my finger, I blew it back in his direction. He abruptly turned on his heel and headed for the elevator.

"Hold on!" I shrugged myself loose from Al and plopped my *Chanel*-covered ass onto the ground. "Seventeen hours isn't a joke in these babies." I giggled to myself, peeling off my heels.

"You good?" Octavia asked, pulling me to my feet.

I shoved open the door to the sidewalk with a shout and darted towards Al's SUV, positioned at the curb. "Yep!" I opened the back door and threw my shoes inside. I then hopped in the vehicle, grabbing hold of the seat before I fell back out.

"You did this." I heard Octavia say as Al held the passenger door open.

The ride from the city to our family compound went by in a blur. Both literally and figuratively as my mind was warm and happy and unable to comprehend anything other than its own blissful ignorance— thanks to those pink snatches… no. Those… tight snatches! It took the edge off my stressful agenda and I was now ready for some blissful sleep.

"Come on, Sienna. Up she goes," Octavia said, hidden behind Al as he fished me and my shoes from the car.

"I got it!" I stumbled towards the door, whispering for them to be quiet since it was late.

Who was I kidding? My father was probably in his office, the guards would be patrolling in shifts and my mother's room was on the other side of the house. Still, I was a loud drunk and a hilarious one at that. I shoved the heavy wooden front door open and skipped into the all white, marble foyer. Soft music came from my right, cascading out of my father's open office doors.

"Daddy!" I skipped inside, plopping into the leather chair in front of his desk.

"Sienna." He smiled at my drunken slump. Walking towards us, he pulled Octavia in for a kiss before she darted towards the stairs. "Where are your shoes?" he asked when he turned to look at me again.

"Here," Al muttered, dropping them at my feet before disappearing out the door with a smirk.

"What is it with you and losing shoes?" my dad asked, his eyes filled with amusement.

"I don't lose them! I always find them… in the end." I grunted.

"Well?" he prompted, and I suddenly sobered.

"In police custody, and as of now, held without bail. From what I gathered, though, their attorney is trying to say due to a medical condition, he should be getting bail." I tucked my hair behind my ear and folded my feet in and under my butt.

"I assume you are putting a stop to that." It wasn't a question.

"Daddy. Am I not *your* daughter?" I smiled at him.

"Indeed. Your mother's beauty but your father's ruthlessness. A killer in designer power suits." He smirked at me before again growing solemn. "We need to talk about something else."

He wandered over to the small fridge that was tucked under his office bar. I used to come in here as a kid, even though it was forbidden. I'd pour water into his crystal glasses before sitting behind his desk like I owned the city. It was a tough pill to swallow as a child… to learn that everything was being given to Lucky. As far back as I could remember, I'd wanted my own power, a city to call my own.

In one sentence my family preached: *You're only as strong as your weakest family member.* The next, you were told that as a woman, you weren't entitled to the keys to the city. I understood it now, and I was thankful it was a title Lucky would proudly wear. Besides, I had decided I wanted more than just New York. *Energia* Holdings was now international and I would continue to take it to new heights… all on my own.

"It appears Lucky has shown some interest…" He started but I cut him off.

"Mirabella Moretti has fallen prey to *il diavolo*." I chuckled at my brother's nickname.

"Yes. Anthony Moretti knows nothing of this… yet. Unlike your brother, you know what gift Anthony is forced to give to me. And between you and me, I've made a decision." My father beamed.

Lucky may have been the future king, but sometimes he was kept in the dark. Five years ago, my father took control over the future of Anthony's daughter, Mirabella. Anthony was given permission to use our docks at a large cost to him—*personally and financially*. However, Lucky's affinity for the girl all those years ago forced my father into silence.

"Lucky wants Bella… you're giving him *the gift*." He nodded at me.

"Yes. Neither Lucky or Anthony know of my plans. But shortly, after your brother realizes his true feelings, I will lock the details into place. However, Anthony did come to me with something else. The son of a bitch assumed he could make demands of me, suggesting that since I am taking his daughter…" He trailed off and it didn't take a genius for it all to fall into place.

"He wants to take yours." Silence filled the space between us. "And Octavia is far too sweet to be handed off to someone in this life. Gio or Dom?" I asked, though I already knew the answer.

"Gio." He dropped the bomb anyway, his blue-steel eyes—so similar to my own—filled with remorse. "You're past the age of marriage, Sienna, and many people have been making offers. I refuse to cower to Anthony Moretti, of all people. But the fact of the matter is… you need to realize the time is now."

In our world, it wasn't uncommon for marriages to be arranged. Men and women in the *famiglia* often strategized over potential matches at the birth of their children. Money and power—they made our world go round and alliances were worth a lot. My father refused to promise any of his children when we were younger, opting to wait and to see what held the most value later on in his reign. And it gave us the chance to make peace within ourselves over our future obligations.

Lucky was falling for Bella—anyone could see that as plain as day. I, on the other hand, had no interest in settling down with some *scemo* who would try to tell me what to do with myself. My company was stronger, and growing faster, than I'd ever anticipated and I refused to share that with anyone. I also refused to become a housewife and sit back while my husband tried running things. I wasn't made for that life. The thought was depressing and filled me with animosity. My parents had built me so strong, yet still expected me to fulfill such a mundane duty.

"Have you chosen for Octavia?" I asked.

"Not yet. But… your mother and I talked about it. It won't be anyone from our world. A politician's son or something, someone that can keep her safe and out of the dangerous Agostino limelight." My dad's admission made me smile sadly at the thought.

"Just not… not the Moretti's, daddy," I implored him, bursting into drunken tears.

"You need someone stronger than that, baby. Someone who sees your worth and won't stand in the way of you achieving whatever it is you want." He smiled proudly. "If you were a man, Sienna, you'd have destroyed Lucky to follow in my footsteps."

"Duh." I laughed, wiping away a lone tear.

"Now, who made you cry?" I shook my head, refusing to answer him; instead, I smiled. "What did Apollo do, Sienna?" he clarified.

My heart stopped in my chest as I raised a curious brow. He had always been such a perceptive man, or was it that I was an easy give-away? He had watched over me my entire life so of course he knew. But I'd kept that side of me—those feelings—all to myself, in the hopes that no one would laugh in my face. The powerful Sienna Agostino capable of falling for the infallible, unempathetic, deadly right hand to the Devil himself.

"Why do you think it was Apollo?" I asked, rising from my seat.

"Because, my darling girl…" He stopped to stare at me in his assessing Agostino way. "He is the only one capable." He smiled soberly, kissing my forehead.

I went to step away from his desk—choosing to ignore his comment—before realizing my shoes were discarded under it. "Oh!" I hopped back in the chair, struggling to slide into my heels.

"I will make you one promise, Sienna." I didn't turn around to look at him, for fear I might get dizzy. "I will do my *best* to arrange someone that can handle you, and is as worthy as possible."

"I know, daddy." The utterance was no more than a whisper. "But it won't be who I want."

I darted up the stairs towards my room before anyone else had the chance to run into me. The tears had finally stopped but my mind and my heart were in a battle over who would come out on top. After all, I was allowed to have my moments of weakness and shatter into a million pieces. I'd sleep it off and tomorrow I'd be back to being *the* boss bitch of the Agostino family.

"Fuck him. He doesn't deserve me." My brain forced the words aloud even as my heart raced faster at the declaration. Besides, my birthday was coming up and I loved any opportunity to celebrate. Without any more words or thoughts, I hopped into bed—still in my clothes—and everything went black.

CHAPTER 6
APOLLO DELUCA

I placed my cell phone in the center console, just as my burner phone vibrated in my jacket pocket. It was the phone that not many of my associates knew about—if they did, they only used it for one reason. Before reaching for it, I stared vacantly out of the windshield as my Phantom Rolls Royce idled—her purr bouncing off the neighboring brick structures around me. The rain was light but constant; it made the streets barren… quiet.

The message would be simple.

The message would be precise.

The message would be a name… an address.

The owner of which would have no idea that they had made my list.

I cracked my neck from side to side before grabbing the phone and sliding open the screen. I didn't care who sent it nor did I care whose name was spelled out in the ominous green bubble.

Michael O'Hare. 2247B Olive Street.

My entire body tensed as I read the text aloud. Pressing the call button, I waited. "Details," I demanded.

"I found him. He's been back in the city for four weeks." My anonymous hacker was the best in the business. No, this wasn't an

Agostino matter; this was my own personal mission—one that I felt compelled to carry out. And that meant I kept it away from the family. My hacker understood my rationale, doing my technological dirty work for his own self-designated reasons.

My mind rattled, memories assaulting my frontal lobe, as I reread the message twice more. He'd spent years ruining lives—acting as if he was God himself—as if he was untouchable. No one was untouchable. I wasn't a deity nor was I the Devil, merely a man with a list. And it just so happened the man on my list had evaded me for over a decade. He knew I was looking for him and I was curious as to why he decided to come back to *this* city.

"Done." I shifted my Phantom into drive and headed towards my destination.

I parked in an underground garage beneath a lavish restaurant several blocks from Olive Street. Once inside, I nodded and shook the hands of each of the many patrons, all offering their regards due to my affiliation with the Agostino's. However, it didn't matter to me if they did so or not—I enjoyed teaching them exactly why I was to be respected. They smiled; I glared. They nodded; I stared them down until they forestalled their gazes and fled.

They were leeches. A systemic plague of insincerity dripped from their smiles as they lay waste to those around them. The frivolity of it all was a goddamned pandemic, throwing the world into chaos and imminent peril. I wanted nothing from men such as these, but they wanted everything from me and mine—especially the things they had yet to earn. They attempted to invoke some sort of imminent domain over the city, as if they could live vicariously through Mario and the empire he'd created. I loathed them and everything they stood for.

When I was sure my face had been seen enough, I slipped through the back entrance and walked to the car parked in the alley. I'd learned the tricks of this particular trade after my unfortunate arrest several years ago—alibis were pertinent even if you despised those in your company. I changed quickly into black sweatpants and a hoodie. I needed to drift into the darkness, not for fear of the light but because I needed my time—as much as I could allocate—alone... with *him*.

Time without the authorities thwarting all of the very palatable ideas I'd conjured up over the years.

I tried to fight the memories as I headed towards Olive Street but I was unsuccessful. It was this man that had created my need to satisfy my lists. He was to blame for my love of spilt blood. Again, I snapped my neck from left to right as I tried to stay in the present, but the memories were too strong. I sat at a red light two blocks away when it all came crashing down around me.

"Come here, you little shit," Michael shouted from the top of the basement stairs.

Cara shuttered on the bed across from me, her soft gray-blue eyes filling with tears. If we were being released from the basement, it wasn't for a good reason. That musty, moldy and rank dungeon was our home unless he saw it fit to punish us for something we hadn't done. Or he sought to reprimand us merely because we were alive... and because he could. I did my best to take all of the beatings—Cara was too small, too fragile to survive his brutal rage.

"I said now!" he roared.

My stomach was empty and it growled as I hit the first step—the aroma of pancakes filling the air. It was breakfast time, but I wouldn't be allowed to eat. He tossed stale bread, unopened cans of soup and other cheap items down the stairs whenever he felt like it. His biological daughter, Sarah, would do her best to steal his keys and feed us leftovers from the kitchen. But after she was forced to watch a beating that stained the stairs with a permanent red tint, she stopped.

"Your ears broke?" he spat in my face. The moment my frail skeletal form climbed to the top, he threw me against the wall—my body pinned in place by a tight hand against my throat. "You push my patience, little shit."

I turned my head as much as possible—his rancid breath threatened to upturn the piece of bread I had consumed yesterday. Michael's eyes flared in excitement. He enjoyed the disgust written across my face; he enjoyed my discomfort. I could see Sarah sitting at the break- fast table with her head down. Her hair, a wall of brown locks, shel- tered her face. The woman of the house sat next to her and stared at me with dead eyes. His wife was just as bad as he was... though sometimes I felt like she was worse. Her lack of concern and action to stave the abuse I was about to endure evoked just as much hatred—if not more.

These people were supposed to shelter and protect me. Instead, I was a slave to Michael's demands... a bag of flesh for him to beat. He was a fat, dirty slob—overweight from the food the state discounted for him; the same food that he withheld from Cara and me. The check he got every month for "housing" us paid his bills and he enjoyed the favor he felt he garnered for doing such a "generous thing."

"I said clean the bathroom, little shit." He squeezed my neck tight once more, seeking to elicit a sound from me. He tried day in and day out, craving a response to the pain, but I refused to give it to him. He growled in my face for good measure before shoving me towards the hall.

I stared at the table overloaded with pancakes, eggs and bacon. My stomach churned in agony as I passed—I'd give anything to even take a large, close whiff. When I started to slow my pace, he shoved me from behind once more, forcing me to lose my footing and fly into the cabinets. The pain enveloped my neurons and stars erupted behind my eyes as I threatened to lose consciousness.

Michael kicked me in the ribs—how many times, I hadn't registered. I rolled over and stared up at him. He was screaming in my direction but I couldn't make out his words. My body was too weak and confused from the lack of nourishment, while the pain in my head left me with the inability to move or think.

He stood over me with a glare so full of hatred that I should have erupted into flames. And I loved it. I loved how much he hated me. I loved that he only did this for the state's money. His lack of empathy had turned his beatings into my cocoon—there was no affection between us. Nothing to get in the way. No matter what he threw at me, I was ready because one day he'd get it back... tenfold. One day he'd beg and plead for me to end his pathetic life just so he could escape the pain I'd inflict.

"In you go, like the mangy mutt you are." His sausage fingers

wrapped around my thin arm and pulled me into the living room. I didn't need to open my eyes to know where he was taking me.

In the center of the small room sat a table with a blanket over it. Only it wasn't a table. Michael removed the covering and unlocked the door to the steel dog cage before shoving me inside. I managed to pull my legs to my body before he slammed it closed. The cage was my home away from the basement. He was a sick, cruel fuck that reveled in watching TV, eating food and using a caged child as a footstool. He'd kick and taunt me from the outside; I remained hidden beneath the blanket and sheltered from any sunlight.

My mind darkened with thoughts of his blood coating my hands as I drifted into a state of near unconsciousness. Though, my solace—the shear nothingness—only lasted for a moment before the cage rattled. He was snickering on the other side of the metal bars. Still obscured by the blanket, he toed the top as he yelled.

"You won't ever be free of me. Not in your sleep, not in this life. I fucking own you." He growled, shaking the cage from side to side—the violent motion forcing my body to slam back and forth against the unrelenting metal.

His words grew crueler before his voice tapered off as he wheezed from the exertion, and I smiled. Yes, one day I would escape this and I wouldn't look back. I'd be stronger, bigger and a hell of a lot scarier when I taunted him with memories of what he had done to me. Once I was capable, I'd be back for him. I'd smile and laugh in his face as his cries fell on my deaf ears. I would make sure that even in death, using his own words against him, he would never be free of me. I'd haunt the fucker.

I shook off the memory as my car idled in the darkened alleyway behind Olive Street. I'd been waiting for this day to come to fruition for years. I'd tormented him from hundreds of miles away. My threats… my vow… merely a whisper in the wind on a cold and lonely night—always lurking in the darkness, reminding him of our fortuitous reunion.

It took a certain type of person—a piece of shit under your shoe in a rat-infested basement—to inflict that kind of pain on a little kid. He had enjoyed my lack of emotions, my lack of empathy—the same as I had his own—when he tried to break me day after day for four years and before I had my chance to leave. When I saw my opportunity, all those years ago, I took it... With a knife to his gut, we fled. Some would say it was a shame that I hadn't had the knowledge then that I do now.

However, I said it was meant to be. Back then, I didn't know anatomy, didn't know that I needed to push the knife in a little deeper and further to the right. He survived that day not because a supposed God was looming over him as a shiny beacon of hope and protection. In reality, karma was a twisted bitch and she had given me the time and the skillset to impart just the punishment he deserved.

And I wouldn't disappoint.

Cara was six when she came to that terror house. Arriving about two weeks after me, she escaped at my side at ten years old. I did my best to protect her on the streets, which in turn, caused a lot of turmoil. Cara was a gorgeous girl. Even malnourished, she was radiant. With her jet-black hair and intense gray-blue eyes, she was an open target as I struggled to keep men away from her.

The emotional, social and physical welfare of young children had a direct effect on their overall development and on the adult they would become. I was a veritable headcase and Cara struggled with physiological growth. The initial lack of nutrients and our later inability to provide sufficient meals prevented her from becoming too womanly. She was shorter and frailer than most, but her beauty didn't falter.

Thanks to Mario's subsidy, I was able to protect Cara from the tortuous path on which life was taking us. She'd manage to finish school and became a counselor for abused kids. She headed for New Jersey when she received information on the *mother* who abandoned her. I had kept my mouth shut after she told me she was trying to *help* the piece of shit.

The woman had discarded her daughter to chase the high of a needle. Forever tainting Cara's life.

The only good thing that had come about—after it was all said and done—was Cara's best friend, the daughter of the President of an infamous Motorcycle Club. Their friendship had earned her the protection of the Rale Bulgarians MC and now she was the old lady of one of their enforcers—a man chosen to protect the family and the club. I still required her to stay in touch, to ensure no one took their revenge on me… through her. The communication was usually passed down from her husband. We shared an unspoken understanding—respect I had garnered due to saving Cara's life. But I would be remiss to say I didn't thoroughly enjoy his discomfort when Cara made me her son's Godfather.

I crept through the darkness to find the apartment on the second story. The fire escape squeaked and moaned under my weight, threatening to collapse at any moment. The window was dirty and the inner contents obscured, but movement and audible screams sounded the second I leaned into the frame. The echo of flesh hitting flesh assaulted my ears and *his* wild grunts and demeaning words ladened the void.

Michael was beating the hell out of a woman now curled up into a ball on the floor. The orange hair told me it was *the wife*—the woman just as guilty as her husband. To this day, I had no idea what her name was. I had never even bothered to do my research. I had always assumed that after he had healed, he would have turned his beatings onto her—a fact, I must admit, that made me smile in triumph.

I raised my hand, my leather glove crackling as I pulled it into a fist and knocked on the glass. It took a moment for him to hear me, his violent assault holding his attention, before he looked towards the noise. He rose to his full stature—unimpressive and still just as portly —walking two steps towards the window with the same glare. He appeared perplexed as we stared at each other for a beat. Then realization settled and the truth sunk in like a heavy weight between us.

Obesity was generally caused by consuming excessive amounts of food with little to no exercise. If you took in an abundance of nonessential nutrients, but did not burn off the calories through outward exertion, much of the surplus energy would be stored in the body as fat. And since Michael's ability to foster children had long since ceased, his BMI was off the charts due to his lack of… *physical activity.*

I stood tall on the stairs and dropped my hood to give Michael an unobstructed view of his executioner. A cloud of impending doom encompassed the fire escape, a proverbial hell fire on my heels as I leaned into the feeble structure of the window. He tried to turn and run but he tripped over the crumpled shell—the waste of a human being—on the floor.

Without a single notion towards hesitation, my body throttled through the flimsy wooden frame, and I plowed into the room. The rain dripped from my hoodie, pooling like a trail of tears from all his victims. He was to make amends for his sins, one fucking drop of blood at a time.

"Hello, Michael." I growled in a low, menacing voice. "It is. So nice. To see you again."

"Pl-please," he begged as sweat beaded at his brow.

"Wife." With a dip of my head, I acknowledged the sack of flesh who watched me with blank, dead eyes. "What exactly are you pleading for, Michael?"

"I'm… I'm sorry." The tears spilled over the edge of his eyes as he crawled backwards, sliding across the dusty floor.

"Every. Single. Day." I squatted in front of his face. "Every one of them inside that cage, I told myself I'd celebrate *you* begging… *me*," I sneered into the darkness.

"I-I was sick back then. I-I have been fixed," Michael sniveled.

When frightened, your central nervous system was flooded with adrenaline—a natural hormone. It caused your heart to pump blood more forcefully to the muscles, and perspiration was secreted as your body attempted to regain equilibrium. You often lost control over your bowels, tears and even nasal membranes. The end result was what I now saw before me as Michael blubbered at my feet.

"Sadistic pricks like you can't be fixed. The only remedy is to be put down like a rabid dog." I smiled. "Curious as to how I know? Because I am that man too. Only I'm strong enough and smart enough to have the upper hand now."

"I-I have some money." He switched tactics.

"I have more money than I could spend in two lifetimes." I flashed a stare at the wife, then back to the prone form at my feet. "The only thing I am missing is your soul ripped from your body… by my hands. You've made it to my list and *il mietitore* doesn't release anyone from the promise of a slow, painful *morte*."

I bounced on my heel for another moment, still squatting—my elbow resting on my thigh—as I leaned over him. Tapping a finger to my upper lip, I rose gracefully. Then in a singular swift movement, my boot smashed into his head with as much potency as I could exact from that angle. I stilled at the cracking noise, wondering if I'd broken his neck. After all these years and at first glance of this son of a bitch, I was already losing my composure. His round body slumped but I could see his abdomen rise and shake with each breath. I made quick work of zip tying his limbs, stuffing his sock into his mouth and covering it with tape. I dragged him to the door before turning on my heel and approaching the *puttana*. I had almost forgotten…

"I've waited for years to learn of your death. I'd assumed you'd have killed yourself by now. But I'm sure you didn't, merely in fear he'd haunt you even in the afterlife." I dropped down, meeting her eye level. "He won't be back. I am sending him to the same hell where you belong."

Her eyes didn't register me but the shaking of her body told me she had heard the declaration. She had allowed her husband to destroy countless kids, her own daughter included. Sarah disappeared shortly after we did, but she turned to a life of drugs in order to escape her reality. She was as weak as her mother, refusing the help I had attempted to give her.

"What's your name?" When she didn't immediately answer, I leaned in closer, sharing her same air.

"An-Annamarie," she whispered, her voice resigned.

"Annamarie…" I chewed on the name for a second before continuing. "You'll never feel freedom even with the peace his death may afford you," I whispered back, placing a 9mm on the floor in front of her. "You had so many chances to free yourself and save so many from the pain this bastard inflicted."

"I-I'm weak." It was the first time I heard her speak loudly and with actual conviction.

"*'Love all, trust a few, do wrong to none,'*" I quoted. "That's Shakespeare, in case you were unaware. All you needed to do was show a little compassion and take care of those kids. So, do us all a favor…" I tapped the firearm with my gloved hand before rising to my feet. I grabbed Michael under his arm and continued dragging him out of the apartment door. I'd barely made it to the top of the steps before I heard the discharge.

She was weak, indeed.

I didn't bother to try to pick him up, instead I shoved him down the staircase, relishing in the trauma the fall would inflict. He awoke just as I dropped him into the trunk, his eyes widening with the realization of his current predicament. His breathing increased as panic took hold and I leaned into him, forcing his body further into the depths of the vehicle. And I knew my bright white teeth were glowing in the darkness as I ran my tongue across them.

"Our fun has just begun, Michael." I listened to his strangled cries, muffled by the gag I had fashioned. "You have so many wrongs to atone for. So many victims who deserve to hear you grovel. Let's start with Cara." His eyes registered her name, igniting my familiar sense of detached rage. I dropped a large wad of spit on his face before knocking him out with a single blow.

I closed the trunk, bracing my palms against it. Hanging my head, I was desperate to rein in some sort of control as my hands shook, as if on their own accord. My mind flashed with the million ways I was going to make him pay for every travesty, every perversion. Hopping into the driver's seat, I turned on the radio and tapped my fingers on the wheel, traveling slowly and cautiously to my abandoned warehouse.

I unlocked my phone and used my security app to open the garage door. As I pulled the car inside the building, I smiled. It had been years —playing cat and mouse with this piece of shit—all coming down to this. Dragging his limp body inside, I cut the zip ties and fastened him into the chains bolted to the floor and hanging from the ceiling.

His chin rested on his chest as he made a satisfyingly pained sound stemming from the depths of his gut. I had so many plans but I wasn't prepared to start just yet. I wanted him to wake up alone and in the dark. I wanted him to be startled by every little noise. I wanted him to pray someone was coming to his rescue. And I wanted him to spend hours stewing in his own filth—all before I played with him. I made sure the chains were secured in the windowless room. I then armed the security system and headed back to the car.

I leaned against the trunk, lighting a cigarette before checking that the nocturnal security cameras were still active. I threw the hood back over my head and enjoyed the silence and the nicotine burning through my chest. My list would never end, but this was the moment I had been waiting for since I had been given the title *il mietitore*. I grabbed my burner phone from the center console, hesitating briefly before dialing the number.

"Hello." Cara answered on the second ring.

"Rest easy," I said, knowing she'd understand me. In a matter of seconds, she gasped in shock, cried in fright and breathed a sigh of relief. A deep voice resounded in the background but she called him off.

"Thank you, Reaper." She hung up without another word.

I flicked my cigarette onto the ground before climbing back into the car. I rolled the window down as the sights and smells of the city aided in my transition to a peaceful calm from a once raging storm. I returned to the alley, redonned my suit and reentered the restaurant.

Everyone buzzed around the room unaware of the threat that had entered through the kitchen. Tomorrow their name could be put on my list, and they'd finally get the chance to learn just how much of a beast I truly was.

CHAPTER 7
APOLLO DELUCA

Lucifer "Lucky" Agostino was like a brother to me; he was my closest confidant… and also my boss. The man was the epitome of strength, patience and the violence that was needed for his position. That being said, to watch him trip over his words and debate his decisions—falling apart at the seams for this sprig of a girl—was pure entertainment.

With each interaction, my respect for the Moretti daughter grew tenfold. After so many years growing up among her siblings, I'd have presumed she'd suffer from the confines of the same dismal gene pool. Instead, she was quite the opposite. Mirabella Moretti was strong and confident with a shrewd way of thinking over all of the possible outcomes of a situation. The information from her arranged security detail further substantiated this assessment. She would be *good* for Lucky.

One look at him and I could see his inner conflict—his errant thoughts intensifying each time she was near. He needed to maintain total concentration on too many things and each new piece of information added a higher level of complexity to the mix. He was on overload where Bella was concerned, with or without all of the *other* issues we were having.

In regards to those *other* issues, I had Gio handled when it came to covering our shipments. My suspicions—believing there was a potential rat in our midst—had turned all information into a need-to-know basis. Shakespeare had said it best: *"Have more than you show. Speak less than you know."* A credence I was currently living by, to ensure we weren't broadsided once more.

The Russians were running interference with our deliveries, a situation we were still navigating through. The last few weeks had turned into a headache of epic proportions as we attempted to figure out how to straighten *them* out. For the moment, our customers—those that had purchased the Russian weaponry—had been patient as they awaited their own deliveries.

In our world, Italians barely tolerated the Russians in any of our business dealings. Lucky extended this olive branch to our local Russian supplier, believing his ties to the *Bratva* were unfounded and nothing more than a rumor to intimidate his other associates. Yuri, our Russian contact, wasn't the brightest human being—but his stupidity was our gain. We were able to funnel in a very lucrative income due to the relationship—this was true—however, we wouldn't hesitate to take the hit and destroy all of them for their misgivings… if needed.

"That was a fucking waste of time." Lucky growled as we pulled out of the warehouse, having just left our meeting with Yuri.

"There is no logical reason for their actions. Why start making waves in a deal that's been extremely lucrative for both sides?" I asked; though, I didn't expect an answer.

After an hour, going in circles over their nonsensical demands, we left even more perplexed than when we'd arrived. Yuri refused to deliver future goods if Lucky wasn't present to accept them. It was a red flag—a goddamned Trojan horse if you asked me—to control Lucky's movements and to take him down.

Lucky had warned Yuri, it would be his head if he broke the current arrangement. The Russian had no explanation, no reasoning behind the demand, so we left with our threat hanging in the air. We would wait and see what they decided to do. However, in that same breath, I scoured over the conflict with Gio, wondering if the incidents were somehow tied. The approach had been thorough… committed. It almost didn't feel like Gio. It wasn't a maneuver pulled by a man with an adolescent vendetta—this was something else.

"Brief me on… Bella." Lucky had spoken her name between gritted teeth, growling when I failed to hide my amusement.

After their "chance" meeting at the coffee shop, Lucky had given up his denial over her. He was so adamant about actually dating Bella, he went as far as to demand that her father hold off on finalizing her impending engagement. That was when we learned the powerful hold Mario held over Anthony Moretti. He had proof that Anthony was the one who had killed Sal Ragetti Junior in order to marry Bella's mother. His silence had cost Anthony extensive dock fees, and Mario now held control over Bella's arranged marriage.

Which in turn, led to Lucky's arranged engagement to Bella and put an interesting twist on all of our questionable issues.

"There is no way Anthony is involved in Gio's mess. He wouldn't take that type of chance, nor risk the Ragetti's finding out the truth," Lucky said, slamming his phone on his desk.

"I don't think we should exclude him from the investigation just yet." I handed him the bank statements Sienna had emailed regarding Anthony's corporation. "He's involved in *something*."

"I agree… One thing at a time—Gio is directly affecting me so I want answers on him first." Lucky signed off on additional items before I switched topics.

"I have set up that arrangement… for you and Bella." I smirked at his scowl. "And her mother has handled all of the details for the blind *date*." And I smirked again at his exasperated huff, but I didn't miss the smile that followed.

"Good. Next on the agenda: you have a skype meeting with Romano from Philadelphia and a few other calls, before Sienna's birthday tonight." I scanned his schedule to make sure I hadn't missed anything.

"What about you?" he asked, rubbing his temples. "What's on your plate?"

"I have a lead on someone close to Gio. I'm going to take a look." I dropped several photos on the desk in front of him.

During Gio's time in Italy, he kept in contact with a crew of street kids back here in New York. Since we were unable to get information from Yuri—and I didn't have permission to torture Gio—they were my next stop. I'd seen their *leader* sniffing around the docks, far too close to the Russian shipments.

"Okay, you're coming to Sienna's party, right?" Lucky asked, booting up his computer.

"Yeah. She'd have my balls if I didn't." I grimaced, rolling my shoulders as my suit pulled snug.

"Yeah, she would. Okay, let me know what happens." Lucky dismissed me with a flick of his wrist, grabbing the phone to call Romano. I left the hotel, hopping into Al's car idling at the curb.

I motioned for him to take off, just as my cell phone vibrated in my pocket. *"It's Britney, bitch,"* screeched loudly and I cringed at the sound. Fucking Sienna—she did this shit all the time. She did sporadic wireless monitoring of all technology and properties for security purposes, leaving behind little Easter eggs, letting us know she'd been there.

Like this fucking ringtone.

"Sienna." I growled, answering to her knowing laughter.

"I happen to enjoy some *Britney* throwbacks." She laughed harder; and consequently, I had to wait for her to calm down before she would continue. "Anyway, I looked into Yuri, like you asked. His 'ties' to the *Bratva* are deadly. As in, he is on the outs… with a very large price on his head."

Apparently, Yuri's deceased wife had a brother that was higher up in the Russian organization. When she died, the *Bratva* turned against him… and his children. He fled Russia with his two sons but Sienna believed the daughter had been left behind. Preferably, the Russian was wanted alive, but dead still paid.

"My assumption… he wants to make a name for himself by taking out Lucky. Once I know more, I will be in touch. Also, tonight I want something sparkly as a gift, you know what I like." In true Sienna style, she hung up before I could tell her exactly what I'd like to give her.

I had the perfect idea.

A mouthy and trying woman such as Sienna Agostino would look impeccable with a diamond-encrusted dog collar locked around her throat—expensive and complete with a leash. When she wanted to run away with herself, I'd choke her back in place. The woman liked to pretend that my patience was infinite when in fact, it was quite the opposite. And she, well, she was fucking impossible.

"Fucking intolerable little shit," I muttered, turning an angry brow towards Al's raucous laughter.

"You didn't get her a gift yet, did you?" he asked, returning his attention to the road.

"Of course I did. It wasn't the gilded cage she needs to put her ass in line, but nonetheless, she'll love it." I'd had something made especially for her, sophisticated… elegant—like the woman herself.

"Do we really think this *cagna bugiarda* is going to have answers?" Al questioned, pulling up to our warehouse.

"Either way, it will send a message." I deposited my phone into my pocket and climbed out of the car. I buttoned my suit jacket and stared at the sign on the building across the street. It no longer read *For Sale* but now boasted proudly that it was *Under Contract*.

"We still don't have answers on that?" Al motioned towards the building.

"Too many unanswered fucking questions." I growled in response. Turning on my heel, I headed inside to take my anger out on Gio's accomplice.

Upon entry, I engaged in my normal routine, removing my articles of clothing and hanging them in the closet. The man in question was bound to the chair and gagged, his lips sealed with tape. I concentrated on his chest auscultations—the indication that respiratory exchanges were still taking place and he hadn't suffocated just yet.

"I have no patience for tears nor the lies they impart. I ask the questions and you give me the answers. I want the truth." I rolled my sleeves up and flexed. "Question. Answer. Immediately. Got it?" He nodded.

His pupils were overly dilated, a telltale sign that he was a drug user. That small realization immediately irritated me because it would make his answers spotty at best. He would whine and he would cry, offering to give me whatever I wanted, but there was a larger chance that it would all be half-truths… and goddamned useless.

I ripped the tape from his mouth and smirked at the resulting yelp. "Gio Moretti…" I said, watching his eyes flutter and his face grimace.

"Y-Yeah?" he stuttered, sweat trailing from his brows. I pulled a folding chair from along the wall and sat in front of him. My elbows planted against my knees, I lowered my eyes to his.

"Tell me about him." I sat back in the seat and watched a myriad of thoughts flash across his face.

"Wh-what do you want to know?" He coughed, trying to clear his throat. "H-he… we used to be friends back in high school, not…" He stopped speaking when I raised my hand.

"Did I not make the instructions clear?" I asked, my voice tinged with displeasure. I didn't have to shout or make threats; my bearing alone displayed my impatience. "I assure you that some questions I ask, I already know the answers to. So, I suggest you assume I know all of them and stop lying."

"O-okay." He looked past me and at the looming figure to my left; Al cracked his knuckle against his palm as he stared back at the boy. "He hired me to do errands and get some information when he was in Italy."

"On Lucky," I stated, signaling him to continue.

"Not all the time. If-if I knew of any word on the street… on what Lucky was dealing in." His eyes flashed in fear, realizing what that meant and what he had admitted—*he was a fucking rat.*

"I see. And what did you tell him?" I asked, his only answer was a shrug of his shoulders. "I won't repeat the rules. Now, tell me."

"I just knew about the guns, that was it!" he cried, eyeing the knife I had pulled from my pocket.

Turning my head to the side, I flicked the blade open and waited for him to finish. When he didn't speak, I smiled. The curl of my lips expelled the air from his lungs as he realized—much too late—that he had fucked up.

I slammed the point of my knife into his thigh, as was commonplace, twisting it inwardly to heighten his screams. However, his guttural moans weren't giving me the normal high I usually enjoyed. I was suddenly enervated, exhausted by an unending series of misleading facts, and the violence wasn't secreting the adrenaline I needed to continue with my line of questioning.

"You've made me lose my patience." I stood tall and turned my back to him. Walking to the closet, I pulled my Glock from the shoulder holster.

"I bought a gun from a corner kid. It was Russian made… Gio put two and two together." Again, I motioned for him to continue. "He wanted names but I didn't have any… since Lucky wouldn't let me into his crew. Gio was pissed. He really fucking hates Lucky."

I growled in frustration before aiming the end of my barrel. I was drowning in useless men with useless information—I was sick of it. The kid kept repeating himself—over and over again, the same irrelevancies—until I couldn't take the sound of his voice any longer. I squeezed the trigger. My 9mm clapped back with a slight jolt and grounded my spiraling impatience. White noise and static echoed off the recesses of my mind. His incessant slobbering was silenced as I watched in my own detached quietude. The open wound on his shoulder had severed the joint but the injury wouldn't kill him.

"Next shot will be approximately seven inches to the left if you don't give me something," I spoke calmly.

I dropped my outstretched arm to my side, listening to him whine that he didn't know anything more. Al stepped in to ask additional questions but the outcome was the same, and the boy was still bleeding profusely. Stepping forward, I examined his wound more closely. The bullet had damaged the deltoid muscle under the clavicle bone in his left shoulder. But the deltoid branch of the thoracoacromial artery remained intact—otherwise, he'd have been dead within seconds.

"He knows nothing," Al muttered, wiping his hands on a rag now tinted pink with blood residue. "I don't think he worked that closely with Gio… to know his real plans."

"True. I just need someone to confirm he's working with Yuri," I growled; the bloodshed had done little to appease the raging inferno inside me.

"I got this." Al motioned towards the whimpering bag of flesh still bolted to the chair, but I shook my head.

I stepped up to him. Ignoring his pleas for mercy, I attacked with an uninhibited sense of loathing. Left, right. Left, right. I beat the ever-loving-shit out of the kid until my hands were raw and I was drenched in a mixture of blood, sweat and tears. My internal firestorm diminished to its normal state and capacity—veritable chaos—but controlled chaos nonetheless.

I'd spent several years trying to calm my inner beast, to release all of the pain and anger from my youth. And Mario had spent several years teaching me how to control the fire inside me, to channel it positively and for his benefit. I had gained the ability to unleash it when it became too overwhelming, but in a way that was practical and of good use—rather than sporadic and unfiltered.

It's okay to allow yourself to feel as if you're drowning in your anguish. But, it's not okay to let it consume you. You are in control. For the first time in your life, you're the one making the decisions as to what happens next. Take that pain… take that rage and release it into something else when it's too much… something beneficial…" Mario said, with a hand on my shoulder, while staring deep into my eyes.

"When it's too much, the only relief I find is in destroying something with my bare hands," I replied, knowing he probably thought I was severely lacking in restraint.

"And that's fine. But unleash that savage beast on those who deserve it. Those who want to hurt you or your family. 'Cause we will do the same. We will always have your back for the rest of your life." Mario's eyes and the conviction they held told me he was speaking the truth.

That was one of the first real moments when I had learned exactly who Mario Agostino was—a murderous fucking dictator who cared only about his family and his business. He opened his home to me and made me part of that inner circle without any hesitation. He said he saw something inside me that day when I was brought to him.

It could've been a kid needing guidance and a home—people that actually gave a fuck about him. But in all honesty, I think it was more than just that… He had recognized that I was a ticking time bomb—a mixture of murder and mayhem that he wanted in his corner, instead of on the opposing side. He wanted a caged beast who he could unleash on his foes.

"Fuck, I am *not* cleaning that up," Al groaned from behind me, snapping me into the present. The word mess didn't paint this picture appropriately. Better depicted, the scene was utterly savage… it was carnage-induced brutality at its finest.

"Call in a crew. We need the entire room hosed down," I said, walking towards the back of the warehouse.

I stepped into the shower attached to our shared office space and glared down at the enclosed floor as the water tinted with blood. It was a stark contrast to the gleaming white of the tile. As the mixture danced and swirled its way down the drain, I continued to stare at it as my mind churned. Taking a deep breath, I knew exactly what I needed.

"You good, brother?" Al shouted.

"Yeah." That was all I could muster in response.

"I'm heading home to get changed for Sienna's dinner before the party. Do you want me to grab you before I head over to *Danza?*" he asked; the level of concern in his voice seemed to heighten. *Danza* was a nightclub Lucky owned, and it hosted the majority of the Agostino birthdays and celebrations.

"No. I have somewhere to stop first." I shut the shower off, grabbing a towel hanging from the bar inside the small space.

Al's movement outside the door stalled my exit. "You sure?" he asked, his question pensive and wavering.

I opened the shower door and stepped inside the office to stare at him.

"I'm good." My tone was a bit harsher than he deserved. But, at the moment, I didn't care.

He stared a beat longer. "All right. Don't be late… you know how she can be." He smirked, turning on his heel and leaving without another glance.

His relationship with Sienna was completely familial. Where I should be thinking of her as a sister, Al actually did. He didn't see her that way, the way I did. But what was I to do? She was a siren, her song calling me to do very unbrotherly things to her. Well, except, she was burdened by those human emotions. The kind that would only lead to the downfall of our amicable relationship—an arrangement that was threatened daily.

Even if my dick wept at the thought of never burying itself hard and fast inside her.

"Fuck. Me." I growled to the empty room. Ripping open the closet door, I changed into a new suit.

Brioni was my favorite designer, if I wasn't having something personally made from Italy. The exquisite material and tailored cuts presented the image of refinement that I so desperately needed. The type of man who was wealthy enough to purchase an eight-thousand-dollar suit and psychoneurotic enough to throw it away when it was tarnished by bloodshed.

Staring at myself in the mirror, something was still eating away at my insides. It was the uncontrollable dread of uncertainty that left me ill-eased. My instincts told me that tonight had the potential to rapidly fall to shambles.

I couldn't face Lucky or Sienna for her birthday in my current mood. They'd annoy the fuck out of me with their stares—and the never-ending questions lurking behind their inquisitive steel-blue eyes. Each of the children harbored dual identities they'd created to conceal the cruel capabilities they each possessed. Those eyes drew your attention, but they only gave you what they wanted you to see.

Marco, the youngest sibling, often hid his brutality behind his sophomoric demeanor and perpetual whoring. While Sienna's came out when she assumed no one was looking, or when she was deep in thought. However, Lucky's ruthlessness was permanently on display; he was deliberate and confident in order to rattle the cages of all those weaker. Then there was Octavia, the most passive of the Agostino children, and the one I'd long suspected had all of us fooled.

I headed towards the garage and hopped into my Rolls Royce once again, this time seeking a different venue. I had a few hours before I needed to be at *Danza*, opting to be a little late. *She* was on at eight, and I knew she was just the distraction I needed before I ended my evening with the Agostino's.

Nonetheless, I should have known better than to press my luck, but I was a fucking idiot.

CHAPTER 8

SIENNA AGOSTINO

"If you do not come, I will be personally offended and I'll have no choice but to fire your insolent ass," I said without looking at her.

Farrah was more of a recluse than my baby sister and refused to participate in such large-scale events like my birthday party. Octavia's own attendance was out of respect and forced familial obligation. Farrah had said she wasn't coming numerous times, but I refused to accept no as an answer. Not now, and not in regards to anything that I wanted for that matter.

"You won't fire me." She smirked, leaning against my office doorway.

I sat back in my seat, depositing my glasses onto my desk and staring at her for a long moment. "I won't just fire you. I will cancel your company Amex card and increase the rent on your precious loft," I deadpanned. Her eyes widening and her mouth dropping slightly ajar, she was unsure how to proceed.

"She's full of shit." Octavia walked into my office, excusing herself past Farrah. "If she does fire you, she'll hire you back by Monday. She won't go through the arduous process of breaking someone new in. You know she hates criers." Octavia then tossed her messenger bag onto my desk with a heavy thump.

"That may be true. Or it may not be. If you don't show tonight, you'll be forcing my hand, one way or the other." I bit back a smile, before tossing my glasses onto my face. "And, Octavia, I refuse to allow you access to my party wearing that!" I pointed to her simple jeans and t-shirt.

"It's Lucky's club." She crossed her arms over her chest.

"And we all know I'll win that battle." I smirked again, entering more data in my software to run after I closed up shop.

I'd just seen the tip of the iceberg that was Yuri Bucharov. His recently discovered ties to the *Bratva* concerned me. The mere mention of him in our city and they'd send their enforcers to take care of him. We didn't need Russian Soviets knocking on our doors. And that's exactly who was after Yuri. Their current leader was old school, like Soviet Union militant old school. As in, they'd ruin anyone in their path just as a show of force. They never accepted defeat; they hid it— like Chernobyl.

I refused to sit back and allow anything to happen in this city that could've been avoided with a little extra digging. I didn't have brute force or bloodied hands in the physical sense. My knowledge was the key to my power and it was more deadly than a bullet to the chest. There was no stifling the blood flow when your entire world was at my disposal with just a click of the mouse.

"Are we having dinner? I'm starving!" I asked Octavia, tapping a few more keys before shutting everything down for the evening.

"I figured. I also figured that since you're doing up your birthday, you'd want a low-key dinner." Octavia motioned for me to exit my office.

"You know me so well." I looked at my watch. "We have a little less than two hours for dinner before the stylists and beauticians arrive at my apartment." I smiled, enjoying the way Octavia was ordering Peiro around.

She was kind and had a good heart, but when Octavia was on a mission… you'd better get the fuck out of her way. And when it came to my birthday, she had set out to conquer the world and I enjoyed watching the wannabe *made men* scurry away from her warpath. I couldn't wait to see what she had planned. I was a little bit classy, a whole lotta money and a decent amount of white trash when I wanted to be.

We rode the elevator to the lobby in silence and climbed into Peiro's car, before he navigated us away for dinner. We made a lot of turns and twists in route as I focused on my emails—I wanted our destination to be a surprise. Before I knew it, Octavia signaled for me to climb out and I stared up at the half-blinking sign.

OAS, was illuminated in bright red letters but the name spelled out was supposed to be OASIS. I wanted to laugh, but instead, I followed my smiling sister inside. The place was low-key and low-rent but it was packed to capacity. The restaurant—if you could call it that—was filled with tables, all crammed into the small layout, and there wasn't much personal space once you sat down. All the furniture was black with black accents scattering the walls, but there were hundreds of white twinkle lights hanging above our heads.

The woman at the door directed us towards the back room, but it hadn't been cordoned off to the public like most private events. Instead, it was surrounded in sheer curtains and elevated above the rest of the room, allowing the remaining patrons to stare up at us in awe. It gave a semblance of privacy, since it was above everyone and enclosed by railings, but we could still see the entire room.

And I fucking loved it.

"Tacky, a dash of grime, and yet still the center of attention." Octavia smirked, gesturing towards the table. Al, Farrah, Marissa and a few of my clubbing girls were seated and already screaming.

"You bitch!" I laughed and pointed at Farrah, who was giggling and holding up a wrapped present. "I was ready to open a job posting for your ass." I walked around the table, greeting everyone who had come. I pretended I hadn't noticed that there were still two empty seats and went about my business.

"Food, drinks and then your apartment has been notified of all of the ladies coming over for hair and makeup," Octavia announced.

The waitresses walked in carrying bright, flashy champagne bottles that shot sparks out of the tops. But it wasn't the pretty lights that had me clapping my hands and hopping in glee. No. It was the plate overloaded with hot wings and dripping in sauce that had me practically drooling across the table. I was ready to be crude and a little cheap before dressing to the nines and invoking my flashier inner drunken hot mess.

We all sat down and began ordering drinks while I attacked the plate like a woman starved for far too long. I licked my lips and fingers as I moaned in near ecstasy around the mouthful of deep-fried perfection. I only stopped to engage my surroundings when Al plopped his big ass into the chair next to me.

"What the fuck are you looking at?" he asked, and I turned towards the recipients of his barred remark.

Across the way, there was a table of four men, openly gawking at me as I enjoyed myself. I sucked back more hot sauce and blue cheese as I stared them down, rotating my gaze from each to the next. They were unimpressive at best, and certainly not worth my effort, but I still wanted to fuck with them.

I slowed down my chewing and moaned louder as I sucked each of my hot sauce-covered fingertips into my mouth. I enjoyed watching the twitch of their seats, their faces awash with satisfaction over my thorough attention, before I stood from my chair and straddled Al's waist. I ground myself down, while attempting to not actually make contact with a certain appendage, and moaned in excitement.

"These wings are so good they turn me on." I flipped my hair over my shoulder and stared at their table. "I want you to impregnate me tonight. I know the hot wings will make it stick. Fuck me raw, baby."

Their repulsed expressions provided me with far more gratification than I had anticipated. They flagged the waitress over, tossing cash on their table before making a mad dash for the door. I climbed off Al's lap as he lost himself to a fit of choked laughter and went back to my meal. We passed around some shots and ordered more food until it was time to head to my apartment for the makeup magicians to clean up this incredible canvas.

"Where are my brother and Apollo?" I asked Al from his front seat.

"Lucky is already at *Danza* ensuring everything is fit to your liking," Al mentioned, glancing at me quickly before returning his gaze to the road. When I didn't look away, he answered my silent question. "He had a lead."

"And?" I asked, knowing Apollo always had a lead or Intel on someone.

"And he handled it." He wiped a heavy hand down his face. "And he's a little... fucked up after."

"Is he coming?" I whispered, too hesitant to ask confidently.

"'*She'll skin my balls if I don't.*'" Al laughed. "His direct quote. So, yeah, Si. He'll be there."

I wanted to smile to myself. Hell, I deserved to smile on my birthday, but something told me it was going to be a disappointment. As of late, there had been a lot coming to light that I felt was lacking in my life. I loved my family to the point that it caused me both physical and emotional pain. And I loved my close circle of friends, though limited, but I drowned myself in work—making little time for much else.

And now, with my father talking about his retirement, Lucky's engagement and potentially marrying me off, I had the deep desire to leave it all behind. I didn't want to be Sienna Agostino, technological genius and successful business owner, who would be a viable bride to bridge powerful families. I wanted to be just Sienna, a girl looking for love and romance with no political—well, mafia—gain.

"Go get dressed, Si. Everyone will be awaiting your arrival." Al tugged a piece of hair behind my ear.

His dark brown, almost black eyes lit with adoration as I pulled him in for a hug. The man was so tall and wide that I struggled out of my seatbelt to reach all of him. His brown hair was clipped short but I still managed to tug a piece on top. I kissed his cheek before climbing out of the car.

"Ladies!" I shouted and they all started clapping, even Farrah—

much to her own dismay. Although, I had forced a few extra celebratory shots on her to help lighten her up.

Octavia ushered our group of drunk ladies inside as a handful of beauticians attacked us with curling irons, foundation and eyeliner. Before I knew it, I was lost in all the mindless chatter and free-flowing champagne.

"What is it?" Octavia asked, pulling me from my wandering thoughts.

"Nothing." I smiled and patted her leg, before saluting her with my glass. She chuckled inwardly and went back to the book in her lap, occasionally throwing me a worried glance.

"They want me gone," she whispered after several minutes of silence, forcing my neck to turn in her direction. "We're only as strong as our weakest family member. With me in the picture, we don't have much strength."

"Octavia, no." She raised a hand to silence me.

"Don't lie, Sienna. I know they are trying to find me a civilian husband. They want me out of the life." She gestured for one of the staff to hand her a glass of champagne.

"It's not because you're weak. Never assume your big heart is a weakness, Tave. Your heart is just bigger than your body and we want to protect you. That's all," I told her truthfully.

"I know I'll never be as strong as you, but I am not stupid either. I know I have a big heart but I am smart enough to shelter it from those who mean it harm." Her words were like a slap to the face.

I could tell by her expression that she hadn't intended to hurt me, but the meaning behind that sentence spoke volumes. I'd once confided in her that I wondered if I'd ever be allowed to choose my own husband, because I would want it to be Apollo. For more reasons than I understood, I wanted someone like him beside me. He didn't try to stifle my strength, opting instead, to add to it with his patient silence while regarding me with speculation.

But he was a man that could never love me—a fact that I had been reminded of on numerous occasions—however, my heart just didn't listen. I allowed myself to get carried away with wishful thoughts and the dreams of being a powerful union. He'd keep our ties to the mafia strong and coordinated while allowing me my freedom to run my own business. It would be a relationship of not only convenience but power and precision, mixed with what I could only assume would be dirty and degrading hot fucking sex.

Time and time again, I fooled myself into thinking his interactions, his concern over my well-being, were more than the motives of a loyal watchdog. But he held no love or regard beyond that, and I still wanted him. I still wanted him to break his emotional ineptitude and claim me like only he could. I still wanted him… to want me.

"Any hot, single men coming tonight, Sienna?" Farrah asked from the kitchen island.

"A glass of champagne and an excessive number of shots were all it took for you to let your hair down?" I laughed, mentally slapping myself for my moment of weakness. "The world is at your feet and ready to suck your toes tonight!" I yelled, and the crowd of girls erupted in laughter.

All except Octavia.

She sat quietly in her chair, the makeup artist fixing her eyeliner while she sipped her champagne and stared over the rim at me. She knew her words had landed with precision and that they were abrasively churning in my mind. All the strength I'd built on the outside was a simmering concoction of self-doubt and self-loathing, spurning into internal woeful cries of loneliness. Her comment wasn't meant to destroy me, but we were both in precarious situations and neither of us liked the intended outcomes.

The girls finished getting ready and I stepped into my bedroom to get dressed. I wandered through my lengthy walk-in closet, all the way to the back—where the dresses I hardly ever wore were housed. I liked to push the envelope with my designers but my outfits were always tailored to the interaction and the way in which I hoped to present myself. Usually expensive power suits and confident, more wholesome ensembles were what was needed for work. But tonight, I just wanted to be a young woman celebrating her birthday in New York.

· · ·

THE ZIPPER on the *Alex Perry* labeled garment bag whispered to me in the quiet space, and the sequins immediately caught in the overhead light. Alex was probably my favorite designer for women's wear and I had to have something special for tonight. He had made this dress specifically for me. The iridescent material would catch every light possible—much as it did here in the light of my closet—and showcase me as the center of attention.

It was short enough to be tantalizing but long enough that I didn't forget my position—and neither would anyone else. It hugged my body like a second skin and looked incredible against my tanned glow. Thin spaghetti straps were meant to hold the bodice in place but it was so tight there wasn't a chance it would fall; while the front was a lower-cut, revealing V that dipped just enough to catch your eye.

"Wow," Octavia whispered, as I stared at myself in the mirror.

"Help me pick jewelry." I smiled at her, ignoring the lingering tightness in my throat from earlier.

"You don't need any," she said plainly. I scoffed but halted when I saw her face. "He may be a lot of things... but Apollo's attention to detail never falls short." He really was the best gift giver.

Before I could respond, my phone began ringing from my bed. As I wandered over to it, I noticed the caller ID was labeled Unknown. I didn't usually answer these types of calls because you just never knew who or what could be on the other end. But my current mood forced my hand and curiosity won out.

"Hello," I sang into the phone, my vibrant mask of pleasantries firmly back in place.

"A beautiful girl like you shouldn't dig through things that don't concern her," came a robotic voice on the other end. "Really... really ugly things can happen." My mind twisted and turned, contemplating the handful of people I was currently investigating. I quickly walked over to my tablet and pulled up my tracing software.

"You'll have to be more specific about exactly who you don't want me digging through. There are quite a few names dropped on my desk each day." I turned the volume up on the call and hit record, listening to anything that could give the speaker away.

"Then maybe you need this lesson more than we thought." The phone shuffled around as sound erupted behind the caller. "There are big things happening and you need to keep your fucking nose out of it, or it'll be your downfall... and your families." A muffled voice echoed in the background.

What was that?

"I don't take kindly to threats nor do the men of the Agostino family. I'd tread lightly if I were you, before you have an unfortunate misstep." I spoke low and with conviction so that they understood my meaning.

"Heed my advice and we'll both be just fine." Then the call ended.

"What was that about?" Octavia prompted.

"An upset customer is all. Check on the girls for me and call the limo around?" I turned to give her a smile but I could tell that my sister wasn't buying what I was selling. Without another word, I turned on my heel and went into my office, locking the door behind me.

The room bore dark grey carpets and muted grey paint but—similar to my corporate office—all of the wall decor and flowers had pops of red. I felt strong and in control with the devilish hue peppering my space. A few clicks later, and with my computer open, I was transferring the recording to my hard drive.

I listened to it three times before slowing it down and using the software to pick up the background noise. There was no doubt in my mind that a door was opened and that sound had traveled inside from some type of overhead PA system. Once I was alerted that the recording was ready, I turned the speakers up and slowed the speed, closing my eyes to concentrate.

"Coming up soon, gentlemen, is the lovely Persephone," the voice announced.

"The fuck?" My mind shifted left and then right, trying to decipher its meaning until it clicked. "Fuck. Me. You little bitch, you actually grew some balls."

I opened an internet page and did a search for *Spogliato* just to confirm that I was indeed correct. As soon as it loaded, it flashed bright with images of the different girls—some on poles, others with professional headshots. There was a list advertising the evenings' lineup of lovely ladies—strippers. And there it was, at the very bottom and proudly announced as the headliner—none other than… Persephone. But the namesake didn't have a picture on display.

"Dominic Moretti, you tricky little bastard. Now you've really fucked up," I muttered the threat to myself, opening a new program before placing a call. "I am sending you several files and I want answers on all of the financials. I also want any digital footprint left on the locations—anything that could be hidden." I hung up.

"We're ready," Octavia said from outside the office door; she tugged on the handle twice before knocking loudly.

"Coming!" I shouted back, locking down all of my systems.

"You okay?" Octavia pushed. I smiled as I tried to get around her. "I'm... I'm sorry for what I said. You're not dumb."

"I am," I admitted, taking the double shot glass she offered and cheers-ing before tossing it back. "But I am the smartest dumbass you'll ever meet. And it's okay—I make it work."

"Sienna! Shots!" Farrah called from the living room.

"You've created a monster." Octavia laughed, walking ahead of me.

"I know but look how fucking pretty of a monster she has become!" We turned the corner and paused a moment to laugh at the scene before us.

Farrah had Al pinned in the corner of the living room, club music pumping through my surround system. She was holding an empty shot glass as she shook her ass. Al had a hold of her shoulder, attempting to keep her gyrating lower body away from his, all while doing his best to maintain a straight face. I really had created a monster but the girl needed to have some fun once in a while.

"You barely escaped with your life." I laughed when he stormed towards me. He quickly hid his huge frame behind mine as Farrah stumbled over to him, still shaking her hips. "We ready, ladies?" I shouted.

"You look incredible, Si," Al said, pulling me in for a hug. "Everyone at the club will be begging for a taste and I'll be getting blood all over my *Armani*." He pretended to scowl, heightening my laughter.

The ride over to *Danza* was quick—over in a flash of shots, champagne and my mind-numbing replays. My brain worked differently than most. I had no idea how to shut it off or ignore the pain-inducing images. My therapist back in the day said it was what made my emotional state so hard to control. I didn't miss a single thing around me and refused to quiet my incessant thinking, even if it was the cause of my inner turmoil.

The club had a line of energetic partygoers that wrapped around the block. The disgruntled patrons yelled at us as we all climbed out of the limo and walked directly inside. Sometimes, being the little Agostino sister did have its advantages. The place was packed and reeked of sex; while the music was so loud, it thrummed inside of my chest. My adrenaline spiked as I watched the crowd sway and dance to the ear-pounding rhythm. Several guests abruptly moved out of our way as Al steered us towards the VIP stairs.

Lucky had an incredible team that changed the interior design of the club constantly to ensure it stayed popular. At the moment, there were a ton of crystal chandeliers with go-go dancers swaying in elevated, jeweled boxes—their uniforms dripping with sparkling diamonds. The crowd below us loved the added light show as the girls shook their diamond-encrusted breasts.

"Happy birthday, Sienna." Lucky was the first to greet me inside his private VIP lounge on the second floor. He pulled me in for a hug, kissing my forehead with a tender smile so unbeknownst to him.

"Thanks, big brother." I held his hand but looked around him. "Where's my sister-in-law?" I taunted, laughing when he shoved my hands away and headed towards the bar.

"What'd I say?" I asked, still giggling to myself, as Marco pulled me in for a hug.

"You're a mess." He chuckled before also wishing me a happy birthday.

"Well, we know that isn't your future bride over there." I glanced at the woman waiting by the bar. She was surveying the room with an inquisitive air about her. She seemed the odd companion at Marco's side—he usually opted for a dumb slut, not an elegant... whatever she was.

"Shots, then dancing!" Farrah announced happily, shoving out of Al's hold.

"Fucking hell..." Al cursed, glaring in my direction.

He seemed annoyed that I wasn't the only one he would have to babysit tonight. But I also noticed the way his eyes never left Farrah, no matter where she wandered off to. There was an entire club of armed men owned by the Agostino family and yet he felt Farrah was his duty.

Interesting.

I happily took the shot from her hands and shook my own ass as they all shouted "happy birthday" and blew air kisses at me. I was surrounded by an amazing group of people but my mind was plagued by thoughts of someone else's absence. He wouldn't miss it—he knew it was too important to me. Octavia's words blared in my head as I followed my girls to the dance floor. Why wasn't I smart enough to protect my heart?

As we shoved patrons out of our way on the lowered platform, I swayed and moved to the music but I still took in my surroundings—I always did. Men lined up around the rails overlooking the sunken dance floor, smiling and waving to get my attention. Many of them were good looking but they weren't what I wanted... who I wanted. And yet, here I was, glancing through the crowd hoping to catch sight of him.

Song after song played, suitor after suitor tried to approach me but my security pushed them all back. My girls came and left the floor—some still dancing, others sitting in the VIP booth next to the DJ. I wandered over to them before hoisting myself onto the raised dance platform, shoving one of the dancers off. It gave me a prime view of the room, in the hopes that I had somehow missed his arrival.

The alcohol running through my system settled a deep warmth

within my bones. Time went on but he still wasn't here. My mind whirled with thoughts of my stupidity and I couldn't shut it off. The end result—my final conclusion—was always the same: he couldn't care about anything. Yet look at me, ruining my own enjoyment at my own party as I searched the crowd over and over again.

Then, suddenly, a large man moving in the shadows caught my attention. He spoke to the guard at the bottom of the VIP entrance. I could see Lucky leaning out of the window of his suite before signaling the large figure upstairs. My mind flung backwards to the call earlier and the threat that was still lingering in the air. This man was a stranger to me, but his imposing stature and excessive tattoos told me he wasn't one to trifle with. But then again, neither was I.

I wasn't one of the Agostino men or their handlers, but I sure as fuck wouldn't sit idly by and allow someone to make threats. Telling me to back off—well, that was a grave mistake. Now they'd turned my entire focus onto them and all of the skeletons in their closet. And I couldn't wait until my crew was able to bring all of their dirty little secrets to light.

Curiosity may've killed the cat but not before she ate the fucking canary.

CHAPTER 9
APOLLO DELUCA

As soon as I walked into *Spogliato*, I immediately recognized the woman on the center stage—Dom's ghost from the docks. Her slender body moved sensuously under the spotlight as she climbed the pole. After the second twirl, I realized she had the same form as the waitress at *Hush*. Now, without her mask, it was clear that the women were one in the same.

And I wanted to see her beg for my dick as she writhed in need beneath me.

I positioned myself at one of the VIP booths closest to her platform. Sitting back and adjusting my cufflinks, I waited. She crawled and roamed about the stage between her pole tricks, the entire room giving their rapt attention. And like a moth to the flame, she drew closer to me. I clenched my jaw to refrain from showing my satisfaction.

"Mr. Moretti would like a word." One of Dom's armed guards leaned into my booth, motioning towards the darkened corner where his boss was stationed.

"Does he?" I asked, my words dripping with malice.

As I sipped my scotch, I watched the guard's fingers twitch

towards the handle of his sidearm. I was making the man falter and fidget, and I loved the smell of his fear—thick and acrid.

I tossed cash onto the table for the waitress and headed to meet the "esteemed" owner of this establishment. Security was on me before I had even stepped through the doorway of the sectioned-off private room. The girls were beautiful and appeared drug free, while the rest of the place looked clean and seemingly upscale. If there was any concern from Dom over his strip joint being under investigation, I didn't see it.

"What're you doing here?" he questioned as soon as I was within hearing distance.

"Enjoying a show. Is there a problem?" I asked. I was calm… bored.

"Yeah. We both know your specific tastes… and it isn't strip clubs… *in any traditional sense*." Dominic glared at me, crossing his arms over his chest.

"And what exactly are you suggesting? Sounds as if someone has been gossiping behind my back." I smirked, earning me a scowl in return.

"The fuck do you want, Apollo?" he groaned, though his voice remained relatively calm.

"As I said. The show." I slowed down to drive my point home. "I heard you had this one particularly fascinating showstopper." I could've laughed at the dangerous expression the mere mention of his blonde-haired, blue-eyed siren sparked.

In our business, especially when dealing with men such as myself, you should never show your cards. And with one comment, I was able to unearth just how much this woman was his weakness… exactly what she meant to him. There was much more to it than what met the eye. The man was boasting a killer hand—attempting to hide his affections—but I was ready to call his bluff.

"Like the Agostino's haven't pissed all over my family enough. Your boss is sniffing around my baby sister and now you're in my private club." He waited a moment before continuing with a huff. "I don't know what Gio has up his sleeve, okay? I know you've put feelers out there and they would've told you that he and I don't interact."

Word on the street traveled fast, but money drove it forward much faster. And I had ensured those I questioned knew exactly who I was, and exactly what I was looking for. I wanted it to get back to the Moretti's and—as Lucky had prompted—I wanted to make them sweat. So, the fact that Dominic knew didn't surprise me, but his sincerity did. I knew he was smarter than his brother, but I had assumed blood was thicker than water.

"He's gunning for Lucky. Always has, always will," he muttered as I was about to turn around. Seeing my sudden change in demeanor, he raised a hand, halting my expulsion of rage before it boiled over. "Doesn't mean I know what he's doing. I just know it's against Lucky —it's always against Lucky." He paused, looking over at the security guard who was walking the blonde towards the dressing room.

"And what will it cost to find out?" I asked, curious as to where his loyalties lay.

"I won't help you—*no fucking way*. He's an idiot, but he's blood. If anyone is going to set him straight, it's me. I won't hand him over to you. I'll teach him my own lesson."

"Your sister is getting stuck in the crosshairs," I said, knowing that would get a rise out of him. "Gio took it out on her outside *Vino*."

"*What?*" The rhetorical question formed as a growl in the Moretti heir's mouth. Briefly, I relayed Gio's assault on Mirabella and the bruises present days later. Dominic seethed, rage radiating off his skin like steam from a sauna.

"Though, slapped around by your brother is better off than being sold to the highest bidder," I said, repeating the rumors I'd heard. But he didn't take the bait; he turned it on Lucky instead.

"Yeah, well, thanks to Lucky it won't just be Gio targeting her. There'll be a whole new load of enemies gunning for her now," Dominic growled, just as the little blonde number sidled up to us.

"Lucky will protect her with his life, as will the rest of the family." I said it because it was true.

"You fucking better believe I'll make sure of that." Dom then turned his full attention onto the girl, pulling her close. "As for Gio, I don't know what he has his hands in, but I plan to fucking find out."

"Be sure you do that," I reiterated, my eyes never leaving the girl. Her breath caught in her throat as we held a silent stare down—the kind filled with filthy promises.

"Yeah. Now get the fuck out of my club." Dominic opened a door, motioning for the blonde to enter. She obeyed, smiling at me before disappearing.

I headed towards the front entrance and walked outside to my car. The girl seemed content with her situation, and Dom was practically marking her as his territory. However, if he decided to turn his back on the Agostino's to save his brother, he'd force me to retaliate. And I had absolutely no qualms about fucking his girl in front of him while the son of a bitch bled out.

I pulled my car up to the front of *Danza,* and the valet—a young kid—walked to the curb, his eyes wide as he took in my Phantom. I remember being his age and looking at the wealth in this city—the same opulence and greed that consumed those who had it—and wondering how I could achieve it for myself.

"Don't curb it. Don't scratch it," I said dryly, opening my wallet and taking out five one-hundred-dollar bills. "And when I come back, this is yours."

He froze, staring back and forth between the cash and the car, before nodding his understanding. Toby was a good kid from what I could tell—he was trying to work off his brother's debt to the Agostino's. But that wasn't how things worked, and the boy would learn that soon enough.

You see, when we found him—the brother—he would still be punished for stealing from the family. In the meantime, Toby had assumed that the money he was earning was going towards that debt. It wasn't. Before we allowed Toby near our operations, I ran a check on him. And the findings were about as bad as my childhood, which made us want to help. His father left years ago, his mother had some mental health issues and his brother was a drug addict.

The kid never stood a fucking chance. So, the money he was

paying us was sitting in an account with his name on it. I was in the process of getting his mom the help she needed. Then, once those wrongs were righted, he would have enough financial backing to buy a home and take care of himself. He was already proving loyal and beneficial—he might even be a good addition to Lucky's syndicate.

I headed into the club and was met with an overwhelming smack to my senses. Heavy bass pounded in my head, the smell of sex hung in the air and a hoard of people sent my hackles rising. I was never one to enjoy crowds in general—let alone one this size. The combination of so many people and their propensity for overconsumption created just too many dangerous variables.

Staring down from the VIP suite's window, Al acknowledged me with a tilt of his head and pointed towards the dance floor. On both sides of the DJ booth were speakers usually reserved for the professional dancers but tonight, it appeared as though the headliner was Sienna. You couldn't miss her even if you tried. Not only was she taller than most of the other women, she also had her designer stilettos on. And yet, she would still only come to my chin.

She was wearing a tight, short sequined dress—no doubt designer and expensive. It bordered on propriety without leaping over the edge. Even if she was in her twenties and reserved, unlike most girls her age, her position in the family required her to behave a certain way. As a result, she acted out in the ways she could control—the woman was a hellhound constantly gnashing her teeth for more.

The crowd parted as I headed towards the small group corralling around her stage. Security ever-present and by her side, they watched me as I approached. Her lithe body was swaying to the beat of the music, her movements both sensual and natural. The girl was sex on long-toned legs. Standing at the bottom of the small platform, I took a box out of my pocket and waved her down to me.

I reached up with both hands. She placed hers on my shoulders as I grabbed her around the waist and hoisted her down. We didn't speak as she smiled her drunk, happy grin. Opening the box, I showed her the piece of jewelry I had custom-made for her. Never being a girl for too much flash, she happily stared down at it as I smiled. The necklace was white gold, with a light trail of diamonds that ended in a decent sized ruby.

I motioned for her to spin as I placed it on her neck. The jeweler had fit it just right, as the ruby sat delicately atop the crest of her breasts. It twinkled in the light, the perfect accompaniment to her birthday dress. She quickly grabbed her phone and took a selfie, her drunken stare glazing over with unshed tears. I liked making her happy… I couldn't explain why, but I did.

"Oh, Apollo," she sighed, as her alcohol-induced sway forced her to bump into me. Her eyes were filled with lust, need—a look far too deadly for my current lack of control. When she stepped up as if to kiss me, I halted her movements, holding her back by her upper arms.

"Happy birthday, Sienna." I kept her at arm's length even when she tried to lean forward again. Once realization set in, that I was turning her down, I watched a flash of sadness pass over her. It was there—only for a second or two—then it flared to anger.

"Yeah, thanks." She went to shove herself off me, but I held firm.

"Don't do this. Enjoy your birthday," I growled in frustration.

"I was…" she muttered, climbing back onto the box stage.

I then left her to her friends. As I turned my back, her disappointment made a second brief appearance for the night, before she started throwing her hands in the air again. Once inside the VIP balcony, I noticed all movement had ceased as everyone set their attentions on me. Lucky had his arms crossed over his chest as he glared in my direction. Al was shaking his head in obvious judgement, and tucked into the corner, Octavia smiled sadly.

On the opposite end of the room, Marco stood next to a barstool bearing a beautiful woman, who seemed to be watching the room and its occupants with an apt curiosity. Her gaze would land on the boy long enough to feign interest in whatever bullshit whispers of sweet nothings he was giving her, before scanning her surroundings again. She was eye-catching, she was poised and she was up to something. A woman like that… with that class and that elegance… didn't pay attention to lovesick puppies like Marco.

"You're a fucking idiot," Lucky snarled, walking back to the window and staring down at the crowd.

"We all saw, man." I looked to Al with a confused expression when he spoke.

"She's drunk," I muttered, grabbing a scotch from the bartender.

"And all those other times you two pant over each other?" Lucky growled, stepping away from the window and into my personal vicinity. "We can all see it. Not just down there, but every day."

"It will never happen." I sipped from my glass.

"Why? What're you choosing to blame it on today? Your inability to connect on an emotional level, or the fucked-up idea that it somehow lessens your loyalty to me?" Lucky asked, being the inquisitive bastard that he was.

"Both. You know I am not capable of taking care of a woman like her—with so many… *feelings*." They didn't understand the time and patience it took for me to determine how someone else *felt*.

"I can't believe I'm actually going to fucking discuss this." Lucky sighed, stepping to my side at the bar. "That sensation that hits you whenever you see her, it's more than the natural need to get off." He cringed as he spoke in *that* regard while mentioning his sister.

"Then what is it?" I asked, genuinely fucking with him now.

"Lust is a feeling, an emotion. An introduction that can lead to the potential of love. You feel loyal to her, right? That you get. Wanting to protect her from everything is more than just loyalty. She can handle herself and has her own security team, yet you take ownership of her. Because it's more than that to you."

With those parting words and a knock on the bar to cement them, he left me and started chatting with some business associates on the other side of the room. Shoving Al out of the way, I walked over to the window and to where Octavia was now sitting. She smiled shyly as usual, and as though I hadn't known her for most of her life. We sat in silence, both staring down at the crowd and watching Sienna hop off the stage and go onto the dance floor with her friends.

Her security stayed close, and near the edge of the sunken platform, in order to give the illusion of space. Her friends were attracting a lot of attention from the drunken crowd surrounding them. She stood in the center, spinning in circles and laughing, all but forgetting her previous moments of sadness. I was about to step away when I saw a group of greasy men surround her. My hackles rose as I watched them circle her like hawks.

"*"A competent and self-confident person is incapable of jealousy in anything. Jealousy is invariably a symptom of neurotic insecurity,"*" Octavia offered, staring at me from under her dark bangs.

"Robert Heinlein? What're you reading?" I asked, amused by her quote. "And it's not jealousy when I see a potential threat."

"Hm." She nodded wordlessly, before replying, "Oh, is that not her security team taking control of things?" Octavia attempted to stifle her giggle while pointing towards the commotion below.

I didn't respond, opting to watch the greasy group of would-be admirers disperse into the crowd. I understood what everyone was saying to me about Sienna but there were factors beyond their intellectual capacity. It was one thing to sit back and watch others as they led their lives inundated with social interactions. And it was another to navigate them on my own—being in a relationship was near impossible for me. It always had been.

Sienna deserved someone who could give her hearts and flowers, opening themselves up in order to bare their soul to her. That wasn't me—even if there was a part of me that grew angry at the thought of someone else touching her soft, olive skin. Of another man owning her sexy, strong and gorgeous body. Without meaning to, I growled audibly at the image forming and obstructing my mind.

But she wasn't mine. And Sienna wasn't the type to be owned.

"I can read you like my favorite book," Octavia said. "All of those thoughts racing across your mind don't have to come to fruition."

"What thoughts?" I sipped my drink, trying to swallow past the dryness in my throat.

"Imagining my sister with someone else. You spend so much time believing you're incapable of some exuberant declaration of love. Have you met Sienna? She'd be content with just having you." This was the most Octavia had spoken to me in months.

"Right..." I muttered, putting the glass down on the ledge.

"I know I've never experienced love myself but I've read about it enough. After all of these years, she understands you inside and out, yet still, she wants you. That speaks volumes… if you'd just open your eyes before it's too late." She hopped off the stool and turned to Lucky before saying her goodbyes around the room.

"Thanks for coming." Lucky kissed the top of her head as she passed Al and Marco, giving them hugs as she departed.

"I've got her," I said, walking her down the stairs to the club.

As always, the sea of people parted as they saw me approach with Octavia tucked closely at my side. Entering the main dance floor, a shadow loomed in front of us, blocking our exit. Grabbing her by the arm, I pulled Octavia behind me, shielding her from Carmine Ragetti. Snarling at his deranged smirk, I didn't appreciate it when he counter stepped to keep Octavia in his line of sight.

"What the fuck are you doing here?" I barked the question, and Octavia jumped in my grasp.

"Calm down, lap dog. Lucky invited me." He laughed, the upside down cross on his face dancing with the movement of his features.

"Then go to Lucky." I gestured towards the balcony, pulling Octavia tighter against my frame.

"Ah! The youngest daughter." He gave her a saccharine grin. "I've heard of Sienna's beauty but I think you're the best kept secret of the family." He reached out a hand—her instilled manners forcing her to respond politely. It was innocent enough, until Octavia gasped at the contact when they exchanged greetings.

"Octavia, this is Carmine Ragetti," I growled, pulling her back towards me when he didn't release her hand immediately. He locked his grasp around her fingertips, forcing her to stumble backwards and the contents of her bag to spill onto the floor.

"My heart be still…" Carmine said, bending down to grab one of the discarded books. "Reading in a club? The Agostino secret has me intrigued."

"Enough," I barked, shoving her belongings into her purse before navigating her outside.

"I-I'm sorry," she whispered as I held open the car door and she climbed inside.

"No reason to be. That *puttana* will be leaving the city shortly." Octavia was captivating and kind—two qualities that could be her undoing in the outfit. Especially, when people like Carmine were concerned.

"*Si. Ciao, puttana.*" Octavia giggled from the open window, smiling as the car rolled away. I turned on my heel, storming back inside the VIP balcony.

"What the fuck is your problem?" I roared, slamming Carmine to the wall with an exacting grip around his throat—an all too familiar repeat of the other night.

"Apollo!" Lucky yelled, storming to his feet. But I held tight, breathing fire at the traitorous bastard in my grip.

"No problem here, lap dog. Just being nice to the family is all." Despite the sentiment, his smirk was filled with sinister promises, the altercation somehow increasing his excitement.

I was lost to my murderous intentions while trying to figure out exactly what game Carmine was playing. Octavia was too good to be graced with the likes of him. She was the polar opposite of his crazy, bloodthirsty persona. I squeezed tighter, watching his eyes light up in triumph at my loss of control.

"Enough, Apollo. I invited him here." Lucky pulled me back. My grip squeezed once more—a silent warning—before I released the son of a bitch and stepped backwards.

"He was flirting with Octavia." I emphasized each word slowly. As consequence, the men in the room all stepped forward, a formidable wall uniting to protect the family.

"Compliments aren't necessarily flirting, lap dog." Carmine lifted a challenging brow. His words said one thing, but his face said another— his interest in Octavia manifesting as veritable malintent.

"And you'll stay away from her." Lucky snarled in his face. Carmine smiled, raising his hands in mock surrender.

"Whatever you say, *boss*." His tone was borderline disrespectful.

"Watch your fucking mouth." I charged around Lucky, reaching out with a closed fist. Al caught me before I could make contact, and he shoved me backwards. I lost my footing, my large frame slamming into the table behind me. Bracing the impact, I landed against Marco and his enigmatic female companion—her resulting frightened squeak, thrumming the blood roaring through my system.

"Or what? Little puppy gonna show his baby teeth?" Carmine taunted as I rushed towards him once more.

"I'll show you my fucking teeth, as they rip you apart." Lucky stepped to Al's back and separated us again.

"I said enough. Apollo, rein it in." Gripping my shoulders to hold me in place, he stared me in the eye.

"I'm good." I shrugged him off, readjusting my suit.

"And you?" he asked Carmine, who was still seething with daggers pointed at my skull.

"Carmine." Lucky shouted his name, snapping him out of his stupor. His mask of indifference dropped back into place immediately.

"Good, *boss.*" Then the cocky bastard winked.

"Now, as I was saying, I asked Carmine here to see if he could help with our little Russian problem," Lucky explained, motioning for us both to sit. I stared back at him, paralyzed and embittered.

Jesus Christ. The Ragetti's help was another headache of debauchery and bloodshed that none of us would want to clean up. Breathing heavily, I sought to exacerbate Carmine's resilient calm. He stormed to his feet, a silent challenge—daring me to make my move.

"Goddamn it. Apollo, go downstairs and cool off. We'll give you both a few minutes." Lucky rubbed his neck, the anger rolling off his shoulders.

Carmine Ragetti was as underhanded as he was unhinged. He was here for a reason—one that I was certain wouldn't benefit the Agostino's. The supposed alliance was nothing more than a farce, and I had a feeling we'd soon see it crumble.

CHAPTER 10
APOLLO DELUCA

The knife under my jacket was long, serrated and sharpened for optimal precision. I pressed it to Carmine's neck, and even a flinch would cause it to slice through his windpipe. The thyroid cartilage of the larynx—the area that formed the Adam's apple and was made up partly by the connective tissue of the cricoid region—housed the artery I was seeking.

The cricoid cartilage was what maintained a person's airway and provided an attachment point for key muscles, ligaments, and connective tissue—that, and it aided in the opening and closing of the vocal cords. In other words, when cut correctly, it rendered a victim absolutely speechless—barely a breathing sound as they internally screamed in agony. Carmine's eyes would flare as he watched his own death on the horizon.

I shook free of my wishful thinking and I charged down the stairs to focus and center myself. I wanted to cut that motherfucker from neck to naval, to rip his fucking intestines out with my bare hands before dropping his innards to the center of the dance floor for everyone to see. The mere sight of blood would send the crowd into a crazed uproar—they'd attempt to flee, but in the frenzy of it all, they'd slip and slide on the entrails.

I took a deep placating breath, grasping for some semblance of control; but it evaporated in a cloud of smoke when I caught sight of Sienna. A soon to be dead man was creeping up behind her, aiming to rub his dick all over her ass. He looked like a California surfer, pussy.

She'd eat him up and spit him out alive—though, partially digested.

I was sure of it... But then acid began churning in my stomach, slowly crawling up and into my throat before burning my mouth. This wasn't Sienna. She pushed boundaries as easily as she pushed buttons, but she wasn't some club slut that ground against total strangers. She had more self-respect and instead, she should have been begging me for a dance.

Fuck. Me.

I watched as Sienna held onto his head and pulled him closer into the crook of her neck, and my calm exterior disintegrated. Concentrating on her amused gaze, I snarled at her. The surfer's hands began roaming from high on her stomach to down lower on her torso. One quick movement, and I hopped over the railing, making it to them before he was able to reach his intended destination.

Sienna's shocked gasp roused his attention and he shook in fear—a reaction that should've mollified my rage, but didn't. Her angered voice disappeared amongst the music; my sole focus was on the man in front of her. She waved for her security team but it was too late. The surfer pulled back his shoulders and stepped in front of Sienna, his pathetic veneer blanketed in mock confidence.

"Leave," I barked as Sienna screamed at me in a mix of Italian slurs.

"Fuck you." His voice was weak and it broke into a squeak at the end.

"Nah, you don't want me to fuck you," I taunted. He glanced once more at Sienna—no doubt wondering if the girl was worth it. Swallowing hard and presumably having made his decision, he stood his ground.

"Fucking leave." He gulped audibly when I spoke. My unrelenting stare exhumed his terror once more, and he cowered away.

And then I struck.

"Apollo!" Sienna screamed. The kid swayed for a moment. Leaning into Sienna, he stared at the knife jetting out from his upper body.

"I barely grazed the infraspinatus muscle of the shoulder. He'll live." I shrugged as her security swept in to remove him. I tugged her close to my body, swaying to a slow melody in my head. "You don't dance like that with men."

"Why do you care?" She challenged me, her voice still trembling.

"I don't." She flinched, hurt raking across her features. "It's not respectable."

She wrapped her arms around my shoulders and her body melted against mine. "Why can't you care?"

"You know why." The seriousness of her question astounded me, especially when she already knew the answer.

"I don't need you to tell me you love me. I just need you." Her words were much like her sister's. "I can handle knowing you don't understand my love. I can't handle you not wanting me."

"But I do want you. That's the problem," I said, watching her blue eyes shoot open. "Don't look at me like that, Sienna. You're fucking gorgeous and you know it. But you deserve more than a life of insecurity and unease." With that admission, she stormed off the dance floor, glaring at me over her shoulder.

You see, once she gave herself to me, I'd never let her go.

When her security was back in place, I ushered my commands and returned to the balcony. Lucky instructed everyone outside of his crew to exit. Once the room was emptied, he went into detail with Carmine, explaining the issues we were having. Lucky's need to involve the Ragetti's filled me with self-doubt. I began questioning my own actions as his enforcer, and whether or not I was able to resolve the lingering conflict.

"A Moretti plot to overthrow the Agostino's." Carmine tapped a finger to his lip in thought. "Guess it's a good thing I stayed in the city a tad longer than planned." He was practically salivating at the chance for more bloodshed.

"And you'll stay away from Octavia," Marco warned—the baby Agostino sibling finally making his presence known with a glare.

Carmine promised to dig deeper into Anthony Moretti, his undeclared intentions becoming clear. His tone and mannerisms told me he'd already been looking into the Moretti's. He was sniffing out leads on Anthony's involvement in his uncle's murder—I'd bet my life on it.

"I want information the moment you get it," Lucky commanded Carmine, who had the audacity to act like it was a suggestion and not an order.

"Got ya. I got some insider shit going on. Once I know, then you'll know," Carmine said, smiling at me like the crazy fucker he was. He laughed at my scowl, wandering towards the bar and flirting with the bartender.

"Should we warn him?" Lucky gestured to Carmine's back.

"I think he should be appropriately introduced to the women in our inner circle." I laughed, watching the show in front of me.

"Do you remember that night at *Striscia*?" Lucky asked, smirking at the memory.

The bartender, Natalia, was married to the club's manager, Nico. A couple of years back, a group of cartel members came into Lucky's strip club looking for a fight. We had them shut down before they could do any real damage. But Natalia impressed us all that day, having incapacitated two key members with her whip and stripper heel.

"Fucking bitch!" Carmine started cackling with laughter while holding his bleeding arm. "You sexy fucking bitch, you just cut me." Natalia stared back at the man with a bored expression, twirling a knife between her fingers.

"No means no, bitch." She lowered the switchblade before stepping around the bar and showcasing her small baby bump. "I did warn him," she said to Lucky, dropping off our drinks.

Powerful men took rejection as a challenge, and his expression was now filled with a savage longing. He was bleeding, denied access and hungry to meet her defiance. I made a mental note to ensure Nico kept a more watchful eye on his wife. Turning on his heel, Carmine grabbed a bottle from behind the bar and sat on a chair overlooking the crowd.

"Where are we with Yuri?" Lucky concentrated on his phone—back to business as usual.

"He pulled the same shit, trying to withhold a shipment. I called the men back and sent word that we need a meeting," I said, shooting off my own text message.

"And?" he asked vaguely. I looked up from my screen, acting as if I didn't understand what he was referencing. "Don't be a dickhead."

I laughed. "You have dinner arrangements at *The Giardinos* tomorrow night." The tension in his shoulders dropped. "Serafina has everything handled. She assured me that Bella is unaware of your intentions."

"Thank you." I watched his jaw clench, trying to hide his smile.

That right there. That was the shit that Sienna deserved that I couldn't give her. I could give her a world filled with all her favorite things. I could spoil her with whatever materialistic trinket she desired. I could fuck her so dirty a year of showering wouldn't suffice. But if I told her I loved her, it would be a lie.

"Fuck," Al muttered, turning from the balcony's edge and heading towards the door. "Sienna just broke some dude's nose. Fights are breaking out."

"I take it back—Sienna may be a pleasant surprise." Carmine hopped to his feet and charged out of the room behind the rest of us.

As soon as the stairs opened up to the dance floor, I spotted Sienna. Her dress was twinkling from the middle of the sunken platform, smack in the center of all of the pandemonium. She was throwing elbows, shouting and knocking people back. Her security team was attempting to keep her covered and away from the physical conflict, but in true Sienna fashion, she just wouldn't have it.

Lucky, Al and I began shouting, shoving patrons out of our way as we beelined towards her. The chaos ended within minutes of our arrival, but the injured attendees would take some time to handle. Sienna was panting heavily, her dress was torn from her shoulder, and there was a madness spread across her face. The epitome of sex and sophistication in a bloodied designer dress with carnage emanating like a strong perfume.

"What the fuck, Sienna!" Lucky shouted, dragging her off of the floor by her elbow. He practically threw her into the elevated booth next to the DJ. "You. Fucking. Said. You'd. Behave."

"I did! He put his hand up my skirt!" She growled, standing up and eye-level; though, she swayed mildly.

"Who?" I questioned with my own savage growl. She didn't hesitate to point out the greasy surfer from earlier. He was sporting a broken nose and scratches marred his face like red warpaint.

"Jesus Christ." Lucky yanked my arm back, stopping me from ascending the stairs to enact the man's death wish. "No!" He grabbed onto Carmine as well, shoving both of us to the side.

"Apollo, take her home." Lucky knocked me towards Sienna. "Carmine, we have more to discuss."

"I don't wanna go home!" Sienna stomped her designer-clad foot like an impudent child.

"Too fucking bad! I warned you!" Lucky snarled in her direction. A look that could make grown men cower only produced a shrug of her shoulders.

"*Fanculo!*" Sienna cursed. She turned back to the booth, ignoring her brother's command.

"Out! Now! So fucking help me, God. Sienna!" Lucky yelled, forcing me to block him from approaching his pouting sister.

"I got her." I stepped up to Sienna. "Keep him on ice for me." I motioned to the son of a bitch who had touched her.

"And me." Carmine clapped his hands together.

"Two fucking psychopaths with Sienna really close to being the third." Lucky shook his head.

"Lucky!" A nasally voice shouted from across the dance floor. I gripped Sienna's arm harder, trying to drag her away from the *cagna* chasing after Lucky. But she fought, scratched and kicked to get out of my hold; Sienna's eyes burned bright with the promise of a come-uppance.

"Bitch." Sienna broke free, charging as Tatianna screamed and fell to the ground. "I told you to stay the fuck away."

"Fucking wildcat." Carmine clapped again, urging Sienna on.

"Fuck you, Sienna." Tatianna snarled through her plastic-infused lips.

Lucky and I attempted to step in the middle but the girls dove for each other, blocking us from grabbing either of them. Sienna had the upper hand in a matter of seconds, showing off the Muay Thai maneuvers she'd recently acquired. Sienna boxed the other girl with a left and then a right—*repeatedly*. After a moment, I pulled her back.

Even in her clumsy drunken state, the woman fought like a beast. She thrashed so erratically she forced me to pin her arms down, her back to my chest. Throwing her head rearward, she slammed into my nose and ripped herself out of my hold. I ignored Carmine's obnoxious laughter, gripping her by her throat and locking her against me in a chokehold. I didn't apply pressure but the silent threat was there, and she stopped moving.

"Fucking hell, Sienna!" Lucky pulled a bleeding Tatianna from the floor.

"Don't you take care of her! Lucky, you fucking promised." Sienna's voice cracked, the only sign that she was close to tears.

"Leave!" Lucky roared at her, and she flinched.

"Let's go, birthday girl." I grabbed Sienna's hand but she slapped it away.

"I can leave on my own, you asshole." She slurred slightly. And when she lost her footing, I had to catch her as she slammed into my chest.

"Say that again without slurring or falling." Grabbing her hand again, I yanked her towards the door.

"I'm fine. I want to dance." She twisted and tugged, breaking free only because I let her go.

"Sure you can handle that?" Carmine stepped to my side. Crossing his arms over his chest, he leered at Sienna. "You hitting it?"

"You're asking for a painful death." But before I could enact my promise, he sauntered off towards Lucky.

Once again, Sienna was in the center of the dance floor, eyes closed and lost to the music. You'd have no idea that she had just beat another human being to shit. Her friends were sitting in the booth, frozen in place as I drew nearer. Ignoring my audience and their stares, I wrapped my arms around her waist and pulled her close for a dance.

"Don't touch me," she ordered. Her voice was exhausted, but she didn't push me away.

"But I like touching you," I admitted.

I liked the feel of her flawless skin under my rough hands. The scent of her shampoo was a mixture of vanilla and strawberries, and for some reason, I found it calming. Her dark hair looked black in this lighting, but I knew it was more brown and softer than silk.

"Will you grant me a birthday wish?" she asked, her expression a silent plea.

"I can't, Sienna," I said, brushing her hair from her face. Her blue eyes burned with unshed tears.

"Can't and won't are two different things, Apollo." And for the second time tonight, she stepped out of my embrace, my fingers tingling at the memory of her in my arms. "I want another drink."

"Can't. We're leaving," I reminded her dryly, watching her sway when she tried to fight me off.

She looked as though she was preparing to spit at me, but when I raised a challenging brow at her, she opted to bite her lip instead. She stumbled back into my embrace as I took her towards the exit. We'd just made it to the edge of the dance floor when her legs gave out from under her. Moving quickly, I swung my arm into the crux of her knees and carried her bridal-style out of the club. Her soft, sleeping breath tickled the skin next to my ear.

My Phantom was already idling at the curb with Toby standing guard. He ran around to the passenger's side and helped me secure the seemingly unconscious Sienna. I was fucked where this girl was concerned.

"Thanks, Toby." Opening my wallet, I handed him a thousand dollars. He gulped as he counted along with me. "You shouldn't fight battles for those who are undeserving." I closed my door before he could respond, hoping my words might somehow make a difference.

Sienna slept the entire car ride back to the hotel and didn't wake until the elevators started moving. She stared sheepishly up at me from her spot in my arms, nestling her head against my chest. My heart pounded, thinking of all the ways I wanted to appropriately wish her a happy birthday.

"I fucking hate her…" she mumbled.

"Pretty sure her new nose read that message loud and clear." I laughed, using my code to open her apartment. "Here." I placed her on her kitchen counter and went to the fridge for some water.

Passing the bottle to her, I watched as she drank the entire thing in one go. I went into her cabinets, and pulling down her favorite cereal, I poured it into a bowl with milk and handed it to her. Things with Sienna hadn't always been this awkward. There was a time when we were just as close as she and Al are.

"Night." I kissed her forehead. "Happy birthday." She smiled and hopped off the counter, before heading towards her bedroom.

Entering my own apartment, I shrugged out of my tie and jacket. I stood in my kitchen, face first in my fridge, when I heard the door open. I grabbed a bottle of water and waited for Cassandra to walk in from work. Instead, the scent of strawberries and vanilla assaulted my senses and I turned quickly. Sienna stood at the threshold wearing a skimpy silk robe. Her long, lean legs were on display and I could see her nipples straining against the material.

"Sienna." I started, pausing when she raised her hand.

"What if I wanted you… just for tonight." Her eyes were so vulnerable I didn't know how to answer.

The truth was, I was ready to strip her down—here and now. I wanted to shred that robe so it would never cover the perfection that I knew was hiding beneath it. I wanted to throw her on my kitchen island and eat her like a late-night snack I'd been craving for far too long. My entire system was giving me the greenlight to own her. *Right the fuck now*. The consequences of tomorrow be damned—I needed a taste of this girl.

Her robe dropped to the floor and my pulse increased at the sight of her. Inch after inch of unmarred olive skin was on display, and her matching black lace bra and panties left little to the imagination. I was a man starving for her affections. She was a siren, calling me to come bend her to my will, and I was losing my hold… my ability to refuse her.

Quickly, I grabbed her by the back of her neck and slammed her lips to mine. They parted on a surprised gasp, allowing my tongue entry. I ravaged her mouth and slowly her body molded to me—the woman was as sweet as she smelled. My leg propped between hers, I wanted to taste the arousal that was warm and wet against my thigh.

I picked her up and tossed her onto her back against the counter. I growled at the dampness I saw through her lace panties. This girl had the power to destroy me. Leaning forward, I ran my nose against her folds, inhaling the most addictive scent—I was fucking salivating.

"Apollo, please," she begged, staring at me from her perched elbows.

"Sienna, baby." My entire body softened at the pleading look she was giving me. She wanted a birthday wish and I was going to grant it. Fuck tomorrow and whatever it meant for us… I was too powerless against her to care about the sacrifices we'd be forced to make.

I hooked my fingers around the thin string of the undergarment that sat low on her hips. Just as I was about to pull it down, I heard the front door open again. Sienna's entire body tensed and her eyes flashed with embarrassment as Cassandra walked into the room.

"Oh, my God. I-I'm so sorry," Cassandra stuttered, turning around with her head bowed.

Sienna shoved me away, jumping down from the counter and snatching her robe off the floor. If looks could kill, I'd erupt into flames. I had expected Sienna's usual temper to flare. But not this time… This was different. Complete and utter devastation was written across her face as her body burned a bright red.

I grabbed her wrist to stop her from fleeing. There were so many words on the tip of my tongue but I couldn't get them out. I wanted to tell her to stay, to explain Cassandra to her. I wanted to tell her how badly I wanted her, and how I would give her everything she'd been begging for, tonight. Except, my brain couldn't work past the sensation that was in the pit of my stomach—it was so strange… *off-putting*.

So, instead of telling Sienna anything at all, I turned to the other girl. "Cassandra, go upstairs," I ordered as she fumbled with her bags. Cassandra practically ran towards the stairs to make her haste exit.

"Sienna." I growled, as she shoved out of my grasp.

"Fuck you, Apollo." She cried… cried, as in tears pouring down her face.

"Wait, Sienna." I tried stopping her, but she surprised me with a knee between my legs, sending me straight to the ground with equal parts precision and force.

"No. I'm sorry that I messed up your fucking night." She angrily wiped the tears off her face, pausing before she left. "These irrational thoughts are done. I won't bother you again." She punctuated her words with a hiccup and slammed the door behind her.

Once again, a good man would have gone after her. But a smart man knew better. And I knew Sienna… She'd lick her wounds, then she'd act like nothing happened. Perhaps this was exactly what she needed anyway—a bullet putting down her silly notions. Fuck whatever this nauseous lump in my stomach was, she needed time to cool off and regroup. Then we'd go back to normal.

"I'm sorry. I didn't know you had company. Maybe it's better if I just go," Cassandra said, re-emerging from her bedroom.

"It's not your fault." I rubbed the heels of my palms into my eyes. I had a debilitating headache creeping in and my balls ached.

"I will call a cab." She turned, attempting to flee but I caught her arm. Her breathing was erratic and her eyes were large.

"Don't look at me like that," I ordered and she immediately casted her gaze downward. "Fuck." I growled, running my hand over my face.

"Please, sir," she murmured, her stare still focused on the hardwood floors.

"Go to the window and strip bare." I enjoyed the way she immediately responded without a fight. Once she was naked, I ordered her again. "Bend and grab your ankles."

And again, she complied without a fight. If this was Sienna, she'd talk back, she'd ask fucking questions and she'd piss me off. As much as I didn't want to think about Sienna, she continued to plague my mind as I stared at the other woman now bent over and dripping wet for me. I was lost to my own thoughts as I slammed my length, hard and deep, inside Cassandra.

My apartment filled with the smell of sex, the echo of moans, and the slapping of flesh on flesh. I grabbed her waist and spun her around. Picking her up without warning, I relished in how quickly she wrapped her legs around me. I slammed her back against the floor-to-ceiling glass overlooking the city.

My mind churned with indecision, and the fact that I hated seeing those much-too-blue fucking eyes filled with tears because of me. I was angry at Sienna for showing up here the way she had. I was mad at Cassandra for walking in at just the right moment and stopping me from making a huge mistake. And I hated myself because as I wrapped my hands around this woman's throat, all I could see was Sienna begging me to take her.

Thrust after thrust, I maintained the terrorizing assault on Cassandra as my hands kept tightening on her throat. My mind was captured by images of being a better man, of not enjoying the pain I caused those around me. I didn't understand sweet or kind. I understood bloodshed and carnage. Even now, in this moment, I only released Cassandra enough to breathe so she didn't pass out before I came. And not because I cared for her own benefit.

It was wrong. I was fucking sick. And Sienna was better than it all. Cassandra's cries were cut off as I wrapped my hands around her neck once more. I could feel my balls tighten as I prepared to release myself inside the wrong woman… I roared in anger as I came and dropped to the ground with Cassandra beneath me.

"You should talk to her," Cassandra muttered after a few moments of labored breathing filling the silence.

"Like fuck I should," I growled, rising to my feet and lifting Cassandra to hers. Something in her eyes was off. Cassandra seemed pleased that I hadn't left her, but the smallest bit annoyed as well.

"And you should talk to her because when you came, you shouted her name," Cassandra threw over her shoulder before flouncing up the staircase.

Yep, I was completely, totally and utterly fucked.

CHAPTER 11
SIENNA AGOSTINO

Demeaned. Dejected. Devastated.

So many words… so many emotions, and yet nothing could do justice for how I truly felt. Apollo had been calling me for days but I ignored every single one—an attempt to drown in my own self-pity—opting instead, to throw myself into my work. To avoid running into him at the compound or my apartment, I had been staying in a hotel room—that is, when I wasn't barricaded inside my office.

On a positive note, I hadn't received any more mysterious and threatening phone calls. I was still on the hunt for answers but I was at least doing it in peace. Well, in peace, if I disregarded the calls and texts from Apollo and forwent that embarrassing trip down my birthday memory lane. There was something broken inside me that was filled with a nothingness, and I needed to let go of the feelings that were slowly killing me.

Andersen Farewell was my stolen engineer from Alias Marks' Corporation. I had employed him to run his software applications and create new patents, and he'd been at my side for the majority of my ongoing investigation. He was a charming computer nerd in his mid-thirties and he was leaps beyond more intelligent than anyone else I had ever met.

He was qualified in four different engineering capacities: chemical, mechanical, biomedical and computer hardware. And he was currently elbow deep in his new program, calculating all of the financial data belonging to Dominic Moretti. We needed the smoking gun to take him down and I knew we were close. Andersen was just like me in the sense that he refused to back down from a challenge. And the man was handsome to boot.

Why? Why couldn't I be interested in someone like him?

He was the quintessential blonde-haired, blue-eyed, muscular all-American boy next door. We worked well together, lost in our laptops and side by side for hours. Yet, he didn't create any type of pull within me, not even when his smile revealed dimples. He was the perfect package, practically leaving hearts and flowers exploding in my office, and I wanted no part of it… or him.

"Holy. Shit…" Andersen muttered. Rising to his feet, he dropped his tablet in front of me. "Look at that."

He tapped play on the screen and a grainy image appeared, revealing Dominic Moretti and John Hardwicke leaving a shipping container. Cash and paperwork were transferred back and forth before Dominic stepped inside the large box once more. When he emerged again, he had a lifeless body thrown over his shoulder as he carried her to his waiting car.

John and Dom continued their conversation while more women were maneuvered out of the container. My breath was caught in my throat as I watched the grotesque truth we'd been chasing appear before my very eyes.

"We got them." Andersen walked towards the window, peering out in silence. "Now what?"

"You don't want to ask questions of people whose answers will go against your moral compass." I grabbed my phone and fired off a text to my father. Normally I would be contacting Apollo to set up a meeting, but not right now. No thank you.

"A moral compass is of little consideration when dealing with men like these." His words caught me off guard and I stopped to stare at his serious expression.

"Good to know." I turned my attention back to my screen.

"I'll leave you to it." He walked out as my phone went off. I straightened from my seat and wandered over to my floor-length mirror. A gray silk shirt was tucked into my tight pencil skirt; it opened at my breasts to reveal a sliver of skin under the bow-tied at the top. My *Manolo Blahnik* pumps were black lace with a diamond buckle across the toes.

Once I had backed up all of the evidence to several different secure drives, I headed out the door to meet my father. I was lost in my thoughts as I left my office and headed to a small restaurant in the city. It was closed to the public until dinner but I could see several occupants inside.

"There she is." My father rose from the large circle table and opened his arms wide.

The restaurant itself was owned by Italian immigrants but it had the feel of modern city architecture and design—clean, sleek lines with a white and black motif while the walls were littered with colorful pops in the form of modern art canvases. Men were spread out around the room; some I recognized as my father's security but others I hadn't seen before.

"I have so much to tell you." I tapped my tablet as he motioned for me to sit.

"First. I need you to understand... I didn't warn you because I know how you are." My back straightened at the realization—*this was a setup*. "After we talked, I put a lot of thought into your future."

"No. Please." He raised a hand and cut me off.

"Not only are things done a certain way in our world, Sienna, but you need protection. I've arranged for..." He stopped speaking when I jumped to my feet and leaned over the table to meet him eye-level.

"You arranged for what... exactly?" I snarled, the anger holding my unwanted tears at bay.

"Sienna." He barked my name, motioning for me to sit once more. His tone and facial expression forced me to back down. "I promised you I would do my best and with Gio Moretti sniffing around, he's caused a stir. Many people have been questioning my indecision in regards to you and Octavia."

"You... You can't be serious." I sat back, my jaw dropping. "You have so much dirt on the Moretti's and yet, you're allowing them to twist your arm with this?" I scoffed, blatantly disrespecting him in front of his men.

"Enough." He barked a second time, and I jumped in my seat. "I have made my decision, Sienna."

"And I have made mine," I responded, my anger now boiling over the surface.

"You were right, Mario." A deep, raspy voice came from behind me. "She is a firecracker."

I turned in my seat to watch the large man walk around the table and stand before me; the sheer size of him forcing my neck to arch in order to get a good look. He unbuttoned the front of his grey suit, revealing a broad chest and a smattering of dark hair peeking out from his opened collar. He had a trimmed beard, dark olive skin, and bold brown eyes that watched me with a reserved amusement. And he was tall—well over six foot.

His face was classically handsome but his eyes were filled with a blanketed brutality that told you just how deadly he was. A silent threat, indeed. His features were chiseled and he boasted a strong jaw with a defined scar traveling chin to temple. The old wound had healed unevenly and the grooves proved it was from a knife hastily slashing through the skin there. But somehow it only made him more handsome.

"Sienna, meet Romano Bianchi." My father gestured and the man extended his hand.

"The new Philly boss," I stated. I knew exactly who he was.

He'd moved up the "mafia ladder" faster than most and had a bit of a reputation for his silent striking capabilities. Physically, mentally or financially—the man had no qualms about ripping his foes apart at the seams. His notoriety also stemmed from his promotion under the previous family patriarch—the man had opted to renounce his biological son in favor of Romano—causing a huge scandal.

"Pleasure is all mine." He leaned over and kissed my hand; the contact sent a slight electrical charge through my system. "Shall we?" He pulled the chair out for me. I hadn't even realized I was standing again.

"Your father has told me several things about you but I've done my own research over the years. And I must say, Sienna, your reputation for hard work and intellectual prowess isn't nearly as stunning as your profound beauty." He smirked at me.

"And I see that the rumors of your premature promotion in place of the rightful heir of Philadelphia are severely overinflated. I mean, now that I've listened to your bullshit." I smiled sweetly in return.

My father looked back and forth between us, his eyes narrowing in displeasure over my insult. However mad he was, I watched the exchange of a simple wink with his head of security and the man stepped closer to me—the entire room seemingly unsure how Romano would react. The silence stretched and he probably assumed I would squirm in my seat, but little did he realize I'd grown up with men just like him. They smelled fear and weakness like it was an enticing perfume, and I refused to cower.

"There she is." Romano roared with laughter. "I'd heard of your fire and I am so glad to see it doesn't easily extinguish under scrutiny." He waved over the waiter and had him pour wine for the table.

"As I was saying, I told Romano all about your… situation," my father continued, for once at a loss for words. Gone was the powerful and precise boss of New York; in his place was a concerned father, who would've melted my heart if not for this unsolicited setup.

"And what situation is that father?" I'd already shown my ugly side —my disrespect—I couldn't mask it down just yet. "The fact that your eldest daughter is still unmarried and that the never-ending list of suitors has grown weary?"

"Sienna…" he growled, the warning clear in his voice. "Show me some fucking respect. I've given you long enough to live your own life. It's time for you to do what is expected. I have spoken with Romano, who is aligned with making an arrangement beneficial for all. There is plenty of open office space in Philly. You can move *Energia* there. Romano doesn't plan on stifling your ability to grow your empire."

"You mean, *rebuild* my empire as a *Bianchi*." I stated the one thing he wasn't saying. "Take everything I've earned on my own and transition it to the Bianchi's." My face was growing hot—the prickly kind of heat that rolled up my neck.

Romano snapped his fingers and one of his guards handed me a packet of legal documents. "If you have your attorneys review this, you will see that—just as I have ensured Mario—I am in agreement with your demands.

The income, the name and the association will never have anything to do with the Bianchi's. A marriage of convenience, a security of combined power and a future of heirs are all I ask. And in exchange, you will continue living exactly as you wish—exactly as you are—in our union."

"I told you I would do my best to take care of you," my father whispered, our eyes locking for a moment before I turned back to the packet.

"I have infinite patience as you thoroughly comb over the documents, and I am open for discussing whatever additions may strike your interest." Romano sipped his wine, his face set in beautifully marred stone.

"But what do you get out of all of this?" I asked. I was genuinely curious about his own ambitions.

"I want the same things as you do—to build an empire. I want a woman who won't hide behind me but stand proudly at my side. I want a legacy and a powerful matriarch to raise our children together and to continue the bloodline we will create." He leaned onto his elbows. "I don't want a wilting fucking flower as a wife. I like fire… I like anarchy. And I don't like when things are easy."

"Easy is boring," we each said at the same time. My father chuckled and sat back in his seat smiling.

"And it doesn't hurt that I find you exceptionally beautiful," he added.

My heart beat harder in my chest as my eyes took in his face, searching for any indication that he was full of shit. But I didn't find any. For all intents and purposes, he acted and sounded as if what he was saying was actually true. Of course, my attorneys would rip this proposal apart to ensure that I was as covered as he said. I was no fool for a pretty face, especially one filled with lies and broken promises.

"I hate to cut this short but I do need to get back to *my* city. I will return to New York in about thirty days. Shall we schedule dinner to discuss your thoughts?" he asked, rising from the table and gesturing for me to follow him to the door.

"Uhm, yes. Thirty days should be enough time for me..." I trailed off.

"Enough time for you to find a million things you don't like and refuse this proposal?" he asked, a devilish smirk on his face. "I've taken the thousands of emails your father has sent me and created this with mostly you... your future... in mind. No bullshit."

"No bullshit..." I repeated, almost amused by his terminology. His only response was an all-tooth smile of perfectly white, straight teeth that made his scar dance.

"I meant what I said." He kissed my hand again. "The rumors of your beauty don't compare to staring into those icicle eyes. I much rather enjoy watching them than the ones on your brother's face." He chuckled, earning him a genuine smile of my own.

Large, warm, calloused hands gripped my face as he stepped closer against my body. His gaze dropped for a moment to the sliver of skin revealing my breasts before returning to mine. His brown eyes lightened with a primal hunger I rather enjoyed.

We stared at each other in silence for a moment longer before he released me with a playful grin and left the restaurant with his entourage of guards.

"Sienna." My father stepped up behind me.

As mad as I was at him for pulling this stunt, especially without a warning, I appreciated his attempt at giving me what I wanted. In our world, no matter the amount of power you allotted, it only took one minute for people to suggest they saw weakness—an act that could destroy everything you'd worked so hard to build.

"I get it. I do. Doesn't mean I like it," I said, refusing to look at him. "I am grateful for everything you are trying to do with this... but it doesn't make any of it okay with me. I will have my attorneys scour the details and I'll be in touch." I turned to leave but the hand on my arm stopped me.

"Once you review it, let's do dinner and discuss it ourselves before he comes back." I nodded and pulled out of his grasp without making eye contact. I didn't even care that we hadn't discussed what I learned about Dominic Moretti. It wasn't directly affecting my father, but regardless, I would send out my evidence to the surrounding authorities in hopes of saving some of those women.

Once I was safe inside my SUV, I let myself collide with the reality of the situation. He was handsome, he was rich and he understood what I wanted without being bothered by my own... strength. But I didn't want to get married to a man who I met over legal jargon with no preamble to actual feelings.

There was a connection—a tingle—that seemed to spark something between us; but my mind was still rattled by the fact that everything I'd been running from was finally coming to fruition.

No matter how hard I fought, I knew there was no alternative. I'd be given away to someone, and I needed to move fast if I wanted it to be a man that would ensure I maintained my own identity.

A woman's worth was so much more than that of the man whose arm she proudly held. At least it should be... Romano Bianchi intrigued me but I hated how my heart wept in misery while a tattooed psychopath danced on it as if it were nothing.

"Your sister called a few moments ago and is on her way." Farrah caught me the moment I exited the elevator. "And Marissa wants a meeting later today if possible."

I didn't respond, just nodded and kept walking. Farrah had been with me long enough to know silence was a non-verbal cue for her to leave me the fuck alone. The quiet allowed me to think. It helped me deal with all the nonsense thrusted my way. And the contract in my bag was several pages of nonsense that weighed heavily on my shoulder.

"I need legal in here, now," I barked, shutting my office door behind me. Not even a minute later, Amy, my lead attorney, stormed inside with Evelyn Campbell on her heels.

"What happened?" Amy asked immediately, depositing her tablet onto my desk, kicking her shoes off and flopping into a seat.

"How are you?" I asked Evelyn, smiling. The girl nodded happily, the excitement over her internship with Amy written clear across her face. "This." I dropped the marriage contract in front of her.

Amy took a second to flip through the pages before she understood the gravity of what it meant and handed it to Evelyn. "No," was all she said as Evelyn started reading through it herself.

"I should be thankful it's taken this long, but sadly... yes. Father has found a man for me to marry." I flopped into my own seat as Evelyn gasped in shock. "Welcome to my world, sweetie." I smiled with no joy.

"How am I proceeding with this?" Amy asked, taking the papers back.

"You know my intentions. Marriage is marriage; he wants sex and kids. I met him today and he actually likes the idea of not having a weak wife, so there's that." I sighed, powering on my computer. "*Energia* and all future businesses are mine and mine alone. I want... I don't fucking know." I huffed in exasperation.

"Full rights to all your businesses and assets, no limitation on anything you personally want to do..." Amy rambled on with the key topics she knew I'd want handled.

"Hey." The door opened and Octavia marched inside, before shutting it in Peiro's face.

"Look at you," I said, causing her to blush as she pushed her glasses back up her nose. She was wearing a black silk blouse tucked into a high waist black pencil skirt. Her red bottom shoes were simple with a strap around the ankle and a tall spiked heel—I highly approved of them. And her brown hair was wrapped into a high professional bun.

"I just left my meeting." Her face was red in embarrassment from all of the attention. That little sister of mine was an enigma. She may have been mild, but she bore a silent ferocity—all while rocking a naughty librarian porn star look. "What's this?" She grabbed the papers from Amy.

She lifted her head and I nodded sadly. "Romano Bianchi," I stated.

"Philly? He wants to send you away from me… to *Philly*?" Her words were a sad whisper that shook my soul.

"Don't do this," I ordered, swallowing past the lump in my throat. Any time Octavia was upset, I lost my battle with my own sanity. I couldn't handle seeing her anything but happy. "I'm dealing with it. Nothing's final. Now… how was your meeting?"

Not many people in the family knew that Octavia was taking a page out of my book and starting out on her own. She owned a small used bookstore, not far from here, and was also entering the publishing world.

She hid the store and the new company away from her real name. She was venturing into being an independent author and had opted to publish herself through her own company, rather than through traditional methods. It was all hush-hush, but today she met with her first round of perspective authors.

Amy muttered that she'd be in touch, leaving my office with Evelyn in tow. Octavia jumped into telling me all about the starting process and the one author she adored. Then we switched topics back to Romano Bianchi and how the first meeting went.

"I mean at the end of the day, if this is what I have to do… Well, then, I mean… I guess it could be worse…" I said, rolling my shoulders.

"Yeah, like it could be Gio Moretti." She stuck out her tongue and pointed to it, making a gagging noise.

"Ha! Gross! And yeah, it could be that bad. But Romano is hot, he's charming and we had a connection," I said honestly.

"Like the Apollo connection?" Octavia asked, her eyes filling with remorse.

"That's its own kind of thing. This wasn't as strong, but probably healthier." I laughed soundlessly.

"Miss Agostino, your appointment is here." Farrah buzzed over the intercom. I scowled as I pulled up my calendar, not recalling anything being on it.

"Sir, wait a minute!" We heard Farrah yell through the door, both rising to our feet as it burst open.

A large man loomed furiously at the threshold; so large in fact, that he had to turn somewhat sideways and duck his head. He was a beast of a man standing over six-five—if not more—and impossibly wide, with muscles that threatened to rip his black thermal shirt. Every available piece of skin I could see was covered in tattoos, even his face.

"Carmine Ragetti," Octavia mumbled. I raised a brow at her admission while the two of them were lost in silence and in what felt like a personal exchange.

"Carmine, huh?" I asked, looking back and forth between them. "Sienna Agostino." I held out my hand for him to shake.

"I met you on your birthday. However, you were beating some girl's ass and taking far too many shots." Carmine finally released Octavia from his dark gaze and turned to me instead.

"Hm." I started assessing him in wordless contemplation. "What do I owe the... pleasure of you interrupting my workday without an appointment?"

He ignored me, forcing my hackles to rise, as he kept his sole focus on Octavia. I didn't like any man paying her so much attention let alone someone like him. I'd heard the rumors of his family all the way from California.

He was the eldest of four kids and his father was an absolute tyrant. The patriarch didn't shy away from dancing in front of the police or the local news cameras, covered in his latest victim's blood or while openly beating his children.

"I want to hire you." His voice was deep and rough—like he gargled glass—with just the hint of an Italian accent.

"Interesting..." I muttered, tapping a finger over my lip as the room grew silent with unease. "To do what, exactly?"

"You're the name everyone says when you need information on someone. I'm working with Lucky while I'm in town on business.

Business that could use your expertise." Carmine glanced at me until he noticed Octavia squirming uncomfortably in her seat.

"I need to discuss this with my father, then I will get back to you with an answer." I didn't even care enough to ask who it was he wanted me to look into. I knew the family history and I wanted him far away from all of us.

When he looked like he was going to argue, Octavia rose from her seat. "I need to get back to work." She swung her messenger bag over her shoulder, bracing herself as the heavy weight shifted.

"I'll see you later tonight." I smiled at my sister, then turned back to Carmine with a blank expression.

"My card." He extended a tattooed hand to give me a black business card with a phone number scrawled in red ink across the center. I was about to speak when he turned on his heel—again ignoring me—to follow Octavia out of the door.

"Goddamn it." I stormed around my desk. I didn't like the way he was chasing my sister.

"Step back, *sir.*" Peiro practically growled from outside my office, his panicked tone causing me to move faster. Carmine said something to him in return but I was still too far away to hear it. However, even from this distance, I could feel the threat he was imposing on Peiro, who was trying to block him from approaching Octavia.

"Step the fuck back!" Peiro ordered again, but Carmine was almost three times his size and unfazed by the guard's commands. The elevator chose that moment to arrive and Octavia practically threw herself inside.

Time slowed down as I watched, unable to stop what I knew was about to happen.

"Call Ton. Now!" I ordered Farrah, and she quickly dialed *Energia*'s head of security. It didn't take an idiot to know what Carmine was going to do.

Before I could separate them, Carmine grabbed Peiro by his jacket, picking him up and tossing him towards me like a ragdoll. I tried to brace myself as Peiro slammed into me and we both struggled to not hit the ground.

Octavia went to step out from the elevator until Carmine forced her back inside, the doors shutting behind them. Peiro and I yelled as we both charged towards the closing elevator, but it was too late.

And I didn't know what scared me more—the idea that a man as ominous as Carmine Ragetti was alone with my baby sister, or the look of intrigue on her face when she realized it was just the two of them.

Yeah… It was her intrigue that startled me the most.

"Fuck! Do we kill the power to the elevators?" Peiro asked just as Ton charged into the room. After a quick rundown of what had happened, he started barking commands at his men in order to get ahead of the situation.

"Downstairs! Now! I need elevator two on immediate decline!" Ton ordered and we followed, hoping his team would stop them in the lobby.

My heart was racing as the next elevator arrived. We watched in tension-induced silence as the car moved down floor by floor rapidly, not stopping for anything.

I tossed a quick prayer to the universe—I prayed that they didn't get off somewhere else. And I prayed even harder that he didn't hurt her.

I knew that look all too well and it would only end in disaster. For as much strength as she claimed she had over protecting her heart, that look told me a tattooed nightmare had just thrown her sensibilities out of the window.

He was cold and dangerous, much like our own men. But where ours were branded to our cause, Carmine Ragetti was the thing that went bump in the night and the psycho held no such loyalties.

CHAPTER 12
APOLLO DELUCA

The Russian and Moretti situations were still spiraling out of control days later. Now, Lucky's newfound romance with Mirabella and her unfortunate namesake added a myriad of additional uncertainties to the mix. I was intrigued by the girl—I respected her. She had more fire, backbone and intelligence than her older brother, of that much I was sure.

Then to top off the veritable shit storm that was already brewing, Sienna had refused to answer my calls. I'd tried numerous times but the infuriating woman had blocked me—cell phone and burner calls wouldn't ring through—and she changed the goddamn security passcode to access her apartment.

Al's never-ending murderous glares confirmed he knew all about our feud, and he was out for blood. He stubbornly refused to address the situation with me, not bothering to say a single word. Instead, he continuously glared and muttered comments he didn't care to repeat audibly.

"Take me to Sienna's office," I ordered him.

"She's not going to be happy." He reached into his pocket, pulling out his cell.

Before he could forewarn her of my intentions, I snatched the phone out of his grasp. My window was already down by the time he reached across the center console. And with no hesitation whatsoever, I threw the cellular device out of the car.

"You motherfucker!" He swerved into the next lane, narrowly missing another driver.

"You fucking rat!" I dared him to continue.

"I was calling Lucky," he lied.

"I sincerely doubt that. You were going to call your *bestie* to warn her of my impending arrival." If I wasn't so disgruntled, his face would've been entertaining. "Instead of sulking in silence, be a man and fucking say what it is you want to say."

"You had a million places you could have taken Cassandra!" he shouted, slamming his fist into the steering wheel. "It was her birthday and she has a set of keys... how are you so smart yet so fucking stupid?" Spit flew from his mouth as he yelled.

Though I did not feel as though I owed anyone an explanation—least of all Al—I briefly summarized why Cassandra was in my home. I was aware that my conduct wasn't emblematic of my true nature, but my logic was of no concern to him.

"Why didn't you tell her? She's been upset for days." Turning off the highway, we headed towards Sienna's high-rise.

"She ran off before I could." I skipped over the part where she kneed me in the balls. "Besides, she knows the score."

"How did she run? How exactly did she get away?" He was amused, clearly reading between the lines.

"Fuck off. And stay here," I ordered as he pulled up to the curb.

I opened the glass doors and walked into the marble lobby, the scene before me rattling the beast within. Sienna and Peiro were pacing in front of the elevators; Sienna's tone was apoplectic when the doors didn't open immediately upon her command.

"What's going on?" I yelled, storming towards them the same moment Octavia stepped from the elevator.

Sienna pulled her sister in for a hug, whispering harshly at the younger girl. Peiro was on the phone, no doubt being berated by Lucky, considering Octavia's well-being was the bodyguard's only concern. Sienna's building security stormed towards me, while the girls argued about heading to the compound before making their way in the direction of Sienna's office.

"Carmine Ragetti trapped Octavia in the elevator *alone*." Ton handed me his tablet and hit play on the screen.

Octavia seemed to be speaking but Carmine just stared at her. And the look was a cross between menace and interest... neither of which was acceptable. When the elevator reached the lobby, security was already waiting, their weapons drawn. The video was void of sound but the picture was clear as Carmine pinned Octavia inside.

One of the men stepped forward, his firearm pointed directly at Carmine's chest but the brute appeared unfazed. The doors started closing again and in the chaos of it all, the security team somehow missed their target—likely hesitant to fire with Octavia so close in proximity. A few words were exchanged and then Carmine left her, sending the girl back up the way she had come.

That video gave me an inclination of another adversary we didn't need, especially now. The elevator doors opened on Sienna's floor and I charged into her office without knocking, the door slamming against the wall.

"I don't have the patience for this shit right now, Apollo." Sienna pinched the bridge of her nose, turning to her computer.

I didn't answer, merely pounced as she sat trapped behind her desk. Aggressively pulling her chair away, I watched as she lurched forward to catch herself, slamming her palms into my chest. I leaned closer, my eyes taking in every detail of her gorgeous face and assessing for any damage Ragetti might've caused her. The silence stretched as neither of us spoke; the only noise was her increased breathing.

"We're not fucking." It was all I could think to say.

"You've made that clear." Her words were filled with bitterness.

"No." I took a deep breath; trying to be kind was a foreign concept. "Cassandra. At my house. Regularly." I clipped each word, attempting to—and failing at—being calmer.

I'd read that facial expressions and tones could ease emotional situations, reducing the other person's discomfort. I never wanted to hurt

Sienna, unintentionally or not. I'd been versing myself on the topic—on how to deal with her—in hopes of lessening the constant feuding between us.

We were opposites—one wishing for daydreams, the other a thing of nightmares.

"Right." Crossing her arms protectively over her chest, she wasn't going to make this easy on me.

"We used to." She flinched at my admission. "Not anymore, not after the other night." *Fuck, here it comes,* I braced myself internally.

"Get the fuck out!" Suddenly pushing her chair back, she shoved at my chest, forcing me to take a step. "I don't want to hear this shit, Apollo. I have enough on my goddamn plate—I don't need your bullshit."

The woman was out of control. She wasn't listening to reason, to common sense. Instead, she stormed to the door and threw it open, barking at me to leave. But my feet were cemented in place, my rage simmering in response.

"*Vaffanculo*! Fucking go!" Her increased volume pulled all eyes to us, and Al barreled towards me.

I beat him to the door, slamming it in his face before locking it. I grabbed Sienna by her shoulders, thrusting her back into the wall a little more aggressively than needed; I was barely maintaining control, as was becoming common ground with this woman. Because that's what she did to me, eviscerated my control—a feat that was supposed to be reserved for my enemies.

"Apollo! Open the fucking door!" Al pounded his fists against it.

"You're irrefutably the most frustrating woman on this planet." My body pinned hers to the wall, as my mind churned at the sensation of her pushed so closely against me.

"I'm sorry I'm not one of your submissive whores." She gave me an all-knowing grin. "Yeah, Apollo, I've heard about *Hush* and your preferences."

"Does it turn you on?" Her chest rapidly rose and fell. "I bet I could own you... every part of you. And what's more..." I leaned forward and whispered into her ear. "You'd fucking beg me for it."

Her eyes were dilated and her breath was coming out in heavy pants, her reception of my words making my cock stir to life. My control evaporated—it jumped out of the top floor window and spiraled to the streets below before shattering into a million pieces. I ground my reaction into her stomach, savoring the fire in her eyes.

"Get. That. Off. Me." She struggled to secure her mask into position. "I don't compete."

I kept her pinned in place, enjoying the way she writhed against me. "There is no competition, Sienna." Her eyes searched for deception.

"Right. Your list of whores has proven that." Her words practically dripped venom.

If I wasn't still affixed to her body there was a chance that I would've missed her muscles tensing—preparing to strike. I shifted my legs between hers, halting her attempt to emasculate me once again. I could practically feel her arousal against my thigh as I shoved her legs further apart.

"Got me once, not again," I whispered.

My nose dove behind her ear, inhaling her soft scent, a hint of floral—a goddamned intoxicating drug. "No one can compete with you, Sienna. But the pain I will cause you is a matter of when, not if."

Her facial muscles, the motor cortex and rostral cingulate motor cortex, quivered; her tears were on the cusp of appearing. It didn't please me that I was the cause of this physical manifestation of her turmoil, not even in the slightest.

"Right." And... the bitch mask was back.

"I don't want to hurt you." Tucking a loose strand of brown hair behind her ear, I propelled myself from the wall. "Just so you know, your brother has a date this evening with Bella."

It was my version of an apology, to set us back to right once more. I had no doubt that the moment I left she'd start harassing him about his affections for the Moretti girl.

I opened the door to Al. "The Russians want a meeting..."

I nodded. "Let's go." I headed for the elevator, smiling internally when Sienna slammed her door in Al's face.

"Fuck, this is boring." Al sighed, flopping back in his chair.

Al was the type of individual that felt compelled to action. If he was lost to his own thoughts, he'd be inclined to kill himself. He had the intelligence of a turkey or a goddamned kakapo, too small of brain to function appropriately. He could use his developed exterior for brute force, but I wouldn't challenge any of his other muscles to flex adequately in dire situations.

My text message alert went off and I opened it. "It's Lucky. He wants a meeting with the Russians immediately."

As of now, our buyers were remaining calm and patient over their missing artillery. Something that wasn't typical in our line of work—patience wasn't a virtue our buyers were keen to possess. And, thanks to Bella's compelling viewpoint, Lucky had finally realized the oddity.

We had a rat that was giving our buyers contact information to Yuri. Then Yuri would, incontrovertibly, offer them the same shipments —our shipments—at a discounted price.

Al went for the car as I stepped into the restaurant. "It's set. We need to go now. I will ensure she makes it home," I whispered to Lucky, interrupting his long-awaited night out with the Moretti girl.

"No, she's coming," Lucky whispered back, staring at Bella. Apparently, she was fluent in Russian and our newest secret weapon.

"We are going to need your help with this." Lucky spoke in hushed tones from the back seat as Al drove us towards the predetermined meeting place.

"You speak Russian, correct?" I asked and she nodded. "Would you be able to listen from the car and report everything you hear?" Lucky went over the plan with her, offering a few encouraging words along the way.

We pulled into the warehouse, Lucky assuring Bella of her safety before stepping out of the vehicle himself. Yuri's men were spread throughout the room, their propensity towards violence evident. It was time for answers or it was time for fucking blood to spill, either would suffice.

"Yuri, Yuri, Yuri. You've broken our deal yet again. I've killed men for less." Lucky morphed into *il diavolo*—his own bloodthirsty alter ego—in front of our very eyes.

"*Da*. This time, not my fault." Yuri's broken English was peppered by a very heavy Russian accent. "Our shipment stolen before get here."

"Do I look stupid to you, Yuri? Do I look like a man to be fucked with? You have tested my patience and now you lie to my face? There is only one way this will end. *Smert'*." The entire room tensed at Lucky's declaration of death.

"Now. Now." Yuri spoke to his men in his native tongue, attempting to quiet their concerns. With his provocation, the Russians erupted into laughter. My spine straightened—I didn't like being left in the dark nor did I share in their sudden bout of humor. Internally, I was even more pleased with Lucky's decision to include Bella.

"Do you truly believe if you keep this up, I will let you live?" Lucky chuckled in response with little concern over their antics.

I had definitely underestimated the young Mirabella Moretti and it seemed, so did the Devil himself. The echo of the car door opening and closing drew everyone's attention as she walked—head held high—to Lucky's side. The men in the room leered, no doubt wondering what it would be like to have a taste of her.

"Are your men even aware of who they are conducting business with?" Bella asked Yuri. For such a petite thing, her voice was surprisingly strong while her posture was unwavering.

Yuri stood mute, refusing to acknowledge the girl or her outburst. The Russians did not take kindly to women interfering in what they saw as the business of men. In fact, his face was twisted in disdain over her audacity in addressing him directly.

She was painting a target on herself; however, this action—facing the Russian adversaries openly and without fear—just ensured the loyalty of Lucky's entire crew. They would respect her for this.

They may have spoken a language I didn't understand but their bodies told me everything I needed to know. Bella's words were causing a major discord among the ranks.

They clearly had no clue who they were in the presence of, but the Moretti girl had made sure to rectify that situation.

"He didn't tell his men the plan or who they are up against. They think you're a spoiled American—they are going to kill you and take your business," Bella told us. "And they knew about me and planned to come for me when you were gone."

This information cemented the fact that we were looking at a bunch of dead men. Threatening Lucky's intended—our future queen—went against everything we stood for, the few ideals our organization held fast.

We would've always protected Bella out of loyalty to Lucky, but her actions this evening earned her, her own.

Yuri started to yell; his men who had once shrunken in on themselves, were now suddenly pounding their chests in pride.

"We need to go. Now!" Bella snapped at us.

Lucky and I shielded her as we darted to the car. A man stepped into our path, earning him a penetrating bullet to his glabella, the skin between his eyes.

"Fuck!" I hissed, falling backwards into Bella and nearly taking her to the ground with me. "God damn it!" The blood from the wound in my arm sprayed across her face.

"Apollo!" She let go of Lucky, turning to look at me as I clamped the resulting hole in the lateral head of my tricep muscle closed.

I shoved her forward. "I'm fine, get to the car, *la mia regina!*"

"Bella, move that sexy little ass!" Lucky pushed her inside the vehicle. "It's bulletproof—stay down, *mi amore.*"

Once she was safely tucked away, Lucky and I smiled triumphantly at each other. Gaping wounds aside, we were set to fucking destroy. We charged after Yuri in perfect precision. One after another, Russians fell to the ground in a frenzy of ill-fated prayers and pleas for death.

"The fuck?" Diving behind a freight of cargo, Lucky and I grunted upon contact with the concrete floor. "These fuckers have a machine gun?" I roared. The sons of bitches had lied about having access to heavy artillery.

"It's a fucking RPK-16, the newest edition from the Russian special forces!" Lucky hid from the heavy fire laying waste to the rest of the warehouse.

"Fuck! Okay, I got this," I yelled, stepping out of the shadows. Darting to the next closest cover, I fired as many times as I could. Even bleeding heavily from my shoulder, I was still a dead shot and one of the RPK's quieted in the distance.

One threat down, however, I was cognizant of the need to tend to my wound. The damage wouldn't be permanent but the blood loss was rapidly increasing. I glanced over my shoulder to ensure Lucky was safe and then darted back towards the car.

"I'm okay. I'm just losing a lot of blood." I placated Bella, ripping off my jacket.

Immediately, Bella leaned across the seat, inspecting my upper arm. She confirmed my assessment of her had been accurate—the girl was by no means squeamish.

Sitting on the center console, and with no semblance of motherly care, she poked and prodded the gaping hole. She then ripped my tie from my neck and wrapped it around my arm, using it as a tourniquet.

Once Lucky was in my line of sight, I attempted to open my door just as a man came from his left. A bloody knife to the gut—three times—had the attacker collapsing on the spot. Lucky was smiling maniacally, soaked in blood and obviously enjoying himself.

"Bella, no!" Snatching the firearm from the console, she rolled down the rear window.

"He's out of bullets," she muttered, and I saw that it was true.

Lucky was crouched low on the ground, but he wasn't going down without a fight. Rearing his head towards the chaos and the carnage, *il diavolo* reflected back in the blood-coated floors.

"Fuck this," I shouted, trying to grab Bella. But instead, she slid out of my grip.

"Pull tight with your teeth. I can't let him die, Apollo." She slipped the end of my tie into my mouth and then she did the most remarkable thing.

With a single deep exhale and one pull of the trigger, silence descended upon the warehouse. Bella had managed to eliminate the last RPK with her deadly accurate aim, and Yuri's men took off in fright. I hopped from the car, shouting commands to our men and ordering them to find Yuri.

"All clear, boss. Yuri is gone but all other targets have been removed," I said, holstering my 9mm and adjusting the tourniquet on my arm.

"I want him found. Now!" Several men took off in different directions, looking for the Russian leader. Lucky stopped to check a blood-sprayed Bella before addressing me.

"What's the damage?" Lucky asked.

"That was incredible, *mia regina*. If not for your fast thinking, I fear we may have lost some of our own men," I said to Bella.

The statement was both clinical and sincere.

This much was true… Her innocence would be shattered by our world with *il diavolo* at her side. Lucky would ensure she thrived and was protected as she found her place as queen. But that was their story to tell.

The story of how a girl was *contracted to the Devil*. Mirabella Moretti had just signed on the dotted line in a trail of her own blood, and the fine print was binding.

Returning to the compound, I took note that my shoulder was still seeping. "It's probably going to need about six stitches," Al said, leaning over me as he chomped down on an apple, the juices dripping from his lips as he talked around a mouthful.

"Get. The. Fuck. Away. From. Me." I ground the words out, the night's events weighing heavily on my back and my patience long since shattered.

"Move." Sienna stormed from behind Al.

This was our first interaction since I went to her office. Though, I wasn't surprised to see her. Our feud aside, she'd always support the family. I respected her for rising above herself and her own feelings to handle business.

She tugged my shirt from the waist of my suit pants and ripped it over my head. Her sharp intake of breath forced me to stare into her eyes, but she remained distant and guarded.

Holding onto my shoulder, she pulled me forward to inspect the wound. Her nimble fingers showed no concern as she poked the hole, smiling when I hissed in pain.

"It's still stuck in there," she said more to herself. Grabbing her leather bag, she brandished a pair of medical tongs. "Deep breath. And exhale," she ordered, stabbing the metallic instrument into the opened flesh and thus, earning herself a string of curses.

"Got it." Clamping the bullet in front of me, she paused as we both inspected it. "Two minutes, only needs a few stitches."

"You… you doing okay?" I muttered, trying to swallow past the ominous lump in my throat.

"Fine. Done." Throwing her instruments back into her bag, she walked to the sink and washed her hands. I explained the night to her, giving details of Bella's involvement.

"She's here," I told Sienna. "He brought her home. She's going to need clothes in the morning." She nodded and smiled, likely scheming over the many ways she planned to annoy her brother.

She briskly walked to the door. Stopping before crossing the threshold but without looking at me, she whispered, "I'm glad you're okay."

I shook my head as the door closed with a soft click and trudged over to the bathroom to shower. That was about as good as it was going to get; coming from Sienna, those four words cleared the air between us. That was how family worked, right…? We hated each other on good days and killed for each other on bad ones.

CHAPTER 13
SIENNA AGOSTINO

At the end of the day and no matter how mad I was at any of the men associated with my family, we always came together for each other. The moment Al told me what happened, I knew I would be needed. I'd patched up Apollo, Lucky, Al, my father—you name it—all numerous times.

After I'd taken care of Apollo, I went downstairs and spent a few hours watching TV with Al and Marco, eventually passing out on the sofa. I felt like I had just fallen asleep when I heard the voices drifting down the hallway from the foyer. I wiped my eyes, pulling my feet out from under Al's oversized ass—I must've burrowed under him in my sleep. When the voices got louder, I shook him by his meaty bicep.

"Fuck! How are your hands always so fucking cold?" Al grunted, moaning as he shook his limbs awake. "The fuck?" His neck cranked to the side, hearing the commotion as well.

"Go upstairs," he ordered.

"How? They're at the stairs?" I pointed towards the foyer.

"Fuck. Move that perky little ass. You stay behind me and dart up those stairs at first glance." Al ushered me to my feet and I clung to his back as we approached the two very angry Moretti's.

"My daughter is not your son's whore! She was to be arranged to be married! Not passed to your son to whore around!" Anthony Moretti echoed around the marble foyer as Al stepped behind my father.

"Who do you think you are to raise your voice in my house?" My dad growled.

I thought I was hidden enough to escape until I saw Gio standing behind his father, staring at me. My hair was down and my face fresh of makeup; I was dressed in linen pants and a comfortable sweater, but the way he looked at me you'd assume I was partially naked. The man was drooling at my breasts like a prepubescent teenager who had just seen his first pair.

Yeah, the look he was giving me was one I had never seen on him. Gone was the errant little boy that flew off the handle and made rash decisions, in his place was someone cold. Someone cruel. Someone with darker plans. A chill went down my spine as he silently told me he was far from done with me.

With everyone thoroughly distracted, I darted into my room and locked the door, thinking it best to ignore whatever that interaction was. I had laid out clothes the night before for Bella so I quickly rushed into the closet to dress myself and add a little touch of makeup. I chose a *Givenchy Grain de Poudre* satin-lapel blazer with a pearl-embellished deep-V jumpsuit underneath. I paired the trim cut bottoms with plain black suede *Jimmy Choo* heels.

I passed Lucky in the hallway as I headed towards his room; his expression was grim as he charged towards the argument. He was as formidable a foe as he was a pushover for his new love interest. Though I must admit, our family's flare for the dramatics always made things entertaining around here.

I let myself into his room and wandered over to his bed. I almost didn't notice her under the covers—she was so tiny. She was having a silent conversation with the ceiling, no doubt chastising herself for spending the night and causing the scene downstairs.

"I assumed you didn't want to greet your father in my brother's shirt," I said, eliciting a surprised shriek.

She stared at me in shock and I finally got my first real glimpse of the illusive Mirabella Moretti, the woman who had tamed *il diavolo*.

She was thin but athletic. She had long raven- colored locks that were shiny with a slight curl. But her eyes were what made you stop and stare. I'd heard about them but didn't understand what was so alluring until I was staring into them myself. One green, one blue—those eyes peered into your soul.

I introduced myself, motioning for her to follow me to the bathroom. I stifled my laughter as she tried to eloquently rise from the bed, failing when the comforter wrapped around her and nearly tugged her to her knees.

She seemed to be at a loss for words so I just pushed her through the motions. First, I dried her hair when she was out of the shower, then I added a slight curl to the end. I completed her makeup, leaving it light and simple since the girl was already naturally gorgeous. Once that was done, I walked her out to get her dressed.

I pointed towards the black *Chanel* dress with a silver *Hermes* belt. Then of course *Louboutin* shoes, earrings and a necklace. I left her in the bathroom to get changed and wandered around Lucky's personal belongings. It gave me a few minutes to snoop before she walked out fully clothed. After forcing her to do a quick spin to give my final approval, I held her arms.

"Thank you. Apollo told me what you did for him and Lucky last night." I smiled at her sadly.

"It was…" I cut her off with a wave of my hand.

"Don't you dare say it was *nothing*. You walked into danger to warn them all. You protected this family and I truly thank you." I grabbed her hand and pulled her towards the stairs.

"Your brother's a real dickhead," I muttered.

Once at the bottom of the foyer, I stepped to the side to watch the rest of the room. Al had told me about her strength and resilience the night before. The girl had brass balls and I loved that my brother was fortunate enough to find such a firecracker. She confidently told her father our cover story—just a girls' sleepover.

"That's not what I fucking heard." Gio's smug voice called out.

"And if I believed the rumors about you, I'd assume your dick had rotted off from all the diseases you've caught. Then I'd tattle to daddy that you are conducting business behind his back." Bella's words came out strong, even as her ears burned bright red.

"I love this girl." I started laughing, enjoying the way Gio turned his mutinous glare on me. The back and forth continued until Lucky officially announced that Gio wasn't permitted near his *fiancée*. Anthony immediately accepted the proposal and ran with his tail between his legs, forcing Gio to follow behind him.

"You are something else, *mia regina*. I have some business I need to tend to, but my mother wanted to show you the gardens." Lucky gave Bella a kiss before she headed outside with our mother.

"Good choice, brother, damn good choice." I grinned.

"I know. She's amazing." My brother smiled back wistfully at the girl's retreating form.

"Let's get this over with, shall we?" I motioned for my father and brother to follow me into the office.

"What do we have?" Lucky asked, tucking his phone back into his pocket.

"You didn't tell him?" My brother looked back and forth between us, evidently annoyed that he hadn't been the first to be informed.

"I've been developing new relationships and your sister is aiding in that," my father said nonchalantly. "Romano Bianchi has submitted a legal proposal of marriage to Sienna."

"Isn't it all just so romantic?" I asked in a fake southern accent. "Contracts of hearts, flowers, babies and leaving my business the fuck alone." I flopped into the chair in front of the desk.

"It ties Philly to New York. When you take over it will be a solid alliance to keep the masses in their place." My father clipped the end of a cigar and took several tokes with a pleased expression.

"You're planning to marry off my sister to align Philly when I step up," he repeated, as if it was a joke. But there was nothing fucking funny about it.

"You're welcome, brother." There were several other things I wanted to say—to throw in his face—but I shut my mouth.

This wasn't his fault. We all had our little roles to play in this terrible show tune we called our lives. He owned his place as the eldest son and the blood on his hands proved the power was one that he had earned. The rest of us had our parts as well and sadly mine was for the betterment of *his* position, instead of my own.

Leave. Leave it all behind. A voice whispered in the back of my mind, forcing me to shake my head and snap out of my heavy thoughts.

"You need strong alliances when we rattle the hierarchy. Romano is feared in Philly and being married to your sister creates a strong alliance. It protects you. Protects us all," my father boasted.

"Apollo already earned me that alliance." My heart raced for a split second at Lucky's words, wondering what Apollo had to do with any of this. "He handed Bianchi a rat and he's already confirmed he'll back me when I take over."

"Charming," I muttered, ignoring my father's warning look. "Are we done here? I'd love to go hang with my future sister-in-law a little more. So many stories to tell and all."

"Sienna." Lucky growled, a silent warning hanging in the air.

"Mom already pulled out the baby books." I started laughing at his scowl, throwing my head back as I caught a shadow at the door. *Fuck. Al.* "This doesn't leave this room, not even to Apollo, or I really will traumatize Bella with stories of your past."

"Go," my father ordered, and I didn't need to be told twice. I waved my goodbye and skipped from the room, closing the double doors behind me. "Don't." I raised my hand to silence him, but Al slapped it away.

"What the fuck? Philly? How long have you known?" he asked, his eyes darkening.

"Long enough to have Amy rip the contract to pieces," I said, strolling arm in arm with him into the kitchen to go find my mother. "Look, it isn't ideal and I am doing my best to handle it."

"Handle as in telling them to go fuck themselves?" he asked, but he already knew the answer. "I'll be coming with you," he stated adamantly, but he knew the answer to that as well.

"Whatever you do, *you* do not repeat what you heard." I stopped on my heel and spun quickly when he didn't immediately respond. "I mean it, Al. Not a fucking word."

"You can't expect… Sienna, he has to know." Al growled, pulling his phone from his pocket.

"Has to know what, exactly? I am *not* his concern and until I figure out my next move, I don't need two growling bears following me around," I demanded. But he ignored me, unlocking his screen.

Without a second of hesitation, I struck. Snatching the phone from his hand, I took off through the back of the house. The chef squealed in shock as I came sliding into the kitchen, barely managing to not break a heel. Before she could move out of the way, I reached over and grabbed a meat tenderizing mallet. Al stormed in a second later and froze at the sight of his phone under the raised cleaver.

"Don't you fucking dare! I *just* got that phone!" Al growled, his large stature too menacing for the chef as she fled from the room.

"Then keep your mouth shut. He's preoccupied with the Russians, Gio, Dom's whore and now his apartment visitor." I slapped his hand away when he reached out again. "I will handle this just like I do everything else. In my own way."

"Sienna, did you not hear what he said at your office?" I shrugged noncommittally in response, refusing to back down from this. "Whatever, he'll learn soon enough anyway. You know Lucky keeps nothing from him."

"Lucky has been coerced into silence for now. You'll do the same and to ensure that, I'll force my brother's hand and he'll make you quiet." I smiled deviously. "And, well, since you said Apollo will find out phone or not…" I raised the mallet in the air again.

"You little!" Al stopped, his mouth dropping wide as I smashed the phone to bits.

"Next time… be my best friend, first." I flicked the scattered pieces at him before strutting out of the door.

"Are you off to work, dear?" My mother stopped me outside the family room and I nodded at her. "We will figure all of this out. The right decision will be made if it's the last thing I do." She pulled me in for a hug.

"Don't you go all mafia mama on me now." I laughed. My mother was stunning and also the sweetest soul you'd ever meet; but she had a cunning and powerful side too. She had to, in order to be at Mario's side and raise a mini devil like Lucky.

"I'll do what needs to be done for you, my love. Now off you go!" She swatted my butt and pushed me towards the door. "Oh! I'll text you information on dinner with Lucky, Bella and her mother!"

I got lost in my emails on the way to my office downtown when I saw a request for a meeting from Amy. My stomach dropped at the subject line. *Bianchi Bullshit.* I loved her and hated her all simultaneously. I needed either a way out of this, or to get over myself and do what needed to be done.

"Thanks," I said, sliding from the car. I was so preoccupied with looking down at my phone, I slammed into a hard chest without noticing. "Oh! I'm sorry!" I stumbled to catch myself when large hands gripped my arms and practically threw me towards the side of the building.

"Not a sound," the man ordered, pulling me into the alley next to *Energia.*

"Fuck!" I gargled out; the force at which he knocked my back into the wall had pushed the air from my lungs. My head made contact slightly, just enough to slow the possibility of a counterattack but not enough to cause damage.

"Quiet." A large hand was placed over my mouth and I finally stared into the eyes of my attacker. "There's that fire I love to see." His other hand gripped both of mine in his and slammed them into the brick above my head, stretching me uncomfortably.

Gio Moretti was dressed in a designer suit that fit him like a glove, all the way down to his ridiculous tailored vest. His brown eyes were filled with excitement and swirled in a deadly combination of undiluted lust. One look now and I knew he never got the memo—*my sincere decline of his proffered relationship.*

"Good to see you, Sienna. You look incredible, as always." He purred into my neck, just below my ear. "I wanted to surprise you but I was unsure what type of flowers to bring."

I quickly realized the struggle to free my hands was futile. I took a deep breath and counted to three before bringing my knee straight up. I swore I was going to make contact but his thigh blocked me at the last second. Then the bastard tsked at me. Leaning forward, he pinned me against the wall with his body and did little to hide the growing erection that was digging into my stomach.

"It's your hot body pressed tight against me; it's you fighting me. It all turns me on." He leaned into my ear and inhaled deeply, ending on a loud groan. "Get rid of Philly."

I blinked a few times and shook my head; his large hand was cutting off my air supply. He shushed me twice before finally removing it and allowing me to suck in a breath. It took me a second longer than I cared to admit to fully grasp the situation. Not only did he think he stood a chance, but he also thought I had any say in the matter of my marriage.

"You get rid of Philly, I get rid of Lucky, and we rule this fucking city like we're destined to." I stared back and forth between each of his eyes, realizing he truly thought he was fit to be king. "I know you want that throne, Sienna. We're one in the same… we've been told we can't have what belongs to us. So, we have to take it."

"You." I coughed to clear my throat. "You think we're meant to run this city? Together?" My body shook in rage as I tried two different maneuvers to break his hold, but he was too strong.

"Every king needs a queen and I happen to see your full potential. Fuck them for not seeing it, for allowing Lucky to be handed this empire. We can improve it and be a power couple who people respect and more importantly… fear."

There had only been a few times in my life I'd ever been left with nothing to say. This was one of those rare occasions. His brown eyes implored me to answer but I was speechless. Usually, he had this look of uncontrolled anger and—well, honestly—stupidity written across his face. But now he was calm, controlled, serious and there was a lingering of something foreboding underneath his glare.

"And how do you plan to do all of this?" I asked, curious if he'd actually tell me.

"I have enacted a plan to have someone else do my dirty work. Once those two, in eventuality, kill each other… nothing will stand in our way." The hair on the back of my neck stood up. *The Russians?*

"I'll be in touch. In the meantime, deal with Philly." Before I could protest, he locked his lips onto mine, pushing my hands further into the brick—the skin scratching open from the abrasive stone. One moment he was there, the next he turned and disappeared into the busy city crowd.

"What the fuck?" I flexed my hands, now throbbing from the open scrapes. "Christ."

I shook off the spine-chilling feeling he left in his wake and headed inside to get some more work done. I needed to meet with Amy about Bianchi and see if there was anything else I could whip up on Gio. My phone alerted me to a new calendar invite from my mother for the dinner she was discussing earlier. Christ! When was it all going to end? There was only so much I could throw onto my caseload before the walls caved in around me.

"I just love that my future sister-in-law has a mighty tongue on her. I'm so thankful she isn't some daisy I have to handle with kid gloves." I lightly punched Bella's arm in mock-anger while she tugged on my long hair in response, sending all of the women into a fit of laughter. We'd only seen each other a handful of times but I'd come to care for and more importantly, respect the girl.

She was stepping out from the Moretti cloud of indignance and falsely placed anger, to shine bright like a little beacon of hope. Hope that my brother would live a happy life with his queen at his side.

Queen. The word immediately reminded me of the impromptu meeting with Gio. I was frustrated that I still had no answers on his diabolical plot; instead, I was left only with my own assumptions.

"How is work, dear?" Serafina Moretti sat next to my mother and was an older replica of her daughter, minus the unique eyes.

"Busy as usual. I have some new contracts that I am reviewing for negotiations with a large investor from Philadelphia. So, my time has been preoccupied with navigating that at the moment," I said inconspicuously, but Lucky didn't miss my meaning.

We hadn't talked much more on the subject but I'd heard whispers of his requests to Romano, asking the man to withdraw his offer. Apparently, Romano Bianchi was keen to create an alliance with Lucky but when it came to me, he wouldn't budge. I had no idea what devious plans *il diavolo* was concocting but I almost felt sorry for the handsome Philadelphia native.

Everyone who knew about the Philly situation had been coerced into silence but Apollo was smarter than all of us combined. His eyes flashed to me and it took me several tries to swallow past the dry lump in my throat when his scowl deepened.

Fuck. You. I said with only a smile, then blew him a kiss with my middle finger. His expression darkened and I knew if it wasn't for the room full of onlookers, he'd have handed me my ass by now. The mere thought of him throwing me over his shoulder with a swat as he carried me out of the room had me squirming in my seat.

"You know, Apollo is single and his eyes practically eat you alive whenever you're in the room." Kicking Bella under the table, I begged her to shut up. Unfazed, she winked and sat back in her chair, hugging her glass of wine. The table gasped as Lucky announced that one of his men had just been murdered, and my heart sank.

If I hadn't been so preoccupied with so many things, maybe I would've found the key to ending Yuri... to ending the Russian threat... to stopping whatever Gio had up his sleeve. I needed to get this handled before someone else got hurt.

"Ladies, I must depart. If you don't mind, I'd like to take my bride-to-be with me." Lucky motioned for all of us to follow, leaving me in a car with Peiro, Serafina and our mother.

The two women were happy with their slight buzz from the wine and the thought of love in the air. As much as I loathed the idea of being forced to move to Philly, I would be remiss to say that I didn't yearn for that kind of feeling. For someone to call my own, to love me the way I wanted. Apollo was a man crazed and yet I still yearned to be his remedy.

"Christ. Down, ladies!" Peiro ordered from the driver's seat. "We've got a tail—car two is coming up on our right to head them off."

Before car two had the chance to separate us, our tail started shooting. I forced my mother and Serafina to the floor and climbed over them, closer to Peiro. With my back to him, I could see the vehicle in question flying through traffic to stay at our rear. The passenger had his window down and was firing off shot after shot. When the back windshield shattered, I heard my mother cry and saw the glass cut into her forehead.

"No!" I growled.

Leaning across the seat for the glove box, I pulled out the 9mm I knew was inside. I slid into the front passenger seat and rolled the window down, ignoring Peiro's demands for me to stay low.

I watched and waited until the car's passenger pulled himself back in, counted to five, and then I leaned out of the car to aim just as he reappeared. I fired two more shots, enjoying the blood spray as he lost his gun and tried aimlessly to pull his arm back in through the window.

"*Fottuta puttana!*" I screamed in his direction. Leaning further out, I dropped my aim low and went for their tires. Peiro started to lose control of the SUV when their tire exploded. I quickly pulled myself back inside as we slid off the road and into an embankment, safely coming to a stop.

Our second car was firing off round after round. The offending vehicle lost control and flipped three times before stopping against a tree on the other side of the road. I turned and saw that my mother and Serafina were relatively unharmed as I opened the car door and got out —despite Peiro's adamant demands to stay back.

I was beyond done with every person who had it out for the Agostino's… for my family. I yearned for so much more than all of this incessant mafia warfare. It didn't matter if I went to Philly or not, there would still be the same threats lingering in the air.

I wanted a love story filled with nicer things and happy endings. I didn't want my father to arrange my marriage; instead, I wanted to be courted and fall in love on my own. I just goddamn-wanted-and-deserved-romance and Apollo to pull his fucking head out of his ass before it was too late!

And I sure as fuck didn't want to fall victim to some Russian piece of shit—undoubtedly on a fucked-up power trip—snuffing out the very life I was trying to build for myself. I slammed the door behind me, stomping in the grass in designer heels, towards the wreckage.

"Sienna!" Peiro roared from behind me, but I couldn't care less.

"Where the fuck are they?" I growled. I wandered over to their car, watching as the heavy cloud of smoke billowed outward.

"Miss Agostino, please!" Rocco—another one of Lucky's men— shouted from car two. He motioned for me to walk around the wreckage and back towards him.

"H-Help me." A voice moaned from under the warped metal.

"Fuck." Rocco growled as I turned my back on him and stepped closer to the voice.

I dropped to my knees and peered under the driver's side door to look at the three men inside. The front passenger and the man in the back seat stared at me with lifeless, dead eyes. But the driver was still very much alive and begging me for help. I leaned into the car, kicking at Rocco when he tried pulling me back. I unclipped the seatbelt and the Russian dropped to the roof like a sack of potatoes. Grabbing him under his arms, I dragged him from the wreckage and placed him on the grass by the now burning vehicle.

"Sienna. Get back, it's going to blow!" Rocco shouted.

"You came for me? For my family?" I asked, my temper rising just as the flames consumed the car. "*Marcire all'inferno*," I ordered him.

His expression soured—perhaps he knew the language or perhaps he could just read my tone and the look on my face; either way, he knew exactly what I was saying. The sound around me disappeared and the heat from the rising inferno ceased to exist as I watched his mouth silently move and contort in anger. I smiled a bright, true, happy smile as I raised the gun in my hand at a slight angle.

"*Cagna.*" I growled, pulling the trigger and watching as his head snapped back—the bullet imbedding itself between his eyes.

"Fuck. Me…" Rocco muttered. I turned to look—just in time—as he adjusted his pants. "Shut up." He laughed.

"Your secret is safe with me." I winked and walked back over to our SUV and to my mother.

"Are you fucking crazy? Do you know what could've happened with that car… those men?" Peiro roared, motioning for me to get inside.

"I'd love to know what concerns you more: what would've happened to me or what my brother would've done to you if it did." I waited for an answer, but his face locked down, giving nothing away. "That's what I thought."

"Sienna." I turned, but he remained silent.

"Just take us home, Peiro." I opened the passenger's side door and climbed in, enjoying that both my mother and Serafina were giggling as they drank straight from a wine bottle—somehow completely unfazed. They were the epitome of powerful wives in the *mafioso* world. I was about to laugh when my text alert went off.

Are you okay?—the screen lit up with the message.

I was run off the road by Russians with a vendetta against *him* and against my brother—repercussions for being in the company of the men around me, and the family I was born into. I could've been taken, raped, beaten or worse. And all I got was a text from Apollo, not even a call from Lucky.

In the grand scheme of things, life pretty much sucked right now. I was drowning between *Energia*'s thriving increases, Romano's dinner and *their* drama. The very same two men who were responsible for turning my red-bottom shoes brown—it was a travesty because they were so damn cute too.

Peiro dropped me off at my apartment in the city. I just wanted an ice-cold glass of vodka, an aspirin and to sleep this fucked up night away. But life was a ruthless bitch when she wanted to fuck with you. I opened my apartment door and froze when I saw the shadowy figure move across my living room.

"What the fuck are you doing in my house?" I asked through gritted teeth.

I guess my shitty night was far from fucking over.

CHAPTER 14

APOLLO DELUCA

In one short breath, everyone who mattered to the Agostino's could've been incinerated. The Russians' brazen attempt to destroy us failed, *this time.* We needed to make defensive strategies and soon. They were ill-prepared and unequipped to take down an organization such as ours. A message must be delivered and I planned to do so… personally.

We managed to keep one of the men alive and Lucky took him to the basement to get information. I was ordered to take Bella home, but much to his dismay, she had no issue ignoring his edict.

"Did she answer you?" Bella asked from the back seat as we headed towards the hotel.

"No," I postulated.

"What?" Her mismatched eyes filled with concern.

"She… She read it but never answered." I clenched my teeth.

We sat in silence for a moment more before Bella fell over in a fit of laughter. I had no idea what she had found so titillating that she was forced to hold her stomach in exaggeration. But it only lasted a minute, until we pulled up outside the hotel and a sense of reality settled in.

I wanted to see how much more il mia regina *could take.*

As we descended the stairs to the basement, Lucky's face soured—

if he'd had a gun in his hand, he would've put it to my head. "I'm sorry, boss. She ordered us to take her or she'd find a way to come on her own." I raised my palms up in the air.

"Bella, *il mio amore,* go home with Apollo." She jumped at his command.

"He threatened our family." Her voice was soft, almost haunted.

"*Si.* Bella, *la mia regina,* I promised you I'd take care of our family. Let me do that. Go home with Apollo." Bella's body snapped straight—her once somber eyes turned angry and fierce. The queen was stepping out of the shadows with her head held high and proud.

"No. He must pay. Lucky, *il mio amore,* I want to see him suffer." She put her hands on her hips.

My palms itched and my heart raced as adrenaline coursed through my veins. My inner thoughts were ravaged with all of the ways I'd make the Russian suffer. The barrage of questions, blood spilling and pained confessions continued to fill the room—though the exact chain of events went by in a blur as I stood and watched. My mind was screaming at me to attack—to end this *cagna* right now. But I remained at a distance as instructed; I did not intervene.

"Boss," I said, getting Lucky's attention and motioning to the red-tinted floor. "Seal the wound."

The average human body had one and a half gallons or less of blood. From his movements and the pool collecting underneath him, we needed to stem the flow before the bleeding man became useless. Rocco stepped forward, pulling a metal pole from the furnace.

The entire room turned to look at Bella, all silently begging Lucky to force her to leave. But the girl stood hard and determined, the epitome of sex and mayhem. With Lucky's nod, Rocco stepped to the Russian, cauterizing the wounds with the hot, steel poker. Screams of pain mixed with the aroma of melting flesh and permeated the air. It was the kind of smell that made weak men squeamish but was better than a fine wine to me.

But not Bella. She stood tall and proud, ignoring the stench and piercing cries.

"Bella. Please, don't stay for this. I know you feel a duty as my queen to stand at my side, to show power and strength. You've done that. You don't need to stay for me. You already have too much blood on your hands," Lucky pleaded, but her eyes held resolve.

They were empty... soulless.

"Bella. Leave with Apollo," Lucky demanded as I stepped forward, nodding my understanding.

Of course... she didn't. Lucky could control the scariest men, but this tiny girl ran wild circles around him.

Turning on her heel, she darted back towards the breathing corpse that was bolted to the floor. Leaning in his face, she was innocently unaware of how her tight skirt rode up just a bit to tease me with the sight of her perfectly-toned ass. Lucky's glare bestowed the promise of murder as he stared into everyone's eyes, demanding that they cast their gaze.

I coughed to hide my amused laughter and turned my attention back to Bella. She was whispering to our captive in Russian. She stood to her full height and smiled, dabbing at the blood under his eye. The entire room tensed, perplexed by her softness, when he started whispering to her again.

"Please. Please." As she picked up a knife, he began thrashing, sobbing and yelling at her. An uproar of cackling laughter left her tiny body and wracked her small frame.

Rocco and I both stepped closer, looking to Lucky for an answer on what to do—he stood rooted to his spot, his concern evident. However, as we were about to intervene, the Russian's shout stopped us in our tracks and we watched as Bella lifted her arm.

"I lied." One fast, confident and precise swoop and the blade sliced through the man's throat.

She dug it in so roughly, she went through the superior belly of the omohyoid muscle and I could see the filleted thyroid cartilage on display. Gagging and gasping, the blood... the very life poured out of him. And fuck if her savagery didn't make my dick hard.

"Rot in hell. *Cagna.*" She whispered and smiled at the corpse.

She had guaranteed the now dead man that she'd protect him if he told her everything. He was doing Yuri's bidding to protect his own family. She had made him false promises and he squealed like a gutted pig. Even I was impressed at the level of deceit she'd displayed when needed.

"We will teach them. Woman or not, Lucifer Agostino isn't weak." She spoke assuredly.

Her confidence had the entire room adjusting their belts as she stood in front of us soaked in blood. Lucky started spouting orders, having lost control and enraged by the heightened sexual tension that had engulfed the small space. He was pissed and a decent amount of that was directed at me as I forced our men out of the room.

"Wait! I have the address. Yuri expects him no later than two hours from now!" Mirabella roared. The Russian had relinquished his scheduled meeting place to Bella just before his dying breath.

"Apollo, handle it." Laughing as we exited, I shoved the men out as moans—Lucky and Bella's to be precise—drifted up the staircase behind us.

Lucky's men remained in the hallway to await orders, rattled in different ways by Bella's actions. Rocco and I were turned the fuck on by her strength and bloodlust—once again to Lucky's dismay.

Lucky sensed the discord when he entered the room and his eyes flared in anger as he took in my perusal of his *regina*. He didn't hesitate to slam a powerful fist into my face, tossing me backwards into the wall. Now, could I have avoided the hit? Abso-fucking-lutely. But I let him send a message, loud and fucking bloody clear.

"She is my queen. You look upon her as such. This is my only warning." He growled and forced everyone to take a step back as I wiped the blood from my face.

"He's totally fucking hitting that tonight." Al laughed.

Now, it was time to maim and mutilate a piece-of-fucking-shit who deserved to suffer for his sins.

The restaurant harboring Yuri was an absolute shithole in a rundown part of the city. He couldn't even hide out with the Russians—that in itself told you he was insignificant. He wasn't *Bratva*, nor did any other Russian family want him around.

"So, we taking him alive?" Al asked. "'Cause I really… really wanna fucking break him."

"He's mine," I said. Al raised a curious brow in response. "He threatened the family."

"You mean he threatened Sienna. Is this your fucked up way of apologizing for always hurting her?" he asked, laughing at my expense.

"Shut the fuck up." I rubbed my temple aggressively. "I need information on his associates. No one comes into this city to challenge us with absolutely no fucking backing. He has to have connections… someone besides Gio."

The air bubbling around us was saturated with the taste of revenge.

"Got it, boss." Rocco nodded, stepping from the car with his phone to his ear.

My heart was pounding heavily and my mind was focused on the end game—Yuri's dismemberment.

"He needs to suffer." Al growled, gripping the steering wheel tighter. "Vinny deserves his due."

Vinny was one of our men, practically a kid, who Yuri had recently executed. One shot—point blank—in the back of his head as he guarded one of our warehouses. Yuri didn't even have the balls to look him in the eye as he callously murdered the man.

"He'll fucking pay all right. Drop by drop until he's bled. Fucking. Dry." I growled each word, staring at the darkened building.

"Movement." Sal chirped on the radio, causing Al and me to look towards the northwest vantage point.

"Young girl. Barely sixteen, throwing trash in the alley." It chirped again.

"Christ." Al pointed to the young girl who appeared malnourished.

"Snatch and grab," I ordered.

A large shadow moved into the alleyway behind the girl, shapeless yet ominous in his precision. That was all of the men attached to the Agostino Crime Family syndicate—each was loyal and deadly with their own skill set. It was this level of stealth, these tactical capabilities that kept Mario in power for so long.

"Target one acquired." The radio sounded again. "Boss. It's bad. She's... she's..." Sal's alarmed voice trailed off.

"Push it aside, Sal," I ordered him.

"Got it, boss. But release isn't happening," Sal returned, clarifying his hesitation.

Fuck, she must be in a really bad spot.

"How do you want to play this?" Al continued to stare at the building.

There were a lot of unknown variables inside. But they didn't compare to our trained ability and firepower. You see, I had no issue with losing men. I would do whatever it took to accomplish what I came here to accomplish.

The back car door opened. "Here." Rocco leaned forward, handing me his cell.

"Who is it?" I asked.

"Nikolai Volkov." Rocco dropped the name with no further exordium.

"The Russian Wolf?" I could hide neither my shock nor my confusion.

Nikolai Volkov was the second in command under Sergei Oblonsky —the current leader of the *Bratva* in Moscow. The enforcer was inauspiciously called the Wolf—both due to his ability to incite a sort of pack leadership amongst his men as well as effortlessly tear at the throats of those who crossed him. Though we circled the same underground as the US-based *Bratva* regime, over the years, we had formed a silent agreement—a truce.

"Yeah," I growled into the phone.

"Apollo Deluca, pleasure to meet you." His thick Russian accent greeted. "I hear you have information on someone I am looking for."

"Please, elaborate," I asked, giving nothing away.

"Yuri. I have a bounty on his head." He answered but I remained silent. "Preferably alive, but accepted dead."

"Well, I don't need or want your money, *Wolf.*" I enunciated his nickname, making it clear that he wasn't a mystery to me. "And he won't be kept alive."

"Look. This is personal, understand? He killed my sister." Nikolai exhaled painfully.

This was news to me. The illusive Russian Wolf didn't have family or friends, or a heart for that matter—all that was known was his thirst for blood.

"And it's personal to the Agostino's. We've maintained an amiable… ignorance of each other and I am sure both sides would like to keep it that way."

"*Da, da.* Sergei won't start a war with New York over my family— we both know that. But I am politely asking you for a chance of..." He started muttering to himself in Russian before continuing. "Closure."

Nikolai explained Yuri *was* his brother-in-law, a disease of a human being wanting an in with the *Bratva*—but the son of a bitch had been denied. Yuri had left Nikolai's sister dead and fled with their three children. The Wolf had managed to save his niece, Mila, before the other two boys disappeared with their father.

"Is this my respective call to warn me about the two sons as well?" I asked.

"Not Alexei, he's always been his mother's son. Alexander on the other hand… he won't stray from his father's plans. The boy is viciously hungry for power." Whispered conversations entered the background. "Yuri ends tonight?"

"Yes," I stated firmly, preparing my refusal—should he have asked me to wait.

"I am coming stateside. Sergei agreed to keep the peace between our groups. I look forward to meeting you, *Reaper*." He hung up before I could respond.

"Yeah." Lucky answered on the first ring.

"I have a little bit of a situation I want to run by you before we proceed." He cursed under his breath, stepping away from Bella as I told him about Nikolai Volkov's impending arrival.

"Was it a threat?" I didn't assume it was. "Then fuck him. End this shit here and now."

"And what about the sons?" I asked, curious as to how he wanted to play this.

"They must be adults by now, capable of making their own decisions. Do what needs to be done. I stand behind you." Lucky ended the call without a goodbye.

"We're a go," I told Al, cracking my knuckles in anticipation. "Wait for my word and then we fucking *destroy* them."

"Hell yeah." Al's hands tensed on the wheel as we watched the restaurant descend into darkness.

Movement on the second story caught my attention. The blackout curtains shifted and the lights from inside shined brightly, revealing the silhouette of a man. My jaw ticked and my palms itched to grab the 9mm holstered at my side.

I was wearing a Kevlar vest with a firearm on each hip and blades on both ankles. My mind cleared and my heartbeat slowed as I focused on the shadowy figure. It was Yuri, hiding out like a *piccola cagna*. I looked to Al. Giving him a malicious smile, I nodded.

I grabbed the radio attached to my chest and spoke loudly. "Let's play." Al muttered a "hell yeah" as the team silently moved from different vantage points. We swarmed like a finely oiled machine of death troopers, merging as one before we attacked.

Every exit was covered and no one was escaping. It was the only way to send a message… to let them know exactly what we could do. The distinct sound of firearms discharging into silencers went off as screams of terror filled the night air. Efficiently and quickly, we charged from room to room, Al on my six as we reached the staircase.

With tactical precision and Al's hand on the back of my Kevlar, we climbed upward, our weapons drawn and at the ready. Our feet were light and the steps barely acknowledged us, but I remained ever vigilant—my instincts on high alert. Just as that thought crossed my mind, someone turned the corner, firing two shots. The bullets hit my chest in powerful, rapid succession—causing my steps to falter as I pressed into Al, who shoved me forward.

"You little motherfucker!" I yelled, firing off three shots of my own and running up the stairs at full speed. Al's gun went off behind me as I slammed my body into Yuri—the same asshole who had shot me.

"*Suka!*" Yuri yelled, trying to keep himself on his feet. But the piece of shit was no match for my size, my fighting skills or my *fucking* rage.

"You think you can fuck with us and we won't fuck you back… harder?" I slammed him to the ground and punched repeatedly, enthralled by the surge of blood leaking from his face. "You want to fucking touch our women!"

The gunfire and yelling in the background ceased to exist as my sole focus turned to Yuri. His first mistake was fucking with our business. His last… was fucking with Sienna. Real men didn't force women to pay for their sins. Real men faced their foes themselves. And real men didn't play fucking games with the lives of those who were innocent.

"You fucked up, Yuri. And now you'll pay for it." I let my anger out on his face, his torso and a kick or two to his balls.

"The *Bratva* come for you! You pay!" Yuri assumed I didn't already know the truth.

"I find your idiocy astounding. As if the Agostino's didn't know the *Bratva* personally. Nikolai sent me his blessing by the way." His eyes went large around the swelling. "He only regrets he isn't here in person. But don't worry… he's on his way… *for Alexander.*" I whispered the last part.

"No! You fucker!" His fight was rejuvenated as he shoved me

backwards. Suddenly, another man charged into the room with a bat, swinging wildly.

As he brandished the wooden implement, I rolled off Yuri and pulled my piece from my side. One shot to the head and the mother-fucker went down—hard—spraying blood and brain particles onto my face. Yuri was still trying to get to his feet when I stood tall. My firearm hung limply at my side, as the real desire to rip him apart with my own hands took hold.

"You Italians… you weak." Holding his ribcage, he stood up. "You so worry for *pussy* you no see straight."

"Oh no, *comrade*, that's where you're wrong. When you fuck with our women, we see perfectly clear." I growled; the outside noises were silenced as Al stepped to my back. "Now tell me what I want to know about your partner and I won't kill you." We both knew that was a lie, but I wanted answers.

"I tell you nothing! *Nichego!*" He started yelling in Russian over and over again. "You lose business and *kiska*." He laughed, wiping blood from the gash across his face.

"Your inadequate threats against women tell me just how much of a sniveling, pathetic little *suka* you really are." My rage was growing at the thought of him touching Sienna, rattling the barely contained beast within me.

"She already gone." Yuri snarled in my face while his smug smile stopped me in my tracks.

"The fuck you say?" Grabbing him by the lapels of his jacket, I tugged him closer. When he didn't answer, I looked over my shoulder at Al, who was already on his phone.

"Keep laughing, you little bitch. It's the last thing you'll ever do." I spoke the promise calmly as my bubbling rage morphed into determination. "Now, I want answers."

"What you give me?" he asked, the blood now trickling down his face at a much faster rate.

"You give me the rat and I'll let you fucking live." Al froze at my words. "For now."

"I know no rat." Yuri shrugged.

"Fine. I'm done playing this game with you. It serves me no purpose to keep you alive." I pulled my piece from my side and jammed it into his forehead.

A kinder, gentler man would end his pain and suffering quickly. But again, I was neither of those fucking things. The right hand of *il diavolo*—the motherfucking crowned *mietitore*—understood nothing other than carnage and absolute fucking bedlam. Yuri's grave was already dug, I just needed to deposit his fucking carcass.

"This is for Vinny, *suka!*" I was about to pull the trigger when his words stopped me.

"You avenge your rat?" He laughed at my confused expression. "You should thank me for killing your man. He play both sides. I shoot him because he greedy and demand more money."

I didn't want to believe him but at the same time, it made perfect sense. I wanted to call him a fucking liar and pull the trigger, but every part of me knew he had given me the answer I'd been searching for.

"Welcome." Yuri tried shaking me off, as if his admission was setting him free. Without a care, I pulled my head back before slamming it forward. His nose erupted into an explosion of red torrent upon impact. "Fuck! You got rat, I live!"

I cocked back my hammer and struck the side of his head, dropping him like a pile of bricks. His nose and scalp were bleeding, and his eyes were unfocused as he tried to watch for my next move. I bent closer to his face. Resting my knee against his chest, I pressed down with all of my weight.

"I fucking lied. Don't act so surprised." I smiled, yes, smiled at him. "The moment you threatened her, you signed your death certificate. The hole is fucking dug and waiting for you."

"Knew she sweet pussy." He wheezed against his constricted ribcage. "So… gave her my son." He spat saliva and blood towards my face before falling onto his back and accepting his fate.

"Fuck. Someone, get eyes on Sienna." I barely heard Al relaying the order in the background. "I want Bella and Octavia confirmed as well."

"You motherfucker!" I launched my assault one after another, powerful fists barreling into his skull. I bellowed out my rage, demanding more answers but he was too far gone to be useful. "Fuck you!" I stood and pointed the end of my barrel at his head, continuously tugging at the trigger long after the magazine was empty.

"Apollo. Man." Al's voice resonated in the distance but I couldn't face him. My mind and sight were still clouded over. I may have gotten one answer but I was left in a different kind of hell. The rat was dead but there was a whole new enemy coming for us.

And that enemy was a fucking ghost with his sights set on Sienna.

"Sienna needs you, man."

I'm coming, Sienna.

Chapter Fifteen Sienna

"Hello." The man moved from the shadows, illuminating his designer suit, though his face remained shrouded in darkness. The voice was so familiar and yet so… different.

"If you're here to enact vengeance against my brother, is it possible for you to come back another night? I'm really fucking tired." I stepped further into the room and dropped my purse onto the sofa.

"The plans I have for you go beyond revenge and anything having to do with your brother. They're about acquiring something that belongs to me. Something that could belong to you… to us." His voice was a prominent, confident tone. The sound was ebbing at the edge of my brain as I attempted to wrap my mind around recognition.

"And what *could* belong to us?" I asked, heading towards my kitchen, which offered a little more illumination.

"This city. This organization. Whatever we wanted." He stepped closer but continued to be swallowed by the shadows. "You see, so many people believe they've punched my ticket. Believe the show I created for them is actually a reality. When it isn't. I own them. One way or another, I own it all."

"And what exactly do you own?" I questioned, growing bored of this cryptic song and dance.

I may have been wandering the tiled floor like I didn't have a care in the world, but the reality was anything but. I was coiled like a snake, waiting for the right moment to strike. The strongest part of a woman was her resilience and no matter what my family, this life or this asshole in my living room threw at me… I would reign again.

"Everyone and everything." His tone was flat and even, as if he truly believed what he said.

"Right. Well, I am beat and I think it's time for you to head on your way." I kicked my heels off in the kitchen, needing to be prepared for the attack. "Show yourself out, like you so unceremoniously showed yourself *into* my house."

I walked halfway into the shadows that surrounded him and motioned for the door. We stood in a silent battle of chicken, each waiting for the other to move. After a few moments, I turned to the door, prepared to open it so he could get the fuck out. I made it two steps before his fingers were wrapped in the hair at the nape of my neck, and he tugged me backwards. His body was hard—strong—and his grip was unrelenting. He enclosed an arm around my stomach and held me to him as I placed each of my hands over one of his.

"Where are those manners I know you were raised with?" He growled and his demeanor changed, making the hair on the back of my neck stand up.

"How would you know?" I asked, trying to scratch my way through his hold on my scalp.

What was it with people fighting girls and always going directly for their hair? Look, I loved having my hair pulled. It was one of those positions I'd heard about—the kind when you hit it just right, the bite of pain sends you over the edge. But in terms of a power play, the action was a tad superfluous, as if his size couldn't do enough damage on its own.

"I know everything about you, Sienna. The issue is you've only seen a piece of me and yet you think you have the right to judge." I gasped, his voice transitioning to someone else… someone I knew.

"I'm done with your fucking riddles. What the fuck do you want?" I growled, throwing my body weight forward to try to knock him off balance. But he was too big.

"You. I fucking want you. And if it destroys the rest of your family in the process... well, that's just a fucking bonus." He growled back, all too pleased with himself.

"I'm not for sale," I spat, the words tasting bitter on my tongue.

"Everyone is for sale. It's my specialty actually. I make my fortune off the backs of those weaker, less fortunate. I take what I want, from whoever I want." He shoved me forward into the couch, forcing me to stumble against the side to stop from hitting the ground.

"Get the fuck. Out of. My house." I yelled, pointing towards the door again while my breath came out in ragged pants of simmered rage.

He stared at me another beat before answering. "And when I take from you, Sienna. When I do... I'll fucking take it all." He started to move towards the door when an unbridled madness overtook me. "The things that went down tonight have moved us one step closer."

Before I could tell myself to stop—to forgo the stupidity that was about to occur—my body started moving. He didn't hear me approach, as my feet barely made a sound on the marble floors. All of the practic-ing, all of the hours in the gym, all of my sparring with the best train-ers... it fled as I threw myself at him. I didn't care what I did. I just needed to teach him a fucking lesson.

He turned as I was about to strike. Reaching out, he easily caught my fist and thrusted me away from him. My bare feet slid across the floor as I caught myself and charged a second time. I bobbed and weaved, tucking my fists under my chin, and avoided the powerful blows he threw my way. I knew one punch thrown with all his muscular rage, and I'd be down for the count. He'd win, having me at a total disadvantage to do whatever he wanted to me.

My mind went blank and I was consumed by my own inner work-ings. I felt like I was drowning. Tears—a mixture of sadness and anger as well as displeasure over the life I was being forced into—flowed from my eyes and down my face. My nails scratched their way from his temple to his chin. He grabbed both of my hands in one of his and lifted me off the ground with a hand to my throat.

My feet dangled in the air, his grip holding tight for several minutes, before he threw me onto my sofa. I bounced against the well-coiled springs and my body projected forward. The glass of my coffee table shattered underneath my weight, depositing me onto the floor with a thud. The breath was expelled from my lungs and I wheezed to gain air, his shadow looming over me and creating a whole new sense of panic.

"Such beauty." He ran a finger down my cheek. I could feel it catching on the blood at my temple. "Why do you want me to ruin it?"

"Don't touch me." It sounded much weaker than I had intended, as unease penetrated my ability to think rationally. Then, as if suddenly, full realization settled in. And I understood how big of a mistake I'd just made.

"I bet even ruined, you'd be a gorgeously fucked-up canvas. Better than I ever dreamed." He smirked at me. The motherfucker smirked.

"And I bet you bleed just the same as I do." I smiled and the motion drew the taste of blood into my mouth.

Without a second of hesitation, I closed my fist around a shard of glass from the table and lunged. The first swipe he was able to avoid but the second, he stumbled backwards holding his freshly lacerated arm. I didn't wait a single beat to charge to my feet and go for him again. With each swipe of the glass, he backed up further and further, avoiding contact as I attacked like a wild animal.

"I don't think my dick has ever been harder." He laughed, enjoying the dance I was so arduously attempting to turn into his funeral rites.

"And I've never wanted to vomit more. Get the fuck out of my house!" I was screaming now. I yelled for him to get out over and over again, wishing for once I wasn't so fucking stubborn and had security around.

Your stubbornness will be the death of you or your family one day. You're not invincible, Sienna. Apollo's words were like slashes to my memory and only spurned my anger forward. I managed to embed the glass into his chest once more before he slapped my hands away. Gripping my wrist tightly, he twisted it behind my back. The pain forced my body to turn and mold to him, his hardened cock rubbing against me in the process.

"I told you, you make my dick hard. Do I need to show you all of what we could have together?" he questioned, grinding against me and making me yelp as he twisted my arm harder. "Not ready yet? Tell me, Sienna, are you a virgin?"

"Fuck. You. *Gio*." I growled.

"No, I don't think you are. Just another rebellion against the position you were forced into. That's what makes you perfect for me, Sienna. I was forced to be second best, forced to play bitch in a role that was beneath me. I stepped out of that expectation and built my own empire. Mine. And I am in need of a queen." He leaned over my hunched body and licked me from ear to collarbone.

"Please. Stop." I hated to beg but I couldn't stand his touch any longer. "Gio, please don't."

"I don't know what is sweeter, your blood or your tears. I can't wait to find out what your pussy tastes like." He ground his dick into me once more, for good measure, before releasing me. "Soon," he said, walking towards the door as I sunk to the floor.

Another figure stood in the hallway by the elevator and for a moment, I held my breath hoping it was someone coming for me. *What a joke*. Of course, it wasn't. Lucky and Apollo were off plotting their world domination and leaving a trail of agony in their wake. Only it never used to be inflicted upon me, not until now anyway.

The two men disappeared from my apartment, locking and closing the door behind their retreating frames. The sick bastard actually double-checked to make sure it had bolted, jiggling the handle before he left. I limped to the door, my leg and back still throbbing from my fall. I stared through the peephole to ensure they both got on the elevator. Only once the metallic doors met, enclosing both of them inside, did I finally release the breath I hadn't realized I was holding.

"Fuck," I muttered. Staggering over to my bar, I poured two fingers of scotch and tossed it all back in one go. Then I repeated the process twice more before pulling out my cell phone.

"What up!" Marco, my little brother, answered.

"I wanna party," I stated, doing my best to hide my pained breaths.

"No way? Lady Sienna wants to let her hair down? And it ain't even her birthday anymore." He laughed and started barking orders in the background. "Car will be there in forty minutes to get you." And then he hung up.

I tapped out a text to my cleaning company, ordering them to send someone immediately to fix my apartment. I needed booze, dancing and most of all, to forget everything that happened tonight. Once I came home inebriated, in a few hours, the apartment would have righted itself and my brain would stop obsessing over my current predicament.

I headed into my master bathroom to take a look at the damage. It wasn't as bad as I expected it to be, considering how I was feeling. The cuts on my face weren't deep nor were they long, though my wrist was starting to change color and my elbow was stiff. I removed my clothes and turned to look at my back—the worst of it all. The lacerations would be cleaned in the shower but the fall to the table left bruises that were already making an appearance.

I showered quickly, styled my hair so it was off my neck but hung a few loose curls down my back, and painted on some exaggerated eye makeup. I tossed on a pair of diamond earrings to go with an all black designer romper and sexy turquoise *Manolo Blahnik* heels. I had just slid my feet into them when the doorman announced my car was waiting. I headed out of the door, double checking the hallway in front of the elevators before locking my apartment behind me.

I stepped into the penthouse elevators and hit the down arrow. I was glancing at my lipstick in my compact when the doors opened under the private penthouses. I paid no mind to whoever was standing there until I smelled the terrible overly-indulgent perfume that practically choked me—it was so strong and so foul.

"You're fucking kidding me." I growled low, my voice full of disdain.

This night couldn't get any worse.

Tatianna and her little gaggle of flocking geese shit were all slutted-up in their best trash-wear, awaiting the elevator. Tatianna was dressed in all white and giggling like the goddamn moron she was—no need for feigned ignorance there. She had a sash on that said bride-to-be and a ridiculously fake diamond crown. Her girlfriends all had matching sashes, proudly displaying "bridesmaid" across their chests.

"Who knocked you up?" I asked, halting the door from closing.

"What?" Tatianna asked in her overly-exaggerated and nasally voice.

"I would never presume someone willingly asked you to marry them." Her eyes glazed over for one second before realization settled in.

"Fuck. You. Sienna." She growled, dropping the fake pitch.

"No thanks. God only knows what depravity you've subjected yourself to for my brother's attention." I shuddered at the thought, urging her little girlfriends to step towards me, as if they stood a chance.

"You're a spoiled little bitch who thinks her big brother is always going to protect her." She crossed her arms over her recently purchased chest.

"Oh my." I stopped the door again and looked all around me. "Well, I don't see him here now, do you?" I stepped out of the elevator.

It was sad really, just how much I hated this bitch. Tatianna was the bully at school who could smell your insecurities a mile away. She enjoyed picking on the underdeveloped freshman, those who looked much younger than their age. Using her mean-girl tactics, she would either train them to be her lackeys or ridicule them out of the school.

She was the reason people said women were bitches.

"Whatever. Take another elevator. We need to go up." She motioned for me to exit.

"Excuse me? Go up where? I don't see a pass or security with you, so where, exactly?" I stepped closer, forcing them back a few steps.

"It's her last fling before the ring. Lucky said he'd make it special." One of her little bitches finally flashed the brass balls in her panties.

"He's with his fiancée, so I doubt that." The look on Tatianna's face was all the satisfaction I needed—that is, outside of hearing her nose crack the last time I punched her. The door closed on her angry scowl before she started screaming.

When the car pulled up outside *Danza*, I wanted to act surprised but Marco was so predictable. The nights always started somewhere else, but like clockwork he ended up here, using the private suites for his latest fling. Security motioned me through the doors and I was escorted to Lucky's VIP balcony.

The suite was quieter than usual, entertaining only Marco's small crew and the girl at his side. She looked familiar and if I hadn't known any better, I'd say he had been seen out with her before. This girl was refined and had fabulous taste in shoes, unlike the Tatianna clones he loved to spend his time with.

"Sienna!" Marco made a big production of hugging me and introducing me around to his little friends.

"Tessa. Tessa Leroux." His arm candy for the evening extended her hand, and I immediately hated her. I didn't know what it was about the girl, but I didn't trust her any further than I could throw her pixie ass.

"Pleasure." I gave her a saccharine grin.

"Hm." She answered with a hum and a knowing smile. She was smart, nearly as keen as I was.

"What is this?" Marco questioned, running his finger down the side of my face where I had attempted to cover up one of the scrapes.

My heart was pounding out of my chest as the room threatened to close in on me. Marco's words drew far too much attention to my appearance. Tessa was watching me like a hawk and I was losing the hold on my limited sanity. The sudden barrage of curious onlookers twisted the knot in my stomach and embedded the knife in my back. Marco was the last person who needed to be concerned with what was going on in my life.

"Seriously, Sienna." He growled, almost sounding like Lucky.

"*Mon cher,* shots!" Tessa beckoned in the background, lifting Marco's focus from me and back onto the promise of a good time.

As he bounced over to her, I watched her lips curl towards me and I could've hugged the girl. I raised my glass into the air, a thanks for saving me from myself. She may have been perceptive, but I still didn't like her, even if she had just called off my interrogation. The distraction had given me the moment I needed to flee towards the dance floor.

There was this incredibly freeing thing about being an anonymous girl lost in a wave of gyrating, sweaty bodies. I was sure the security, the bartenders and the dancers all around me knew exactly who I was. But to the rest—to the hoard of people shaking their asses and letting their hair down—I was just some girl in a designer dress, dragging myself to the center of the floor. I was just some girl lost in her own world, in her own thoughts, as she swayed with a sea of strangers.

So many thoughts ran rampant in my mind as I ruminated over the events of the night. The realization settled into my brain that I was nothing more than a pawn in the game my father and brother owned. The great Mario Agostino was selling me off to Philly—no matter how handsome the man may have been, he was still not my choice. And my brother was so engrossed in his own business, he didn't notice his repercussions trickling down onto me.

I could pry and dig into whatever they asked but at the end of the day, I was the resource they used to uncover the treachery among them. And yet they refused to give me my due. I had the information they needed about Dominic Moretti and no one allowed me the chance to explain the situation. Instead, I was accosted in my own home by an individual who was set on destroying Lucky. I was literal collateral damage when it came to my entire family's dealings.

The crowd around me buzzed with the type of energy that would normally fuel my high. But right now, it just added to my anxiety. Tonight showed me what I already knew—it was just written out in clearer terms. No matter what I did to create a name for myself, I would only be as strong as the man on my arm, as the name on my birth certificate. And no matter what way you looked at it, it sucked.

I felt my phone ringing a time or two but I couldn't bring myself to answer it. I continued to sway and dance amongst the crowd. However, instead of releasing my tension, it exhausted me both mentally and physically, and I craved something far more entertaining.

I walked into the VIP lounge and saw the occupants had dwindled down even more—there were only a few stragglers with Marco and Tessa. Natalia, the bartender, made me another drink and I offered her a smile before moving forward and sitting on a stool by the window. The glass had been left ajar tonight, doing little to hide the VIP attendees and forcing me to lower my gaze to the crowd.

My phone started vibrating again and I knew it wouldn't stop anytime soon. I answered it, steeling my spine at the adamant demands on the other end. Al and Apollo were an obnoxious pair and any other night I would have loved to mess with them. But tonight... tonight I was too fucking tired.

Just as I was about to toss back my drink and call for Marco to order me a car home, I saw him. Everything inside me should've told me to continue with my plans and leave. But everything inside me for the last several years had told me to toss my inhibitions to the wind and beg him to claim me. To show him exactly what he was fucking missing and demand he handled it like the savage lover I know he'd be.

But the sober part of me knew that if I tried... I'd be lost forever to the misery of his rejection. And the sober part of me also knew that I'd already tried it a few times drunk and each time, it ended in my embarrassment and blue lady-balls. Our eyes locked as he stared up at me as if the half-naked girls dancing around him didn't matter. As if only I mattered.

But outside of being Lucky's sister, I didn't matter. Outside of being an Agostino, I didn't matter. And as much as my heart told me I wanted to matter to him, I knew it was wasted breath. As much as his face contorted in agony until he saw me, I was nothing more than a pawn in the scheme that was the Agostino empire.

I was a trophy meant to be displayed on a shelf and gawked at, never to be touched, and with no real value outside of that which others placed on me.

CHAPTER 16

APOLLO DELUCA

"**S**he's fine," Al said, throwing his phone up on the dashboard as we climbed into the car. "Pissed off that I interrupted her date… but fine."

"Fuck!" I pounded on the vehicle interior. "Fucking bitch!"

"Who the fuck are you calling a bitch?" Sienna's angry voice clipped through the Bluetooth speakers. "I know you did not call to ruin my fucking date and then call me a bitch!"

"I'm not fucking talking about you, Sienna." I rubbed my temples.

"The fuck you aren't. I'm alive and well, so what do you two want?" I could hear club music and shuffling, until a door closed and sealed off the noise.

"Where the fuck are you, Sienna?" I queried as Al pulled the car into traffic.

"None of your goddamn business." But Nico hollering in the background gave her away.

"Right. *Danza*, we'll be there in twenty, so I suggest you get rid of your little fuck boy." I reached over to the steering wheel and ended the call. "Bothersome little brat."

Al busted out laughing, and now wasn't the time nor the place for it. He wheezed as he attempted to gain his composure, making my blood boil.

"Are you done with your impetuous entertainment at my expense?" I internally debated cutting his fucking throat.

"Oh, don't use your fancy words with me. It was fucking funny." He glanced over before pulling up to the curb outside the club. "She didn't have a date. She's out with Marco, but I find it hilarious you're so—" He started coughing and gagging, unable to finish his sentence as the ball of my fist made contact with his Adam's apple.

"And I find that shot to your trachea absolutely uproarious. Now I assure you, one more fucking word and I will damage your vocal cords with the next one." I spoke calmly—evenly—as I watched him writhe in pain. Slobbering on his steering wheel, he was unable to respond. I climbed out of the car and shut the door softly before adjusting my suit and heading into *Danza*.

I charged up the stairs and slammed the VIP door closed behind me. Marco ignored my entrance but his *date*, the same one from that night before, startled. Her eyes widened the moment I walked into the room. I was intrigued that Marco was still *dating* her.

I ignored them both and went to the open window where Sienna was standing. Natalia came from around the bar and placed a drink in front of me. I grabbed her shoulders before she could walk away. Staring at her belly, I dismissed her from working until after the fetus was delivered.

"You do realize you don't always have to be a dick, right?" Sienna watched the girl storm from the room, Nico silently thanking me behind her.

"I sent her home to avoid potential concerns for the fetus's health." I stated, unsure why she was acting overly accusatory already.

"Baby. Normal people call it a baby." She sipped on her drink before turning her bright blue eyes on me. "And the reasoning was sweet but the delivery was... *dickish*."

I fought the smile that only Sienna could pull from me. Her vocabulary was always farcical and amusing. Looking down at her, I watched her smirk around the rim of her glass before taking a sip. Her long, gentle neck worked slowly as she swallowed. The scent of lime and vodka permeated my nostrils as I leaned into her.

"Enjoy yourself tonight," I said as I tucked a piece of hair behind her ear, earning myself an elegant, honest smile this time. "It's your last night out until we get a loose end handled."

I watched her closely for some kind of tell, any inclination of what was going through her mind. At the end of the day, she could be as pissed off as she wanted to be but the fact of the matter didn't change —her safety greatly outweighed her proclivity for partying.

"Then I guess I should get to enjoying my last night of freedom. You can go now." She threw back her drink, the disco light illuminating marks on her face.

"What is this?" I grabbed her chin, turning her profile towards me. "What happened? Tell me. Now." She cringed at my tight grip.

"Nothing." I pulled her closer, wrapping my arms around her waist and tugging her flush against my body. "What the fuck?" Yanking down the back of her romper, I saw that bruises and scrapes marred her spine.

"I handled it." Her shoulders slumped in exhaustion.

"I'm almost amused that you think that answer will suffice," I stated, impatiently waiting.

"A little mishap at my apartment. Nothing more. Nothing less." She tried shrugging me loose, only winning when I saw her flinch in pain.

"That's all?" Her silence forced me to put my phone to my ear. "I want the last twelve hours of surveillance at Sienna's apartment reviewed for unwanted visitors."

She stormed to the other side of the room, putting as much distance between us as possible. Her girlfriends, who were standing in the corner, welcomed her with open arms while passing around shots. The ring of my cell phone stopped me from dispersing her little party and sending her home.

"Both the elevator and door feeds were deleted for approximately two hours. The bank on the corner picked up Gio Moretti around that same time." My gaze zoned in on hers. Her throat moved quickly as she swallowed several times.

"You motherfucker!" Al's misguided fury barreled into the room.

His voice was raspy and damaged, evidently the force I had exacted on his throat was harder than I realized.

"Not laughing anymore?" I asked sincerely. His chest puffed in and out as he tried to calm himself, but he was close to losing it.

"Come dance with us, Al." Sienna walked up, standing between the two of us. "It's my last night of freedom—let's get drunk."

He stared me down for a beat longer, then finally retreated with her. I'd allow him a moment to cool off before alerting him of the news.

I sat opposite Marco and his date—I used that term loosely. He never *courted* the same woman twice. Each was merely a distant memory before he moved on and hunted his next conquest. But this girl was different from his normal variety and it was all in her eyes. It was in the way she stared through you, as if calculating every possibility—every threat—before you made it.

She was a small little thing at five-foot-nothing, while her prominent cheekbones and soft pale skin made her appear almost innocent. She had light brown hair that was in a high and tight ponytail cascading down her back.

But none of it compared to those damn eyes. They were green… an olive green. They had a strange aura, a resounding speculation. She watched everyone with a naturally inquisitive air. And she was exactly the type of person the mafia didn't need sniffing around. She was giving me what she no doubt assumed was a coy smile while simultaneously batting her lashes.

Whatever this *little girl* wanted, it wasn't sex—at least not from Marco. She threw her head back to let out a throaty laugh, seductively running a finger over her chest as she did so. She wore a large yellow ring on her hand. *Ostentatious and a bit out of place*, I thought. But with the way she played with it, I knew it was important to her.

"You can stare all you like, *mon cher*, but at least buy me a drink?" she asked, leaning over the empty stool between us.

"Sorry, little girl, I don't promote alcohol consumption in minors." I tossed back my whiskey, savoring the flavor.

"Looks can be deceiving. I assure you... I am old *enough*." She practically purred. "My name is Tessa *Leroux*. And you are?" She overly annunciated her last name, making her lips wrap around the word as she exuded erotic promises sealed by a French accent.

When I didn't answer or lean forward to shake her proffered hand, she seemed taken aback but instantly regained her composure. The girl was dressed like sin and smelled like expensive French perfume, the scent lingering in soft waves of hot, hot sex.

"What're you doing here?" I asked and if I were anyone else, I would have missed the way she tensed at my tone. But again, her recovery was quick, almost undetectable. *Almost.*

"Doing? Well, I could be doing anything you like." She twisted in her seat like a wanton sex kitten, practically rubbing against me.

"Anything, *mon beau*," she repeated, reaching out a hand to run her fingertips across my chest. But I caught her wrist before she was able to make contact and tugged her forward.

I held it tightly, leaning in close enough to press my mouth to hers. Her breath peppered my face as she gasped. Only I didn't kiss her, just stared deeply into those olive... now almost jade-green eyes.

"Not so fun when the roles are reversed, are they, little girl?" I motioned towards Marco as her jaw dropped open in surprise. "Stick to playing with little boys. You're ill-equipped to handle a man, let alone one like me." I released her wrist and rose to my feet.

She was smart, but apparently not smart enough to know when she should be afraid. A fact that I was certain would get her into trouble one day. And it would be the kind of trouble she wouldn't be able to talk her way out of. But today, she was Marco's problem—I had enough of my own. She straightened herself back in her seat but the harsh movement of her throat showed me I'd succeeded in rattling her.

Something told me it wasn't the last time I would be seeing this girl.

"Marco." I barked out his name without any regard for his frightened date, who was still trying to recuperate from our little interaction.

I nodded towards her and raised a brow at him. "Your actions always have consequences. The Agostino name comes with a show of strength... power. Accordingly, those in the gutter will seek to destroy anything they can get their hands on, in an attempt to take what you have for themselves."

"Yeah, yeah. You sound like Lucky and Pops." He smirked, his boyish charm flashing as his dimple popped out.

"Lucky and Mario are trying to prepare you for taking over as Lucky's right hand." I stepped further away from the bar, out of earshot of the girl.

"And what're *you* preparing me for? I thought you were happy as Lucky's right hand?" That dimple begged me to slap it. Instead, with a hand on his neck, I pulled him close.

"I am forewarning you that those seeking to take what doesn't belong to them... Will hurt or take what doesn't belong to you." I motioned to the potential collateral damage adorning his arm for the evening. "If I've noticed she's been around more than once, so will they—she's unprotected."

His smirk vanished as his blue eyes burned in anger—only now realizing the burden his last name carried. We didn't live this lifestyle in anticipation of things being freely given to us. You didn't run the entire east coast by asking politely. You fucking took what you wanted and fuck anyone that got in your way. By consequence, it was the same mentality shared by our enemies and those weaker than us. And it was exactly what led them to target the people we were responsible for.

And Marco's yet to take responsibility for a single action.

"Do better. Be better," I said as I released his neck, smacking the boy's cheek a little rougher than necessary.

I reached inside my suit jacket as I descended the stairs into the club. The crowd gave me a wide berth as I stormed across the dance floor, pulling my cell from my pocket.

We got a squealer—the screen read.

Rocco was able to save me a rat from Yuri's crew. This night just got that much better. I could feel the tingling sensation slowly drift over my body as *il mietitore* prepared to show himself.

Sienna caught my attention as she shook her ass on a walking dead man. Her eyes told me she saw me and wanted me to step up to her—to murder an innocent drunk. She was playing a tedious game of cat and mouse; one she didn't realize she was unable to win.

I met Al at the bar and informed him that we had two stops to make before our evening was over. I directed his questionable gaze to Sienna, watching as her movements were slow and tensed by pain. He had questions I didn't have the answers to, so we left to go find them.

We charged the two blocks, pulling our Glocks from under our suits and disengaging the safeties. This visit was not sanctioned by Lucky; therefore, I was unable to kill *him* yet, but he'd get the fucking message nonetheless.

Stepping into the dimly lit restaurant, patrons took notice and darted towards the exits as we passed. Gio's men moved to block us but they were too slow—we had them on their backs within seconds. Gio stormed to his feet but Al raised his gun, the barrel pointed at the son of a bitch's chest.

"She didn't tell you it was me," he stated so confidently my body coiled with tension. "What camera did I miss?" He smirked.

"Leave her. The fuck. Alone!" Al clipped, cocking his hammer back.

"I can't. She belongs to me and her time is ticking away." His words lacked their usual rage and idiocy. The man before us was different—a breeze of certainty poured off him. "Come on then." He waved his hands in a come-hither motion. Walking around the table, he rolled up his sleeves and widened his stance.

"I don't have much time so I will make this quick." I charged forward, my fist cocked back at the ready. I snapped his neck to the side, blood spraying at the contact.

He answered me blow for blow, most of which I counter blocked. This wasn't a death match; this was a comeuppance, repentance for all of our past sins. He was bleeding from the nose and lip, while favoring his right ribs. I had a gash across my cheek and my shoulder was sore, but this wasn't what I had expected.

This new voice, this stance of a stronger man, all showed a side of

Gio we hadn't anticipated. Just as more of his men charged into the room, Al pushed me back to separate us. We were outgunned and outnumbered, while the odds of us leaving alive had quickly dwindled.

"I gave that to you because I didn't mean to hurt her. That's on me, and I *allowed* you this moment to send her my sincerest apologies." I didn't answer, just turned on my heel and left the restaurant with a thousand new questions.

Rocco and I stared down at Yuri's weakest link. We didn't even have to spill blood for the man to tell us the interesting tale of Yuri and his son, Alexander. The weaponry was only the beginning as the Russians merged into a relationship with the new man leading the sex trade in our city and dealing in women and children.

Dominic Moretti was confirmed as the east coast flesh kingpin.

Rocco leaned over our captive, knife in front of the man's chest—the same knife I'd seen the mafia soldier destroy many lives with. Rocco continued to question him but the fucker had turned mute suddenly, holding back the most important information and the answers we needed. Instead of words, a large wad of spit landed on Rocco's face and the rage and control he had once exhibited was gone in a flash.

Rocco reared back his fist and slammed it into the rat's face—over and over again. Not a single one of us moved, knowing the rage was warranted and that we'd already gotten all we were going to get anyway.

"End it," I ordered Rocco, who looked over his shoulder at me with a haunted and blank expression.

We all had skeletons in our closets… some just hid them better than others. When you were able to witness a moment of extreme emotional outlet, allowing an individual to release their pent-up pain… it truly was a beautiful sight, filled with bloodlust and redemption—that is, unless you were on the receiving side.

"Hear that?" Rocco asked, leaning over the pitiful figure. "This is the end…" he whispered, jamming his knife into the man's abdomen before pulling it north.

The Russian released an agonized moan as the blade slowly, but precisely, ripped through his torso from navel to neck. His flesh separated, exposing his entrails, while his mouth gurgled and his body shook. I smiled down at the creature, wanting to haunt his eternity in hell… to ensure he never forgot who ordered him there.

One day, the Devil and the Reaper would make their own descent into the fires of the afterlife. Lucky might have been the crowned prince —the veritable dictator of burnt flesh and bedlam—but I was the monster who would surround you as you were engulfed by the flames and burdened by the brimstone… I was no fallen angel. I was fucking hell-born.

"*Fino a tardi,*" I taunted as I watched the light dim from his eyes.

"Motherfucker spit on me." Rocco scoffed, wiping his bloody knife on his slacks. Al laughed from the other side of the room, and Rocco turned to glare at him.

"Well, you are an asshole," Al offered with a shrug

"The fuck is that supposed to mean?" Rocco's confusion caused him to laugh harder.

"Weren't you just bragging about fucking some girl in the ass and her crying because all you did was spit on it?" Al roared and the rest of the room followed suit. "Exactly. Asshole." He confirmed, pointing in Rocco's direction.

With that, Rocco charged and I didn't intervene. It was comical, but Al still deserved to get his pretty face damaged. He'd been talking a lot of shit lately and I myself wanted to knock the man's fucking teeth out. I let them go at it for a moment.

"You little bitch!" Al yelled. I stepped between the two of them, but they kept lunging at each other.

"You wanna be my bitch?" Rocco punched Al in the face, busting it open and dripping blood on me.

"Enough. Both of you!" I clipped. "We need to update Lucky."

"Fuck. You know he's gonna be pissed." I raised a brow at Al's comment. "It's Bella's birthday," he clarified.

"Fuck." I hadn't even realized that was here already. "And I still need to deal with Dom."

Women and children were the innocents of the world and should be protected at all costs. Dom's days were numbered—his only saving grace so far was his fucking sister.

One day, Bella would learn her beloved brother's truths and we'd deal accordingly. I held absolutely no qualms over being the one to end him—a woman begging for anything other than a man's dick was irreprehensible. She should never be cowering because she feared for her life.

I ordered the team to clean up the mess and send the corpse directly to the last known location of Yuri's crew. I hoped it would send a message to this Alexander, warning him to get the fuck out of our city. I headed home to sleep; tomorrow was going to be another long fucking day.

I barely closed my eyes before it was already sunrise. I had awakened early, heading to the elevator to take me to Lucky's floor.

"What was it you needed to discuss with me?" Lucky asked as he continued getting dressed for the party.

I went into detail, explaining the rat's confession and how Dom was selling women from the streets and the poles. I elaborated on the Russian's intent to hunt down Sienna and potentially use her as leverage against us. We agreed to meet with Mario later in the evening and create a plan of attack.

Tonight was to honor Mirabella Moretti's twenty-first birthday and it was also the official announcement of her engagement to Lucky. He'd tell the entire room of *made* families that she was his and fuck them all if they came for her.

Like goosebumps racing up your arms, my entire being warned me tonight wouldn't be as easy as we all hoped.

CHAPTER 17
SIENNA AGOSTINO

"Hello, love muffin." Al chirped loudly in my ear—I wanted to murder him and beg for coffee… simultaneously.

"Go. The fuck. Away." I groaned from where I was buried underneath my pillow and blankets. Without even looking up, I knew the motherfucker had opened all of the blinds.

"Nope. You're stuck with me," he said before unceremoniously flopping onto my bed.

Bella often called him Big Al—well, because he was fucking huge—a sentiment I normally loved. Until his ass was hopping all over my bed, making the alcohol in my system slosh around internally. It was also a painful reminder of the abuse my body had endured at the hands of Gio.

"I need some hair of the dog, a shower and to be away from you." I groaned again, rolling over and shielding my eyes from the unforgiving attack of sunlight. "And shut the goddamned blinds."

"Nope. Punishment," Al announced, without a hint of remorse in his tone.

Fuck. He knew about Gio's assault.

"Fuck. Off." I growled—I was in no mood to deal with his load of crap.

He was my best friend but he was also the reason I was hurt yesterday. Well, not the sole reason but he was loyal to the cause that made Gio feel it necessary to target me. I also found it comical that it was Al here, not Apollo or my brother. *The engagement party!* I wanted to mentally smack myself for almost forgetting.

"Not a chance in hell. Why wouldn't you call me? You're constantly trying to deal with stuff on your own. When will it occur to you that we're stronger as a family?" He forced me onto my back and stared down at me. "Shit happens to this family… because of this family." He drew out the words.

"Right. So why would I lean on the family, when they're the reason it happened in the first place?" I shoved him off me and slowly threw my legs over the side of the bed. "I'm dealing with him."

"No. Apollo dealt with him." Al gloated, sitting back with a smug smile on his face.

"Dealing or dealt?" I asked. His smirk grew larger. "Doesn't surprise me. Whatever. His allegiance to the Agostino cause, unfaltering as usual."

"Dealt. And it wasn't just the cause that had him jumping into action. He cares, Sienna. In his own fucked-up way, for his own fucked-up reasons, he assumes his motives are anything but emotional baggage when it comes to you." He paused a moment. "Now what the fuck is the deal with Romano Bianchi?"

"Right, he cares." I scoffed, blowing off the tingle the admission caused in certain parts of my lady bits. "And the alliance is yet to be determined." I stood up and grabbed my cell phone, motioning for Al to follow me to my office. I called Amy and she answered on the second ring.

"Girl! You didn't tell me he was loaded and sexy as hell." Amy chirped before answering my hello.

We spent the next half an hour discussing what she'd uncovered from her review of the contract and any changes she'd want to make. Apparently, in regards to keeping my best interest at heart, there wasn't much he missed and that fact pissed both of us off. Even Al muttered his comments about the man being a "lying, ass-kissing little sneak" while shaking his head. Romano had spoken with and met Lucky on several occasions and never offered up any information on this arrangement—a big red flag to Al.

Amy continued with the details. The contract actually protected my company and income from being touched by him. He was willing to leave all of my assets and anything previous to the marriage intact with the expectation that in the future, any new businesses would be explored with him. But he had left *Energia* and all future dealings within the corporation to me. He literally just wanted a future with me... that was it.

"Bullshit. There is something buried in this contract. Something else he wants." Al growled, leaning over my shoulder to get into view on the video chat.

Amy remained unfazed. "I assure you, Alvin, there was nothing I missed. Evelyn is quite thorough and will be a tremendous asset to our firm." She stopped and smiled off screen. Her coaching and overall assessment of the girl made me happy. "And I did a double check. I'll happily lay down my sizable salary if you actually have the balls to not only challenge me, but find something I missed, Alvin." She smirked.

"Christ," I muttered, rubbing my eyes with the heels of my hands. "Say it, Amy."

"In retrospect, since we knew something like this was coming... You honestly couldn't ask for more, Sienna." She gave me a sad smile. "He missed no detail when it came to honoring all that your father laid out for him."

"Read it again. She isn't moving to Philly," Al demanded, crossing his tree-trunk arms over his chest with an aura of finality.

"I assure you, Jolly Green Giant, I have her best interests at heart and evidently, so does Romano Bianchi. You of all people know what is expected of Sienna. And out of all of the suitors, this is the only one who has come forward *with* a willingness to protect her interests."

"So, he just wants me..." I stated out loud, the realization of those words settling into my heart.

I was looking for hearts and flowers, looking for a man who *wanted* me. With my birthright, this was the closest I would get to something like that. To be so cognizant of all the emails my father sent, of all the demands I expected to be met, and still he managed to offer so much more.

It faltered my reasoning to continuously fight him. He *wanted* me. He didn't want my name, didn't want my money, didn't want my company.

Just me.

"There are plenty of other men in New York who want you, Sienna." Al's argument fell on deaf ears as Amy said goodbye and disconnected. "Ones who won't shy away from showing you they… care."

"Right. And why would any of them interest me now, when they've failed to do so before?" I asked, knowing he didn't have an answer.

"Give me a chance to talk to him," Al begged, his face growing redder when I refused.

"He needs to come to me because he wants to, Al. Not for anything else. Not because of anyone else. He needs to come to me for no reason other than *he* wants me." I could tell he wasn't listening so I cranked up the attitude I normally wouldn't drop on Al. "And you received a direct order from Pops and Lucky… keep your mouth shut."

He didn't like my threat but he nodded like the good soldier he was. He was stuck between a rock and a hard place, as several loyalties threatened to tear him apart. Of course he was loyal to Lucky and my dad, loyal to the cause, but Apollo was his *other* best friend.

He had been rooting for us from the start, trying to insert himself between us and build something he knew Apollo wasn't capable of. But my heart could only take so much more turmoil before it shut down for good.

"Are you going to be my date tonight?" I asked, showing him the dress that I planned to wear to the engagement party.

"Sienna, I just ask that you try tonight… Tell him without telling him, okay?" Al's eyes implored me to continue embarrassing myself. Because when all was said and done, that's what I would be doing… again. I nodded but moved around the room, further dismissing him as I started the arduous task of getting rid of my hangover and dressing for tonight.

"I am here!" Octavia shouted from the foyer, and Al and I laughed at her ridiculous singsong entrance.

"I'll leave you ladies to get ready. I'll be back to escort you both to the party." Al walked out quickly while Octavia used her large blue eyes to assess me.

I downed a few glasses of champagne before telling her about the *very* stupid plan I'd just concocted to try to bring Apollo to heel. I would throw myself before him but in a different manner than normal. This time I would use indirect truth to see what he had to say.

If he *assumed* that one day I would leave and he'd be left with nothing, how would he feel? You see, if I did in fact go to Philly—out of respect for Romano—I wouldn't speak to Apollo again.

"Christ." Al walked back into my apartment to escort us to Bella's birthday-engagement extravaganza.

I went all out for the evening ahead of us. My hair was pulled up off my shoulders, boasting the curls pinned to the back of my head. My makeup was light and simple—I had opted for a magnetic natural look so the focus was on my dress.

Even my jewelry was only a simple pair of diamond earrings. *Oscar de la Renta* had made this dress—and I would argue he only had my body in mind when he designed it, as its fit was pure brilliance.

It was black and tight, hugging my curves with a low, deep V between my breasts. It was tight on my hips and flared around my legs from the high slit on my thigh.

We wandered downstairs to the festivities and I swooned from the sight before me. All of my hard work had come to fruition—I'd arranged the perfect party for Bella.

Every table was covered with black linens and black vases, dripping with crystal diamonds and filled with bright red roses—which were displayed expertly. All the tapestries were black and showcased the sparkling chandeliers. And every tabletop and open space had diamond-encrusted candles lit brightly.

All the staff and attendees already present were in black-tie; the women were in black gowns. I had made it clear in the invites: if you were in any color other than black you would be barred access. Bella was the only one who was permitted to wear white; she was the sole focus of the party, a fact that should have been clearly emphasized.

"I don't like it," Octavia said from our table while she glared across the room. I stopped for a second, thinking she meant the party I'd worked tirelessly on. But then I saw her expression and I knew what she was referring to.

That was the thing about women… we were resilient. We could withstand so many storms, but there would always be that one that had the ability to destroy us. Hurricane Apollo was a Category Five—the storm of the century—with the capacity to wreck me from a distance, before I was even able to bunker down and shelter myself.

This *one chance* tonight—the Lord knew he had plenty of chances before this—would determine whether or not I would accept Romano's proposal.

"How is the intended bride-to-be?" I asked Lucky, interrupting his conversation with our parents.

He smiled. My brother, the future of the Agostino Crime Family and famously dubbed *il diavolo,* was smiling. It melted my heart and in that same moment, it filled me with so much jealousy I threatened to erupt into flames.

I wanted that. I wanted someone to take their villainy, their obsession with power, and throw it all aside. I wanted a small semblance of a smile, a semblance of love, while we battled side by side for a throne.

Then suddenly, as if the angel to his devil had heard us speaking, she appeared. She was dressed in a white strapless gown with a sweetheart bodice that hugged her slight curves. Her neck boasted an elegant heart-shaped emerald necklace—it hung low just above her breasts and was an heirloom in my family, having been passed down for several generations.

It looked flawless against her porcelain skin… My mother had selected the perfect piece to give to my brother. Her long black hair was swept to the side, layering silky curls that were held in place by a pin that shined from the diamonds in the light. My brother's eyes lit with a fire of possession, and I couldn't help the happy giggle that escaped from my lips.

Apollo caught my attention out of the corner of my eye. He filled his expensive suit with a thick, dark menacing aura that consumed those who dared come close to him.

The danger he emanated was palpable—it was in the way he walked, the way he approached the crowds with a sinister glare and the way he was always prepared to fight. My breath caught in my throat as I watched his slow, precise movements. He devoured the people in the room and smiled when he saw a chance to spill blood.

My brother met Bella at the stairs and he began showing her off as his newly announced fiancée—Apollo and Al right behind them, scanning the crowd. As our family made their way over to the table, Apollo remained off to the side, his presence a formidable warning against any potential threat.

I tried to look away but my heart was in my throat as I watched his eyes slowly turn towards me. I could feel the damned thing beating against my chest while the seconds passed.

The air escaped from my lungs as I pleaded with him to acknowledge me. To show his appreciation for what he was seeing.

His glance met me for a moment before it was gone. His eyes didn't even take me in; instead, it was as if he checked to make sure I was breathing before moving on. My hands shook, my pulse raced and I started sweating, agitated by his blatant brush off.

I didn't spend four grand on this dress and even more on hair and makeup to be dismissed like that. He was lost, his expression vacant, until he took in the presence of someone behind me.

I glanced over my shoulder and froze when I saw the blonde waitress pouring wine into Bella's glass. She was gorgeous—that much was true—but it wasn't until her eyes came into view that I realized why she seemed familiar.

The Moretti Whore. It was the goddamned ghost, the girl from the docks who had somehow remained unidentified. Yet here she was, playing the slutty little server.

Dominic and Anthony Moretti were at the opposite end of the table, whispering amongst themselves, but I didn't miss the glances Dominic kept sending her way.

Apollo left Lucky's side quickly, stalking towards the blonde mystery girl, and my grip tightened—threatening to break through my wine glass—as I watched the interaction.

The same man incapable of feeling anything lit up with lust right before my very eyes, and the little display turned me murderous. *Fuck this bitch.* I had put in my time, my dues and tried to make this work between us.

Everyone had warned me off him but now, he laid it out clear as day right in front of the entire family—he felt something all right, it just wasn't for me. The more I thought about all of our conversations in the past, the more I criticized myself for being so emotionally inept. I hadn't even seen the disaster I was creating for myself.

A resounding gasp and a flurry of commotion brought my attention back to the moment. I watched in terror as the blonde bitch spilled wine on Bella's hand. It only took Dominic a second before he rounded the table and yanked the girl away from his sister.

The look of fear on her face should've made me feel sorry for her, but it didn't. Maybe it was the wine. Maybe it was my broken heart. Or maybe—just maybe—I was a terrible human being... one that everyone saw beneath my perfect smile but no one dared to point out.

"Dominic!" Bella gasped, hopping from her seat and grabbing onto the girl's arm, in an attempt to stop Dominic from rushing her away. "Take. Your Hands. Off Her. Now!"

"She almost drenched your white dress, Mirabella. She's incompetent." Dominic growled back in a low menacing hiss, his hand firmly positioned in a death grip.

"What has gotten into you? Since when do you behave like Gio?" Bella whispered, turning my stomach at the mere mention of her brother's name. Dominic's head snapped up, seemingly shocked and appalled by her comment. His mouth opened and closed in silence.

"Isn't this the kind of shit Gio would do?" Bella motioned towards his hold on the girl, while the bruises on my back threatened to burn me alive. They were all the same—the Moretti men—they were cruel, self-centered and ruthless bastards.

The blonde scurried off and Apollo's gaze followed the sway of her hips. I tossed back my glass and snatched another from a passing waiter before I returned my attention to Bella.

She was practically glowing between the wine and the love of her life claiming her for the entire room to see. I smiled at her happiness—she deserved it after a lifetime under Gio's watch.

I polished off another glass of wine and took a big gulp of Al's scotch—much to his disdain. Laughing at my father's jokes, I smiled a moment more before wandering off in the direction of the mysterious blonde.

I saw the door close to the staff bathroom at the end of a dark corridor. Unsure of exactly how I was going to play this, I took a deep breath. Then, choking down my pride and holding my head high, I stormed into the bathroom.

"I never would've believed it if I hadn't seen it for myself. A ghost right before my eyes." I crossed my arms over my chest and leaned my back against the closed door.

"I'm sorry?" she questioned. Her beautiful eyes swam with unshed tears; no doubt, she had been crying alone in the bathroom.

"No one and I mean no one can escape my investigations. So, clearly you must be a ghost to not show up on any system. Which means... you're up to something." I placed my wine glass on the table by the door and stepped closer to her. "When Apollo asked me to research some pretty... little doll on Dominic Moretti's arm I didn't expect to find... well, nothing. So, tell me, little doll... what're you hiding, exactly?"

I was taller than her by several inches and my red-soled shoes ensured that now it was almost by a foot. I knew, as she took me in from head to toe, that she could tell I could hold my own.

My defined arm muscles and prominent stature told you that I was a powerhouse draped in fancy wrapping.

Any other woman would be intimidated by sharks like me, circling their prey. And those sharks... well, they had sharper teeth than little guppies like her.

"I need to get back to work." She practically growled, stepping to me in a deliberate show of dominance.

"Why is Dominic Moretti's little plaything working at his sister's birthday party?" I asked with a snarl. "I guess he loves playing in the gutter and fucking the help." I had no idea what overcame me or why I suddenly felt so vicious.

I was filled with such hate and animosity for this girl that I lashed out. I kept replaying images of myself as I built a life in Philly with Romano. I would be happy to an extent, but it wasn't what I wanted, with who I wanted.

She smirked, snarky and unapologetic, and my spine straightened as I waited for her to strike.

"What is your problem, exactly? Is it my mere presence here? Or is it that the help is competition?" she countered, squaring her shoulders.

"What the hell are you going on about?" I growled, my hands on my hips.

"He had you research me because I am the mystery he wants in his bed. Our encounters are filled with sexual tension and the promise that he could, would and will fuck me dirty." She waited, and it was obvious that she was enjoying the control I could feel slipping from my grasp.

"Watch your fucking mouth." My words were quiet. Coated in gasoline, they seeped into the air before bursting into flames.

"Maybe later you can watch it for me. As I swallow his cock… whole." She smacked her lips together and winked before stepping around me and leaving.

"What the fuck?" I muttered to myself. Turning to face the mirror, I cringed at the woman before me.

This wasn't me. I wasn't some weak girl who had to prey on the innocent. I was stronger than giving into this empty and callous behavior. I was better than twisting myself away from the elegant woman I truly was.

I adjusted my breasts, whispered a self-directed admonishment and opened the door. And then I strutted my ass in a perfectly composed rhythm of sex and strength back through that darkened hallway.

I'd just stepped through the swinging doors—ready to flag down the closest waiter for a glass of wine—when a hardened grip wrapped around my wrist and pulled me off my feet.

The other hand clamped over my mouth, and using my own body against me, the figure dragged me to a janitorial closet. The door slammed behind us and he pressed me into the wall, effectively forcing me to trip over a mop and bucket.

"You look absolutely radiant, Sienna." Gio pressed himself into me, his erection showing his pleasure at my appearance. "It should be you being celebrated, not my sister and her announcement as Lucky's whore." He rested one palm against my chest to keep me in place while the other moved away from my mouth.

"You're messing up my hair." I growled, annoyed at the pressure at which he was forcing my head into the wall.

"I wanted to tell you I was sorry; in case my message wasn't delivered through Apollo." He clicked on the overhead light, pointing to the cuts and bruising across his face. "He assumed he won, but I told him it was merely my apology to you. You didn't deserve my anger, even if it was your fault it was brought to the surface."

"Who are you?" My question made him falter. "You forget I've known you for years and the man before me... Well, I don't know who he is."

He stared at me for a long moment, stepping back and crossing his arms over his chest with a devious glare—one filled with cruel promises. He looked me up and down from my red-painted toenails to the top of my curled updo.

It made anger swirl in my belly at the realization I could literally make the enemy give me what I wanted, but Apollo was immune. The answer to my dilemma—to what my future held—was standing before me in a broom closet and the combination of bleach and painful truths burned my eyes.

"Or maybe you never really knew me." He stepped closer, his palms flat against the wall beside my head. "We're all forced to play our little roles in this life. We hide behind who we're expected to be and sometimes we don't even know our *real* selves when we look in the mirror."

"And what game is this?" I motioned back and forth between us.

"This is me dropping my mask and showing you the real me. And I am asking you to do the same." He tucked a loose strand of hair behind my ear. "Who are you—who is the real you, Sienna?"

"I-I don't know…" I answered honestly.

"I don't think it's the intelligent girl with a *Fortune 500* company and a mean right hook doing her daddy's and brother's biddings." He stood up, returning to his towering form while the flickering bulb above him offered an eerie shadow. "I think she has all the makings of a queen with a light so bright she overshines anyone else in the room. Let me help you shine, *bambina*." His voice was low but held so much promise.

"I. I." I hesitated, suffering from another rare occasion where I was at a loss for words—though, I guess it was becoming far less rare…

"As I said, I have someone working on the minor details for me, doing my dirty work. But your brother removed one obstacle from our path. I just need to deal with his *son* and then the city is ours for the taking." He turned as if to leave before swooping back in and grabbing my face.

He tugged my mouth towards his and before I could protest, his lips latched onto mine. His tongue begged for entrance but I resisted, unsure of what exactly was happening.

His hand left my face, dropping to my neck and squeezing. The movement caught me off-guard and I gasped, just long enough for his tongue to swirl inside.

"Every part of you tastes so good." He moaned, releasing my neck and standing tall. "Time to go play some games." He smiled before opening the door and motioning me out first.

I stepped into the hallway, now bustling with waiters and chefs—a flurry of movement that seemed to stop and stare as we emerged. Gio halted a passing waiter and grabbed a goblet of wine and a rocks glass.

Handing me the wine, he watched as I took a large gulp. His eyes were glued to my neck, his gaze darkening as I swallowed.

An evil sneer lit up his face as he took a sip of the amber liquid before dabbing a napkin inside. He deposited the glass onto a ledge and held the damp cloth to his mouth and chin, soaking the liquor into his pores.

"Time to have some fun." He turned towards the hallway I'd followed the blonde through and disappeared, his voice echoing as he went. "Come out, come out, wherever you are," he taunted, leaving me frozen in my place. The fucker had no semblance of sanity left in him —I was sure of it.

"What's the matter?" I asked Marco as I walked back up to our table.

Bella's face looked ashen, Lucky and his men were gone and Marco sat at Bella's side. He gestured towards the commotion—Apollo and Al were quickly maneuvering Angelo Fioretti out of the ballroom.

To anyone else it merely looked like they had their arms around an old friend, but the tension in their shoulders told me differently. I was about to ask what happened when I saw *her*.

My invitations were specific—no one was permitted to wear white —but she *hadn't* been invited. Tatianna was dressed in a white gown that bordered on propriety and stretched over her plastic curves.

She must have been Angelo's date for the evening because she was also being escorted from the room in a flurry of large men, followed by the promise of recompense. Her shrill giggle flounced behind her and I watched Bella cringe at the sound.

"Stupid. Bitch," I muttered around the rim of my wine, and Bella laughed. Leaning over, I clinked our glasses together before raising mine and slamming it back in one gulp.

"My father just nodded. Game. On." I clinked glasses with her again, motioning for the waiter to refill both.

The rest of my family swarmed to her side in a show of solidarity. The Agostino's against anyone that decided to fuck with us. But in the back of my mind as I stared at everyone around me, I wondered why I felt so opposed to allowing them to help me.

All the bullshit that was happening could be handled by my family. I had no idea why my mouth was sealed—not a goddamned clue as to why I felt so determined to end it all on my own.

Perhaps it was the fact that I was just a woman and considered collateral damage when all was said and done. I was a contracted alliance between Lucky and Philadelphia.

Whoever they chose for Octavia—whatever civilian in the outside world—they'd be some sort of politician or financier who would also better the Agostino's. I loved my family but I created this strength on my own and I would do all of this on my own, too.

More commotion sounded as Lucky walked back into the room, nodding at attendees as he passed. He immediately pulled Bella out of her seat, sweeping her off her feet and onto the dance floor.

My mother and father were canoodling in the corner, Dominic and Anthony Moretti were whispering amongst themselves and Marco was schmoozing the poor women on the waitstaff.

"No." I laughed, glaring at Octavia two seats over. Her head shot up and her cheeks burned bright with embarrassment—she had been caught. "You are *not* at an amazing party and sneaking a book under the table."

"Shut it, Sienna!" She snapped, tossing her book onto her seat and walking towards me. "What the?" She paused and pointed.

"Fuck, Gio Moretti is coming in hot," I said, trying to flag down Lucky's attention. Looking around, I could see neither Al nor Apollo in the crowd.

"He's drunk…" Octavia muttered as we watched Gio stumble and sway onto the dance floor.

"No, he isn't…" I whispered more to myself. His actions earlier seemed off—insane—until this very moment.

He was playing a game and whatever it was, he was ensuring he'd win.

The man was one hell of an actor…

CHAPTER 18
APOLLO DELUCA

All of the high-ranking families were present for the Agostino celebration of the century. But none of these callous, illiterate, monopolizing jackasses could give two fucks over what we were here to celebrate—their attendance was about their desire to rub elbows. Lucky had pulled out all of the stops to make this an incredible evening. Until now. Until *her*.

I had no idea why Lucky hadn't killed Tatianna yet. But her actions tonight, they sure as fuck cemented her feet at the docks—she was a goddamned dead woman. Sienna looked at me from across the room, running her pointer finger across her neck. I nodded before turning on my heel and heading to the basement.

"Fuck her! I had you first, Lucky! She doesn't deserve you. She can't fuck you like I can! She doesn't have the same bloodline I do!" The little bitch rose to her knees, all of a sudden having a backbone. "You can't hurt me! My father would have your head."

The room erupted in laughter—Tatianna actually believed her father could protect her from us. I ignored the conversation that transpired as I circled her. I could practically taste the destruction I'd lay on her flesh—it melted in my mouth as if I was already able to savor the moment. Her eyes kept flashing to me as she realized how well and truly fucked she was. I was ready to see how quickly I could break the bitch.

Her father was in politics—a senator maybe—and he was as dirty as they came. The Agostino's had so much on the man, he'd hand his daughter over on a silver platter if it meant saving his own ass. Her biggest nightmare was right in front of her and she was welcoming it—welcoming us. We didn't hurt innocents and this *abomination* in a pair of designer heels was anything but.

"In other words, you dumb bitch, your daddy can't do shit. You're ours now," I said before pulling her off the floor and pinning her against my chest. I wasn't hard from the feel of the girl under me. No, it was her terrified screams that had awakened my arousal. "And Tatianna… Lucky's version of domination is child's play compared to what I like."

She continued to struggle against me as if she had a chance of fleeing. One slap to the face and she froze in my grip, equal parts shocked and appalled. That was the thing with silver-spoon-fed-trust-fund-babies, they had no idea how the real world worked. They'd never been spanked, gone hungry or seen the true filth that society had to offer. Tatianna was trying to play our game, but she hadn't bothered to learn the rules.

Al pulled a chair into the center of the room and sat. I placed Tatianna over his lap while Lucky and I shredded her dress down the center. As she lay bare-assed and in full view, I stretched her over his thighs before yanking her waist upwards into the air. I stepped to the side, removing my jacket and rolling up my sleeves. Glaring at the underside of her ass cheeks, I frowned at the prominent red incision marks I observed there.

"You didn't." I laughed.

"Oh, she did," Lucky answered—the remaining men breaking out in hysterics.

"Tatianna, is any part of you natural?" Her response was mumbled —incoherent—as we continued to chuckle. "You're a spoiled little brat and you need to be punished, Tatianna. And I am going to enjoy it." One after another, left then right, I painted her ass a glorious shade of red under my palms. She thought, like most, that a little spanking was foreplay but I didn't stop until I saw the skin start to split—her screams only inciting the act.

"Fuck, I'm getting hard." Al twisted his hold, pulling her against his erection.

"Hear that, Tatianna? You're making him hard. Are you going to take care of him?" I didn't relent as I waited for her response. "Answer me!" My palm was burning from the assault and the *demoni* that lurked in the dark recesses of my brain begged to come out and play.

Smack. Smack. Smack.

"Yes! Yes! Please, just stop." I slammed my hand down once more before stepping back as Al dropped her to the floor.

"Now you won't fuck with Bella again. Or next time… I'll really play with you." The fear in her eyes earned the girl a smirk—I enjoyed how she crawled away from me.

Al showed her the bulge at his zipper and I shook my head over her sudden pleased expression. Psychologically, girls like Tatianna degraded themselves in an attempt to seek acceptance from the opposite sex. Daddy issues, if you will. She climbed to her knees and opened her mouth—not a fucking moment of hesitation before happily suckling his cock. I wanted to take my anger out on her throat but Angelo—having passed out after meeting the back of Al's hand—spurned my attention. The man was starting to come to.

"The fuck do you think you're doing? My father will kill you for this!" Angelo rubbed his fingertips over his split lip.

"Real *made men* don't need their daddies to do the killing, Angie. No. In fact, real *made men* make pussies like you, bleed." One punch from Lucky and blood, bones and screams erupted on impact. "Daddy said I wasn't allowed to kill you and out of respect to him, I will oblige. But you will be taught a lesson, Angie."

In a flurry of movement, Lucky lost his goddamned mind. It was a blur of growls, bones snapping and fists meeting flesh as he took his rage out on the man who was sniveling at his feet. I saw the light start to disappear from Angelo's eyes, but I gave Lucky a few more punches for good measure before stopping him.

"Boss, he's out." Lucky took a minute to return to the present. "Go back to Bella. We got this," I said and I passed him a towel to wipe the blood from his hands.

"Take out the trash," Lucky ordered the men at the stairs before motioning towards Angelo.

"Do we get a turn?" One of them pointed to Tatianna still on her knees as she hungrily took Al deeper into her mouth. The front of her was soaked in saliva as Al roared with his release.

"Well, Apollo has next." Lucky shrugged as he ascended the stairs.

"But he always breaks his toys," the guard whined.

And Tatianna's smile dropped immediately. The girl stared at me as I approached, her eyes widening when I removed my belt.

"You wanted to play, didn't you? Tell me now. I only take my women willingly." A wave of uncertainty washed over her face before her smile returned and she nodded. "Now's the only chance to leave, Tatianna. Only chance. Make your decision now."

"I'm staying." I sneered at her words but relaxed when I felt my calm, rational exterior flee. The psychotic side—buried under all of my ink and expensive suits—was coming to the surface. And the bitch had no idea what she was in for.

"Apollo," she whined. Her voice was obnoxious and grating, the sound sticking to her nasal passages before exiting through her pursed lips. She took two steps forward and placed her palms onto my chest— the gesture burned against my skin.

"Did I give you permission to touch me?" Her fingertips immediately jumped away. "I've never understood the allure of fucking something so... *inconsequential.*" I waved my hand in a circular motion as I positioned myself behind her.

"Apollo, I—" She paused when I clamped down on her shoulders —her back now to my front.

"I wasn't done." My lips pressed to her ear, I lowered my tone. "Does it make you feel special? To have their hands on you? Men who have made it clear they don't think of you. Not for a single moment. After they've come down your throat?"

Her soft cries echoed in the basement, the sounds reverberating back—likely causing her to cry harder. Women like Tatianna just didn't get it. If she wanted to enjoy her sexuality and have some fun—so be it. But to act like a common whore and think the future leader of the mafia would marry her… *it was fucking pathetic.*

"The plastic… the silicone… it's all so frivolous. I don't understand—can't you see what you've done to yourself? There has to be some semblance of intellect behind this overly coiffed hair." I paced until I stood directly in front of her again, leaning into her personal space. "Do you think if you swallow my cock, I'll put in a good word for you with Lucky?" I smirked as a new rush of angry tears sprung from her eyes.

"No. But I want… it, you." She let out a fake moan, but the spark in her eyes told me she had a hidden agenda.

"Knees," I ordered.

I cringed at the way she dropped down so quickly onto the cold concrete. Her body was clearly used to the abuse. I nodded as she raised a brow in question before undoing my button and removing my dick from my pants. I was barely hard and had to fight to sustain it when her excessive perfume hit my nostrils. Sienna always wore a faint mixture of strawberry or vanilla—sweet and light. She didn't need to hide behind expensive labels.

Don't fucking go there, I chastised myself.

"Shield those fucking teeth and get your hands off me," I ordered, grimacing as her canines scraped down the sides of my dick. I didn't do love songs and pretty words. I got what I wanted and that was it—and it usually ended in pain. "Fucking Christ." I growled in agitation as Tatianna's overly exaggerated moaning only heightened.

The sound threatened to make me take a jump off Lucky's penthouse terrace.

I placed my large hands around the sides of her head and yanked her forward—the thickness of my cock stifled her noises. I hunched over her and got a good look at her bright red ass. Admiring my own handiwork, I watched as her bottom hovered in the air, avoiding contact with the red welts.

"The funny thing about asphyxiation, *cagna,* is people underestimate the level of terror it can induce. The nervous system starts firing off warnings and panic sets in when something is blocking the airway. And a cock like mine—wedged deep in your throat—impedes the exchange of oxygen. Your tonsils are located at the base of your throat, quite a ways up from your esophagus—which I'd love to say I was reaching but I am not *that* endowed." Her gasping increased and her nails dug into my thighs as she struggled to push me away.

"Take it." Holding her by the back of the head with one hand, I bent forward and using the other, I added more welts to her ass. The thrashing, the tears and the smell of fear were calling my orgasm to approach far more quickly than I'd like.

"Now, if you calmed down and ignored the sudden rush of adrenaline, you'd realize you could inhale just fine through your nostrils." She started snorting as if finally realizing she had a nose. "But! Your pharynx at the end of your nasal passage—just above the throat—has too much pressure on it. Between the overextension of your jaw and my head buried so deep… nothing can get past my dick. It's kind of empowering as a man, to think to myself—*I could kill this bitch with my dick*. And I could, Tatianna."

Her body shook with relief as I pulled back—just enough for her to inhale—before slamming home again. The small reprieve wasn't going to solve her need for more air but it would sustain her a little bit longer. The crew wasn't joking when they said I broke my toys because after this, she'd be a whole new level of fucked up. Lucky warned her. Sienna warned her. Bella warned her. Now I was *fucking* warning her.

"Oh, fuck. I'm close, Tatianna. Just keep the tears coming… show me exactly how afraid you are—it's so fucking hot." With each muffled whimper, my inner beast awakened. "Don't worry, your body can't go past three minutes without air and I'm only a minute and a half away. Two tops." I rotated my hips and her throat worked me just the right way.

"Fuck!" I roared as my orgasm took hold and I shot my load down her open throat. I pulled back and she immediately flopped forward, choking and gagging for air. Her makeup was ruined, her hair was a mess, and her bra was soaked in saliva. Her body wracked with muted sobs before she found her voice again and began wailing.

I squatted before her and grabbed her chin, forcing her to look into my eyes. I did nothing to hide the true nature that lurked within me—and I could only imagine what she saw reflecting back at her. The moment she gasped and fell backwards onto her tortured ass, I knew she understood exactly what I was. And I was *the* fucking monster. I was the goddamned grim reaper that loomed in the shadows with a list of names… men that would endure a terrible ending. Tatianna just so happened to be celebrating her lucky day because even though that part of me clawed beneath the surface, just skin deep, today she left with her life.

"Fuck! Look at her eyes!" One of the guards wandered over. "I fucking told you… he always ruins them for the rest of us."

"Fuck, dude. She looks haunted now." The other laughed, leaning over my shoulder as I tucked myself back into my pants.

"Did we learn a lesson today, Tatianna?" Her lost, vacant eyes stared back at me—her irises absolutely empty. "Next time, I won't pull out before three minutes. Stay in your fucking lane and leave this family alone." I straightened and turned to the guards. "She's all yours… if she has anything left." A wad of my spit landed next to her leg, seemingly snapping her out of her haze. I made it to the bottom of the side staircase before she spoke.

"I'll have to tell Sienna all the rumors about the size of your dick are true." Her nasally voice was gone, replaced by the ruthless savage tone of a *dead bitch*. "From personal experience." She sneered at me.

"You dumb whore." The guard shook his head laughing, stepping aside as I flew back in front of her. I grabbed her by her neck and pulled her to her feet. I grinned when her startled gasp turned into a choked whimper.

"You can't be that fucking stupid." I roared in her face, my hand on her throat, pinning her against the wall. "I should bring Sienna down here to fucking murder you with her bare hands." Her eyes lit up in fear.

"Want me to get her?" the guard asked, and I enjoyed how my delayed response rattled her plastic frame.

"You know we don't kill women. Even the guilty ones we allow freedom." She slumped into the wall, no doubt filling with relief. "Except when it comes to women killing women… all gloves are off."

"Pl-please." She choked for air as she begged.

"But you see, I won't allow a queen such as Sienna, down here with the *peasants*." I dropped her to the ground in a plastic heap of daddy issues. "You may make her cry but I will comfort her. Shakespeare said, '*Weep not, sweet queen, for trickling tears are vain.*' And I will make sure she overcomes anything you fucking throw at her." I lingered in her space for another minute before turning on my heel to leave.

"Get her the fuck out of here!" I ordered, grabbing my jacket and heading back to the party. "I've got better company to keep." Her apoplectic threats faded into the distance with each step I took. I opened the door and stared at the guard on the other side.

"Trash taken care of?" he asked; I nodded as I adjusted my cufflinks and rejoined the party.

The trash had indeed been taken care of… for now.

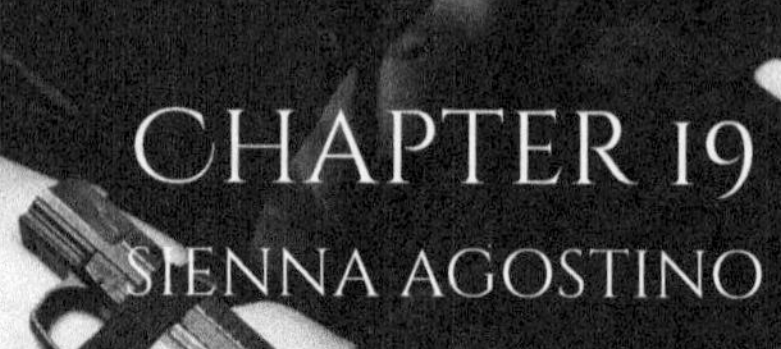

CHAPTER 19
SIENNA AGOSTINO

I was at a loss—I had no idea what Gio's angle was as he stumbled towards us. I knew he wasn't drunk from his little bravado earlier, but he was really acting it up now. I'd just started to relax and devour enough wine to drown an angry cow when Gio interrupted. I realized Apollo and Al were off to the wings; however, their attentions shifted as they, too, noticed his arrival. They swooped in a circle around Lucky—vultures ready to pick apart the dead man's bones.

"I'm here to congratulate the lovebirds. Surely you don't-don't t-t-think I'd harm my own sister?" Gio played up his supposed drunkenness.

I stumbled backwards into Octavia as Anthony and Dominic charged towards the third Moretti male.

"This fucking idiot." Apollo stifled his laughter from behind Gio, who continuing with his antics, feigned surprise. His father and brother shouted, attempting to corral him away from the fight he'd started.

"Fuck you, D. Our little sister got engaged… to this! This monster pretending to be a dignified man in a suit!" Flicking his hand out, Dom caught his brother by his shoulders to keep the man upright. "This… this *stronzo!* He's not g-g-good enough for her! Fuck this family."

"Gio!" Bella swung around Al, getting within an inch of Gio's face. "Enough. Goddamn it. You think Lucifer cares for me enough to keep you alive? After all you've done! You're breathing on borrowed time, you idiot!"

Apollo wore his normal unreadable mask but the tension in his shoulders and the spread of his legs, mimicked a fighting stance. I sipped my wine as the men went tit for tat with their insults and ominous threats. It was like a goddamned ping-pong match—back and forth, they went. And sip after sip, *I* went. Then just as suddenly as it started, I watched Bella's head drop in defeat.

"Enough. Please go." A tear ran down her cheek at her whispered plea, begging her brother to leave. I wanted to go to her, planned to go to her, to console her… until *his* voice stopped me.

"No one makes *mia regina* cry!" Apollo was two steps into attacking again with Al on his tail, when Bella stepped between them.

Everyone. Everyone came first but me. I may have been strong enough to fight my own battles but at some point, this is the Apollo I would've loved to have seen for myself. For him to so gallantly step up to destroy whatever was making me upset. I knew I hadn't been forthcoming about Philly and now I realized why. I wanted him to fight for me, for once, not just because I was an Agostino—but because I was me. I wanted him to *pick* me.

I was like a weeping heroine in a romance novel, the one where you just wanted to tell the bitch to shut up and grow a pair. But that was so much easier said than done when you're hiding behind the spine and hundreds of pages, and not stuck in this mess that was my life. This was my fucked-up story, and I'd cry with no balls in my designer panties all I wanted.

The conversation heated up around us as both sides continued to fight. Then suddenly—for just one single moment—Gio turned his attention towards me and winked. My spine straightened as I realized no one else had seen it. *What was he about to do?* I stepped forward in an attempt to do—I didn't even know what—but something. He turned his sights on his sister and verbally attacked her.

"You don't tell me what to do, you stupid bitch! You're just a whore! *Stupida cagna!* Just a pair of legs father brought back from Italy to wrap around the Agostino eldest son. To make him weak! You're weak!" My jaw dropped at his insult. I was prepared to speak up when Lucky reached out and snapped Gio's finger back, twisting the joint in an unnatural angle.

I pulled Octavia behind me to avoid the onslaught of people shoving their way free of the altercation. Marco was still at the table, flirting with a waitress—though she was focused on the fight and not on his advances. Between all of the back and forth, Apollo had gripped Gio up and began pulling him towards the exit. In true slow motion, Bella stepped forward in an imperfect cadence, taking the blow her brother had intended for Lucky.

It felt like the entire room collectively gasped then froze, until Bella spoke. Her voice was loud and confident, though peppered with an undertone of malice I'd never heard from her.

"Enough! Listen to me clearly, Gio. You are done. You're not welcome in *Lucifer's city* anymore. As an engagement present, I am asking him to spare your life this last time. If he sees you again, Gio, I guarantee you it will be your death."

Whatever this charade had all been about, Gio Moretti looked almost smug—like somehow, he'd won this round. If I did actually know anything about him, I'd say he had just gotten what he wanted. Both Lucky and Anthony—Gio's own father—looked like they wanted to set the man ablaze. To make sure he died a fiery death and then—only after he took his last breath—they'd piss on him to put the flames out.

"Now get the fuck out of my party because, dear brother. You. Are. Dead. To. Me." Bella growled, turning on her heel and stomping her way back to the table.

The party reignited around us again as the fight ended, and Gio took off with Apollo hot on his heels. Al was hanging in the shadows behind me, never too far from Bella. Even with the mass chaos that erupted, Lucky and Bella cuddled close to each other, smiling. I finished *another* glass of wine and smiled to myself as well—the fermented grapes made my current predicament almost amusing.

"Shots!" I shouted, motioning for Octavia, Marco and Al to indulge with me. Al hesitated for a moment. Turning to follow his gaze, I saw my brother whisking Bella out of the ballroom—to go to pound town, I was sure. Ha! "Off duty, while they get it on." I handed Al a shot, laughing harder at my own joke than he was, but at least I was having fun.

"To sexy panties and the sexy ladies who wear them!" Marco shouted and without a second thought, I finished off the liquor. Laughing mid-swallow, I tried my best not to choke.

"I can't believe I toasted to that." Octavia shook her head and rolled her eyes.

"Sienna." My father called over the music, motioning for me to come to him.

"Another! To brutal contracts and sex with the same person for the rest of your life!" I cheered but all three of them stopped to look at me as I tossed another one back. "No? Just me? Right." I spun in a circle and shook my hips as I approached my father.

"Enjoying yourself?" he asked, amused, as I leaned against my mother who wasn't much more sober than I was.

"Dandy. Call the meeting," I said, turning a sad smile to my mother.

"Sienna. We can wait a little…" I raised a hand and paused him.

"The reasoning behind my procrastination is childish. This is as good as it will get for me. Call the meeting." I dropped my empty wine glass on his table and with my same sad smile, I went back to the trio of devious alcoholics… well, except Octavia.

"What the fuck?" Al growled.

"You know, contracts and whatnot." I ignored him and called over the handsome bartender. "Another round please, but something with a little fire." He smirked and pulled a fresh bottle from the ice bin.

"Dah, dah, dah, dah, dah, dah!" I sang out, trying to imitate the beat to that *Pitbull* song. "Fireball!" I passed the glasses around, opting to take Octavia's myself when she so rudely declined.

I ran out to the dance floor after one more shot, pulling all of them along with me. My red-soled shoes were killing me but pain was beauty and I looked damn good shaking my ass to the music. Song after song played, and I enjoyed myself for what felt like the first time in months.

"Let's go," Al ordered, standing behind me with his arms crossed.

"Nope! I don't wanna!" I whined like a disobedient child—the obnoxious foot stomp and all.

"Now!" he commanded once more, grabbing my arm when I went to sway and hauling me back to the table for my clutch.

"Every party has a pooper and that's why we invited you!" I sang loudly, and Octavia and our mother laughed. "Party pooper!" I danced and pointed both fingers at him, giggling until the room spun and he had to hold me upright.

"Christ," Al muttered, wiping a hand over his face the same time my father chuckled. "Here we go, Sienna." Al tried picking me up but I swatted him away.

"I can do it all by… myself!" I snagged my purse and started to walk—albeit a little sideways—to the elevators.

"It's true what they say you know." It was a statement, not a question, and boldly offered in the most annoying of voices.

"Fucking Christ. Why're you still here, you fucking bitch?" I growled at Tatianna, staring at the elevator and silently begging the doors to open.

"Apollo's dick, it's as big as everyone says it is." She wiped her lips for added effect, and I saw red.

The picture had been painted and I wanted to fucking vomit. I turned to Al but his flushed face told me all I needed to know. She wasn't lying. When they'd taken her from the room, she no doubt fucked Apollo and the guards to save her own ass. First, this bitch had broken my dress code and then—for that extra "fuck you" factor—she had shit all over the unspoken girl code.

"Thanks again, Al." She smirked at him, rubbing a hand down his arm.

The backstabber at my side, my best friend, openly returned the gesture. The knife Apollo had firmly planted in my back was twisted in a circle—Al's grip on it was relentless. This fucking cunt had been attempting to interfere with everything I loved my entire life. It was bad enough Lucky kept her around for a while, but now... Apollo and Al too?

"Sienna..." Al prompted and I shrugged off his hold. "Don't," I grunted.

"Now, now. They both did talk about you afterwards. They were worried about how you might react—delicate feelings and all." Tatianna gloated, and I stabbed the elevator call button angrily.

"Get the fuck out of my face," I growled at her. I tried to take a deep breath but I choked.

"Sienna." Al stepped between us, but the action only served to further piss me off—*was he trying to protect her?*

"Oh man, this is fucking rich." I laughed humorlessly. The sudden ding alerted me to the elevator's arrival and I stepped towards it with Al following at my heel.

"Let me know if you want me to suck your dick some more after you put the little Princess to bed," Tatianna propositioned behind Al's back, and his large frame couldn't twist fast enough to grab onto me.

I dove around him and once free of his interference, I pummeled into her poorly-doctored frame, taking her down in a pile of fake tits and lip-fillers. I rolled her onto her back and twisted her hair into a tight grip. Tugging her forward, I made sure we were eye-level—I wanted her to see the punch as it landed. The resulting shriek that escaped her, as her nose burst wide open and leaked red pools onto her white dress, did little to soothe the anger coursing through me. However, I only got the one punch in, before Al was on me, pulling me into the elevator as another party guest went to Tatianna's aid.

"Do not fucking speak to me. I am spending the night in my apartment, alone. We'll talk tomorrow," I ordered Al. I could tell he wanted to argue but his phone went off, and he muttered something about Lucky needing him.

I didn't hesitate when the door opened on my floor, and I charged to my apartment. I ignored his subtle hints, indicating he wanted to talk, and he sighed before calling out his goodnight. Once in my apartment, I went directly to the bathroom and kicked off my heels under the sink. The room started spinning as the adrenaline of fighting with Tatianna wore off. I was still pretty fucking drunk, and in my infinite wisdom, I decided I didn't want the party to end. I walked right back to the elevators, taking them up to Lucky's floor.

"My eyes are covered and I am not exiting the foyer until you tell me you're dressed!" I shouted, opening Lucky's door enough to hear Bella's giggles. "Lucky, she's giggling and that isn't a good sign in the throes of passion!"

Obscuring my vision with my hands, I wandered around his entryway as I mumbled to myself and knocked shit over. When I hit the wall and almost fell, Bella started laughing and I uncovered my eyes. "How long have you been standing there?" I asked her.

"Long enough to question your sanity and the color of the bottom of your feet." She motioned downward, and I realized I was still barefoot.

"Fuck!" I stumbled again as I scratched my head. "Where did I put them? They were brand new… and super fucking expensive." Looking around like my shoes might somehow randomly appear, I stumbled once more.

"I'm sure you'll find them somewhere." Bella escorted me into the kitchen and handed me a bottle of water.

"Or Tatianna fucking snuck back in and took them, that treacherous troll." I snarled around the rim of the bottle, and both of us broke out in hysterics.

"Where are your shoes?" Lucky's question reignited our incessant laughter. "You've both lost it but, my love, I need to go debrief with Apollo. I won't be long."

Just hearing his name, I cringed and I knew Bella saw it—but like the kind soul she was—she didn't say a word. With little regard for what was up and what was down, I started to slide off my stool when Lucky pulled me upright with a scowl.

"They were three-grand, Sienna. They better not be lost." Heading towards the elevator, he waited.

"I didn't fucking lose them!" I yelled as he stepped inside. I waited for it to close before I spoke again. "I just lost where I put them!"

Once we fought through another bout of laughter, I replayed the altercation with Tatianna downstairs. I tried to breathe deep but I almost lost my composure as I begged Bella to tell me when it was *my* turn. I was strong in so many things, but I was still a woman and for once, I wanted to be taken care of. Poor Bella was at a loss for words as I unloaded onto her, and I was unable to hold back my own tears any longer.

"You were told to stay in your suite!" Al stormed into the kitchen. "Sienna… are you crying?" he asked, his concern evident.

"Fuck off." I growled, swatting at the offending tears.

"The hell happened?" Bella demanded from him.

"We left the party and waited for the elevator when Tatianna walked up. She made a few snide comments and Sienna whooped her ass. She yelled at me in the elevator and said she was spending the night on her floor. I checked the cameras when the alarm alerted me to the door opening and I saw her stumbling her ass here."

"Fuck you! I am fine in the tower with the Queen. You can fuck right off. I'm sure Tatianna will swallow your cock even easier now that I knocked her teeth loose." I winced the moment the words left my mouth.

"Fucking hell, Sienna, you love Apollo. What's the deal?" To that, to his bold retort, my head snapped up. Hobbling off the stool, I charged past Bella and into Al's face.

"Anyone! Anyone could suck your dick! Not her! You're my best friend. You know how much I hate her!" I roared.

Bella and Al exchanged a few more words while I—still somewhat in a drunken emotional haze—ignored the rest of their conversation. "You can stay here. I will escort her back," Bella offered and Big Al relented, his eyes openly apologetic.

"How is she still alive?" Bella muttered in the elevator, and I snorted in response.

"Not even officially an Agostino and so bloodthirsty already." I feigned shock with a hand to my chest.

Once back in my apartment, Bella stayed with me for a little bit as I found my shoes and got ready for bed. When she left, and I was alone again in my own silence, I realized how unnecessary I'd behaved to Al. He was my best friend and could do as he pleased, but it still stung that he touched her. I needed to go back upstairs and apologize. I shoved my toes into a pair of socks just as my phone rang from an unknown number.

"Sienna. Get the fuck out of your apartment." Gio's voice thundered through the receiver. "I've called your security detail but they won't make it in time."

"What?" I pulled the cellular device away from my ear and stared at the screen in confusion.

"You fucking heard me. Shit is fucked up." His respirations were strained while the panic in his voice was disconcerting. "They know about you, Sienna. I need you out of your apartment—go upstairs to Lucky. Stay on the phone with me until I know you're with his men."

Something in his tone told me not to question him and I darted for my door. Thankfully, I'd changed into comfortable yoga pants and a light sweater after Bella had left. I snatched my sneakers as I ran, my phone glued to my ear. My brain was on autopilot, forcing my legs to move in an effort to save myself. I peeked out of my door and saw that the hallway was empty. I hit the button to call the elevator, and darted back into the apartment to wait, in case they were already riding up to my floor.

"Where are you?" Gio asked.

"Elevator is two floors away," I whispered, exhaling with relief when it opened and it was empty. "I'm inside now."

"Good. Good…" he muttered, sighing deeply. "It wasn't supposed to be like this, Sienna. I had it all handled until the Russians lost their shit over Yuri."

I was shocked he was so forthcoming with his information; information that would ultimately lead to his demise *when* Apollo and Lucky found out. Then it all clicked as I fumbled to enter the security code in order to ride up to my brother's penthouse—*Yuri had two sons.* And Al had confirmed that the Russian leader had been removed from the equation and his sons were blaming Gio for it. I was *again* collateral damage in the stupid games that men played.

"I'm here," I announced, unsure of how to respond otherwise.

"Confirm you're with Lucky. Your detail is two minutes away." Gio shouted to someone in the background, the sounds of passing traffic echoing through the speakers.

"Oh, my God…" I mumbled, as I took in Lucky's foyer.

"What is it?" Gio demanded, but I was rendered mute by the shock.

There was broken glass everywhere. The tables, potted plants and anything else that was neatly arranged in the foyer had been flipped, smashed and scattered around the room. There were red fingerprints on the wall and streaks of blood across the tile leading into his apartment. I could hear a man groaning and my heart dropped into my stomach when I recognized the sound—*Al.*

"Bella!" When she didn't answer, I growled. "Fuck, Gio. The place is a mess, there's blood and I don't see your sister."

"Motherfucker. It was a ploy, goddamn it." I could hear what sounded like him punching something. "Your security is close. I need to go—they didn't want you." *Though, at the time, I missed the irony of his words. Because the funny thing was… no one ever wanted me.*

"Get her, Gio. Please…" I said just before I heard his command— he was headed to Dominic's place.

I tiptoed into the apartment, looking at every corner in the room in case someone was still there. I didn't hear anything outside of the pained moans, so I carefully followed the trail of blood. I took a few more steps and I thought I heard another voice but my mind was playing tricks on me—no one was there. Just then, I realized I hadn't called anyone on our team. I was trusting a fucking Moretti with protecting me.

I tucked myself into the shadows, so that I could still view all possible vantage points, and pulled my cell phone to my ear. I called Lucky first but it rang and rang, with no answer. I hung up and immediately called him back but I got the same result. The motherfucker wasn't picking up, and again I was left to deal with the consequences of *his* actions. As much as it killed my pride, I dialed Apollo next.

Just as he answered with his crude tone, I saw movement. Al had slumped over onto his back. He was covered in so much blood and his eyes were closed, but even from this distance I could see his chest rising and falling. I charged towards him, ignoring the broken glass crunching beneath my feet as I slid on his blood to get to him.

"We're busy, Sienna…" But Apollo's cold hiss softened when he heard me yelling and sobbing.

"She's gone! Bella isn't in the apartment and Al's barely holding on! Don't die on me, damn it, Al!" I begged, holding my hands to the wound on his chest.

"Miss Agostino!" I heard the familiar voice of my security detail shouting from the foyer, and I dropped my phone next to Al.

"In here!" I yelled, and the team created a protective circle around me, while a few others swept the apartment.

Moments later, my brother darted into the room, shouting orders as the medical technicians followed. He looked me over quickly before barking at my team and disappearing into his surveillance room—with me hot on his tail. Apollo was clicking away on the computer as I pulled out my phone. I sent an email to Andersen, demanding he start tracking the phone number Gio had called me from.

I was lost in the shuffle when my father and Anthony Moretti stormed in. We made eye contact for a few seconds and my body shuttered in disgust at the man's glare. *He knew—Anthony Moretti knew.* He knew what his son had planned. I could see it all in his eyes. He was lying through his teeth about being kept in the dark. His anger was genuine—that much was true—however, it was over Bella being taken instead of me. Somehow, I just knew it.

Motherfucker.

Lucky and Anthony started yelling and shoving at each other as my brother blamed Gio. The pissing match was getting old and my phone beeped with an incoming text from Andersen. He confirmed that he needed to talk with me but would get me the details I had requested.

"Maybe he didn't physically do this. But sure as fuck, his actions caused it!" Lucky roared at Anthony, while Apollo and my father scoured the computers frantically for information.

"What do we have?" Dom barreled into the room, just as his cell phone rang. Apollo stepped closer to listen, still all but ignoring my presence. *Asshole.*

"Fuck!" Dom started cursing up a storm, punching the walls and freaking out. "I want them both back. Right fucking now!" He seethed in rage.

I had overheard the entire conversation, and I watched in anger as Apollo's hackles rose and rage contorted his face. You see, during Gio's little impromptu visit to Dom's, he had stolen his brother's pretty little blonde plaything. He had taken the girl in an attempt to trade the Russians for Bella.

It was pretty fucked up when the enemy had protected you more than your own blood.

I was about to announce I had an active tracker following Gio when my father whispered that he had eyes on Bella. They continued in hushed tones amongst themselves for another minute as I caught Anthony staring at me again. Everything inside me cringed at the attention he was paying me, and I couldn't stand it. Another scuffle erupted and my brother shoved Dom back, while Apollo grabbed my wrist and pulled me from the office. Lucky motioned for his men to lock it down with the Moretti's trapped inside.

"Go to the compound," Apollo ordered; though he still did not meet my eyes; instead, he gestured for my security detail to escort me.

I didn't even fight them. I didn't even have the will to do it. Rocco stood tall with a solemn expression on his face as he handed me my shoes. Al had already been removed from the room and panic filled me for a moment. But then, Rocco told me he was fine and I exhaled the breath I didn't realize I'd been holding, and a weight lifted off my chest. Apparently, Al was already in the car with Lucky and Apollo.

"Hey." I answered my phone when I was safely tucked into the car with Rocco.

"Are you all right?" Andersen asked, genuine worry lacing his tone.

"Yeah. Thanks. I appreciate all you did to get me the information so quickly," I said; he started to speak twice and stopped.

"Sienna, I need you to stay safe. Something, everything, in my gut is telling me this isn't over. Those men will clearly not hesitate to hurt you." He sounded so concerned and so sincere, my heart wanted to weep. I promised him I would, and disconnected before he could pester me further.

I went back to the compound to ensure my mother and Octavia were okay. It didn't take a genius to know that they were probably sick with worry. Rocco kept looking back at me with questions in his eyes, but he knew better than to ever ask them. He knew I handled shit in my own way.

The car had barely made it to the center of the horseshoe driveway when two female blurs hightailed it to me. I could hear the whimpers and the hushed prayers of thanks directed to God. At the end of the day, it was family who brought it all together; some members just didn't want to participate.

"I've died a thousand deaths since I got that phone call!" My mother ripped me out of the car, crying harder when she saw me limping on my bloodied feet.

"I'm fine, *madre*," I whispered as I held tightly to her, allowing my own tears to finally descend.

CHAPTER 20

APOLLO DELUCA

I couldn't even look at her. Chaos had broken loose and she stood there, so asthenic and dispirited. After the engagement party, I'd followed Gio home to send him a message. It was a brutal warning to haul his ass out of the city and to never return. He had expected me, of course—suddenly very sober *and* very forthcoming with the information on his darling brother.

Gio planned to use Dominic Moretti's only weakness—Persephone, the blonde girl—to take the man down; a plan I was by no means in agreement with. I warned him to let sleeping dogs lie… to let the big boys handle it. But I could tell by his face—before I smashed it in repeatedly—that there'd be no accordance between us.

The ride to Bella's location was filled with ominous silence. Once we got eyes on her, I was being sent in first to extricate her before full-out pandemonium ensued. We were on the outskirts of the city, surrounded by trees and foliage. An old farmhouse was in the center of the clearing. The water lines around the foundation explained the unkempt condition—we were in flood lands.

As I wandered the building in the shadows, I could hear Gio demanding his sister be returned in place of the blonde ghost girl. I could only hear so much as I remained hidden, but evidently, none of this was going according to Gio's plan.

Yuri's son, Alexander, had taken Bella and Gio was slowly losing control—his alliance with the Russians was falling apart at the seams. I gained entry through the rear door and remained silent as Gio and Alexander argued further down the hall. I accessed the room in which we had suspected Bella was being held—there were no windows and tactically it made the most sense. And I flinched at the sight of the Moretti girl—Lucky's fucking fiancée—restrained to the bed.

Downtrodden. Beaten. Destroyed. She was covered in her own blood and bruises were already coloring her exposed flesh.

"Fifth door, target acquired. Go, go, go," I ordered, closing off the room behind me as gunshots erupted from the surrounding perimeter of the house.

Bella was a tiny thing on a good day, but laying handcuffed to this bed—open wounds and bruises peppering her—she looked beyond fragile. Her shirt had been pulled up around her head to expose her bra, while her breasts were haphazardly being held in place. She was incoherently mumbling to herself, telling the air that her saviors had come for them *both*. I'd just managed to get her hands free and put her shirt on when I heard the whimpers from the closet.

"Are you all right?" I yelled through the door, hearing Lucky's voice and two more gunshots erupt in the distance.

"*This* changes nothing. You're still fucking dead," Lucky growled from the hallway.

"I didn't do it for you. Tell Bella I'm sorry," Gio replied.

I opened the closet to find the source of the whimpering, and a slumped body rolled over to look at me. Through the mess of dirt and grime, two of the shiniest—yet broken—blue eyes I'd ever seen opened. Persephone stared back at me, a stark contrast to the woman I'd seen at the docks.

"Fuck." I growled, startling the tiny girl still curled up in my arms. From the ground, the once fiery blonde stared vacuously past me. It was the mental wounds that would haunt her for the rest of her life, not the physical ones—an outcome I myself knew all too well.

"Persephone…" Bella mumbled in her haze of half-consciousness. Lucky charged into the room, beelining for the one person in this world he could not breathe without.

"We're safe now, Bella. They've got me. I'm okay," Persephone assured her.

I announced our exit strategy to the team and we made it out safely. Men flanked each side of us, as we slid through the rear door and into the idling SUV.

Lucky and Bella climbed into the third row of seats and I placed Persephone down on the second row, next to me. She was covered in the filth of her previous surroundings—something that would normally trigger my discomfort. But now, for some reason, I didn't care. She cuddled herself into a ball against the window, slapping my hands away when I tried to inspect her wounds.

I turned to the rear and saw Bella curled into Lucky, seeking his warmth and protection. Gio and Alexander were in the wind, but the mission wasn't a total failure now that the two innocents had been saved. Persephone was a gorgeous little spitfire, whose tiny frame did little to match her big attitude—she wasn't easily broken. That meant the longer that Alexander had her, the more extensive her internal fracturing would be.

"Drop me off at the first gas station you see," the blonde-haired, blue-eyed seemingly soulless girl muttered.

"No." I barked out the singular word and ordered Al to keep driving.

"Yes," she retorted. "One prison for another and another. Charming."

"You're not a prisoner any longer. You will have your own room. A private doctor to treat you and the lap of luxury while we figure everything out." She knocked my hand away when I tried blotting the blood on her chin.

"Rest assured the actions I've witnessed are of no concern to the police. I know who you are and how this goes. No threats are needed for me to keep my mouth shut. A simple thank you to you both for saving me. And a goodbye at the gas station is my only consolation prize." She sat perfectly poised, staring straight ahead.

"It doesn't work like that. You will stay until we say you can leave." My tone was harsh and clipped. She was already getting under my skin, and the next words out of her luscious mouth burrowed her even deeper.

"*'Though those that are betray'd do feel the treason sharply, yet the traitor stands in worse case of woe.'*" I could feel the heat from her glare, and it burned more powerfully than the sun. "I'm not stupid. I'm not a fucking snitch and I won't be your plaything."

"A lady after my own heart, knows her Shakespeare." Gripping her wrist tightly in my hand, I tugged her face to face. "And you'll be whatever the fuck I want you to be. Now how about we start with you being thankful and quiet."

The car filled with tension—the simmering rage she ignited inside me eviscerated the patience I sought to bestow. She was exhausted but she didn't feel safe enough to drop her guard. She assumed that because I wasn't letting her go, my intentions were anything other than honorable, which of course they were—well, to an extent anyway. I'd most honorably destroy what I could only assume was an addicting enrapture between her legs.

"You're safe. You can sleep." Propping herself upright and crossing her arms over her chest, she ignored me.

When her head dipped a second later, she shook herself and sat straighter. "*'Therefore was I created with a stubborn outside,'*" she said, her tone laced in boredom.

"You're more akin to Shakespeare than I presumed," I laughed. "Hmm, let's finish that saying, shall we?" A scowl lit up her face. "*'With an aspect of iron, that when I come to woo ladies, I fright them.'*"

A crazed cackle left her as confused silence filled the car. "You can be stubborn and made of iron, but you don't scare me. I have nothing left to give so I don't dare presume to be frightened anymore." Sliding down the bench and further away from me, she acted as if the added distance between us would protect her when *il mietitore* came for a bite.

"They're both out," Lucky acknowledged, the car pulling into the driveway of the compound.

"I'll put her in my suite. Lock her down until she's well enough to start talking." I opened the door when we came to a stop and slid the meager girl into my arms.

"The doc is five out," Al announced, heading inside where I could see Sienna was waiting for him.

Her face was bare, clean of makeup, and her eyes were filled with unshed tears as she watched us enter. Once she seemed pleased that I wasn't hurt, she looked at the girl still in my arms. With a soft pattering of bandaged feet on the marble floor, Sienna stepped to Persephone and wiped her dirt-tinged hair from her face.

I carried her upstairs to my room. The moment the door swung open, I inhaled a calming, purging breath. The odor of disinfectant and the feel of the organized space brought my spiraling mind back to the present. I placed Persephone in the center of my bed, to await the doctor's arrival. My California king basically swallowed her whole. She was so little, compared to my size, I could easily break her apart.

Terrible thoughts echoed through the confines of my mind as I questioned just how pink and juicy her pussy really was. The girl was riddled with abuse and tainted by trauma but there was something about fixing my broken toys, just to break them again, that left me salivating. I was a monster among men and this girl was going to get a front row seat. I'd have my fill of her lush body and find out some answers along the way.

Within a short time, the doctor arrived and looked her over. She awakened during his examination, and her bedeviled gaze stared at me in silence as he poked and prodded her. We would've examined her for signs of forced penetration, but the moment he tried to take a peek, we were both greeted by a vicious wildcat. She masticated, clawed and thrashed against our hold.

"Calm the fuck down," I ordered, but she ignored me.

I threw my large body on top of hers, pinning both of her hands in one of mine above her head. Sitting on her hips, I used my legs to hold her down, her writhing frame doing little to calm the raging erection pushing against my slacks.

"Oh. Daddy." She moaned, dragging her tongue across her upper canines seductively before snapping and snarling her puppy teeth in my direction.

"Do it," I ordered the doctor, gesturing to the syringe in his hand and at the ready.

"Oh. No. I'm so much more fun without the drugs." When the tip of the 27-inch gauge embedded into her arm, she didn't react at all. "Need me sedated to get it up? I get it. Pussy." She hawked her saliva back, but my free hand latched over her mouth before she could eject it.

I ground my erection into her stomach. "Clearly, I have no issue with you being awake and crazy... or silent and sedated." I smirked at her gasp of breath. "Now, you're going to learn to be a good little girl, because good little girls get what they want... after I get mine."

The doctor stepped to the other side of the room, offering a semblance of privacy as I basically threatened the girl with rape and bodily harm. Her eyes started to grow heavy and the fight dwindled from her limbs. I sat back and released her arms—they slowly drifted down and protectively wrapped around her torso. I climbed off the bed. Pulling the covers over her, I was caught off guard.

Her right hand raised, and reaching across the sheets, she slashed my left cheek with her nails. "I-I-I'll neverrrrr tell..." she whispered with a cheeky grin and closed eyes, before collapsing back onto the bed. I hovered above her, dropping spots of red across her porcelain flesh.

"Fuck." The doctor stepped forward to assist me until self-preservation won out and he fled the room.

I entered my attached bathroom and stripped off my suit, along with what felt like the last shards of my sanity. I turned the shower as hot as it would go, steam billowing in heavy clouds. I didn't wait to test the temperature before stepping inside—the pain gave me the moment of concentration I needed.

I was always calculating the best outcomes, devising future endeavors and the roistering of blood that would be spilt. My dick got hard just thinking about it, growing erect and landing heavily mid-torso. I tilted my head back and let the scalding water clean my freshly-delivered gash.

Persephone passed out in my bed meant I couldn't appease the heavy hammer between my legs—not with her anyway… not yet. I gripped my dick hard in my right hand and pressed my left to the glass wall. After a good couple of strokes, my body went tight. I closed my eyes and let my thoughts devour me whole.

Persephone's face burned brightly behind my eyelids—her blue eyes so lost and confused but filled with fire. Her flirtations and endless taunts pushed against the fence that protected her from the proverbial hellhound, buried just beneath the surface and threatening to crash through it and destroy her—piece by delicious-fucking-piece. I'd bet she'd make the sexiest noises when she came, like a cat purring in satisfaction but I prayed it sounded like a terrifying lion's roar instead. I pumped a few more strokes and then my mind altered course.

And suddenly I saw Sienna standing in the security room, absolutely broken. It was the way her eyes filled with a haunting sadness before planning to enact her revenge. The girl was a fucking savage against those who hurt the ones she loved.

There was something different in the way I responded to Sienna. She had so many sides to her and each was more attractive than the last. She was a challenge and at the same time, she was my forbidden fruit. Temptation served as the only barrier between all of mankind and its destruction, and she made the sin that much sweeter.

"Oh, fuck." One last image of Sienna covered in blood, a body—her foe—at her feet and I came… *fucking* hard.

Taking a deep breath, I rinsed off in the shower and stepped onto the damp tile floor. I stood at the sink and stared at myself in the mirror. The room was clouded in steam, and as I approached my obscured reflection, all of my intricate and dark tattoos rose from the heavy air like a *demoni* coming out of hell fire.

I looked closed off, shut down. My eyes struggled to focus and I knew I was still teetering on the edge of collecting myself and plummeting to the depths of my insanity. I had one more thing I needed to do to screw my head on straight. Once I dealt with Persephone, I needed to handle Michael—my dearly devoted foster father—who was still on ice and waiting for me. I was a busy man but the Devil always finds work for idle hands. I managed to spend a few hours getting time in at the warehouse before Persephone woke up.

Vacant. Disoriented. Lost. Submissive.

I opened my mouth to direct her to the shower when she did the strangest thing. The thing that normally, I would've rewarded her for with my hard cock parting her lips or plunged between her ass cheeks. The thing that I normally sought in the women I fucked. Except in this moment—in the here and now—she was so damaged... the sight made my stomach turn.

"Get up." I motioned for her to rise from her position at my feet, where she had knelt and dropped her head in the perfect submissive pose. "Get up, Persephone," I ordered again.

She rose to her full height, eyes down casted, and in one fluid movement, removed all of her clothing. My entire body locked into place, every single muscle frozen, as my brain tried to remind my dick that she was too damaged to play with. Only the message was intercepted and my dick pushed against my grey sweatpants. Persephone didn't hesitate to reach inside and grab hold of me. And I jumped and snatched her wrist.

"The fuck are you doing?" I growled. Her grasp was tight and her bottom lip pouty.

"You know you want it." The bitch had the balls to tease me, as if I would leave any piece of her unscathed.

"No, but *you* know what it is that I do want." I held her wrist tighter than was necessary, enjoying the way she flinched in response. "We can get to this... later. I have some questions you need to answer first."

I lifted her upwards, watching as her handful-sized breasts bounced. I grabbed my discarded suit jacket and draped it over her shoulders, willing myself into my camouflage of control. She twirled from my grip and galloped—literally—to my bed. She spun in the very center of it several times before tossing the jacket to the side and flopping onto the sheets—her white porcelain skin a shiny beacon against the black comforter.

"Once upon a time, there was a beautiful Princess who the Kingdom forbade to ever leave her castle." She curled into a ball, somehow making herself appear even smaller. "All around her, the townspeople were worked to death, beaten and starved. But she had no clue in her ivory tower in the sky—the Princess never knew true pain a day in her life."

"I need you to answer a few of my questions in regards to Dominic Moretti." I paused to see if she'd react, but she kept stroking her dirt-ladened hair while humming to herself.

"See that's the thing about pain… The King and her Prince brothers thought they were protecting her but they made her weak. If you've never experienced true pain, then when the sky starts falling, you're unable to protect yourself." She smiled sadly, before turning to me with a devilish grin. "Those who have felt true pain, shall not falter. And I…. Well, I'll never tell."

"You'll talk. You'll give me what I need. You see, little girl, I have absolutely no qualms about administering extreme pain in whatever way I see fit to get what I want. And you have what I want, just here…" I knelt on the bed and tapped her temple. "And you'll give it to me."

She shot out of bed, as if burned by scalding hot water. I stepped back as she started walking in circles around the room—some twisted nursery rhyme chattering her lips on repeat.

Each time I tried to step in her way, she pivoted to go the opposite direction and her little song got louder. I grabbed her by her arms to bring her movement to a halt.

But it resulted in the counter effect; suddenly the wildcat had returned and she thrashed against my hold with enough force I lost my footing.

To avoid falling on top of her, I pinned her back to my front and locked her arms down, as I turned and landed on my spine. She felt like a small child within my grip but the rest of me didn't get that memo, and I grew even harder as she twisted and wriggled to get away from me.

Then she spun, smashing her chest to my stomach and throwing her legs around my waist to straddle me.

"Just like that." She moaned into my ear.

"Enough, Persephone!" I blustered and shook her, causing her to sit up straight while her breasts lifted higher. "Dom is missing and I know you have an idea of where he'd go."

"I'm not his keeper." She threw her head back to stare at the ceiling, attempting to grind her hips on my lap. "He's mine."

"Christ, enough." I gripped her neck firmly in one hand and jerked her back and off me. I shook with anger as her little nails clawed at my hands. Her limbs swung and kicked as I walked her over to the closest wall and pinned her in place, my hold on her throat unrelenting.

"Please." She gurgled and I released her, just enough for her to inhale deeply.

"Please, what?" I asked; *il mietitore* had pried himself from his cage. "Don't fuck with me, little girl. You'll have my dick when I get what I want from you. Once you answer my questions, I'll fucking own this." My free hand traveled down her body to grip her dripping pussy.

"Please…" she clamored again.

"Give me." I leaned closer to her face, biting at her cheek. "What I." I inhaled her neck, just under her ear. "Want."

She wanted to see how hard she could fuck with me, but she had no clue just how hard I liked to fuck.

Her little games wouldn't work. I'd get what I wanted and then she'd milk my cock until it was empty of. Every. Last. Drop.

But life had a funny way of giving you the middle finger. She collapsed into my arms and passed… right. The. Fuck. Out. "Fuck." I growled the singular word before grabbing the hospital gown the doctor left behind and carrying her limp form into the bathroom.

I filled the clawfoot tub with warm soapy water and slowly

dropped her inside. I held my breath, waiting for her to wake up again and start thrashing.

Instead, she mewled in a pleased release of air and seemed to settle as I cleaned away the blood, dirt and who knew what else on her. Her broken body told a thousand tales of abuse and trauma, but what had me gritting my teeth to stay calm… were the open wounds on her back. Whip marks.

Once she was tucked back in bed, she woke up, then passed out. Then woke up again. A vicious cycle causing my mind to churn with murderous intent, to thread my next course of action uncontrollably into a pattern of dark thoughts and despair—something I hadn't felt since my very first kill for Mario—the inability to collect myself.

Over and over, we went.

She rattled on, trying to seduce me, and when I declined, she returned to her singing bullshit. Sometimes she'd start walking again but she mimicked as though she was going to climb up the walls.

She was holding all of the answers and I was running out of methods beyond physical abuse to obtain them. A light knock on the door startled me from my reverie and I opened it to find Lucky.

"Why are you rattled?" Lucky asked, slightly amused.

"I'm not fucking rattled. I'm fucking murderous," I said, shaking my head.

"You forget, brother, I've seen you murderous. The room around you will be bathed in blood and carnage. Yet, we'd find you in the center of the chaos… immaculate. *That's* not *this*." He motioned up and down, and I took in my untucked and wrinkled shirt in shock.

"I don't hurt women," I said and he nodded. "But she makes me want to."

"Okay." He placed a comforting hand to my shoulder and I quickly pulled away.

I stormed around the room, practically crawling up the walls myself while tugging my hair out from its root. "I want to murder her with my bare hands. Watch the life drain from her eyes and then revive her to do it all over again. I want to bury my dick in her and wait until the light goes out in those pretty blue eyes. Only letting her breathe when I feel her orgasm writhe beneath me."

"You didn't do any of those things to her though… right?" I wanted to throttle him for such a question, but his concern was valid.

"No, you fucking asshole. That's probably why I am crawling out of my own skin," I scoffed as he walked up to her prone form.

"Persephone. Hey!" he probed; however, arousing her attention nicely didn't work. "Get her in the chair." I did as Lucky instructed, trying to hide my amusement at what I knew was to come.

"Before you touch her, just be prepared…" I warned. Her eyes were dry and vacant. No one was home; the girl was just an empty cavern of mumbling nonsense.

"Big bad Apollo scared of the little kitten's claws?" Lucky taunted. My only response was a smirk, as I waited for the show.

And just like that, the tepid girl turned into a vicious animal, striking out against him. She thrashed and screamed as he forcibly threw her into the chair.

I handed him straps to hold her down, but I made no attempt to help him any further. If he wanted to laugh, to act as if I was incompetent in my handling of her, then the son of a bitch could suffer while his poorly made assumptions were used against him.

"Ow! Fucking bitch!" He tugged his bicep from her teeth. He tried to talk over her yells and spewed curses, but it was to no avail.

"Let her tire herself out." Stepping away from the assortment of colorful expletives being hurled around the room, we sat down at the small table next to the window.

"She's been like that the entire time?" he asked and I nodded.

"Why do you think she was laying on the floor? The moment she woke up, she ran circles in the room. She tried getting into my closet and when I stopped her, she dropped like dead weight. Hasn't moved since."

"Jesus, they put her through the paces…." he muttered. "Bella and I are pushing up the wedding. We are going to get married in a couple of days. I don't want to wait anymore."

"Congratulations." I understood he wanted to give her some light in the darkest of her days. He went further into the specifics of it all. The ceremony would be held in the backyard, here at the family compound. He stopped mid-sentence when we heard Persephone start her story time again.

"That little girl had shimmering blonde hair that glinted with strokes of silver in the sun. Everyone envied those silver highlights, wanting pieces for themselves. But they'd take and take… till there was nothing left of the little girl."

"It's been nonstop stories of a little blonde girl," I said, shrugging on a heavy sigh.

"Persephone, I need your help. You have the answers that could save so many other girls from what you went through." Barren eyes stared back at us. "If you tell us all the places Dom held you, we can stop both bad men." Silence stretched on for minutes, her unaesthetic gaze staring at nothing and no one.

"Both? Not all?" Her questions were barely above a whisper. "You want answers to help your problem. Not fix the bigger problem."

"One step at a time, my dear," Lucky responded.

"You're all the same," she mused.

"We are *not* the same." My thunderous voice boomed then echoed across the space. I locked my hands around the arms of the chair, our noses almost touching. The vacancy in her dead eyes was replaced with an icy blue fire. "There she is," I muttered with a knowing smirk.

"Prove yourself differently then. Tell me your plans for destroying the greater evil? Do you have a plan outside of taking down those who wronged *your* family?" Silence met her question, and she answered my smirk with a matching one—just as disturbed but perhaps more depraved. "You only care to hurt those who hurt *you*. When there are thousands more being hurt every day."

"Do you honestly think, today, we can stop them all?" Lucky said, and her head snapped in his direction.

"The biggest offender of them all is related to your future wife. Will you kill him too? Will you destroy the last of her family because of their travesties against strangers? She won't be able to see their destruction as I do." Her eyes were somehow both hardened and chillingly aware.

Lucky opened his mouth to speak, but she ignored him and looked back towards me. "You heard my whispered cries. You saw the bruises on my skin. More than once, you watched and saw his anger, his wrath against me. And you did exactly what you are... *nothing.*"

"Says the girl shacking up with the worst of them. We're giving you an out here, if you help us, and instead you protect him," I challenged her, but she smiled even more cruelly.

"Is he the worst? How would you know? Maybe he is trying to be king at what he does so he's the only one, narrowly saving millions of lives?" Her logic made absolutely no fucking sense. I started to tell her as much, to contest her disillusioned words, but I watched her light fade as she tucked herself back into her happy place.

She rose from the chair, once I unhooked her, and stripped again in front of both of us. When she went to drop to her knees at my feet, I stopped her and ordered her to shower.

Lucky and I agreed we needed to push her... but I was unsure how much more the girl could take. She walked out of the bathroom, dripping wet, just as Lucky was about to leave.

"Persephone. Get dressed. I showed you where your clothes are." Rising to her feet with a muttered *"yes, master,"* she sauntered off.

Her coping mechanisms and unsettling behaviors were clear signs of extensive psychological and emotional distress. Repetitive and severe injury to the girl's psyche, after surviving extremely traumatic events, had resulted in the impairment of her daily functioning and life skills.

But at the end of the day, she wasn't the bigger problem—she was just a clue, a piece of the puzzle. Dominic, Gio and Alexander still had sins they needed to atone for. And *il mietitore* was happy to oblige.

CHAPTER 21
SIENNA AGOSTINO

"You can't be serious?" Octavia asked as I descended the stairs and headed towards the foyer.

"Work doesn't end just because there is a new threat to the family," I stated, my tone dead and flat—I needed to get out of this house.

"Sienna. You… you almost." She paused when I turned to look at her.

"If I am going to be taken out, the least I can do is be a dead *Fortune 500* CEO and look damn good doing it." I winked with a slight smile—one Octavia clearly didn't buy—as she scowled at me.

"What're you doing here?" Andersen asked the moment I stepped off the elevator.

"Uhm. Working." I shrugged my shoulders and turned towards my office with him on my heels.

"How are you?" he asked and his concern threatened to shatter my resolve.

"I'd be better if you told me that things with the Rockwell matter have been addressed." I powered up my computer and started reviewing emails.

"Sienna." Andersen slammed his fist into my desk, startling me and forcing Farrah to spin right back around and leave us.

"How. Are. You?" He ground each word out, the sincerity in his eyes resounding.

"Honestly?" I questioned.

"No, lie to me," he mumbled.

"I don't know how I am. There are so many things outside of my control with my family and yet here I am, the target of those very things. I just need to get a handle on here and this Philly business. Then I might be okay." I smiled, throwing on my glasses and returning to my computer screen.

"I told you I will move to Philly to set up the new home of *Energia* with you. I just want to know… why the move?" Andersen pulled his suit pants up a bit before sitting down.

"I am…" I stopped short, unsure of how to explain.

My office door flew open, and Amy barely looked up before she started speaking. "How can he be such a sophisticated and successful businessman when he agrees to every—and I repeat—every counteroffer." Amy growled, shoving her tablet into my face.

"Every demand?" I guffawed.

"Every. Goddamn. One." Amy crossed her arms and stormed to the floor-length windows—no doubt upset that she hadn't gotten the chance to show off her legal prowess.

"Shit." I didn't have anything better to say.

"Is Philly food even any good? How is the shopping? Like, what does this mean for me?" Amy asked, turning around with unshed tears in her eyes.

"You can do remote, Amy. I told you I plan to still keep this building and to come back when needed. It's not a far drive." I tried to smile.

"Right…" she murmured, sitting in the chair next to Andersen. "I need, at minimum, a trendy loft overlooking something nice with a good-sized home office. Close to the retail district, and preferably a coffee shop within a one-block radius."

"I'll get right on that for you." I laughed.

I looked to Andersen, who was ignoring Amy, his sole focus on me. I couldn't tell what he was thinking but it was clear something was plaguing his mind. My team didn't need to relocate with me—what we did could be done virtually. I understood their allegiance and the dedication created by our tight bond. But to be so committed, to actually uproot their entire lives to follow me... it warmed my heart.

"So, what is your answer to this?" She tapped her tablet.

"Fuck. Me." I growled, rubbing my forehead.

"My advice is to do that first before you sign on the dotted line. You know... to make sure *that* is as accommodating as the contract." She winked at me and I laughed, while Andersen scowled.

"Schedule the meeting for when he's back in the city," I conceded with a wave of my hand.

"He's here now. He wants to meet before he leaves," Amy deadpanned.

"Fuck. Farrah, come to my office," I ordered over the intercom. Farrah ran into the room with her tablet.

"Mr. Bianchi's assistant and I coordinated dinner for this evening." She waited for my nod before continuing, "Okay... I'll schedule his suggestion for *Vino* tonight at eight?"

I was shocked at how quickly all of this was moving along. The last twenty-four hours had been a whirlwind, and now I was meeting to sign my engagement contract. Farrah scurried off to schedule every-thing, Amy agreed to be present before leaving and Andersen continued to stare at me.

"What?" I asked, refusing to glance up from my emails.

"Nothing. Just... what can I do?" I lifted my head to glare at him in confusion. "You called me yesterday to hunt people down for you. Today, you're scheduling a meeting to get engaged and start your move to Philly."

"And? That's just another day in my world, Andersen." I pulled up the files on an acquisition for the new security monitoring system I was attempting to patent. "Where are we on this?" I asked, nudging the conversation away from me and towards business.

We lost ourselves in hours of contracts, systemware applications and future endeavors. Before I knew it, Amy walked into the room holding her purse. Andersen opened and closed his mouth a few times to speak. Then, shaking his head, he smiled sadly and left the room. I moved to my closet and fixed my hair, freshened my makeup, and smoothed over my dress.

We didn't speak, as we descended inside the elevator and climbed into my car to be taken to *Vino*. The hostess smiled and motioned for us to follow her into the private back room. As soon as the door opened, my heart rate increased. Romano rose to his full height, and it didn't take a fucking idiot to see the man was handsome.

His dark eyes sparkled with an undisclosed emotion, and I could feel my face burn brightly during his slow perusal of my body. With a hungry smirk, he started at the top of my perfectly curled hair, down the deep sheer V-cut of my dress, faltering on the cinched waist showcasing my figure and ending at my peep-toe designer stilettos with my red nail polish on display.

"Now that you have thoroughly eye-fucked my client, shall we?" Amy stormed past him and tossed her paperwork down next to his lawyer.

Romano circled the table and held out the chair for me. Ever the gentleman, he motioned for the waitress to come take my drink order. The room was scattered with his security detail, two of his lawyers and a few of the waitstaff. I had to do a double take when a large shadow caught my attention in the corner. Peiro had a tight grip wrapped around Al's bicep—he was snarling as he stared daggers at Romano. I gave a small shake of my head and a warning glare, hoping he'd stay out of it.

Amy didn't hesitate to speak up, confirming all of my demands were, in fact, being met. Romano sat back in his seat to my right. His suit jacket was draped over the back of his chair and his button-down shirt was open at the collar, revealing a tanned chest with a smattering of dark hair. He didn't say a word—his dark eyes continued to stare through to my soul—while his attorneys handled Amy.

It was this—the way he looked at me—that stalled my breath. And my core tightened—he was fucking hot, okay? This arrangement didn't come down to any money or power, just me. He wanted a strong wife to give him strong kids. He promised faithfulness and from that damn glare, I'd bet he was a top-notch fuck.

"I told you what I wanted," Romano whispered. Leaning into my personal space, he inhaled deeply.

"Me," I stated, and he nodded. A filthy smirk lit up his face, holding all of the dirty promises I'd practically begged Apollo to give to me. His gaze filled me with a sense of perpetual longing being sated; something that I hadn't even known I needed so badly.

"What do you say?" He reached into his pocket and pulled out a velvet box, setting it down silently on the table.

"Jesus Christ." Al growled from the corner, dragging my attention to him. Peiro was holding him back, whispering harshly.

"Someone isn't too pleased, I see," Romano said, tilting his head to glare at Al. But his blatant disregard only made Al's anger worsen. "Is this something I need to know about?"

"Well, you are getting a bride but not a virgin bride, if that's what you're asking." He scoffed as if unfazed. "But no, Al is my best friend."

"You will have your own guard when you come to Philly. No offense to your family, but I will only trust your safety in *my* city with *my* men." He waited a beat. "And I promise not to murder whoever was able to taste what I am sure is the *sweetest* nectar any Goddess could possess." I coughed and shifted under the weight of his glare, straightening my spine and ignoring the last comment.

"I understand. But all of *Energia* will be coming with me," I said, to which he nodded without further explanation.

"And again, I ask… what do you say?" he prompted, resting his hand on my thigh. The intimate gesture forced me to swallow back my sudden urge to jump to my feet.

"So romantic…" I growled, crossing my arms in annoyance.

"What? This?" He opened the box, revealing a gold, retractable pen. "This is merely to sign the contracts now. Ask Amy about the visit clause." He smirked.

I looked to Amy expectantly. "You sign now, and if at any point during your visit to Philly you opt to decline the proposal, the contract is no longer valid."

"Fuck." I sighed.

"I told you what I want." He tugged a stray curl away from my face. "No surprises. No gimmicks. I want you to be happy and content in my city."

"Okay," I conceded and took the proffered pen, much to Al's dismay.

"Leave." Romano growled, and the deep sound caused me to jump. He motioned to his men and they began shuffling everyone out of the room—everyone except Al, who stood chest to chest with Romano's right-hand man.

"Al. Stop. I'll be fine," I muttered, refusing to meet his eyes. He stared at Romano a beat more before exiting and slamming the door behind him.

"I want time with you, before I have to leave the city." Romano motioned for the waitress to refill my glass, while another started putting plates in front of us. "Normally I wouldn't presume to order for you but the chef made this recommendation."

Silver serving trays were laid out in front of me; the heavenly aroma of chicken parmigiana covered in homemade mozzarella and piled high with pasta made my jowls water. I worked out hard in the gym specifically to enjoy my life. And food was life. My eyes lit up and Romano chuckled. Leaning back in his seat, he picked up his own utensils.

I found the interaction between us profoundly… *settling*. All of this unnecessary drama that had surrounded me my entire life ceased. Because with Romano, it felt *easy*. My heart still wasn't in the right place about all of it, but this calm, comfortable quietude took away some of my nerves.

Our dinner conversation was light as we shared our likes and dislikes, what music we loved, what shows we were embarrassed to admit we'd binged and even what we were allergic to. He was a quiet man, reserved—he thought heavily before he spoke. And when he finally gave you a part of himself, you could tell his words were deliberate, almost reticent.

I'd heard the whispers around Philadelphia about his cutthroat tactics; he was known as the silent threat. However, the longer I sat with him, the more I started to notice small similarities between us—like the brick walls we built around ourselves. And when he'd lower his a hair, I was surprised to see how quickly I dropped my own. I wasn't exactly an open book, but he impressed me enough to offer him a few chapters.

"I heard your brother is arranging a private wedding to the Moretti girl." Romano wiped his face with his napkin, depositing it onto his empty plate.

"Of course, as if your fiancée being kidnapped and almost murdered wasn't enough of a reason to want to run away and get married."

He smirked at me. Leaning back in his seat, he took a sip of bourbon. The movement of his mouth caught my attention—it was an act so simple when conducted by anyone else, except him. His lips were heart-shaped and looked smooth, inviting. My chest thrummed loudly in my ears, and my cheeks heated at the perceptive glare he was offering me in return.

"I know you're chomping at the bit to invite me to the wedding." He sunk his teeth into his lip to hide his smile. "Sadly though, I will be in Italy. But why don't we schedule a tour of Philly after the wedding, when I return?"

I couldn't hide the stupid grin that was stretching across my face. "Have your secretary call my secretary." He chuckled at my response.

It was a low and deep sound, and the small hairs on the back of my neck came alive while my lower extremities tingled. I stood up from the table and he motioned for me to exit in front of him. I was about to open the door when he grabbed my elbow and pulled me back. A harsh, calloused hand pressed against my neck and he tugged me to his body, pinning me to the wall. I went to cry out when his tongue sought entrance, his large frame holding me in place.

The taste of Romano mixed with expensive bourbon might just have been my new favorite drug.

"I knew it," he whispered, licking his lips—mere inches from mine. "So sweet." He growled and pulled away from me, before thrusting the door open.

I stumbled ever so slightly as I wandered into the main dining room of the restaurant.

Romano's men stood close to Al, and his glare turned deadly when Romano grabbed my hand and escorted me outside. As we approached my waiting car at the curb, Romano stepped into my space, his calloused thumb stroking my lower lip. With a tap on my nose, he turned on his heel and made his exit.

"Get in the fucking car," Al hissed at my back.

"I know you aren't speaking to me like that." It wasn't a question. I tossed my hair over my shoulder and slid into the back seat as Al climbed into the front passenger's side.

"What the fuck, Sienna!" Al shouted, while I swallowed down the minor twinge of terror his voice invoked. "That looked more fucking cozy than some bullshit dinner."

"We all have our roles to play, Al." I pulled out my phone to respond to my father's request, asking me to return to the compound.

"Yeah, well, no one said yours was to be a whore," Al ground out his words, and my neck snapped up to glare at the back of his head.

Without a second thought, I cocked my hand rearward and swung. My phone flew from my grip, landing with a satisfying smack to his temple. I kicked off my shoes in the same movement and dove over the center of the console towards him. However, the array of expletives he relinquished in pain did little to ease my anger. Throwing a right hook, I watched the skin around his eye break open.

"Fuck. You." I growled, shoving against Peiro's attempt to hold me back as he drove. "Don't you. Ever. Fucking. Ever! Speak to me like that again."

The beating organ in my chest felt like it was submerged in a pit of anger and embarrassment—my inner turmoil all too real. He was supposed to be my best friend, who *should* understand I was doing what I had to in a fucked situation. The rest of the car ride was filled with silence as Al sulked and blotted at his face.

"Sienna, I'm sorry," he muttered, as we pulled down the driveway to the compound.

I jumped out of the vehicle before it came to a complete stop, ignoring Al's heavy footsteps behind me. I stormed into the marble foyer and froze when I saw Apollo standing at the bottom of the steps. My heart did that annoying thing where it skipped a beat and my eyes greedily took him in from head to toe.

His shirt sleeves were rolled up, revealing the tattoos that my tongue begged to trace. His eyes held a darkness, somehow shrouded in sorrow. He looked back and forth between Al and me, silently questioning the blood on his face. Without allowing either of them to start in on me, I stormed up the staircase towards my room.

"I said wait!" Apollo ordered when I made it to the top landing. I turned to glare at him. "You did that." He dipped his head towards Al at the bottom of the stairs.

"Yes." I swallowed audibly, staring at his opened collar—laid back wasn't his style.

Apollo was a man who despised dirt and disorder, yet here he was looking much like the poster child for a stressed millionaire. I covered my mouth to stifle my laughter but failed horribly. He held a sandwich and a glass of water in his hand, and the happenstance confused me. The man refused to eat or drink in his room, requiring cleanliness and structure at all times. The realization of it sullied my mood once again.

"How is she?" I asked between gritted teeth.

"Sleeping mostly." He shrugged, seeming to take in every detail of my face.

"Do we have the answers we need yet?" His eyes told me no. "Then, why is she being fed sandwiches when she should be bleeding?" I crossed my arms over my chest.

"We don't hurt women, Sienna." With that, I threw my head back in mocked laughter.

"But I do. So, shall we?" I motioned towards his end of the wing.

"No? Right, then." I turned on my heel, leaving him to stare at my ass, before locking myself in my room to wallow in my own misery.

Fuck both of them.

"Peace offering." Al's voice woke me suddenly, his large body shaking the bed. I was about to tell him to fuck off when I smelled the sweet aroma of coffee.

"You're still an asshole." My head remained under my pillow but my arm raised up in acceptance of the warm cup.

"I'm sorry, okay? The thought he'd take you away from me, from your family—it pissed me off." Al breathed heavily.

"Who said he isn't what I want?" I asked, popping my head out, but he refused to look at me. "I deserve more than some bullshit tale of unrequited love, Al." I took a sip of the coffee, practically moaning in delight.

"You deserve the world." He tugged a piece of my hair with a goofy smile on his face. "Besides, you haven't seen him these last few days. He's a loose cannon. Yet, I swear that two-second conversation with you last night made him breathe easier than I've seen in a while."

Goddamn Al and his fucking honesty. I knew Apollo *needed* me for several reasons, but I *needed* him to *want* me. Maybe his recent actions showed things were changing between us? And maybe I was just a dumb bitch.

I finished my coffee and shooed Al away so I could shower and get ready. I opted to wear tight, high-waisted workout pants and hid a matching *Nike* sports bra under a zip-up hoodie. Heading downstairs to join my family for food, I smiled at the banter echoing down the hall.

"Hello, family." Wandering around the kitchen, I gave my mother and father each a kiss, before smiling at Serafina Moretti.

The conversation continued to buzz about Lucky's fast-approaching nuptials and everyone's mission to ensure it went flawlessly. Of course, I was handling all of the details and making a dream wedding for my big brother.

Al lurked outside the open French doors, staring at me in silence. I mentally replayed all of the potential reasons Apollo and I were doomed to fail, yet prayed that maybe, somehow, there was a chance. Why, might you ask? Because I was a girl who was drunk on the possibility of being loved by the one man in my life who was totally incapable of doing so. The never-ending, vicious cycle of hope was on repeat in my head as a bruised Bella entered the room.

"You look like you went ten rounds with Mike Tyson." I laughed. "Well, if Mike Tyson was a sniveling little bitch like that bastard who did this to you." I pulled her in for a tight embrace, wincing when she gasped in pain.

Once everyone had their chance for a greeting and a hug, we all joined together to sit around the table. Bella's mother, Serafina, placed a plate of food in front of her and it took everything I had in me to hide my chuckle. Bella was the tiniest little girl, but to see her devour her meal with a gluttonous rapture was thoroughly entertaining.

"I see we haven't lost our appetite. Better heal quickly so I can beat your ass back into shape in the gym," I taunted her, enjoying the way she laughed around a mouthful of food. The conversation picked up, as we commingled like the girl hadn't just been kidnapped.

"Any word yet?" Bella turned to look at my father expectantly; though the shake of his head had her smile faltering.

"I'd love to flay that man alive," Serafina whispered harshly.

"So bloodthirsty in this family. I'm appalled!" Bella muttered in mocked sincerity, just as Lucky and Apollo joined us.

Apollo was back in his pristine, designer suit but the haunted expression on his face remained. My hands shook as my body fought the urge to go to him. It didn't matter what Al said or what my heart wanted, because my brain knew Apollo would reject the sentiment. Then I'd have to face the reality that I was truly meant to head to Philly.

"Any updates on our houseguest upstairs?" My dad pointed the question at Apollo, but it was Lucky who answered. "She's got a lot of physical and mental healing to do."

"I will be moving her into my home once the doctor has cleared her. She won't be your problem," Apollo said, glancing towards my father before returning to his plate.

I was having a conversation with Octavia when his declaration slapped me close-fisted across the face, and my response stuck in my throat. He was… taking her home. *Home.* His special domain, where no one was welcome. He was taking her *there.* Some blonde whore was going to be cared for and under his protection. In his *fucking* home.

How fucking stupid could I possibly be? I allowed myself to weaken the strength that roared within me for a man that didn't fucking deserve me. I was worth more than what Apollo was willing to give. I was dumb enough to think I stood a chance at making him see what was right in front of him. But now, now I was done.

I rose to my feet, my head held high and my poker face locked in place. The only telltale sign I was rattled was the dishes that clamored in the wake of my exit. I needed to fucking destroy something. And since his little blonde-ghost-slut-bitch upstairs was under lock and key, I'd have to settle for a pair of gloves and a punching bag.

Al attempted to follow me to the gym but my raised middle finger stopped him in his tracks. I moved on autopilot, taping my hands and stretching my arms before I attacked the bag like a mad woman. I concentrated on my breathing, while forcing the unwanted emotions to leave my body with each jab. My rage, my sadness and my stupidity slowly dwindled, as my body burned off its adrenaline.

"I leave for Philly after the wedding," I told my dad, feeling his presence at my back. I just couldn't tell myself to slow down—I was scared my pain would catch up with me as soon as I did.

"I'm sorry…" He said the words with so much pity, I screamed in anger and increased my pace.

"Just stop. Things with Romano are right. It's what I deserve. Maybe one day, it will turn into love but for now, at least it's respect." I froze when he stepped closer.

"What do you need from me?" His softness made me want to break down and cry.

I wanted to be the little girl he used to wrap up in his big arms and hold tight to his chest when she had a nightmare. The little girl who found solace in the scent of cigars and whiskey because it reminded her of the safety her father offered her. I didn't want to be the adult who was creating an alliance. I wanted to be the woman who was swept off her feet by the ill-fated man she was in love with.

"For now, nothing." I embraced him, and in return, he placed a kiss to the top of my head.

I needed to find a way to say goodbye without actually saying it. I didn't want to worry them with everything going on in the family. So, I'd bide my time and wait for the right moment. It wouldn't be easy. No matter how close Philly was to New York, it wouldn't be the same.

"I've got work to do. Love you, daddy." I smiled and kissed his cheek.

"Of course." He hugged me tighter, then let me go with an ominous glare.

I darted through the house and up the stairs, in the hopes of avoiding the rest of my family. There were only so many solemn expressions I could take in a day. I made it to the top of the landing before Apollo's voice stopped me in my tracks. He was ordering someone around on the phone. Turning the corner, I stared at his muscular back.

"I want you fucking naked. Wet and waiting for me," he commanded through the receiver. My stomach plummeted at the sound of his lust-filled voice. "Cassandra, I need you."

"You have got to be fucking kidding me." I growled under my breath. Pivoting on my heel, I retreated to my room and slammed the door closed. I leaned my back against the wooden frame as I caught my breath.

"Sienna." Apollo knocked a second later. I ignored him, clicking the lock into place before heading to my desk to video call Andersen.

"Well, aren't you a sweaty sight for sore eyes." Andersen's handsome face popped up a second later.

"I was kicking the shit out of the bag." I smiled, grabbing my cell phone and pulling up my notes.

"What's the matter?" he asked, once again, his concern faltering my attention. "I know you, Sienna. Beating the shit out of the bag means something is up."

We'd only been working together for a short time, but he knew more about me than most. He saw the good and the bad side of me when it came to business and now, he had front row seats to my family drama. He was one hell of an asset to *Energia,* and our time together had proven his personal value to me.

"Philly is a go. I have a couple more things to deal with here, then I will be heading there to scout out my new life." I smiled even though a part of me wanted to cry.

"Sienna." Andersen snarled between clenched teeth.

This was an attribute of his I hadn't seen before. A man like Andersen played the boy next door because of his outward appearance. But lurking deep within him was much more than what met the eye. Men felt a sense of ownership in the best of times and a sense of entitlement in the worst.

"What the *fuck* are you thinking with Philly?" He growled at me, running an exasperated hand down his face. "Leaving your family, your company and your protection behind to uphold some bullshit agreement that your *father* decided on."

"Andersen, I get what you mean, I do. But it's how…" He cut me off.

"How things work in your family. Did you ever think that maybe the separation from them is exactly what you need to find out who *you* truly are?"

His eyes softened, while his words made me falter—my mind was trying to play catch up. *Maybe you don't know the real me.* Gio's insight resonated back, and I struggled as my own thoughts wandered.

Did I really know myself? Was I being allowed to find out who I was? To an extent, yes. To another, absolutely not. Gio was a threat to the family because he wasn't accepting the life he was dealt. *Yeah, Sienna, it was totally the same thing.*

"It's not that easy. You have no idea what it would entail." The whispers about my father rang true—he was of course the head of the mafia—but that didn't mean I shouted it from the rooftops.

"Trust me. I have an idea." He straightened in his seat, his demeanor completely altering. "But like I said, I am willing to follow you."

I had enough on my plate, and adding Andersen's little tirade had not been on my radar. It wasn't that I didn't enjoy a challenge in my life, and going against my father would be exactly that. But it would also be the greatest disrespect I could ever show him—refusing his wishes and turning my back on the family.

In the mafia, you didn't get to leave just because you didn't like what the boss said. The only way out was in a body bag. Did I think he'd kill me? No.

However, even though I may have been daddy's little girl, I had no doubt that the *boss* of New York would ensure I followed orders in whatever way he saw fit.

CHAPTER 22

APOLLO DELUCA

"**I**'ll bring Bella in when she wakes up. This one should be out for at least eight hours," Lucky said, then suddenly he stopped. "What are your plans with her?"

"Get the answers we need from her then send her away. Somewhere safe. Somewhere of her choosing. No cost to you. I'll set her up." As I stared solemnly at the bed, something had stirred inside me. I needed to protect her.

"She's not right in the head, Apollo. I don't know if she ever will be. Do you really want to deal with all that entails?" Motioning towards the mumbling under the covers, Lucky raised a questioning brow at me.

These last few days, his words repeated over and over in my head as I dealt with Persephone's antics. Her despondence and borderline psychosis were beginning to take me down with her—my own mental deterioration was on the horizon.

"What's so funny, *amore?*" Lucky asked Bella, pulling me from my thoughts as the three of us stared down at Persephone's sleeping form.

"Just amused at this little girl being troublesome." Looking over her shoulder, she smirked at us. "Something dark and lurid lurks within this tiny, but beautiful soul."

"How is that funny? If you think she is trouble, she's gone. We don't need more to deal with." Lucky all but yelled his frustration, and I growled in response.

"Now-now." She walked towards Lucky and put her palms to his chest. "Not too much trouble for Apollo." She turned her attention to me.

"I'd never allow a threat to *il mia regina* to live under the same roof. You know this." I couldn't help the anger I threw Lucky's way.

The stress was creating a rift between us, and anatomizing my loyalty wasn't helping our plight. The family's safety was my top priority, regardless of this damaged girl tucked into my sheets.

"I agree. And she seems taken with you. Whatever crazy is lurking behind those beautiful eyes, I have no doubt you will be able to handle it. You're capable of helping her get back to the girl she once was." Bella looked back and forth between us, thoroughly amused.

"I'll let you men discuss your business alone. I am in need of some comfort food. And a lot less growling masculinity." Her preservation kicked in and Bella wanted to flee as Lucky and I breathed fire at each other.

"I'll send someone to your room with your favorite…" Lucky started to say, but Bella cut in. "No-no! I am sure I can manage without anyone's assistance. I already hear the family downstairs. I'll be fine, *mio amore.*" Shutting the door before he could speak, she disappeared.

"You'd assume for someone so sheltered her entire life, that a kidnapping would diminish that attitude." Lucky smiled at the closed door. "Now. What's the deal? We still have no answers."

"She's too damaged to coerce, Lucky." I knew where his line of questioning was headed.

"Get the answers. In whatever manner it takes," he ordered, before turning on his heel to leave. "And she needs to go. *Soon.*"

I checked to make sure Persephone was still sleeping, then I followed him out of the room. I had to refocus my growing animosity into a more positive outlet, such as bending someone to my heel—someone that actually listened. I wasn't used to feeling this out of control and I needed to regain some of my composure; a wet pussy offered that solace.

"So smart and yet so fucking dumb." Al growled from the front door.

"What is your problem now?" I adjusted my tie, pulling it snug against my collar.

"You really don't see it." He waited for an answer but I offered him none. "Sienna!" He shouted as if her name alone was an explanation.

"Yes?" I seethed.

"She's going to leave," he deadpanned.

"Then you and Peiro take her to her office. I'll organize with Ton to ensure she's covered after drop off." I grabbed my phone and turned to the stairs.

"*New York*. She's going to leave New York, you fucking idiot." He shoved at me from behind.

Without a thought for the repercussions, I charged towards the threat. Grabbing his left arm, I twisted it at an odd angle, forcing him backwards. His heavy weight crashed into the wall, while his angered, flushed face contorted in discomfort.

"Grow up and put your foot down—her vacation is denied. Simple as that. No matter what she says, she isn't permitted..."

"For good!" he yelled. And instantly, I dropped his arm and continued adjusting my suit. "If you've ever cared—or whatever the fuck that twisted mind of yours is capable of—for her... do something about it. Don't let her go." His voice broke at the end.

"She isn't permitted to go anywhere, and Mario will handle it if she tries. As for the rest..." He cut me off again.

"Never-fucking-mind. *Gesù Cristo! Così fottutamente stupido.*" He turned around and stormed through the front door, slamming it behind him.

There were times I wished my life was easier, that I wasn't so emotionally inept and forced to pretend to understand others and their *feelings*. Then there were times like this, where I was thankful that I felt nothing. Watching the way his body filled with anguish over Sienna baffled me. Then, when she didn't answer her door, I left for the penthouse.

"Sir." Cassandra's soft voice whispered, hidden in the shadows of my apartment.

"My bedroom. Now." I removed my jacket and watched Cassandra's pert ass sway as she followed my commands. "Did I give you permission to get on the bed?"

"No, sir." Again, she whispered her response.

The four-post frame was calling me. I grabbed Cassandra by her arm, enjoying the way her breasts bounced. I pulled down on the chains that sat at the top of the columns. Turning her away from me, I secured her arms first, then her legs. I tugged tightly and watched her quiver as the bindings pulled her into a tight X-formation. She panted in need as I silently stared at her rear.

"This isn't about you." Sweeping her hair to one side, I bit down on her shoulder. "It's about your master tonight."

"Yes, sir." My hands explored her body—the tight skin of her ass felt soft under my calloused touch—my erection pushing tight against my clothing.

I took off my shirt and removed my belt before opening the button of my pants. I landed a hard smack to her ass. She didn't make a noise as I rotated back and forth between each cheek—ten sharp strikes. Her porcelain skin turned a dark red, the welcomed sting in my palm begging me to break flesh.

I wrapped my hand around her throat—I needed someone to feel the pain, the torment and the chaos within me. I tightened my grip, while my other hand reached between her legs to find her entrance soaked.

I released my hold, counting to ten before I clamped it back in place. I pinched one, then the other erect nipple, growling as they stood taller. Her ass ground against my dick as she trembled from the combination. Rotating my attention, I pinched, plucked and pulled. There was a link between pleasure and pain—biology stated that pain caused the central nervous system to release endorphins. The hormone acted as a natural analgesic, working in a similar fashion as opiates by inducing feelings of euphoria.

Again, I loosened my grip on her throat and yanked on the chains, dragging them down the length of the bedpost—her arms were forced to drop and tightly pull out at her sides. I positioned her shoulders forward and placed her head onto the mattress, her ass held high in the air and her legs spread-eagle.

I dragged my nails from the top of her neck all the way down her spine, her flesh breaking out in goosebumps upon contact. I stepped out of my pants and grabbed her by her hair, lifting her shoulders and head off the mattress. I slid my massive frame under her stretched arms and sat on the bed in front of her.

I nodded—a silent command—and she bent forward, licking my thick cock from balls to tip several times before finally closing her mouth around it. *Fuck.* At the end of a bad day, there was something rapturous about a woman's warm mouth wrapped around your dick. It silenced my internal monsters as I sought absolution.

During sexual intercourse, the human brain worked overtime to release a variety of different hormones and neurochemicals when you orgasmed. Dopamine was responsible for the sensations of pleasure and lust—the only two feelings I was akin to.

Sienna's saddened face popped into my head. Growling in agitation, I grabbed Cassandra's hair and held her in place. Thrusting my hips, I drove my dick deeper into her mouth. She struggled to keep her composure—my pace was too fast—but I didn't give a fuck.

My balls tingled, threatening to plummet me over the edge into the metaphorical abyss, however I couldn't reach completion. I was unable to get the high I needed from Cassandra. I pulled free of her lips and stepped under the chains to stand behind her. I lined up my aching cock and rammed it deep inside her—her screams of pleasure ricocheting off my bedroom walls.

My thrusts picked up pace. Hard, fast and relentlessly, I pounded into her. Her needy cries surged me onward, as I took everything that she had to give. I reached around to the front of her and pinched her clit, offering her the pain that I knew she needed. A few more pumps and her pussy squeezed me tightly, before she screamed into the comforter as she came.

"Fuck, Cassandra. Will you give me this?" I asked, rubbing my thumb over the puckered skin of her ass. Her willingness was confirmed in a garbled mess of both verbal and non-verbal pleas.

I pulled a glob of saliva in my mouth and slowed my thrusts, as I parted her cheeks. Slowly, the spit dropped from my lips onto her inviting skin, I stroked it with my thumb over her opening before inserting my finger—in and out. Once I felt her relax, I gradually entered the tight hole and growled as it gripped me like a vice. *The high I needed was finally on the horizon.*

"Fuck." My orgasm threatened to rip me apart from the inside out, sending white hot signals coursing through my system. "Shit." I quickly untangled Cassandra—she was a pool of sedated female limbs.

"Interesting," she muttered, as I gently picked her up and carried her to the guest room.

"What? I've fucked your ass frequently." I deposited her onto her bed.

"You called out for Sienna again." I stalled briefly, before dismissing her observation and exiting.

I shut off the light and stormed for the door. Locking it behind me, I headed back to the compound. I needed to deal with Persephone and have a conversation with Al.

"Who pissed in your Cheerios, dude?" Marco asked, stepping back as I charged into the family home.

"Where's Al?" I answered his question with one of my own as I darted up the stairs.

"He left," Sienna said from her bedroom door. "He took Octavia somewhere." She shut and locked the door behind her as she glared at me in the hallway.

"You're not leaving," I commanded. Her steps faltered and her spine straightened—I knew she was ready to throw an attitude. I pressed forward, into her space, forcing her against the wall—she was pinned by my body.

"Like fuck, I'm not. I have work to do, thanks. Rocco is taking me, all mighty one." Her typically entertaining commentary was very much void of humor this evening.

"New York." Her face gave her away—she wasn't telling me something. "Whatever you're planning, I'll find out and I'll fucking *destroy* whoever it is you are planning it with. New York is your home."

"You have no fucking clue." Her sudden laughter was grim. "*Maledetto idiota.* You know nothing." She leaned into me and inhaled, her eyes growing round in consternation.

"You're not leaving," I repeated. She pushed against my chest, but I refused to let her go.

"You smell of whores and lies. Leave me the fuck alone." She shoved harder. "*Maiale disgustoso!*"

"What is going on here?" Isabella Agostino, Sienna's mother, charged into the hallway. "Apollo, your *guest* has been causing issues. If you'd please go tend to her before she sets the house on fire."

"Christ." Sudden exhaustion swept over me, settling into my bones.

"And you, young lady. How proud I am of your elegant Italian— that being said, I do not appreciate the words you shout. I raised you better." Isabella stood tall and formidable, a beautiful older version of her daughter.

"*Mi dispiace, mamma...*" Sienna muttered, leaning in to give her mother a kiss before turning a fiery smirk to me.

"*Sarai la mia morte.*" Isabella smiled and hugged her daughter. *Yes, Sienna would be the death of all of us*, I thought to myself.

"What's the matter?" I stormed towards the guard I'd posted outside my door. "You want to climb the fucking ranks, yet a little girl has you confounded."

"I was told not to touch her." He held his hands up in surrender.

Barging into my room, the damage done faltered my steps. There were holes littering the walls, the bed was stripped of the sheets and one of the bookshelves was ransacked. She was sitting on the windowsill in the corner, stroking the glass while mumbling to herself.

I opted to ignore her and headed for the shower instead. Sienna's comment left me *rattled*—I'd barely washed my balls before hauling ass out of my apartment. I set the shower to scalding before I stripped my clothes off and stepped under the harsh spray. The sting erupted across my skin and my mind shut down, reprieving itself from my mental anguish—wiping the slate clean. I pressed my palms and forehead against the glass, allowing the water to cascade down and loosen my muscles.

The sound of soft footsteps forced my eyes open. Persephone stood naked before me. Her gaze hungrily roamed my body, stopping at my thick cock. Though her eyes were distant and lost, my cock didn't get the message, hardening at her perusal.

"Leave." My command echoed off the walls but did little to shake the girl of her reverie.

"Sir," she mumbled, opening the glass doors and stepping into the large enclosed shower. She was the littlest thing compared to me—I felt like I swallowed up the space.

"Persephone." I grabbed her wrist. "I am not a man with much patience, let alone when you grab my dick. Get the fuck out." I shoved her away from me.

She took a step back, melting against the wall and watching me as I washed. Her breathing increased as I stroked myself, her eyes focusing on the motion and burning with a need.

"Sir." She stepped forward, her blonde hair matted to her face. "Please." She licked her lips and dropped to the floor.

Though I didn't like to repeat myself—*I must say this again*—I was not a good guy. Never fucking claimed to have a decent bone in my body. But when a woman was on her knees and begging with her warm lips around my cock, who was I to turn her away? She was fucked up, but Persephone used sex as a different outlet.

Her entire life, the only way she had received gratification from the opposite gender was through the use of her body. She manipulated and schemed with her feminine faculties, coercing people into doing what she wanted by promising to fully give herself over to them.

I grabbed the blonde locks in front of me tightly and fought my urge to take charge. The girl was talented, welcoming me deeper into her mouth. I assumed control, swinging my hips forward and back. I held tight to her hair as she swallowed my head with each thrust—over and over and over.

I didn't give her a warning or a chance to argue as I came down her throat. I froze for a moment, wondering if I called out for Sienna again —either I hadn't, or Persephone didn't care enough to mention it. I pulled her to her feet, staring into those two blue orbs, filled with so many secrets. She smiled lightheartedly, stepping under the water and washing her hair while once again humming that annoying nursery rhyme.

"Christ." I finished washing myself before opening the glass doors. "Finish up. We're leaving," I ordered her.

"Taking me to your torture chamber?" She offered me a playful-yet-demented smirk.

"Trust me, you have no desire to see *il mietitore's* torture chamber." I patted myself dry with the towel. "It'd destroy even those as damaged as you."

One moment. One single look. In a flash, it was there and then gone. That spark of fear—the walls dropping and allowing me the chance to see the damaged, scared and shaking little girl that lurked under all that insanity.

"Now let's go." I left her in the bathroom and quickly changed into a new suit. I'd just tied my shoes when I heard her scurrying around the bedroom.

"Look!" She pulled a garment out of the bag of clothes. "But I don't like dresses." She pouted at the offending material.

"Beggars can't be choosers." I growled, forcing her to stop her incessant dancing. "Now get changed. I've got pressing matters to attend to."

"Are these matters…" She dropped the clothing and pinned her chest to mine, before trailing her fingertips lower. "Pressing against your zipper?"

"Enough." I shoved her backwards. She snatched her bag and

skipped into the bathroom. "Christ." I was checking my cell phone when she finally reemerged.

The dress fit her perfectly while the royal blue color made her luminous eyes pop. Her blonde hair was curling at the ends as it dried and she wore cream-colored flat shoes. She was so fucking small that she looked like a little porcelain doll with flawless skin and big fucking eyes.

The moment I crossed over the threshold into the hallway, Rocco and Al were at my side. They'd escort us out of the city before returning to their duties, once we reached my personal compound. We made it to the bottom of the stairs where Isabella and Mario were waiting, arm in arm.

"Thank you for the safe refuge in your home," Persephone whispered, giving a disbanded smile.

"We'll ensure your safety, if you give us what we need to make it possible," Mario commented, causing her spine to straighten.

"These men have their ways of making all of the bad go away. We just need to open ourselves up to them, and allow them to chase away the demons." Isabella smiled, reaching out with a tender hand but Persephone shrunk away from the older woman's touch.

"They only remove the bad that doesn't agree with their demands. Are they not bad themselves?" No one answered her. "You're all so blinded by your own greed and love for *your* own family that you can't see beyond them, to the bigger picture."

"And what picture does Dominic Moretti paint for you? Sex or servitude?" Mario spat, stepping closer to the girl.

"*'All that we see or seem is but a dream within a dream.'*" And with that quote from Edgar Allan Poe, she turned on her heel and exited the front door, Rocco right behind her.

"What the fuck?" Mario asked, running a hand down his face. "She's beyond repair, isn't she? She's not capable of helping us."

"I think she is." I stared at the door she'd exited. "Her paranoiac antics are a form of self-preservation. But there is more to her."

"I'll follow at the rear—I need to get to Sienna's office," Al said, walking outside.

"Is there a problem?" I questioned.

"Nothing for *you* to worry about." He slammed the car door shut.

Fucking hell.

Persephone sang quietly in her seat for the first twenty minutes of the drive. Then, as the scenery changed, her attention turned towards the window. As the city slowly disappeared behind us, the mountains and foliage replaced them.

My private home was my personal refuge when I needed an escape from the demons *il mietitore* burdened me with. No one came to it. No one stayed with me.

Trauma came in many forms: mental, physical, emotional. The issue derived from the disruption to your body's natural equilibrium. It was known to freeze you in a state of hyperarousal and awareness, a state of fear—the individual becomes trapped, unable to expel themselves from their own internal prison. Exercise and a reduction in stress were often key elements in releasing adrenaline and endorphins, subsequently repairing the central nervous system—a metaphysical reboot, if you will.

A calming environment away from the city and the danger surrounding her would be the best way to start. There was an enclosed swimming pool, hiking trails behind the cabin and walkways along the Hudson River.

The car came to a stop at the edge of the driveway, and I could tell she was about to run. She hesitated when Rocco opened her door and roughly pulled her out. Her preservation instincts ignited against my entourage as she fought to get free.

"She'll tire herself out in no time," I muttered, securing the lock to her room in place.

"You motherfuckers! I'll never tell. Nothing. Not a damn word. And he'll... he'll come for you!" She pounded her little fists against the door.

"Good! Let him come." Her knocking stopped for a second, before turning into a frenzied uproar.

"What the fuck?" I heaved as Rocco and I stared down the door.

The incessant hammering transitioned from fists, to her entire body, before…

"Oh, fuck!" Rocco muttered. "That was definitely her head."

"Jesus Christ. Call the doc." I growled as I slowly unlocked the door.

Sure enough, her blonde hair was caked in blood and matted against her forehead. She was on her back on the mattress, her arms stretched out wide. A closer inspection alleviated my concerns of long-term damage. When the left and right hemisphere of your brain shut off, both at once, you lost your state of consciousness. And she'd rattled the hell out of them.

Fucking hell.

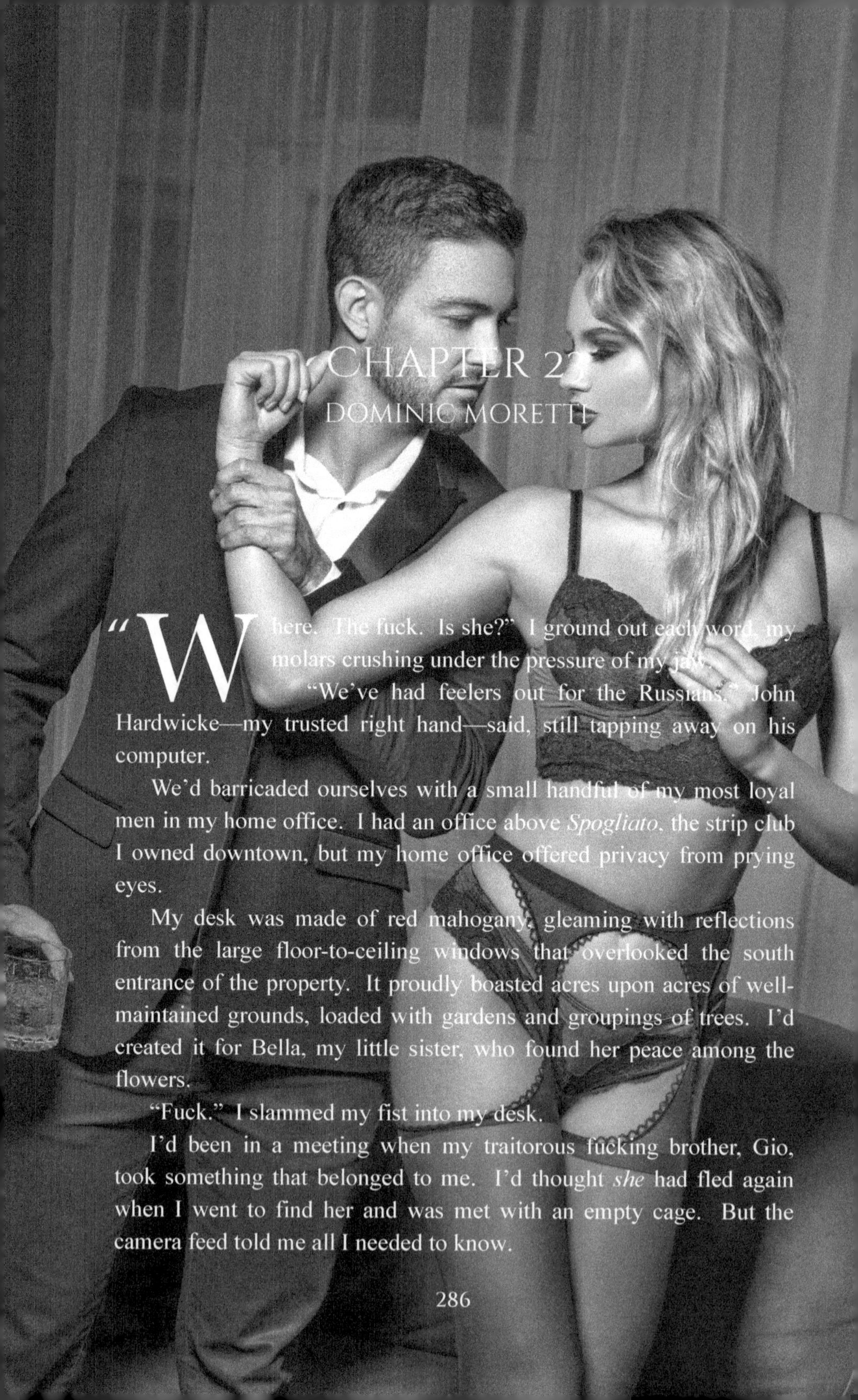

CHAPTER 27

DOMINIC MORETTI

"Where. The fuck. Is she?" I ground out each word, my molars crushing under the pressure of my jaw.

"We've had feelers out for the Russians," John Hardwicke—my trusted right hand—said, still tapping away on his computer.

We'd barricaded ourselves with a small handful of my most loyal men in my home office. I had an office above *Spogliato*, the strip club I owned downtown, but my home office offered privacy from prying eyes.

My desk was made of red mahogany, gleaming with reflections from the large floor-to-ceiling windows that overlooked the south entrance of the property. It proudly boasted acres upon acres of well-maintained grounds, loaded with gardens and groupings of trees. I'd created it for Bella, my little sister, who found her peace among the flowers.

"Fuck." I slammed my fist into my desk.

I'd been in a meeting when my traitorous fucking brother, Gio, took something that belonged to me. I'd thought *she* had fled again when I went to find her and was met with an empty cage. But the camera feed told me all I needed to know.

286

The *stupido figlio di puttana* stole her right out from under me. His extracurricular activities had been a focus of mine for quite some time. And now, because of this, I was going to destroy everything he cared about.

"Where the fuck is my brother? I want her back." I growled, losing my patience with each minute that passed with Persephone missing.

She knew too much.

The girl was a loose cannon and knew far too fucking much about my business to be lost in the underground with the Russians. She could give up what she'd assumed was only a tiny detail and in turn, unravel my entire organization.

She was crazy on her best days but under duress, she was the epitome of total destruction. And it could be that of herself... or me. Or potentially my entire fucking empire I'd worked so hard to build. I had made a huge mistake by keeping her under personal lock and key.

I should've locked her up with the rest of them, if only she hadn't gotten under my skin. I let her get too close and now her disappearance stood the chance of ruining everything.

All because my fucking brother got in over his head with the Russians. Persephone had her own mission in life that she wanted to surpass, and now all of that was going to hell right along with me.

I still didn't know the entire story of what Gio was doing with the Russians, but none of it would be good. He had this ridiculous obsession with destroying the Agostino's since we were young.

I was unsure if there was an ulterior motive in it, or if he just hated that our family didn't own the city like theirs did. Add in his odd obsession with Sienna Agostino, and he was firing on all cylinders to get himself killed. Bella and Persephone wouldn't be his collateral damage if I had anything to do with it.

My phone rang and grabbed my attention—an unknown number flashed on the screen as I answered it. "Brother, I hear you've been trying to find me." *Gio, that son of a bitch.*

"You have something of mine and I want it back. Now." Each word held so much disdain, I was waiting for him to hang up on me.

"I needed a trade for Bella—she was the easiest option at the time," he gloated, knowing damn well he was the cause of this mess.

Our innocent little sister should've never been involved, but like the fucking idiot he was, Gio planned to trade her for an alliance—one ill-fated decision from the moment he started reaching out to this... Yuri Bucharov... for meetings.

I'd learned too late in the game what he was doing, and now it was out of my hands. I exhibited control in all things in my fucking life—this was no exception—and I would have it back shortly. One way or another. My brother's blood on my hands or not.

"Yuri is dead. Your deal is dead. I want her back. Now." I snapped my fingers at John, making sure he was trying to track the call, and he nodded.

"Yuri's sons are *not* dead. The deal is still on. But your little plaything is neither with me nor the Russians," he said, almost amused at my silence. "The Agostino's found Bella. Your little toy is with them."

"You've got to be kidding me!" I yelled into the phone, my limited patience long since spent.

"Afraid not, brother. I tried... for your sake. But she was taken to their family compound and my *eyes* lost sight of her." He chuckled when I growled.

"Lucky has her." It wasn't a question but a grunted affirmation.

"Actually... it seems his second took her from the property," he corrected, waiting a moment until we both said the name at the same time. "Apollo."

"What're you planning, Gio?" I asked, doubting he'd actually tell me anything.

"Nothing you need to worry your pretty little head about, brother. I have some things up my sleeve." He laughed again.

"The FBI is sniffing around you, Gio," I warned, as John's neck snapped to me.

"Have been for years. Don't worry about me, Dom, get your little toy back before she's broken beyond repair." He shouted an order to someone before returning to the receiver. "You know the rumors say Apollo breaks all of his toys."

He disconnected before I could ask him what he meant by that. Apollo had whispers swirling around the city about him for years. He tried to hide all of the bad inside him by doing these good deeds here and there, calling himself *il mietitore.*

He could possess the souls of those deserving all he wanted, but he was still a calculated, cold and murdering psychopath.

I myself was no innocent man—my soul was purged in the blood of my enemies, those I'd destroyed with my own hands, but even Apollo put me to shame. I had a conscience. Well, partially. I still handled my business with an iron fist, and bore no shame at the whispers spread about me. The sad truth was no one truly understood me besides John.

Fuck me. And Persephone.

"What do you want to do?" John asked, rubbing a tired hand down his face.

We'd been burning the candle at both ends for days. Before Persephone was taken, we'd been preparing for a huge takeover in *my* industry. I was about to sign my life away to become un-fucking-touchable. Now, with her disappearance and Gio's mess, the plans were stalled for the time being.

"Apollo Deluca has a lot of fucking enemies," I announced to no one in particular. "And he just fucked up by taking what's mine. Now it's time I take something of his."

"What're you thinking?" John asked, a sardonic expression on his face.

"Get me eyes on the daughters. I want to know their every move." I twisted in my chair to look at the men in my office. "He may have a lot of enemies, but he just got targeted by the worst one of them all." *Me.*

I snapped my fingers and my men took off to follow orders. The fucker took something precious of mine—it was only fair I returned the favor. Everyone in our circle knew he was extremely close to Sienna. Gio wasn't the only one who would leap at the chance to take her.

I turned in my chair to stare at the window as the sun began to set. The gorgeous orange and yellows dropped below the trees, coming close to plunging us into darkness.

I'm coming for you, Apollo Deluca. And I can't wait to see you fall at my feet to get back what you think belongs to you.

Eye for an eye, tooth for a fucking tooth, you sick son of a bitch.

CHAPTER 24
SIENNA AGOSTINO

"It looks great, team. Good work." I smiled into the camera at my programmers.

"Have a good day, Ms. Agostino." My lead on the project grinned back in excitement before disconnecting.

"Who does that smile belong to?" Andersen asked, waltzing into my office without knocking. I guess this change of pace was better than him ignoring me, like he had been since our little disagreement.

He couldn't understand how my life of *mafioso* men didn't compare to normal dating woes. My choices—if I had any—were limited and if I opted to run, I'd be dragged back by my hair. Apollo's threats about me leaving the city weren't idle chit chat. He didn't know I was headed for Philly but the hidden message was still received. There was no running from this life.

"The new program is finished three weeks early," I said, as I typed away on my computer.

Andersen walked to the window and stared out at the city below, silence stretching between us—the only sound was the tapping of my keyboard. This was the most awkward I'd ever felt with Andersen, since he onboarded with *Energia*, and I couldn't shake the feeling. It wasn't so much what he said to me, but *how* he said it. It created this unspoken tension in the room that mixed with something... *menacing*.

I'd been around dangerous men my entire life and until this moment, I never caught a whiff of it off Andersen. But the room was stifling with this buried animosity, this unbridled anger that lurked under his forced smile.

"Are we okay?" he asked, still staring out at the city.

I huffed in agitation as I took my glasses off and pinched the bridge of my nose. I didn't want there to be any hostility between us. Andersen was an amazing asset to the company and previous to this, he was someone I would have considered a friend. But to succeed, to live fully in the life I was raised, you needed a certain set of skills in order to ascertain who was friend and who was foe. Now that there was this *something* in the back of my brain, I couldn't drop my guard around him—not just yet.

"We're fine in a sense. I understand you have your worries about me and I truly appreciate that. But I am *still* your boss just as much as I am your friend so at the end of the day, we may disagree, but I have the final say." He smirked at my tone.

His face washed over with relief and my spine straightened. I was confused by how easily he fell into line. I typically got my way and people either respected or loathed that about me—I was a mouthy and confident woman. Between the telecommunications business and the mafia, both being comprised of solely male leaders, I was used to battling against sexist and self-assured assholes. I went in prepared to win and I did, often.

Men like Andersen were inherently predisposed to alpha-like tendencies. They would claim to be fine, even when they weren't, wanting to lick their shattered pride in privacy. Our discordance seemed to curtail in light of the conversation, but I wouldn't hesitate to put him down like a rabid dog if he tried to interfere again. I didn't obtain this success by sitting idly by and allowing a man to control me.

Even if Apollo controlled my heart and my ever-loving-mind all too much. That was something I couldn't change, no matter how hard I fought. But this, this I could and this I would.

"How are your brother's wedding plans coming along?" he asked, switching topics.

"Well, I am the coordinator, so incredible of course." I winked, tossing my glasses on my desk. "It's all falling into place perfectly. I am just finishing up a few minor details."

"Like picking a date?" He chuckled, our usual banter back to normal.

"I would never purposely put that type of unwanted attention on someone, by asking them to accompany me to a family affair." I laughed, returning my gaze to my computer.

We spent the better part of the day working together, side by side, in my office. I was happy our professional affairs were being handled. I even laughed at his jokes and smiled when I was supposed to. I kept my mind busy with finalizing what needed my attention, but I kept my hand near the 9mm strapped under my desk.

There was something my mother said to me once—after my first scuffle with a man trying to step on my toes when I started *Energia*—and it resonated still. *You'd assume men had deep pockets, because where else would they hold all of their audacity.* No matter how kind. No matter how understanding. No matter how hard I fought. Men were men, and they assumed because they were the larger of the sex— typically anyway—that they were the rule makers.

Not in my house.

Mario Agostino ran New York City and Isabella Agostino ran the family compound. I was raised by a powerful man that believed his family was only as strong as their weakest link. My mother had a voice, and that voice was heard above his men. Ironically, however, that didn't matter for his two daughters, who were fighting for lives of value outside of the mafia. Whereas, I *wanted* out, Octavia was the one being thrown that way. We were the most valued prize possessions when it came to obtaining a stronger foothold in New York, forced to marry our way to the top. *Energia* was much the same, just a mix of vultures vying to take a piece of what I'd created.

Andersen left, and I began packing up my stuff to head out for the evening. "Before you leave, there are a few things to update you on."

Farrah started reading off her list, as I bustled about the room. "Oh, and Ton left a message for you to see him on the first floor, conference room B, before you left today." I nodded and grabbed my phone to head downstairs.

"What did you need?" I asked, closing the conference door behind me with my nose buried in my cell phone.

"You. Always you." I froze at the voice.

"What're you doing here, Gio?" I asked, tossing my phone into my bag and hiking the strap higher up on my shoulder.

"I needed a moment of your time. You look ravishing as always, Sienna." The bruises on his face were still visible, but he held his head high. "Word on the street is you're planning my sister's wedding to your brother."

I kept my head in the game and swallowed the flinch his admission threatened to gain. It was supposed to remain a secret, but his knowledge didn't surprise me. Who the fuck was telling him this shit? He knew about Philly's offer, the wedding, and what the hell else?

He stepped towards me, and I mentally chastised myself as I took a step backwards, almost bumping into the wall. Men like Gio, they enjoyed the hunt. He also clearly loved chasing things he assumed were his to begin with. Each visit he'd thrusted upon me, he seemed to unravel even further. His eyes were filled with a wild energy as he stared back at me with an expression that chilled me to the bone.

It was a mixture of undiluted lust, increasing menace and an infinite lack of sanity. When I attempted to step to the side, to get out of his potential embrace, he matched me—step for step. The more I moved, the closer he pinned his body to mine. The wall behind me was an unrelenting barrier withholding my escape. He was coming undone at the seams in his pursuit, and the scent of my fear only urged him onward.

"What's the matter? Not happy to see me, *tesoro*." He purred the pet name, leaning in and sniffing my neck. "Is it because you didn't end Philly, like I had commanded?"

I didn't respond. Instead, I swallowed deeply, internally empowering myself to be stronger in front of him. He was trying to exert his dominance over me, as if caging in a wounded animal half his size was something to be proud of. I steeled my spine, released an angry breath and stared back—my gaze penetrating deep into the recesses of his brown eyes.

"You have no hold on me, nor can you tell me what to do." I placed my hands on his chest and shoved. When he didn't immediately move back, I swung my knee.

He blocked the attack on his testicles by pinning my leg with his own. "Tsk, tsk, *tesoro*." His eyes filled with the same insatiable hunger as a snake about to feed on a mouse.

I was trained better. I was raised better. I learned to fight better. And yet, I didn't see it coming. I froze when his body moved in slow motion towards me. All of my training, all of my defensive maneuvers fled as my mind slowly wrapped itself around what was about to happen. His right hand gripped my neck—with a force I hadn't anticipated—knocking me into the wall. His grip tightened and he held me prisoner as the air escaped my lungs.

"Apparently, I've been too *fucking* gentle with you. I have no patience for disobedience, Sienna." And he squeezed—my nails digging into his skin went unnoticed as I felt the warmth of his blood on my fingertips. "You run around this city with a freedom you haven't earned. I wanted to give you that freedom, to reign at my side, but clearly you aren't ready."

He let go and I gasped in fresh gulps of air. I trembled, and I hated that I had to hold onto his arms to keep myself from crumbling onto the floor. His eyes and large frame held me captive as my brain refocused on breathing, and how the *fuck* I was going to get myself out of this mess. This malicious intent to break me was yet another side of Gio I hadn't seen before. And with it, I knew he would enjoy my ruin.

"Gio, I…" I stopped to clear my dry throat. "What do you expect me to do? I said yes to Philly—I didn't have a choice."

He watched me for a moment before he smiled. "Then I suppose I need to remove that *choice,* now don't I?" He sneered but his words dripped with excitement, while the hair on the back of my neck rose in warning.

"You can't... Gio, you can't go to war with Philly," I stuttered.

"It won't be war when I destroy their leader and send the city straight into the gutter." His eyes glittered with the lingering promise of more bloodshed.

"Gio..." I started again, but he turned his head and attacked my lips with his own.

My hands—which were holding onto his biceps—twisted to his chest, pushing to remove him from my space. His large hand gripped both of mine before slamming them into the wall above my head. *We had to stop meeting like this,* I thought to myself as the force of the movement made me gasp. He plunged his tongue inside the sudden opening of my mouth. He moaned and rolled his hips against me, his growing erection digging into my stomach.

I tried to tug my hands free but it was to no avail, so I opened my mouth wider and his tongue attacked mine even harder. I braced myself but kept my body lithe against him. When I finally felt the opportunity come... I *fucking* took it.

When I didn't think he was prepared, I bit down. He growled in pain, squeezing my jaw agonizingly hard with his thumb and forefinger —forcing me to release my hold. I tasted the metallic flavor of success. His blood pooled in my mouth and poured over my lips, leaving a streak of victory down my chin. When his body coiled to defend itself, I lifted my knee again. He turned slower this time, but I made enough contact to jar his balls.

I darted for the door, prepared to scream my fucking head off for security to come kick his fucking ass for me. But the door barely opened before I was tugged backwards by my hair—the momentum of which threw me onto my back and against the conference table. Gio stepped between my legs, pinning me down. Fight or flight had fully kicked in, and I refused to be raped by Gio-fucking-Moretti.

I clawed, thrashed, kicked and bit anything that I could make contact with. He roared above me, gnashing his teeth like a beast possessed when I refused to kiss him back, the blood from his tongue dripping on my face and chest.

"You make me crazy, *tesoro.*" He moaned before shoving off me and stepping back. "Fuck, why did you make me do that? Christ, Sienna. You're different. I need to be better for you. In apology, I promise to handle Philly for you."

Before I could respond, he turned on his heel and left the room. I scrambled off the desk, adjusted my breasts and snatched my bag off the ground. I pulled my phone out but my face ID wasn't working—it took three attempts to enter the code in order to unlock it. I darted through the lobby with my head down. I didn't want to be questioned.

"Sienna." His deep voice greeted me on the other end, but my rapid breathing cut him off.

"Romano. There's a threat," I huffed, my heels echoing around me. "Gio Moretti knows... and isn't happy. He said he'll take care of..." I ran smack into a hard body with an *oomph* of surprise.

Without looking up, I started thrashing, in fear that Gio had overheard me. My phone was still in my hand, but it was the tattooed grip on my wrist that halted my attack. Time slowed, and my mind finally caught up with the fact that it was Apollo who was yelling at me. His eyes morphed into a mixture of rage and confusion. I stopped my fighting to give Romano a few more details before hanging up.

"What the fuck, Sienna?" Apollo growled, staring at the red droplets coating my face and chest.

"It's not mine..." I whispered. He used his thumb to wipe some of the blood from my cheek, as a sudden sense of exhaustion swept through me. "I need to go." The adrenaline was rapidly diminishing and I could feel my hands beginning to shake.

"Then let's go." He wrapped his arm around my shoulders, turning my face into his chest.

A feeling often so simplistic in action meant the absolute world to me. I'd spent so many years fighting to prove how tough I was, it was hard for me to allow myself a moment to be weak. Apollo put me in the back of the SUV idling at the curb. I sat back into the warm leather seats and listened to him order Rocco to wait.

"Take me home and I will tell you everything," I whispered, forcing Apollo to hesitate. "All of it." I waved at my blood-slathered face.

"Okay, let's go." Apollo slid into the front passenger seat and Rocco pulled out into traffic.

"Apartment. I don't want to deal with the ghost girl lurking at the compound," I ordered.

"Compound," Apollo corrected Rocco. "She's not there."

"No? You took her home already, then?" I asked, and I could tell he was debating on his response. "She's a fucking ghost I doubt she has one of her own." He didn't answer but his labored breathing told me he was pissed.

Good, 'cause so was I.

The rest of the car ride out of the city was in silence. I was covered in blood and utterly defeated with life in general. Apollo was twitching in his seat, and the farce of maintained control was slipping faster than I'd ever seen before. That's what pissed me off the most about the entire dilemma that was Apollo and me. I was what he *needed*... who he needed... if he'd just stop with these stupid-ass games.

I used to wipe the blood from his skin when he'd come back from brawling on the street corners as a teenager. I'd stay by his side as he fought with the demons inside his mind, no matter how many times my father ordered me away. I became powerful in spite of Apollo, to give him time to empower himself under my father's rule. I knew every-thing about him. Even when he was unraveling faster than belts in a whore house.

The car had barely stopped in front of the compound when I jumped out. Storming inside, I watched as the maids scattered out of my way as I carried my heels and oversized work bag. I was pretty sure my family was mixed in among them, but I didn't stop to appease their concerns. I was absolutely defeated and exhausted. I opened my bedroom door and stepped inside my own slice of heaven, not even bothering to close it.

There was no reason to—he'd be right behind me. Apollo was a dog chasing a bone, and my promise of answers was the reward he was panting for. I didn't speak when I heard the door close, just dropped my shoes and removed my clothing. I stood before him in my matching set of undergarments—a lacy, sheer black bra and thong. We stared at each other for a moment while his eyes completed their slow perusal—he did little to hide his enjoyment at the sight before him.

Something that would normally twist my belly in excitement now felt solid and heavy, buried deep in my gut. *I deserved so much fucking more than all of this.* I said it before and I reminded myself again. Instead of demanding that he left, I slowly stepped out of my thong—the fine material pooling at my feet. I glared at him a moment longer, my hands on the clasp of my bra at my back, waiting to see if he'd stop me. When he didn't, it landed beside my thong.

Gio's blood was still on my skin, drying in pieces across my bare chest and drawing in Apollo's savage attention. Like the previous encounter with Gio at my apartment, my body felt sore and bruises were already showing on my skin. Apollo's angered expression softened as he stepped closer to me—a gentle finger whispered across my skin, tracing each mark.

"Tell me." I exhaled my breath at his command—I wasn't ready to do this now, let alone naked.

I spun on my heel and walked into the bathroom, turning the shower on as hot as I could take it. I looked over my shoulder seeing that he had followed me. The zipper of his pants was pulled snug as a large bulge caught my attention—I licked my lips as I stared at it, and he growled. His face was that of a hungry lion staring down its meal. I clamped my legs together to stave off my own desire, forcing myself to step into the shower.

I wanted to give him no mercy, to allow him to bleed his soul across the floor in front of me. I refused to make this easy for him. I moaned as the harsh spray traveled down my body, my fingers slowly tracing and following the trail of the droplets.

"Either join me or leave," I offered, not bothering to look at him as I did so. It was another moment before I heard his retreating footsteps escaping the room.

I dressed in comfortable linen pants and an off-the-shoulder sweatshirt. Wrapping my wet hair into a messy bun and foregoing shoes, I wandered into my room. Apollo was on his phone—seated in front of my desk—as I wandered around behind it and turned on my computer.

"Explain. Now." He clipped each word when he spoke.

Inhaling deeply, I leaned back in my seat and stared at him for a beat before exploding with everything. Gio's reign of destruction, as well as his vendetta against Lucky and his plan to take over the city with me at his side. All of his visits to see me. The call that warned me to get out of my apartment when Bella was taken and the visit today. I was about to open my mouth to tell him about Philly, but for some reason, I couldn't. I wasn't cancelling my visit to Romano after the wedding, but I wasn't ready to tell Apollo either.

"Why didn't you come to me?" he asked, his voice held a taste of uncertainty in it.

"Oh, I don't know." I flopped my head back in the chair and stared at the ceiling for a moment. "Persephone, your houseguest slut, Lucky, Bella, Al and all of your adventures as *il mietitore*. When would you have time for little ole me?" I kept my voice flat and my eyes void of emotion.

"I'm astounded that you'd assume a threat of this nature was some-thing I wouldn't pay attention to." His statement was matter of fact.

"You've been busy. Your allegiance to Lucky and protecting Bella comes first. Add in all of your time spent between the two women you are keeping… And well, I handled it… *myself*." I crossed my arms over my chest in defiance.

"Evidently," he said, running his fingers down the length of his throat—my own peppered in bruised fingertips.

"It's handled." I sighed. "I have plans in place, don't worry about me."

"Sienna, there isn't a day that goes by that your actions don't concern me," he muttered, sitting forward in his seat.

His black suit was paired with a white, crisp shirt and no tie—the top opened just enough so that I could see the beautiful ink beneath it. His honey brown eyes shimmered under the glow of the light above him. He really was a masterpiece of pure masculine perfec-tion to behold. It almost seemed wrong to call such a deadly man beautiful, but for all of his misgivings in life, God did make him gorgeous.

"I assure you—I am not your problem. Nor will I be an inconvenience for you much longer." I smiled at the rage that took over his face.

"We've had this discussion… you're not leaving." His words were so blatant and so calm—they sat like a storm of heavy clouds ready to pour over my head.

"What're you going to do for me if I stay?" I was poking at the flame, but at this point, I didn't care.

"Sienna, don't play games you aren't equipped to win." He rose to his full towering height. And leaning over my desk, he rested his palms flat against it. "We both know it's not something either of us will win once we start *really* playing."

"I don't play games I know I'll lose. And with you, Apollo, I'll never fucking win." I turned around in my white leather chair to stare out of my open windows.

My room overlooked the vegetable garden my mother had built. Isabella Agostino was a generous soul and donated the entire garden to feed the needy all season. That thought alone made me smile as I recalled my youth, and how she'd drag me outside to help pick the spoils of her labor.

Just because we are privileged enough that we want for nothing, doesn't mean we turn a blind eye to those less fortunate.

My mother was an incredible woman with a big heart, far too large for her small body—much like my sister. She controlled the house, her children and her husband with an iron fist and high expectations. She pushed us to never settle, yet that's what I seemed to constantly be doing.

I reaped all that the men sowed and yet, I received none of the reward. But such was the burden of women. And I was fucking over it.

"What do you want me to do?" I sighed, ready for him to make his exit.

"See if your man can find Alexander, like he did Bella." He turned to look at me, his eyes seeming as though they had so much to say and yet, not speaking a word of it.

"Andersen." I addressed him when he answered. "I need your help again. You were able to uncover the whereabouts of my sister-in-law—well, now I need your magic on the man that took her."

"No. This is too dangerous, Sienna." He barked, literally barked at me.

"Who are you to tell me no?" I questioned, my spine straightening as I heard muffled voices in the background.

"Fuck." He sighed into the receiver. "Fine, Sienna. But know this, I can guarantee these men are worse than the men you've grown up with."

"Trust me, I know." I ground out my words, unsure why he felt the need to act so superior to me.

"No, you don't, Sienna. These men have no moral code when it comes to hurting anyone who gets in their way. You were already in their crosshairs once when your sister-in-law was taken. What happened to her was child's play compared to what they are capable of. But since it is you asking, I will find them for you. But warn your rabid dogs that they can't let you out of their sight for a second."

"I am protected," I said; the ferocity in Apollo's gaze had me squeezing my thighs together—searching for the release I wouldn't find. Not from him.

"This wedding couldn't come at a worse time," Apollo muttered, crossing his large arms over his chest.

"Falling in love is never perfect, nor does it ever seem like the right time. But why should they hold back their union just because people want to take it from them?" He halted his exit at those words. "If we faltered in our plans just because someone wanted what we had, the Agostino empire would cease to exist."

"Contrary to what you might believe about your fairytales, true love can die at the hands of one good shot. Romeo and Juliet perished, to spend what they saw as an eternity together." His expression darkened, the reality of his words settling heavily.

"I guess it's a good thing you're so incapable of love then. While everyone else drowns in it, you can sit by and keep watch." I walked to my door, opening it wide. "I think we have a damn good chance of surviving with *our* best shot being so emotionally inept, don't you?" He walked through the door and I slammed it behind him.

Apollo and I were a hot-fucking-mess, which I didn't have the time nor the mental capacity to deal with at the moment. Instead, I was off to plan someone else's happily-ever-fucking-after.

CHAPTER 25
APOLLO DELUCA

My interactions with Sienna were growing more and more hostile. It was like parking your car on train tracks and ignoring the blinking lights of the large vessel shuttling down the railway towards you. You watched as it approached, the headlights getting brighter with each breath you took. Releasing the brake would avoid disaster, but there was something so exquisite and so entrancing about the spotlight, you were unable to move.

Of course, then you died—slowly and painfully because life was anything but easy. I was just unsure which one of us was the conductor and which one of us was sitting in the car. Every time I felt like we made amends, I somehow tipped the scales again. Regardless of all the studying I had done, I would never be equipped enough to avoid feuding with her.

I'd hurt her, and she refused to ask me for help because of it. The woman was staring death in the eye—perhaps worse than death—and she didn't falter, not once. In unrelenting silence.

"Boss," I clipped into the phone. "We've got a problem." I relayed all of Sienna's confessions to Lucky.

And we agreed that Dom was a looming threat. I arranged additional security for all of our women, and then decided I had one last loose end that I needed to handle, personally. An unwanted flashback assaulted my mind.

"Cara, enough." The ache in my empty stomach was too much to bear—I needed sleep.

"You've learned the alphabet and how to put the letters together. You can do it." Cara's soft voice calmed the raging embarrassment inside me. "You've been doing good with Macbeth*; you get it better than I do."*

Cara always acted like our foster father was wrong, like I wasn't just a "dumb fucking kid" as he had so eloquently put it. I didn't know how to read because I wasn't allowed to go to school once I moved into this house. When he was asked about it by our social worker, he claimed we were being home schooled, and well, you know how the system was—overcrowded and underfunded. But it didn't matter to me… I already knew I'd never leave this place alive—Michael would see to that.

It had gotten to the point where I no longer felt physical pain when the son of a bitch attacked me. I took his abuse to protect Cara. I wouldn't let him take her away from me. She was the light in the dark of this rat-infested basement.

I sighed and rolled over, taking the book and shifting towards the rays peeking through the small window. Macbeth *by William Shake-speare—it was tattered and left in a mold-ridden box but the pages themselves were okay. I liked when Cara read to me, and when we talked about the underlying significance of the story. But she kept wanting me to try my own hand at deciphering the letters.*

"Fine. 'False face must hide what the false heart doth know.' That's it. Huh." I chuckled.

"What does it mean?" Cara asked, her eyes filled with wonder.

"They're planning to kill the Scottish King so Macbeth can become King." I pushed the book under my blanket and flopped back to stare at the ceiling.

"Will you?" Cara whispered the question.

"What?" I turned to look at her, but she remained silent—she was

too kind to say the words out loud. "I will. I'll kill him one day. We deserve to be free."

"And one day, you will be King." Cara giggled, the sound making my heart race.

"I don't want to be King. The King can't live in the shadows; he has to be seen. I like the shadows. It's where I belong..." I muttered.

"Why do you think that?" Cara yawned.

"I don't think like you. I don't feel what you do. The shadows are for the men who do the dirty work for the King, so he can continue his rule." I returned to my back, once again studying the rusted metal pipes above me. "But I will find a King who deserves my loyalty."

"You deserve some light, too." Cara rolled over, turning away from me.

After a few minutes, her breathing evened out and she fell asleep with barely audible snores. The sound of her at peace calmed me. She was too broken by Michael—she wouldn't last much longer. I had yet to grasp the meaning behind the looks he gave her, but I knew they were wrong.

It felt like only minutes had passed—my eyes had just closed— when a heavy boot made contact with my side. I acted on impulse and bent inwards, attempting to shield myself. I refused to give him the satisfaction of making a noise.

I opened my eyes to see Cara had moved further into the basement, hiding in the darkest corner. But her light gray eyes were staring at me —they harbored a brightness that drew too much attention to her. She needed to close them; she shouldn't watch. They filled with unshed tears as she stood to her feet. I tried shaking my head, telling her that it wasn't worth it.

But this time felt different and maybe she felt it too. He was out for blood. Something snapped inside me when I saw Cara take a hesitant step forward. I wasn't worth her protection... wasn't worth the pain she'd suffer at his hands. When she ignored my silent pleas, I relented and Michael got exactly what he wanted from me.

"Ow!" I faked a cry, garnering his attention enough to pause his foot in the air.

"You little shit." He smiled down at me, but there was only hatred curling those lips. "Shut the fuck up."

Time itself stilled. Cara retreated to the shadows as he pulled his foot back again. I watched it coming, staring at the steel toes of his boot still coated in my blood. When the tip made contact with my head, darkness descended immediately and I too was finally at peace.

I exhaled a deep breath as I shook the memory away. Taking in my surroundings, I was startled. I was standing outside the warehouse. I didn't remember getting here, but I knew it was time. Michael O'Hare had filtered his disease into the air for far too long. When I sent him to hell, I'd bury all memories of the man along with him.

I disarmed the security system and walked into my office first, removing my jacket and rolling up my sleeves—I needed this routine. Once I crossed over the threshold into the room where he dangled from the ceiling, the scent of blood and broken men filled the air. Michael's chin rested against his chest, the slight roll of it the only sign he was still alive. I flicked on the overhead light and he startled awake—his moan bouncing off the walls before laughing back at him.

"Hello." I approached the table of implements. "You've held out longer than I expected, Michael."

He mumbled incoherently, while his head continued to bob. His nose hooked at an odd angle—a side effect of knuckles fracturing his nasal cavity and mending too far to the right. The rest of him was tinged in shades of yellow and purple and dotted like a canvas with an artist's slathering of dark red. He no longer held a power over me; he was no longer capable of hurting anyone else. The memories of him that shook loose every so often were showing their grisly faces for the last time.

First, I pulled the IV from his arm. Then, cracking my knuckles, I went to work with a few combinations of jabs and hooks to reignite and release my adrenaline. He was naked and the fresh blood poured in vibrant streaks down his body, while his flaccid cock hung limp between his battered legs. His cries were euphonious, echoing around the enclosed space and serenading our familiar song and dance.

I grabbed the scalpel from the table. And circling his pathetic floating form, I administered precise swoops of the blade in the most excruciating anatomical locations. More and more of the fluid turned bright red as it met with the oxygen in the air and pooled downward. I had closed off the floor drains, enjoying the sound my shoes made as they amalgamated with the feces and drying gore. I'd just raised the sharpened implement above my head—to end it all—when my phone started ringing.

"Cara," I answered—I found irony in the fact that she chose this moment to call.

"What's the code?" she asked, though I didn't understand her meaning.

"What code?"

"We're out front—your normal code isn't working." When I didn't respond, she sighed. "I knew it. Apollo, let us in."

The phone disconnected and I pulled up my outgoing log, noticing a four-minute call with Cara from a few hours ago. I guess I wanted her to know I was on my way to end the nightmares… our nightmares. I dropped the scalpel and headed to the doors. Punching at the keypad, I watched as it opened to Cara and her husband.

"Jesus…" Cara muttered, dropping her eyes down the length of my blood-spattered body. "Did we miss it?"

"No," I said as she stormed past me.

Her husband stepped in behind her, surveying the exterior before he secured the door. He lurked around the room, close to his wife, watching every corner and rightfully earning himself his road name. Edge, the man didn't know how to relax. He was an efficient enforcer and protector for Cara. He nodded at me, before again stepping to his wife's side.

"Fuck." She coughed, covering her nose. No doubt the fumes of urine, feces and blood were unpleasant… *when you weren't used to it.*

"Christ, you're sick." Edge smiled, hugging Cara to his chest. He meant it as a compliment.

Cara walked to the spicket and turned the faucet on, grabbing the long hose that was wrapped tightly to the wall. Standing in front of Michael—tall and proud—she blasted him with the water. He spluttered awake, writhing and shaking to avoid the cold onslaught pelted his way.

"Look at me," she ordered as his head swayed slightly before turning to her. "Remember me? I bet you fucking do." Her voice broke at the end and I watched Edge tense up, shifting on his feet.

"Cara." I ground out her name. Neither Edge nor I wanted her to get in over her head.

"I'm fine. I've waited for this moment for as long as I can remember. Years I've spent, wondering what I would do or say to you when I got my chance. But now I realize... you ain't worth it. None of it!" She screamed, drawing out the sound until all of the air had left her lungs.

"Baby." Edge walked up to her and wrapped her in his arms. "It's okay. Breathe, baby, it's over."

"I will do this," I said, stepping aside so they'd leave the room.

"No." Cara pushed out of her husband's arms, storming closer to the monster that plagued her dreams. Edge and I looked at each other with concern—neither of us wanted her to be the one to do it. "Fuck you, you piece of shit." She snorted, heaving a wad of saliva directly in his face.

"Nice." Edge laughed, earning a quick smile from Cara.

"My brother and my husband will be the ones to end you. Rot in hell, you dirty son of a bitch!" She lifted her hand to reveal a pair of scissors that I hadn't even seen her pick up, before jabbing them into his chest. "I loved my long hair!" she shouted, stabbing at him several more times. Only when she calmed down, when she had her fill, did I speak.

"It had lice anyway," I stated with a shrug. Cara turned around so quickly, she had to grab the table to stop from sliding.

"It did not!" She looked back and forth between her husband and me.

"It did. He didn't need to cut it off the way he did, but it did have lice." I nodded to Edge, crossing my arms over my chest.

The first thing I remembered about her was her long, dark, silky hair before Michael had lopped it all off. What were once dark raven-colored locks that made up half of her body, he hacked into a short, uneven mess.

"You shut your mouth," she muttered, knowing it was the truth. With one last glance at him, she smacked the end of the scissors to push them further in, before turning to us. "I'll be in the car."

She pivoted on her heel and headed out the doors, leaving Edge and I to stare after her. Long gone was the scared little girl hiding in the shadows of that basement. In part, it was thanks to Edge and her best friend, Fallon, as well as her own fire that had somehow always burned beneath the surface. She was tough as nails and I was proud.

"Fuck me. To this day she makes me hard with the shit she does." Edge adjusted his pants.

"Shut up." I punched his shoulder, and he laughed. "That's my sister."

"Pretty sentimental for a sick bastard, who feels nothing. Maybe you feel a little more than you realize." He turned towards Michael. "What's the plan?"

I stared at him for a second longer, annoyed by the unsolicited observation. It was a shame that such trivial commentary could ruin a good moment. Luckily, my need to end Michael kept me satiated. I was suddenly filled with exhaustion—I just wanted it to be over. Once his heart stopped beating, it would be an end to a lifetime of hunting.

"I think we should keep the scissor idea," I said, motioning to another pair on the table.

"How many holes do you think it'll take for him to die?" Edge asked, picking up the rusty shears. I shrugged and we both stepped closer to him. "Was it that bad?" he probed.

"Her head was covered in them," I said, and he shivered.

We went to work and my mind turned itself off. Cut after cut, we went. His cries soon died out but he was still breathing so we continued. With each jab to his torso, I felt lighter. But then as the life drained from him, in turn, my soul darkened. Together, we counted aloud with each wound we inflicted until he gurgled his last breath.

"Really? One hundred and one would've been so much better than ninety-eight," Edge muttered, dropping the shears onto the table.

"Take care of her," I said, not looking back as he turned to walk away.

"Always." He opened the door to leave but stopped. "We'll bring the baby by sometime soon. He forgets what his Godfather looks like." And then he was gone.

Without much thought, I ordered a cleaning crew and I left the warehouse behind. I needed to get away from it, to let it be a distant memory—one that would no longer follow me. I was confused and I felt like I was drifting above reality, suspended in time.

I pulled up to the compound, and most of the lights were out—it was so late. *The wedding.* Fuck! My mind churned, obsessing over the potential disaster as I crossed the foyer. My dress shoes slid with each step, leaving behind red footprints on the white marble floor.

I bent down to remove them when a startled gasp halted me. I looked up to find Sienna standing at the bottom of the stairs, wearing a silk nightgown and holding a glass of milk. She stared at my bloodied and disheveled appearance. We were frozen in this silent stare down—neither of us moving—waiting to see what the other would do.

"It's okay. Come on, Apollo." She reached out a hand to me.

My body moved on its own accord, while her tanned skin practically glowed against my stained knuckles. She didn't say anything, just pulled me up the stairs and down to her room. I couldn't stop her if I wanted to. I was unable to do anything but follow her sweet scent.

She closed the door softly behind us, depositing her glass onto her desk. She knelt down in front of me, and untied then removed my shoes and socks. She rose back to her feet and stared at me for a moment—a silent request for permission—before unbuttoning my shirt and pulling it over my head.

Her brows pinched as she stared at my blood-soaked chest. Traveling her hands down my stomach, she removed my belt. She tugged my pants and underwear down in one motion, my erection springing free. Her cheeks tinged in red but she didn't stop there. Looking back into my eyes, she smiled encouragingly.

"Let's wash it all away." She took my hand again and guided me into the bathroom. At first, I thought she was going to fill the tub—the idea of sitting in that sick bastard's blood made me draw back. But then I followed the hum of her voice. "Here we go."

The shower was running as she held her hand under the stream, waiting for the temperature to rise before motioning me inside. I was incapable of doing anything other than following her orders, and I crossed over the threshold and under the spray. The warm water bathed my cold, aching bones and I sighed in relief. When I didn't immediately move, she turned the shower head away from the door and stepped into the large stall.

She scoured me from my head down to my toes. I watched her closely; though her mind was focused on taking care of me, one appendage at a time. Her pink tongue poked out as she scrubbed my chest arduously, my torso having taken the brunt of the blood splatter. She focused all her attention on removing the foreign skin fragments stuck to mine.

I felt her hesitation as her fingertips trailed towards my erection before skipping it and moving to my legs. With each motion of her hands, I felt lighter—the dark clouds clearing away after a destructive tornado. Only Sienna, only this woman, could calm me in the middle of that raging storm. Only Sienna, in the middle of a wild brush fire, was able to bring me relief.

"I'll leave you to... that." She nodded at my hard dick, and handing me the washcloth, she turned to leave. "What?" she muttered, when I grabbed her wrist.

We stared at each other in silence, while the tension between us crackled in the air like a fireworks show. She stood before me, an innocent yet captivating woman. Absolutely beautiful—ruinously beautiful—because she wasn't for me. I couldn't... no matter how much the urge to own her roared through my system.

We had both sworn to stay away from each other. She knew it. I knew it. Yet the look on her face told me she didn't give a fuck about what we knew.

My hands trembled and my breathing increased as those forbidden thoughts coursed through my brain. All the ways I planned to break her, just because I could, just because I craved it—craved her—played on repeat.

"Fuck." I growled before storming towards her

Like the true powerful queen that she was raised to be, she didn't cower under my harsh attack. My hand gripped her neck—with a softness that was a complete contrast to my typical brash behavior—and I pinned her to the wall. Her small but formidable frame quivered beneath me, while the smell of her arousal breached my nostrils, and I had to stop the consuming need to drop to my knees before this Goddess and taste her.

"You fucked up." I growled again, biting the flawless skin of her neck—*that* perfect spot just under the ear. And noting her legs threatening to crumble, I used my body to hold her in place. "I warned you to stop these games. Fuck. Me. You truly are ruinously beautiful..." I repeated the words that I had spoken internally. "I just don't know who it is that will be ruined beyond reparation. You. Or me."

I took a step closer, pulling her almost against me. My eyes searched hers for anything that showed hesitation as I prepared to strike. But there was none, not a single indication or doubt, only her and me. Her blue eyes filled with such wonder, a part of me ached to turn back time and offer myself to her sooner. Wrapping my fingers around hers, I twisted her hands to grab my erection and guided her to stroke it the way I liked.

I kept my gaze glued to hers as she moved, her expression tinged pink as she followed my lead. If I hadn't known better, I'd compare her demeaner to the unconfident fumblings of an inexperienced virgin. But Sienna was far too beautiful to have remained untouched for so long.

I maintained the rhythm with hard strokes, relishing in the sensation of her tiny hands on me while her own heavy breathing told me how much she was enjoying herself as well.

I dropped her hand, using both of mine to grab the sides of her face. She startled as I pulled her under the water with me, my mouth assaulting hers like it was the air I needed to breathe. Her lips and tongue matched mine, move for move. She had such a natural sexuality about her that I couldn't help but growl with need.

She had always turned me on—there was never a doubt about that. She was an incredible woman, who exuded a confident and carnal prowess. I pulled her slick chest to mine and lifted, and her long legs wrapped around my waist, neither of us allowing the kiss to break.

I walked us into the bedroom, setting her down on her feet next to the bed. With one last kiss to her lips, I pulled back to stare at her. Her eyes were soft and filled with passion, her mouth swollen and her nipples hardened peaks against her drenched nightgown. I grabbed the hem of the silky material and pulled it upwards. Sienna was a Goddess—her picturesque body was the epitome of what was written in Greek mythology. She was pure perfection in tangible form.

I guided her backwards, dropping her onto the bed and hovering above her. Imparting another gentle kiss, I worked my way down her neck to her nipples, sucking each one into my mouth. She moaned as I bit down, drawing out her pleasured pain and enjoying how she writhed beneath me. My trail continued down her stomach to her hips, my trimmed beard tickling her during its descent.

When I got to the apex between her thighs, I licked up her slit before burying my nose and inhaling. She smelled like she tasted, like sweet, fresh strawberries at the peak of summer. This woman was turning me into a man starved for her touch, for her everything. I returned my mouth to her core, and skimming my hand downward, I sought to insert a finger and froze.

"Sienna." I snarled, dumbfounded as she hid her face in her hands. "Sienna, look at me."

"Please…" she moaned, still hidden. "I-I want it to be you. Please, Apollo." I tugged her hands away from her eyes and saw the vulnerability she'd worked so hard to hide.

I had always assumed… I mean, from the way she carried herself, we all had.

"I can't be gentle, Sienna. I don't know how to *make* love." I cringed at the mockery in the sentiment.

"Who wants love? I want it hard and fast." She had no idea what she was asking for. "I trust you, Apollo."

I should have left. I should have grabbed a towel and walked right out the door. I should have allowed someone else to take her innocence, someone who actually deserved it—deserved her. Because I sure as hell didn't. I was nothing…

Maybe it was the thought—the ending to a perfect day as I laid to rest so many demons that afflicted me over the years. Maybe it was the look she was giving me, begging me to take her. Maybe it was just that Sienna was what I needed, what I didn't want to admit to anyone —least of all myself. Maybe it was because I was a cruel bastard and the darkness within me wanted her virgin blood on my cock.

And with that, I stopped thinking and attacked her mouth with yet another harsh kiss. She was too tight and I was far too thick—no matter how much I prepared her, she was going to be in pain. That thought engulfed my cognitive senses and for some reason, it left an unsettling weight in my chest. *Weird.* I licked and tasted her through three orgasms. I was shaking in need as I listened to her cry out in ecstasy.

"This is still going to hurt," I said, lifting onto my elbows before climbing back up her body. I tucked a loose strand of hair behind her ear. Her face was flushed with happiness and her eyes, dilated with need.

"Do it," she ordered breathlessly, as I held myself at her entrance.

With a shake of my head, I growled and slowly entered her taut supereminence, her walls squeezing tightly around me. Her face pinched and I stopped, but she gripped my shoulders and urged me onward. Kissing her once, I pushed hard and fast. I broke through her barrier with a snarl on my lips and a cry on hers. Once I was buried deep inside her, it was like I was given a taste of heaven. And it was fucking addictive.

"Fuck, baby." I dropped my forehead to hers, gritting my teeth as I fought my urge to thrust.

"Okay." She gasped, her chest heaving beneath mine. "It's okay."

I positioned myself above her, watching as her flawless olive skin wrapped around my sinfully inked torso. I lifted her knee, faltering when I stared down at the apex of her thighs. *Blood.* Her barrier of innocence snapped and wept all over me, coating my cock like an offering to *il mietitore.* My hands trembled and my body vibrated with desire. Pulling back slowly, I slammed forward, burying myself deep once again.

Research showed that some women had more hymenal tissue than others, which could cause a girl to bleed when first penetrated. I was very much aware of the girth I was born with and therefore, I knew Sienna would take time to adjust. After a few more sexual interludes, her body would adapt and conform.

Sienna caterwauled with each thrust, and her body coiled tightly from the onslaught. I dropped her knee and pinched her clit, before swirling my fingers around the sensitive bundle of nerves. Her inner walls clenched and trembled, threatening to squeeze the life out of me.

A few more strokes against her clit and she screamed with release.

"Apollo!" she remonstrated, deep and breathy, as she came around my dick. Her pussy clasped so tightly, I practically saw stars as I bayed under the rush of my own climax.

"Christ, Sienna." I growled, my chest heaving as I kept coming, unsure if I'd ever stop. "Fuck."

Transcendence.

Her body glowed underneath mine from postcoital bliss as her own chest palpitated for several minutes. Our breaths evened out before I slowly withdrew my length, still tinged in her virginal blood. She swallowed audibly, staring at my dick standing tall and hard. I wasn't anywhere near settled with her. One taste and I was sentenced to hell for fucking the Devil's sister… I'd be damned if I wouldn't enjoy her a few more times. And I was already damned, so fuck it.

"Come here," I ordered, raising an eyebrow with a diabolical smirk.

She came all right. And fuck, so did I. Repeatedly.

The sun was rising when we collapsed, side by side, both of us spent. I rolled over and pulled her closer to my side, needing to touch her. But when I looked into her eyes something seemed off—her gaze harbored a sadness.

A moment later, her breathing evened out and she fell asleep wrapped in my arms. Something heavy settled on my chest because of that look. It was almost as if she was…

Saying Goodbye.

CHAPTER 26
SIENNA AGOSTINO

Nothing seemed to fit the expression on his face when he walked in covered in blood, not a single word in my vocabulary. Whoever died tonight—their remnants coating his skin—they seemed to take a part of him to their grave. I had the image of a frightened child standing before me. I couldn't tell myself to walk away, to turn my back on him, not like that.

When he noticed the thin barrier that was pushing back on his finger, I thought he'd flee. Instead, he finally lost his resolve—giving me the one thing I needed from him—before we said our goodbyes. I had dreamt about this and prayed that he would be the one, a memory we'd always share.

The initial pain sucked but he made it better. His dick was so thick that the first deep plunge threatened to break me apart. But I was insatiable and the moment we came together, I needed him again. When I saw that his erection hadn't gone down, a tingle of satisfaction—knowing that I did that to him—enveloped me.

"Come here." He smirked. The look on his face made my core clench in need. It was a part of Apollo I hadn't seen before, his devilish intentions as clear as the sky after a storm.

I stood up, cringing a little at the pinch of soreness between my legs. But that hesitation too was gone, the moment he eye-fucked me from my bed. I crawled on my hands and knees across the mattress, grabbing his dick with two hands and stroking him. His brown eyes melted into small pools of honey, dripping with desire and watching me like I was heaven-sent.

Without thinking about it too much, I leaned forward and took him into my mouth. He was warm and smooth, and his thickness parted my lips wide, bordering on uncomfortable. I dropped to my elbows with my ass in the air—letting him control the oral penetration—as he thrusted forward and back. I could taste myself on him, but it was his heady scent that made my own arousal spike. My jaw started to ache from his size, but his groans of pleasure urged me forward.

"Sienna." He pulled out of my mouth before settling in behind me. With one lunge, he buried himself inside me, a new angle that took him even further into my depths. I groaned against my comforter, losing control as a white-hot fire burned its way down my spine. Apollo was like a drug and I was chasing the most delicious high.

The sound of slapping skin, his deep moans and my muffled pleas filled the room—he smacked each of my ass cheeks twice before rubbing my clit. I came on a scream and he followed with a roar. But I was far from spent, rolling onto my side as he once again pulled out of me. We lay next to each other, catching our breaths.

When I felt his erection against my leg—pointing north like a strong arrow—I pinned my legs together to satiate my need to have him again. My body was beyond sore but it was fighting with my brain to have more. I climbed to my knees and shoved him onto his back, straddling his waist as he pushed himself into my entrance. Once seated deep inside me, I leaned backwards. My hands on his thighs, I tossed my head and moaned.

His warm calloused hands grabbed my breasts as he lightly stroked and tugged my nipples. I started to roll my hips and move against him, a little awkward at first, before finding my rhythm. He played with my clit and my hips jerked faster as I found myself teetering on that delicious edge once again. I rode the wave harder, jerking with uncoordinated movements as fast as I could.

When I slowed down, a rough grip latched onto my neck and pulled me forward. My long hair dropped in a curtain around us as he stared up at me. The expression on his face was so tender, then pulling me closer, he kissed me with a softness that almost made me cry. His grip tightened as he swiveled his hips and started fucking me with a powerful force, my breasts bouncing from the intensity. I moaned as I felt myself build up again. Staring into his eyes, I shuttered—this orgasm threatened to break my heart into a million pieces. That look held promises that I knew he wouldn't keep, but it told me things I wanted to hold onto forever.

His grip on my neck tightened, and just when I thought I couldn't take anymore, I fell over into the abyss, with Apollo flying high right behind me. Spent and thoroughly satiated, I climbed off him and lay down. He looked like he wanted to say something, but I shook my head and pulled him closer. Cuddling and Apollo seemed like oil and water but it felt just right. His hold was strong and protective, and though it didn't make sense, I felt powerful in his arms.

Only the sunlight of a new day could threaten to crush this dream we were living in. Tomorrow we'd go back to our reality, to being friends with an undercurrent of sexual attraction. I'd drown myself in work, and he'd drown himself in blood and whores. It wasn't a romantic fairytale by any means. But for just one night, gone was the woman I was raised to be, replaced by the woman I wanted to become.

I forced my body to relax, cocooned in the comfort his arms created. I fell asleep for a short time, but woke as the sun blared through my windows. I slid from his grasp and climbed out of bed, careful not to wake him. He was still naked, and Christ, was his body a chiseled work of art.

My jaw went slack when I looked at his dick resting against his thigh. He wasn't aroused but it was still a mighty sight to behold as my brain screamed for me to back up, my body fully spent and incapable of taking more. I brushed a light kiss to his lips before glancing down at the blood on my sheets and smiling to myself.

Last night, I gracefully handed my virginity to a cold and calculated killer. Today, my brother was marrying the love of his life and I was creating their nirvana. Once showered, I threw on some sweats and darted down the stairs to monitor the staff. Bella and Lucky would have the perfect day, even if I had to kill someone to make sure of it.

I felt a moment of guilt for leaving him naked and alone in my room, but soon those thoughts were shoved to the back of my mind and I was lost to wedding coordinating. Besides, I refused to allow him— or anyone else for that matter—to burst my bubble of happiness by making today awkward. I got my wish and I said my goodbye. After the wedding, I would head to Philly to meet Romano, finally granting Apollo his reprieve from the inelegant tension between us.

Several staff members were already running around when I came downstairs. The moment I made eye contact with the caterer, she called all of the staff to attention and awaited instructions to ensure the wedding started at sunset. We had a lot of work to do but it would be worth it—at the end of the day, despite our differences, my brother was worth it.

At one point, my mother tried to gain my attention, and when it didn't work, she shoved food in my hand with a motherly glare. As the final preparations fell into place, my brother came down to check everything out. He and Apollo followed me across the aisle, paying attention to each of the details I reviewed with them. I had expected to feel distressed by *his* presence, but instead, my body was enlivened by his close perusal.

"Sienna." Lucky whispered my name as he gaped in awe at what I had created. I smiled happily to myself and glanced at Apollo, who was already looking at me with a peculiar expression painted across his face.

It wasn't filled with unfiltered exasperation or curled with murderous intentions—as was its tendency. In fact, he almost looked at peace as he paid close attention to everything that I showed them. I was filled with pride over their outward approvals.

The theme was my recreation of Lucky and Bella's first date at the restaurant *The Giardinos.* Bella loved gardens, flowers and vibrant colors, therefore I sought to emulate her "perfect date" as she called it. The tall cocktail tables were spread around the brick-covered terrace with flowers on every available surface. The moment you stepped outside, your senses were bombarded by the aroma of fresh flowers.

The walkway to my mother's garden was littered with candles, lighting the twirling path to the hidden pergola, where hundreds of red and white rose petals bestrewed the ground. I added more gigantic waxed pillars in every corner inside and around the enclosed space, while the final part of the aisle had large lanterns illuminated behind the glass so that the ground twinkled.

I spared no limit on my attention to detail and I believed that I nailed it. Bella deserved the happiness she'd spent her life fighting to achieve. Lucky called out for Apollo, but he remained in front of me.

"You left," he said after a moment.

"I had to get things done." I smiled, unsure what exactly was behind those eyes of his.

"Sienna." He sighed and it was like a punch to the gut.

"Don't." I growled. I didn't want to hear his bullshit, and I turned to walk away.

"Wait." He grabbed my arm and stopped my flight. "Thank you. For giving me the honor. For giving me such a gift. I know, without a fathom of doubt, that I didn't deserve it." He held my face in his hands, tenderly stroking my cheek.

"I've always wanted it to be you." I smiled as a single tear dropped, knowing this—this moment here—was our goodbye.

"I don't deserve anything good in my life but after tasting something so sweet, I want more." My heart stalled at his words—perhaps hanging onto hope. "But we can't. You know that it's not my choice." *But it was his choice to keep Persephone at his cabin, right? Funny how that worked out,* I thought to myself.

That being said, I honestly wanted to believe his words—hell, a part of me knew they were true. I wanted to slap and to shake him, to demand that he stand his ground and tell my father he was claiming me. And I wanted him to kick that girl out on her ass—both of those girls for that matter. But it wasn't in Apollo to rattle the tree that had given him life. I understood his loyalty to a point, but it was what kept us apart. It was his *choices* that kept us apart. We both wanted this… I could read it clear as day on his face.

"I'm not good for you." He kissed the tear that was staining my cheek.

"Apollo!" Lucky shouted again, pulling us from our private confessional. He smiled and turned on his heel to follow after my brother.

"What was that?" Octavia asked a moment later.

"Fucking Christ," was all I said as I left her in my dust, darting inside to get ready.

By the time I made it into my room—locking the door behind me—my mind had managed to twist the meaning of his words in several directions. Of course, he *wants more*. We both *want more*. After all, we came numerous times.

But it wasn't the same sentiment I shared, the same plea I'd been giving him for years. I steeled my spine and shoved the thoughts away —I knew this was coming, but it didn't mean it hurt any less.

I rinsed off in the shower and wrapped myself in a towel to style my hair. I pulled the tendrils back and off my face, added some curls to the ends and pinned it to hang over my right shoulder with my grandmother's diamond-encrusted, vintage hairpins.

I did a little contouring to make my high cheekbones pop and added a smoky palette to draw focus to the blue of my eyes. I had probably the nicest tan of my life going on, so I knew exactly what dress I wanted to wear.

A *Herve Leger* metallic fringe maxi dress that I'd been saving for a special occasion. It was a glimmering silver, which looked perfect against the tone of my skin, and bore a tight bodice that clung all the way to my mid-thigh, before turning into dangling fringe pieces and ending at my feet.

It was form-fitting but the bottom flare made it fun and easy to move around in. Then, of course, the hemline sat atop my new *Jimmy Choo* Romy Glitter Pumps.

One last look in the mirror, and I went down to greet the guests. Apollo and Lucky were nowhere to be found, forcing me to play the gracious hostess alongside my mother while welcoming family and business acquaintances.

We'd kept the list small and close, to avoid any issues with this Russian-Moretti mess. I checked the decor once more and laid fresh petals down the walkway, just in time for Bella to appear on the arm of her mother.

My heart pounded in my chest and tears burned the backs of my eyes. I looked away for a second to collect myself, but was startled when I noticed that Apollo was already glaring at me.

His expression was odd again—not closed off but blank... confused. I smiled at him, turning back to Bella and Serafina as the pair approached the altar. Anthony Moretti was still MIA, like the rest of her family—the poor girl.

She was wearing a gorgeous white *Vivienne Westwood* gown with a delicate drape corset and Theresa skirt lined in silver lace. It was cut into a halter neckline and boasted a tight bodice waist before flaring out perfectly.

The makeup artists did an incredible job of hiding her slight bruises and ensuring her mismatched eyes shined. I smiled encouragingly as they stopped at the altar and Serafina stepped forward.

"The future King of New York or not, this woman I am handing over to you is more than you deserve. She needs to be loved and cherished like no other. She deserves the world, the moon and the stars. All of which you will deliver to her on a shiny platter. No tears, unless of joy. No sadness for a single moment and nothing more than happiness for you both." Serafina relinquished her daughter's hand to Lucky. "Because *il diavolo* or not, I promise you this. I will. Fucking. Destroy. You." Her words were delivered so damn happily that it made the small woman that much more terrifying. My parents and the guests started chuckling but I looked at the quiet, timid Serafina Moretti with a whole new light.

"Your mother's sincere threats or not, I promise you this: you will never know another day without love and happiness. I will give you a house filled with fresh flowers every day, with love and laughter of a warm and caring family to cherish you as much as I do. Anyone who ever wishes you anything other than love, I will destroy with my bare hands. You're my love, my life and my future. And fuck, if I'm not the luckiest bastard alive," Lucky announced tenderly.

All of our guests and family laughed at the impromptu speeches that had been delivered. We were *mafioso* after all. We didn't give a damn what people thought. We lived by our own code—promises of love and threats of violence went hand in hand.

Just as my brother and his bride went to lean in for the kiss that would seal their union, I chanced a glance at Apollo. He mouthed that he needed to talk to me and as I was about to nod my agreement, a figure moving across the lawn caught my attention.

A man dressed in all black approached from the south end of the yard, only he wasn't one of our waiters. I looked down at his tactical gear and shouted, signaling Apollo towards the ominous threat coming our way.

I jumped to my feet, shoving my mother and sister to the ground. I grabbed the table with flowers and lanterns, flipping it over to shield them.

I turned to Lucky as the gunfire started to erupt but it was too late. Bella hung in his arms, red pooling in the center of her perfectly white dress. I started to scream and charge for them, stumbling when a burning pain sliced the skin at my side.

Apollo darted towards me, tackled me to the ground and dragged me back behind the table.

"Sienna, fuck." He growled, ripping at my gown to examine the wound.

"It's fine! Look, the bullet came out." I pointed to the seeping hole in my side. "Now, go!" He confirmed it was just a through-and-through before handing me a gun and ripping a piece of his jacket off to pin it to my gash. With one last glance, he took off towards the threat.

"This can't be happening." I heard Octavia mutter.

I crawled towards her; she was still hidden behind the makeshift barrier in fright. Seeing that my sister was unharmed, I breathed a sigh of relief. Serafina was leaning over the upturned table, firing cover as my dad charged away with Bella in his arms.

I had expected Octavia to be cowering under a chair, crying and freaking out. Instead, she was wide-eyed and angry, grabbing my side to inspect my injury—just as Apollo had.

"It's out," she said, and I nodded. "Backup is almost here." She tapped her cell phone with a bob of her head, but I didn't understand the reference. And I didn't have time to figure it out.

"Motherfucker." I growled, finally spotting the source of the fire-power raining down on my family.

"Alexander Bucharov," Octavia muttered, pointing at the man in question. He was tall with familiar features, features that I'd seen before. He must've been stalking somewhere around me...

Lucky was storming towards Alexander with Apollo and Al on his heel. It took them mere moments to hurdle over the table and take the Russian down.

I breathed a sigh of relief when I saw they had the situation taken care of, and everyone scrambled to help the injured.

"Come on, dear, we'll get you stitched up." I looked down to Sera-fina Moretti. Her eyes were filled with devastation, and I couldn't help myself as I started to cry.

I turned to grab Octavia but she was already across the yard, standing around the corner of the house and talking to an obscured figure. By the profile, I knew it was a man, but he remained hidden by the curvature of the stone siding.

She stomped her feet before turning around and taking off in a full run towards me. She wrapped her arms around my waist, helping me to the car with Rocco and Peiro.

Rocco stepped on the gas and we darted down the driveway,

surrounded by two other cars. Serafina was crying softly to herself, holding Apollo's jacket against my gunshot wound.

"I'm so sorry," I said, tears peppering my own eyes.

"Why're you sorry, dear?" she asked.

"Because Bella is hurt, her dream wedding is ruined and you're all alone." I didn't mean to unload like that, but my heart bled for the woman.

Maybe it was more than that, maybe it was like a vision into my future. I didn't want this life for myself or for my children. Philly seemed much quieter since Romano took over, but the threat would always be there. None of us would be safe when the war over power began.

We pulled up out front of the hospital and Serafina took off towards my parents. Octavia and Rocco walked me inside and called for a doctor to come give me stitches.

I tried to wave off their concern but they demanded that I be looked at. I was taken to a small room shrouded by curtains and assisted by a hot, young male nurse.

"Beautiful dress for a beautiful woman. Even soaked in blood." He smiled at me, but it did nothing. He had a stunning smile of straight white teeth, a surfer's tan and blonde hair.

"Stitch her up and keep your mouth shut there, *nurse*." Rocco stepped behind the curtain with his arms crossed over his wide chest.

"My apologies, sir. I was just trying to make your wife smile." He winked at me and I snorted. He made quick work of my stitches and stepped out to grab more gauze. Upon his exit, I glared at Rocco expectantly.

"It's handled. They're on their way. Besides Bella, only one of the waitstaff was hurt and he'll live," Rocco confirmed.

Once I was cleaned up, I went back to the waiting room with the rest of the family. A short time later, Lucky stormed in with Apollo and Al. I darted for my best friend, who gladly pulled me in for a long hug followed by a slew of encouraging words.

We gathered around each other and my heart wept at the thought of losing Bella. It would destroy my brother and break our family apart.

I wanted out of this life—it wasn't for me anymore. Well, maybe it never really was.

I deserved better than gunshot-riddled designer dresses and beautiful brides fighting for their lives. I looked to my sister, then over at my mother and Serafina.

We all did...

CHAPTER 27
APOLLO DELUCA

There was something to be said about watching someone you're close to fall apart. To have no way to help them in their despair but be a silent ally at their side. The strongest person I knew, who seemed to rule his world with an iron fist, was a shell of the man he once was.

After Bella's shooting, his revenge on the Russian didn't satiate the pain in his chest. Sending Alexander off to the basement with a few of our men, we headed to the hospital where his bride had been taken. The car ride was ominously silent as thoughts of death and loss hung heavy in the air.

Her mother and his parents sat in the waiting room, all with the same bleak expressions. Mirabella was the glue that held these two families together; a girl with no trepidations latched onto the Devil himself and she inspired us all to be better… to do better.

"What's the news?" Lucky asked as we approached, the women bursting into tears at the sight of him.

"She was taken into surgery. We've heard nothing yet," Serafina Moretti was an older model of her young daughter. Years under the Moretti name and yet her fire still burned bright.

"Does anyone want coffee?" Sienna rose to her feet, turning her back on me. Several "please and thank you's" were announced before she angrily strolled away.

"I'll help her." Leaving Lucky to his weeping mother and business with Mario, I followed the dark-haired beauty.

Stepping into a small alcove of the lobby, there was a coffee dispenser and several vending machines. Twirling in her towering heels, Sienna offered me a fake smile. "I'm good, thanks." She turned her back on me yet again, aggressively punching the numbers into the keypad.

Her skin tight dress was torn and coated in her own blood but it did little to dwindle her beauty. Images of her writhing beneath me, begging me to dissolve her innocence swirled in my mind—my dick craving another taste. Her altered disposition was expected as she built her protective walls back up around her. However, she didn't need to direct her line of fire at me. It had been a fuck of a day and this attitude wouldn't work.

Snatching her wrist, I spun her around to face me before pushing her up against the vending machine with my body. Even with the added height of her heels, I looked down at the delicate woman before me—fire brewing in her eyes—and she was a sight to behold.

"Get. Off. Me." I could hear her teeth grinding between each word.

Yeah, she was pissed.

"To what am I owed this attitude, pray tell?" She liked to pretend she hated how I spoke to her. But I was so attuned to her body, I could hear the spike in her breathing when I'd quote Shakespeare or Mark Twain.

"This isn't about you, Apollo. My sister-in-law is getting surgery on a wound that should've been prevented." Tears began filling her auspicious eyes. "The chances of her survival are slim to none and I know it will kill my brother. Right now, all I care about is getting a fucking cup of coffee."

She shoved me backwards, out of her way, and spun around. Jabbing the dispense button several times, she lowered her head as small, barely visible wracks of pain shook her shoulders.

"The coffee is already in the cup." Stepping around her, I took it out of the proffered machine and started a new one.

"Thank you." Her words were barely audible as she held the warm Styrofoam in her hand.

"Whatever happens, we will get through it, together. Just like this family has always done." Tugging her to my body, I allowed my heat to comfort her small frame.

Whenever strife hit the Agostino's, they banded together to share their strength, showing the powerful force they were. It was peculiar to me—their inability to shut off their emotions to deal with the problem at hand. But then again, most social interactions were peculiar to me.

I understood Sienna's comments—Lucky would be destroyed by his enemies' travesties. On the off-chance Bella didn't survive, a piece of him would die with her. As much as I didn't grasp that feeling myself, I could see the devastation on his face.

"We won't get through this together," she mumbled, pushing away from me.

"The hell we won't. I am here, Sienna. I will be the strength you need." Spinning on her stiletto, she stepped away from me and to the furthest corner of the vestibule.

There were many sides to this girl. Even now—standing in front of me in her ripped designer dress with a hole at the hip revealing her fresh stitches—I wondered which part was about to attack. Hidden behind an expensive label, a frail Italian woman cliché and a too-smart-for-her-own-good persona was a wildcat.

She was an enigma—one minute she'd flay you alive for fucking with someone she cared about and the next she was crying over a romance novel. She had what would make other women envious. Yet here she was hiding behind her coffee cup, looking into the dark liquid like it held all the answers. She was upset about her family—true, but there was something else stinging that overwhelming heart of hers.

"Fucking spill, Sienna." Her eyes burned brightly, as she prepared for her verbal retribution.

"We won't get through this or anything else *together.* Once all of this is handled, I am leaving." Raising a brow at her outburst only fueled her rage. "I want more than murderous vendettas. More than old school Italian facades and men attempting to gain power at the whim of others' misfortunes. I am craving more, someone offering more."

Both at a loss for words, we each stared deeply into the other's eyes as the silence stretched on for a few more moments. I was aware of her dislike for the parts of the mafia world that disgraced women outside the Agostino household. But the mere mention of leaving everyone... leaving all of it behind was something else. Especially after last night, after the way we had both dropped our guards...

"Sienna." Raising her hand, she stopped my words and stepped into my space.

"I've always hidden behind your lack of emotional capacity as the reasoning to why we'd never be together. Loyalty to Lucky and the family was the only real thing you felt. I was okay with that... with believing one day, emotions aside, you'd see we were a good fit." Setting her coffee on the counter, she moved closer and peered into my eyes. "But I was so wrong."

"Sienna, the loyalty..." Cutting me off again, she spun on her heel before halting at the exit.

"I hid behind your apathy because I thought it was hardening my heart against the feelings you stirred in me. Inside, it brutalized every-thing I had believed. But once I saw the emotions that you'd truly kept hidden, I realized I was an idiot."

Indeed, Sienna was riddled with a very tempestuous presence, allowing such feelings to make her see things that weren't there. Whatever sentiments she had were totally irrelevant. I didn't know anything outside of the loyalty I'd given to the Agostino's—even when I thought I did. Seeing the devastation at the wedding made me realize what I thought I felt must have been nothing more than postcoital endorphins. And perhaps if I hadn't allowed them to cloud my senses, I would have seen the men coming up our rear—but all I had seen at the time was Sienna Agostino simultaneously staring at me and through me.

"You know my clinical diagnosis." Her chest rose and fell aggressively, her ample breasts heaving at the motion.

"It's bullshit. You're bullshit." Breathing angered flames, she drew out the suspense before asking me a question that felt like a slap across the face. "Did Persephone settle into your home okay?"

That was what this attitude was about? That girl had several issues, none of which stirred anything substantial inside me—other than the rage that burned under my skin and the desire to rip her fingernails off to keep her from singing that stupid nursery rhyme.

"The fuck that have anything to do…" Lucky's painful roar in the next room stopped our conversation.

"No!" Sienna stormed past me and towards the inconsolable screams.

Heading back inside the waiting area, I watched the family collapse before the surgeon, his green scrubs covered in blood. The man shook his head and apologized—she hadn't made it… Bella hadn't made it. Serafina and Isabella were holding onto Octavia, crying in heaps of heartbreak on the floor. Lucky stood, pacing as he tugged on his hair, a mess of anguish and brutal fury.

"Fuck." Shaking off my reverie, I started towards my makeshift family.

Mirabella Moretti was the glue now removed. She had been the calm that rendered the Devil tame. Her sudden death created an odd feeling I was unfamiliar with inside myself. No doubt, it must have been a sense of foreboding as Lucky tore through the hospital exit.

Passing Mario, the only real father I ever had, I noted that his face was a mask of indifference. As he hugged his wife and Serafina Moretti against his chest, his demeanor bothered me. It was bordering on guilt as he took in the destruction the loss had created.

After all these years working beside this man, nothing about his current expression made sense. I knew for a fact that he'd seek vengeance for her, but there was something else lingering under the surface, too. The way he locked his face down told me he was plotting, and his future plans wouldn't be what we expected.

Shouting outside alerted us to a scuffle, and the chaos sent security charging through the exit to stop Lucky's rampage. The scene I was witnessing—Lucky punching, kicking and throwing hospital guards around like ragdolls—would have been comical, if not for the pain and sheer ruin etched onto his face.

Once I was able to separate Lucky from his destruction, I ordered Al to take him to Alexander. The only way Lucky would be able to have a semblance of peace was to put the fucker down like the rabid dog he was. Lucky climbed into the back seat, a part of him—his very soul itself—left behind in that hospital room.

"Apollo, hold on a minute." I turned at the sound of Mario's voice.

"Take him. I'll meet you there," I ordered Al; however, we were halted by yet another shout.

"Boss!" Rocco boomed as he ran out of the hospital, holding his phone to his ear. "The Wolf is in New York—he wants a meeting."

A sinister smile washed over Lucky's face, and in an instant, his pain was masked by savagery and a slew of commands. Out of respect for the Russian enforcer, we'd hold off on murdering his nephew until he was present, but that didn't mean a warm up wasn't in order.

"He needs you now more than ever," Mario said, staring at his son before turning to me.

"I know. I've got him." It was a promise full of sincerity. He was my brother; this was my family and we protected each other.

"Apollo, there isn't a day that goes by that I don't think of you as a son." His words gave me pause, and I turned towards him with a curious stare. "It's the damnedest thing being a father. Unsure if the decisions you are making are right for your family. The pain and anguish they feel… wanting to free them of it in any way you can. But sometimes… it's just not that easy."

I didn't say anything—I didn't know what *to* say. He'd been a parent to me since the day he pulled Cara and me off the streets. His face, mannerisms and tone were of a man I didn't recognize. I was unsure if it was the guilt that he felt for not protecting Bella—but that fell on all of us—or if it was something else… I thought about it for a moment longer and then I realized, Mario was indeed burdened by something other than the girl's death—I was sure there was much more to him than what met the eye.

"Cara called me," he admitted. "Why didn't you tell me you had *him*?"

"It wasn't your problem—it was ours to deal with." Cracking my neck from side to side, I refused to make eye contact.

"She told me it's done." We both turned towards the car as Lucky started punching the seat in front of him. Shaking his head over his son's grief, Mario continued. "I still remember *il mietitore's* first kill. A new man was created that day—empowered and in control. Do you remember?"

"Eugenio Affanad." I smirked. "How could I forget that day? It's what cemented me into place, calmed me."

"I've never been prouder of the man you've become." His face boasted a smile while I was left in silence. We watched as the doors opened and Sienna walked out holding a weeping Octavia. "Speaking in the sense of legality, I'd be happy to call you my son—of sorts—if you wanted that official title." He nodded towards Sienna.

Frozen in a state of reticence, neither of us moved for a few minutes as Sienna helped Octavia get into the car. She walked back over and hugged Mario, her blue eyes clouded by unshed tears. He smiled at his eldest daughter, giving her a squeeze before turning a solemn expression to me and raising a brow, as if in challenge. I didn't speak as he whispered in her ear. She nodded in response and headed back towards the car.

"Sometimes things happen that force us to open our eyes before it's too late. I made a tough call for this family, one now filled with the kind of regret that I have to live with for the rest of my life. Don't follow in my footsteps, make the right choice while it's still an option to make." He stepped towards the entrance of the hospital. "Watch your back with the Russians. The Wolf seems like a man true to his word, but Sergei Oblonsky is a fucking snake in the grass." I nodded, before darting to the car to meet up with Lucky and Al.

As I marched down the stairs towards the basement, Mario's words played on repeat in my head. I had to force myself to lock them away as I focused on ensuring that Lucky had his revenge. Bella was gone and it had fragmented all of the good that had been left in his soul. I was concerned that my best friend was going to be forced to face the same dark reality as I had, and live with his demons in the shadows.

"Lucky. Nice to see you. Shouldn't you be on your honeymoon." Lucky didn't speak, staring absently. "No? How is the blushing bride?" Spatting blood-tinged saliva on the floor, Alexander smiled triumphantly.

"She's well, thanks. She sends her regards." The fucker anticipated a reaction, but in defense, Lucky had locked it away.

"Pity, she didn't come herself. Why is that?" The Russian knew the shot to her chest had done its job, but Lucky wouldn't grant him the satisfaction of saying it aloud.

Instead, the growl that left him echoed off the walls as he pounced at our captive. Left, right, left—Lucky attacked him with such ferocity, such anguish, no one was able to look away. We needed to keep the son of a bitch alive long enough to appease the Wolf, but Lucky was owed this recompense. After several minutes, Al and I stepped forward to call him off. He was covered in blood while his knuckles were nothing more than cracked teeth and broken flesh. Like a cornered beast, his eyes drowned in misery as he continued to fight against us.

"You're fucking dead." He spat in Alexander's face before pushing away from me and my attempt to clean him up. Charging upstairs into the lobby, he barreled forward while residents and employees alike ran from his barbarous appearance.

"Fuck..." Al muttered, watching Lucky disappear into a waiting car.

"Come. We need to meet with the Wolf," I ordered our small crew.

"We're going without Lucky?" Al asked, and I had to refrain from punching his face in as he doubted my volition.

"Does it look like he is capable of conducting business in his current state?" It was a question that didn't need an answer. We drove silently into the *Bratva* territory downtown, pulling up to the curb outside a Russian restaurant.

If their *Pakhan* didn't attend, the meeting should be uneventful—Sergei Oblonsky, the portly man in question, was known to create chaos with little to no preamble. With Lucky off his game, I needed to be the voice of reason with the Russians... to ensure Bella got her justice.

"You sure about this?" Al asked, looking out the window with an aberrant expression.

"We need to maintain peace. From what I know of Nikolai Volkov, we should be able to handle this matter amicably." I took my 9mm from its holster, loading a round into the chamber.

"And if Sergei is there?" Rocco probed, following suit with his own firearm.

"We stay calm." Opening the door, I slid out and walked towards the restaurant.

Several men in expensive suits lingered at the threshold, blocking our entrance. I stepped forward—Rocco and Al a formidable wall at my back—and nodded to the man who appeared to be in charge. The Wolf had come to the US with an army, to do what still remained to be seen.

"Where Lucky?" One of the Russian men addressed me, his accent weighing down each of his words.

"Busy at the moment." I reached out a hand, in a gesture of peace.

He stared at it for a moment, smoking his cigarette, before offering his own. I took stock of the tattoos on his neck and hands: the skin of each of his fingers was banded by several dark rings while a poorly sketched manacle encompassed his wrist; the shackles stretched up his forearm and adorned what appeared to be an Orthodox cathedral of some sort. With this in mind, I knew the heavy canvas of ink was indicative of several years spent in a Russian prison.

"Come," he said, turning on his heel as he spoke to his men in his native tongue.

The small army was spread throughout the room and in the center, at the only occupied table, was the Wolf. Nikolai Volkov was fair-skinned; he bore bright gray eyes with dark blonde hair buzzed short, and he maintained a neat beard. His suit was expensive, tailored to him, but he forewent a tie and his collar was unbuttoned.

"I'd know those tattoos anywhere," Nikolai stated, rising to his feet and extending a hand.

"And I yours." Our clasped palms tightened—a silent pissing match—while I took note of the ink visible on his neck and chest as well as along the outside of his knuckles.

"Lucky couldn't make the time to see me?" He motioned for a waitress to come over. A young girl smiled sheepishly as she filled our small glasses with vodka.

"He will join us when we're ready to deal with Alexander." At my words, he raised his drink and we threw them back.

"You have him already?" he asked, to which I nodded. "Interesting. And I assume Lucky is tending to his new bride?" He smiled, not a hint of deceit in his words.

"Alexander was captured during the wedding." Rocco and Al shifted behind me, uneasy on their feet. "The bride… she didn't make it."

Nikolai's eyes went large, the round orbs smoldering with rage and turning a shade darker—almost black. It was one of the many reasons he was nicknamed the Wolf. You see, the way he looked through you; it was animalistic… it was soulless.

"Women suffer enough for our sins. They should be protected from the games men play." His words were very telling, something had happened to a woman of his, something bad.

"Now, as for Alexander, do you know where his brother is?" I watched his facial attestation at my line of questioning—I needed confirmation. I looked for any sign that Nikolai knew more than he was letting on.

"What of him? From what I understand he's had little to do with his family over the years. As I said, he is his mother's son." And there it was—the slightest twitch of his eyebrow and a heavy swallow. He fucking knew where the boy was.

"I won't allow anyone who has had a hand in this to go unpunished," I stated dryly.

"I have no plans to interfere. I am merely here to ask my nephew a few questions before Lucky does as he sees fit." Though there was no indication he was holding back this time, the man was Machiavellian by nature and I couldn't count on his word alone.

"Deal. Let me speak with Lucky and I will be in touch." We both rose to our feet, shaking hands in shared agreement.

"Please send my condolences to *il diavolo*. We will make this right." The men around the room all straightened as we turned and made our way back to our vehicle.

The ride to the penthouse was monotonous, each of us lost in the perplexity of our own circumstances. Rocco dropped us off at the door, while Al and I rode the elevators to the top. As we approached the hotel cutoff to the suites, the sounds of an altercation drifted into our space. Readying our firearms, I motioned that I'd step out first.

Lucky was hollering and we could hear anguished cries—female cries. The doors opened to an empty vestibule, but I could see Lucky's reflection in the distance.

He had a hold of Tatianna, slamming her head against the elevator mirror—over and over again—as she clawed at the fingers clasped around her neck. Al and I were on him in seconds, pulling him out of the enclosed space.

I shouted at Lucky but his auditory functioning seemed to cease as he launched out of my grip. Tatianna was stabbing at the buttons trying to flee, but he wasn't having it.

"I fucking warned you last time. You never speak of my fucking queen again." He was screaming in the girl's face.

"I wanted to show you I was sorry. I could take away your pain." She was a blubbering mess, cowering on the floor of the elevator with her hands raised in a gestured plea.

"The only way you could truly be sorry would be to die. To allow me the chance to watch life slowly drain from your disgusting body." She trembled beneath the weight of his voice.

"You were mine before her. I wanted to be yours after," she whimpered.

Lucky had pulled his firearm from under his jacket, aiming it dead-center—a kill shot. His shoulders bounced up and down while his eyes remained distant as he loomed over her. Al and I looked at each other, unsure of how we should proceed. I stepped towards him when the elevator next to us opened and froze us in a perpetual state of shock, as if the world itself had turned on its axis.

"When will you learn, Tatianna?" I stared, slack-jawed, in the direction of the ethereal voice. "He will never be yours. I'm done with people trying to take what belongs to me." Mirabella Moretti (or was it Agostino now?) grabbed the 9mm from Lucky's grip—there wasn't an ounce of hesitation as she unloaded the magazine into Tatianna.

"Bella!" Lucky finally realized his bride wasn't some fucked-up mirage just as she collapsed into his arms.

When we'd extracted Alexander from the wedding, he was armed with a 45-caliber. A cartridge of that size would've gone straight through her abdomen, producing a smaller hole at the entrance and a larger one at the exit. In order for Bella to be standing before us, the bullet had to have missed all of her major organs and arteries, a feat that was incomparably rare. A damn near miracle—if I believed in such a thing

"I told you I didn't want you to hate me." Mario spoke up as if appearing from the air. "But I saw an opening and took it. To draw them out of the shadows."

"Welcome back, Bella." I stared at her pale face; I myself was wide-eyed and confused. "Boss, I got this." I motioned to Tatianna's body before the doors closed in front of the unfathomable reunion.

"Holy. Fuck." Al said the words we were both thinking. "She's alive."

"And *she* isn't." I nodded towards the motionless form at our feet. "Wanna give a hand there, princess?" Al grunted a response before stepping into the elevator and grabbing one of Tatianna's arms.

Mario was a man on a mission and it was clear, his family's mental health be damned, he was ready to do whatever he needed to protect his city. He had called the sheep out to pasture, so the goddamned wolves could attack.

CHAPTER 28

ALEXEI BUCHAROV

This man, the very sound of his voice, bored me. He'd done nothing but drone on for the last hour about his contempt for the Agostino's. I had attended this meeting because I knew for a fact that the Italians had my brother. If he was still alive—which was merely an assumption—then Alexander was currently in a world of pain while drowning in remorse. Not for his actions, of course, but merely because he was caught before he could taste his victory.

My brother had spent his entire life believing that because he was the eldest son, he was responsible for the family's success. However, instead of hard work and planning, he followed the path my father was infamous for taking; the stupid one, paved in villainous intent while scheming and stealing from those more powerful than us.

It was those very ideals that built my entire life up until this moment. My father liked to tell tales of his childhood in Moscow. The mighty and powerful Yuri Bucharov, tyrannist and malicious leader over the *Bratva*. He boasted about being one of the original soldiers in the country, forging an alliance from jail while imprisoned for murdering a man in my mother's honor.

I suppose he forgot that Alexander and I remembered what happened the day we fled Russia.

My parents fought nonstop; this time was no exception to the depravity we witnessed when they argued. It was winter and cold. It was always so cold—one of the many things I didn't miss about that country. I was playing dolls with my little sister, Mila, while Alexander sat in the corner sharpening one of his many knives.

Alexander liked to think he would rule the family in my father's stead, but there wasn't anything for him to rule. My mother hated my father; he only used her for my uncle's connections to the Bratva. Our family struggled to live, let alone thrive; a fact that Alexander turned a blind eye to. I couldn't remember what they were fighting about. Perhaps I didn't want to remember. That, or I just didn't care because I was so used to it.

But I remembered the roar—stricken, terrifying and belonging to my father.

Alexander and I went to take a glance into the living room but our father blocked our paths. He coerced us into packing a bag and into leaving the apartment through the fire escape. Alexander went first, while I ushered Mila out of the window. Looking back over my shoulder, I stopped myself from following to momentarily grab her favorite doll. My father was securing the bottom of the pane open with his elbow, yelling at me to hurry up, when I saw my mother's lifeless eyes staring back at me. He'd killed her and like a coward he was fleeing. He knew my uncle would come for him...

We'd just made it to our shitty little car and pulled out of the parking lot when we saw several SUV's come flying in behind us. We somehow narrowly managed to escape as we headed for the train station. My father had refused to tell us anything, but I knew none of his plans would be good. We'd barely managed to survive in Russia. I could only imagine what he was thinking, taking three children to an entirely new country.

One look at my baby sister's innocent face and panic overtook me. What type of life would she live if we were on the run? Mila was too gorgeous for her own sake, my little Russian doll. She had hair dark as night and pale blue eyes like little clouds mingling with the hues of the sky. She was an exact replica of my mother, a natural beauty. She would be a target, a means to an end, in my father's climb for success. I couldn't—I wouldn't allow that to happen.

We'd pulled into the train station as the final whistle blew for everyone to board. My father shouted for us to hurry up but Mila was little and slow. I stopped to lift her into my arms when I saw my Uncle Nikolai's black Mercedes enter the parking lot. However, I knew he was too far away and wouldn't make it to us in time. He was a terrifying man but he loved my mother and he adored Mila.

"I love you, zaika," I muttered, looking down at her big bright eyes surrounding her button nose. She was my little bunny, my baby sister, and I'd die for her.

"I'm cold..." she whined, burrowing herself into her oversized jacket.

"Uncle Nikolai is here, zaika," I said, watching her expression light up. She loved him, probably more than her own father, and that look told me all I needed to know—it was the right decision.

"Mila!" Uncle Nikolai roared, running through the snow to get to us.

"Go to him, zaika! And know I will always love you!" I shouted my affirmation, turning her towards him and helping her little legs run faster.

Uncle Nikolai watched me with an intent gaze, and once he understood what I was doing, he nodded. He bent down into the bitter snow and opened his arms wide as Mila barreled into his embrace. I smiled as tears poured down my face.

"Take care of her!" I yelled, before stepping backwards and fleeing towards the tracks.

"Stay, Alexei. You're not like them!" my uncle ordered, but it was too late—I'd already made up my mind.

"Someone needs to watch out for them." I gestured towards the train car where my father and brother were waiting. Then, without another word, I boarded, leaving my little sister behind with the most feared member of the Russian mob.

Neither of them ever asked where Mila went or what happened. They seemed almost relieved that they didn't have to deal with the burden of the small girl. I wanted her safe and I knew I had done right by her. And in turn, I would follow my father and brother wherever they went and attempt to keep them out of trouble. We did eventually split up but we always stayed in contact. I had valuable skills—skills they needed—and that fact ensured I could do my best to protect them.

However, this... this they didn't contact me about. If I had learned about their plans to align themselves with the Moretti's and overthrow the Agostino's, I would have warned them against it. Until now, they'd only managed to amass a small gun trade while dabbling in drug running. I was able to keep them out of the crosshairs but I had always made my intentions clear—I would do my best to help, but when they got in over their heads, they were on their own.

Tampering with the Italians' shipments and spying on their organization had been stupid enough. But kidnapping the future bride of the eldest Agostino—the heir for god's sake—well, that was like swimming with cement shoes. I'd learned all of the details too late, and now my idiot brother had gotten himself captured for shooting up a wedding. He was as good as dead, practically dug his own grave like our father... may he rest in hell. I wanted to mourn for the man, to cry for him, to feel something. I really did. But I couldn't. My father bore no love for me and the feeling was mutual. I had kept my tabs on him for business purposes only. And now my brother was just as lost... just as damned for killing the Italian bride.

"I'm sorry for your loss." I offered my condolences to Anthony Moretti.

"I'm losing millions!" He pounded the table in front of me, freezing when I raised a curious brow. "Thank you, yes. She was a sweet girl."

Selfish bastard.

"What can I do for you, Anthony? Why have you reached out to me?" I had an idea of what he wanted, but I needed to hear him say it.

"Alexander, may God rest his soul," Anthony said, even going as far as to make the sign of the cross, "told me that you had connections to Sergei Oblonsky."

"And?" I steepled my hands in front of me, leaning back in my leather chair.

"I would like an introduction. I am confident that I can finish what my son and your brother started. A lucrative business connection, if you will." He sat back pleased with his attempt at *bargaining* with me.

"Sergei doesn't work with anyone outside of the *Bratva*. He is old-school, traditional in a sense. No one is as powerful as the Russian man, and he only makes deals with people that have things he wants. So, tell me, what is it that you have?" *Nothing*. Anthony Moretti had absolutely nothing.

"I am going to destroy the Agostino's, one family member at a time." His words had me sitting straighter in my seat. "They took my daughter from me; my sons are on the run and I refuse to cower. I have a plan to ensure that they bend to my will." He smirked, his eyes clouded by greed and thoughts of destruction.

"And what good is that for Sergei, exactly?" I asked, curiosity urging me forward.

I—in absolutely no way—had a direct connection with Sergei Oblonsky, the leader of the Russian *Bratva*. My uncle Nikolai had grown in the organization to be his number two. But other than checking on Mila and occasionally warning my uncle about my father's plans, I kept to myself. I ran my own life, my own business and created a future for myself in the states—a future outside of my family's hunger for power.

"Sienna Agostino." He clipped the girl's name—all too fucking cheeky with himself—as I tensed.

"And what of her?" I urged him on.

"My traitorous wife is partnering with the Agostino's and planning my daughter's funeral. Sienna will be present, to pay her respects of course. I will pick them off one by one, then I will take the Agostino girl as my prize. Once I have no additional use for her and have successfully taken over the city, I will pass her to Sergei as a gift, in exchange for an alliance." Anthony sat back, and the smile curling his lips told me just how pleased he was with his proposal.

"I thought your son was planning on keeping the girl," I mentioned.

"Gio isn't capable of doing what needs to be done. Hell, his younger brother has a successful trafficking business while Gio runs around talking a big game. But the fucker has no backbone." He grunted.

He had no clue just how wrong he was about his two sons.

"So, you will contact me after the funeral? When you've obtained the girl?" I asked.

"Yes. Are you…?" He paused to smirk at me. "Are you interested in her for yourself?"

"I will be honest with you, Anthony. Sergei won't be the type to do business with you… simply because you're Italian. Sell you some shit weaponry… maybe. But an alliance won't happen. Now, with me… Well, if you bring me the girl and gain my favor, I can act as your liaison. Which quite honestly is much safer for you. Sergei doesn't like double-crossers and that's exactly what you're doing to your sons."

"And you? How do you feel about that?" he asked, his hand leaving the table, as if I'd allow him the chance to reach for his firearm.

"Calm down." I chuckled. "I like money. Plain and simple. I came to this country from an impoverished and cold land, where I had nothing. Now, I want for nothing." I held my hands up, gesturing to my large office. "I've known for some time that I need to start my own family to build my empire, so I think we can help each other out."

"I think we can indeed." He rose from his seat and I followed, offering my palm. "I'll be in touch when I have the girl," he confirmed and I nodded.

"She is to remain untouched. I don't want sullied goods." I made my demand loud and clear.

"Of course." He faked what he thought was a sincere smile as I ushered him out the door.

"Fuck." I growled, that man was as slippery as they came. I grabbed my phone ready to make a couple of calls when I saw that the screen was already blinking.

"Nephew." The clipped voice greeted me in Russian.

"Uncle Nik, how nice to hear from you. How is Mila?" I asked, my heart aching at the mere mention of my little sister.

"A terrible teenager, just as you were, but gorgeous like her mother." Silence stretched between us for a moment, both lost in thought over our dearly departed.

"It's strange you reached out… I had plans to call you shortly," I admitted.

"Interesting. I am in the states. I think we should meet up." His tone was clear—it wasn't a request; it was an order.

"You're here?" I repeated. Then, pausing for a moment, I realized, "You're here for Alexander."

"Yes," he admitted dryly. "We've discussed this, Alexei, so don't tell me you're bothered by it now."

"Of course not. I just didn't think you'd come to the states for him. My father, yes, but not Alexander."

"He had the same opportunities as you did, Alexei. Instead, he betrayed the brotherhood and stole three of our shipments." I cursed under my breath before he continued. "And I am looking to make an alliance with the Agostino's." It made sense—after all, the Italian family controlled the city.

"Understood, uncle. Is Mila with you?" I asked, hopeful at the chance of seeing her in person for the first time since I left Russia.

"Yes. We can discuss that later," he responded, pulling away from the receiver to speak to someone in the background. "Now, why were you planning to contact me in the first place?"

"I have some information you may be interested in."

"Let me work on the details and I will message you with a time and place. Mila will be excited to see you." He offered and I agreed before hanging up.

My heart was overwhelmed with a mix of emotions. The loss of my father felt like nothing to me. My brother's assumed death stung a little, however, he had numerous opportunities over the years to change. But the idea of seeing Mila, after a decade apart… Well, that stirred up painful thoughts of my mother.

I didn't have time to wander down memory lane as I went about the preparations of securing my new wife. Anthony, of course, would do all of the groundwork by procuring her; while I planned to kill him when he made the delivery... that's if the Agostino's didn't do it first. I sat back in my seat, watching the moon light up the sky over the city.

It was by a random happenstance that I came to New York looking for work. But now that I was here, I'd grown to love it and to call it home. I had planned to potentially move once more, but with the way everything was falling into place, I might just stay. The pawns had been maneuvered around the chess board. Now, I could sit back and watch them destroy each other before I was handed my *queen*.

Like father, like son, I suppose.

CHAPTER 29
SIENNA AGOSTINO

"You truly are the most gorgeous corpse on your funeral day, Bella." I tried to make a joke but it fell on stressed ears.

"Sienna!" My mother gasped, shaking her head as tears rolled down her cheeks.

"Sorry…" I mumbled. "Death, even fake death, makes me uncomfortable," I grunted, feeling like I was crawling out of my skin.

It had been a fucked-up couple of days. Bella was dead; then she wasn't. Then Tatianna was dead. Thankfully that bitch stayed that way. My father was using Bella as a sacrificial lamb to draw out the Moretti's, and her "funeral" was the perfect place for it. I had to admit, as fucked up as it was and as much as it hurt, it was a damn good idea.

"Well, *I* thought it was funny." Bella elbowed me and I smiled. "Time out," she said, causing me to turn back in her direction.

Except, she wasn't looking at me. She was looking at Apollo who had just entered the room. He stood tall and angry, surveying the group and softening only slightly when he saw me.

"Not now," I growled in a hushed tone.

"Sienna," he clipped. Then grabbing me by my arm, he practically dragged me away.

We hadn't talked since my hospital meltdown. I wasn't kidding about leaving it all behind. Tomorrow I was heading to Philly, where I planned to discuss safety measures with Romano. And if his answers didn't sound right, I wasn't staying.

I had the capabilities to go off the grid, hidden away where no one could find me, if needed. I was glad Bella was alive, but what if she wasn't? That was the threat I lived with every day because of my last name. And I didn't want it anymore. Romano would either handle my concerns or I was gone.

I followed alongside Apollo as he pushed me into the security room. He locked the door behind us, pinning me to the wall with a pointer and middle finger against my chest. He'd actually texted me a few times to ensure I was safe, which was more than he'd normally attempt. We were doing a fantastic job of hiding from the reality of our actions.

"Are you, oh—" I stopped when he lunged for me.

His large hands gripped the sides of my face, tugging me closer. I didn't hesitate to latch onto him, our lips molding together perfectly. We let our bodies speak all the things we didn't know how to say. For reasons I couldn't explain, I started crying silently as I drowned in his kiss.

"Fuck me, Apollo. Please, I need you," I begged, causing him to growl as he pulled away from me. He took one look at my face and his expression softened. Leaning forward, he pressed his lips to the two stray tears trailing down my cheeks.

"Sienna," he snarled, gripping my shoulders before turning me around and lifting the back of my black *Givenchy* funeral dress.

He dropped to his knees, his tattooed hands feeling their way up from my ankle to my panties. His finger traced over the fine lace covering my pussy and I quivered in need, gasping at the sensation. Ever so slowly, he pulled the fabric down my legs, his nails dragging along my skin as they went, before I stepped out of them. He quickly shoved my relinquished undergarment into his pocket and leaned forward, swiping his tongue between my folds.

His large hands gripped my thighs to hold me upright as my legs trembled and threatened to give way. The sensation was so overwhelming I thought I'd fall apart at the seams. Back and forth he tasted and explored, his beautifully inked knuckle rubbing over my clit as another finger stroked inside me. I was biting my lip in an attempt to hold back my screams of pleasure.

"The sweetest fucking pussy I've ever tasted," he said, before wrapping his lips around my clit and sucking hard. The slight burst of pain sent me over the edge, and I shoved my hands over my mouth as my orgasm rattled me to my core.

"Fuck." He growled, licking me a few more times before rising to his feet.

I arched my ass out further, widening my stance as I looked over my shoulder to see him pulling himself out of his pants. A new need surged through me as I watched him stroke himself once, then twice before aligning with my entrance. My thighs shook as I breathed deeply, trying to prepare myself. But no amount of preparation would work, his dick was just so *fucking* big.

He moved slowly, cautiously, with a gentleness that was still so unexpected. Once he was pushed all the way inside me, I breathed deep and pushed back. The erotic feeling as I stretched to accommodate him sizzled down my spine, my body enlivening with the force of his penetration. Back and forth, slowly he thrusted his hips, an even and measured pace. Apollo locked his hand over my mouth, increasing his speed as I fought to hold on tight.

"Christ, Sienna, you drive me wild," he groaned.

"I-I'm coming, Apollo." I moaned under the cover of his hand.

"Do it, baby. Come for me." He increased the power of his thrust while his hand wrapped around my hair and yanked—hard—sending me spiraling into an intense orgasm. "Fuck." He grunted as he came, still pumping into me relentlessly.

"Lucky! Do you like my shoes?" Bella's loud voice rang out.

"Why are you yelling?" Lucky asked, sounding like he was right outside the security room door.

"Bet they look even better wrapped around you." Bella giggled, again elevating the volume of her speech.

She knew we were in here.

Apollo quickly tucked himself back into his pants and straightened my dress. I asked for my panties but he refused, offering me an enticing smirk instead. I could feel myself starting to tingle back to life, and the fact that I had no panties on was a little disconcerting at the moment.

We listened at the door and when it sounded like the hall was empty, Apollo kissed me once more before I ducked out under his arm. I walked back into the living room, and Bella crossed her arms over her chest with a big cheesy grin painted along her lips. I rolled my eyes and looked at my sister, who was discussing a new book with Serafina. I caught Apollo's entrance a minute later, looming over the crowd with that silent intensity he somehow naturally possessed.

His eyes slowly traveled down my body, forcing a blush to warm my cheeks. He smirked and that little smile was so fucking hot that my mind drifted to images of sitting on it. He raised his hand, deliberately aiming his index like a gun before pulling the trigger with a slight wink in my direction. Then he dipped his pointer finger into his mouth—the same one he'd inserted inside me—sucking on it.

"Oh, fuck." I jumped at the utterance, looking at Bella, who was staring at Apollo with her mouth ajar.

"Shut up." My face burned with fire.

"What?" Octavia asked innocently.

"Nothing!" Bella responded, smiling deviously in my direction. "Who's ready to go bury me?"

"Bella!" Our mothers gasped and scolded her name in unison.

The family corralled together, leaving in three different cars. Bella and Apollo were hanging back, because in true badass style, she planned to show up to her own funeral gathering respectably late. I would be lying if I said it didn't amuse me that she had my brother wrapped around her tiny little fingers. Anyone else would've been locked away and under guard at home.

Not Bella.

No, my darling sister-in-law was riding shot-gun alongside Apollo. Everything inside me said we shouldn't be doing this. Dominic Moretti would want to pay his respects but my family would take him down, while Gio and Anthony would use the opportunity to seek an advantage.

"This is insane…" Octavia muttered, as we stood by the empty gravesite, listening to a priest drone on about Bella's aforementioned *life*. "Sienna," she gasped, nodding towards the foliage alongside us.

Gio was standing about a foot into the tree line and staring directly at me. He had a high-powered rifle dangling at his side. His trademark suit was gone, and instead he had donned all black tactical gear, a pair of military boots replacing his dress shoes. The fucking audacity of this man—showing up to the funeral he caused and acting as if he gave a damn.

No. I mouthed the singular word in his direction. I shook my head, fearing what he might be planning to do to any number of my loved ones now present.

Run. He mouthed the warning in return.

I was about to scream when, grabbing Octavia's hand, I froze. Gio had turned away, before lifting his gun and pointing it beyond us. *Beyond my family.* Leaning in, he aimed the end of the barrel and focused the scope. Instinctively, I turned, searching in the direction he was preparing to fire. I was shielding my eyes from the penetrating sunlight, when I saw it… Saw *him*—a prone figure on top of a mausoleum, pointing a sniper rifle at our small gathering.

"What the fuck?" I whispered more to myself, but Lucky heard it, pivoting on his heel before calling out a warning.

"Get down!" he roared, tackling Octavia and me—we hit the ground just as the rapid gunfire sounded off.

But the shots were echoing from our side, not behind us. And Lucky was already on his feet and charging towards the mausoleum, where the shooter lay limp. A shadow loomed over me as everyone panicked and took off in different directions. Reaching out a hand, Gio's expression was solemn and rather… *curious*. I took the offer and he pulled me to my feet.

"You're welcome," he said, staring at me and then Octavia, who was watching our interaction with wide eyes. "You've been targeted,

Sienna. I need you to stay safe. My father wasn't the only one with plans to take you."

I stilled at the realization, my eyes darting between Gio and where the fallen figure lay. He had killed his father to protect me. I stared at him in shock, unsure of how to proceed or how to even process this information. He had saved me, again. That being said, I guess technically he put me in this precarious situation in the first place. It was a never-ending vicious cycle with Gio Moretti: wanting, taking, regretting. After all, he was the reason his sister was "dead".

"I have to go. Tell Lucky he needs to protect his sister better than he did mine." His expression morphed into one of anguish. I opened my mouth to tell him she was okay, that she was alive, but it was too late—he had disappeared into the crowd.

"Come on." I grabbed Octavia's hand, silencing her barrage of questions. "Get to your car." I shouted over the white noise and the screams.

I turned to Rocco, watching Peiro grab my sister and pull her towards the SUV. I made it to my own door, stopping to check on my family. Everyone appeared to be fine, now that the immediate threat was gone. I was hovering above the ledge of my car when something caught my attention. A large shadow towered over Octavia's SUV, before the unknown figure slid into the front passenger seat.

I didn't recognize him—he was too far away and obscured by the crowd. However, a man of his height and width would have been hard to miss traipsing around the grounds. The additional security had been fully vetted by Lucky and Apollo, and so, I dismissed my tendency to over scrutinize, realizing I was still shaken from the constant emotional roller coaster that was my life. Rocco called out, ushering me into the car and effectually stifling my troublesome thoughts. I was so lost in them that I hadn't noticed my feet were still hanging outside the door.

"Apartment, please," I said. He nodded, motioning me inside.

"Apartment, then Philly?" he prompted.

"Yes." His eyes were watching me in the rearview, and I could tell he wanted to say something—he wanted to ask questions. "And I know for a fact your order was given under secrecy, Rocco."

He nodded again and for the rest of the ride, we both sat in tension-riddled silence. We pulled up to the penthouse and I darted inside to retrieve my bag. I'd packed it the night before, knowing my window to get out of the city would be limited. No one was pleased about my decision to keep up with my end of the deal.

I grabbed my phone and dialed Octavia. I needed her to tell me not to go, that she wanted me to stay. But it rang and rang and rang. I left her a message to call me back—*ASAP!*

I shook my head; it was time to put on my big girl panties and commit to the deal I'd made. *Panties!* I'd spent the entire day with no panties, feeling naughty and free. Touching my fingers to my mouth, I still felt his kiss as fresh as if he were right in front of me. I could even feel the soreness between my legs and I relished in it. Shoving down the ache in my chest, I threw on a new pair of underwear before changing.

I opted for comfort over business for my trek today. This was—in a sense—a business meeting but I was going to be walking a lot. I donned an all black romper, sleeveless and cinched at the waist. Gold-embellished thread ran throughout the seams and I paired it with black and gold *Jimmy Choo* pumps. *Fashion is pain; pain is beauty.*

I was filled with a mix of emotions as I texted Romano, letting him know I was on my way to him. *On my way to a new city.* I wanted to smile, but I also felt like throwing up. I wanted to be excited, but I also felt a sense of loss. I was a bipolar mess in a four-thousand-dollar romper. The sound of my phone ringing stopped my whirlwind of thoughts and internal whining.

"Romano," I greeted, watching Rocco's eyes snap to mine in the mirror—that one name told him everything he needed to know.

"Sienna," he answered with his deep, raspy voice. "I just heard. Are you all right?" The sincerity of his concern, of that simple question, made my heart hurt. This man was so willing to make me happy, the least I could do was give him an honest chance.

"All is well—none of *us* were hurt," I said, staring out the window to avoid Rocco's murderous gaze.

"Very well. I would've accepted a reschedule... if needed." I heard someone voice themselves in the background but Romano silenced them.

"It isn't necessary, but thank you. I am ready for my tour of this incredible city you are trying to sell me. You know, the one you promised me. I do feel it necessary to offer a word of advice, come with your A-game because I am a beast with negotiations." I chuckled, enjoying the sound of his deep rumble. We said our goodbyes and I disconnected.

"Just like that…" Rocco mumbled, before I asked him to repeat himself. "Nothing to no one? You're just going to disappear without telling us… *him*?"

"We all have our parts to play, Rocco. Mine is to be sold like cattle, and his is to protect the herd. What would you have me do? Stay in New York to look like an idiot, time and again," I challenged.

"Bullshit. We both know that shit's changed." He cracked his neck from side to side, white knuckling the steering wheel.

"A few days out of many years is nothing to boast about. I said my… goodbye to him in my own way; now I have my duties." I swallowed roughly, hating the way I had chosen to do so—to say goodbye —without telling him everything.

"I know this is none of my business, Sienna. And I'd be remiss to say Apollo wasn't a challenge; however, the man was a damn viable choice. Leaving your family behind to fulfill some sense of duty is bullshit," he growled.

"You're right. It's none of your business." I pushed past the tears.

"I-I'm sorry, Si. You're like a sister to me and the thought of you leaving kills me." His voice softened.

"Nothing is set in stone yet, not until after the trip." I checked my makeup in my mirror as we merged onto I-95. "Besides, what doesn't kill us makes us stronger."

I gave him a fake smile and Rocco started to laugh, flicking his eyes between my reflection and the road. He opened his mouth to speak just as something collided with the back of our vehicle. The impact was too much for us to maintain control on the road, and we spun out. My seatbelt held me in place as the SUV tipped and rolled several times before slamming into a concrete barricade.

"Si-Sienna..." Rocco moaned.

I looked around, and seeing the damage, I was surprised we were both still alive. Rocco had red gashes across his face and I could feel blood trickling from my temple. I braced my arms and legs before unclipping my seatbelt and rolling onto my knees. My head was woozy and I had a violent urge to vomit. Rocco was pinned against the steering wheel, the mangled metal frame refusing to budge.

"Fuck, they're coming." Rocco drew his weapon, pointing it towards the sound of scuffled feet. I reached into the glove box and grabbed the spare gun. Holding my finger in front of my lips, I pointed towards the sound.

The moment the first silhouette appeared, and I knew I had my shot, I pulled the trigger. One of them went down, while the other hid behind the engine. When the second male chanced a glance in our direction, I fired again. I grabbed Rocco's seatbelt and tugged. It released and he slid sideways from his seat but the engine block held his leg hostage.

"Come out, Sienna, and we promise not to kill your lackey." A voice shouted in the distance.

"Don't even think about it!" Rocco ordered, but he was in no position to make demands.

I reached into the back seat and took out my cell phone, pressing it into his hand. "Okay, don't shoot!" I shouted back. I pulled a gold locket out of my purse and threw it around my neck. "Call Andersen, he can..." A hand reached into the windshield and grabbed me by my hair, tugging hard. I screamed as my body was ripped from the remnants of our car.

Without thought, I lifted the gun at my side and shot the asshole holding me. The bullet embedded in his chin and he relinquished his grip. I hit the ground hard as his body slumped on top of mine. The 9mm slipped out of my hand and the two other men knocked it away. Removing the dead weight now pinning me to the ground, one of them kicked the side of my face. My neck jerked on impact and pain erupted immediately while blood spewed from my mouth.

"Sienna!" Rocco screamed from his prison inside the car.

My movements were sluggish. I rolled over and screamed as one of the assailants went to lean into the car with his gun raised. I was defenseless and there was nothing I could do to save my friend. Gunfire erupted and the man flung backwards to avoid Rocco's hail of bullets. He cursed and I finally got a good look at his features. None of our attackers were Russian. If I didn't know better, I'd say the sons of bitches were homegrown… in fact, they were fucking Italian.

"We need to move, now!" A new voice came from behind me.

I rolled over towards the sound of it, my entire body aching. I blinked several times, before my brain finally registered, and I peered through the bright lights of the sun. The figure slowly appeared as the hazy cloud evaporated and my eyes went wide with recognition.

"You motherfucker!" I screamed, trying to tell myself to get up and attack.

"How nice to see you again, Sienna." A wicked smile greeted me.

"You've got to be kidding me." I grunted as one of the men picked me up from under the cusps of my arms and threw me over his shoulder.

My head bounced uncontrollably and I dry heaved from the rattling motion, wishing I could puke all over his back. However, I took solace in the fact that the second man left Rocco alone to follow behind his counterpart. Two of the assailants sat in the front seat as my third remaining captive slid in the back beside me.

"I'm so happy you remember me, Sienna." That same smile peppered the statement with so much malice, I could feel the words burn against my skin. "Now be a good little bitch and shut the fuck up."

I had so much I wanted to say, so many ways I wanted to hurt all three of them but I was powerless. My head ached and I knew I needed to bide my time until the right opportunity presented itself. Rocco was alive, my family would be called and I was sure Andersen would be able to find me easily. I let myself drift off into a suspended place of foggy dreams, comforted by my thoughts of enacting my future revenge.

My family would come for me. And they'd fucking destroy these people who had the audacity to fuck with us. I would walk out of this prison with their blood all over my six-thousand-dollar *Jimmy Choo's* and I'd save them as a reminder…

No one fucked with the Agostino's and lived to tell the tale.

CHAPTER 30

APOLLO DELUCA

"Out of all of the ways I saw this funeral going, that ending was not one of them," Lucky commented, the car ride home ironically grim.

"He killed… *our father*…" Bella said, staring out the window. "Why?"

"He was next to the family at the ceremony. He could've easily killed us but he didn't. Anthony had planned to take us out and would've, if Gio hadn't interceded." Lucky was as bedeviled as I was.

"I think he did it in your honor, *mia regina*. What he said to you, checking in on you, it makes the most sense." Bella turned to look at me, her mismatched eyes red and swollen.

"He's done a million things wrong, *il mio amore*. He didn't know you were alive and still wanted to give you something in death." Lucky pulled her in for a kiss and I turned back around, glancing at Al as he drove in silent contemplation.

Her brother had not only saved the family, but he ended his father's tyranny in a series of precise tactics that ensured he was the new patriarch of the Moretti's. However, this act alone wouldn't be his saving grace. He still needed to die; he needed to be taken down like an uncontrollable beast that mauled anything in his path, after having deliberately slipped his leash.

"Call Nikolai—Alexander is going in the ground today. No more loose ends; this shit is over." Bella was monotone and distant as the city lights lit up her face.

I could see Lucky straighten in his seat, his eyes filled with pride—the girl had become a formidable force, ensuring this family's reign would be successful. I sent out a group text. The women were to be put on lockdown, and I wanted Persephone back at the compound. Mario had agreed; we'd set a trap for Dominic Moretti.

"Call the Russian." Lucky repeated Bella's orders. "And take us to Alexander."

I was unsure of the Wolf's motives but his anger towards his nephew was undeniable. He had insinuated, at first, that Yuri's two sons were victims of their father's decisions but he seemed removed of any guilt when it came to planning Alexander's death. He wasn't here out of mercy; he was keeping an alliance amongst us—he knew he was unable to sway our decision.

Bella gasped as she took in Alexander's swollen features and blood-tinged shirt. Even beaten half to death, his face lit up with a battered smile when he saw her enter the room. She charged towards him, but Lucky stopped her halfway.

"I knew you were too strong to kill." His chuckle turned into a labored cough, spewing blood upon exhale.

If I had to guess, he was suffering from traumatic pneumothorax. The direct and repetitive impacts to the chest—between fists, a knife and I believe a foot—more than likely produced a punctured lung. In layman's terms, air had collected in the space between the two layers of the tissue lining the lungs and impacted his ability to breathe.

His body was purging the damage that had been done to his internal organs, attempting to mend itself. It was futile, of course, we'd inflicted irreparable injuries to heighten his suffering, before death could release him from it.

"Ravishing as always, Bella. Oh, how I wish Gio hadn't interrupted our moment in Italy," he taunted her.

My gaze snapped to Lucky, his body rigid like a panther ready to strike, while his focus remained on Alexander. Whatever the Russian was insinuating, it had Bella enraged and thrashing against Lucky's hold. Once I inspected his bindings, I nodded for Lucky to release her.

"It was merely my attempt at one-upping my controlling father. You were never special, a convenience and nothing more," she sneered, leaning into his face. "You mean nothing. You will die... as nothing. And I will feel... nothing."

"The *Bratva* will come for you, *suka*. You will cry and beg for them to end you! All of you!" The lies dripped from the darkest depths of his cowardice.

"You speak for the *Bratva* now, nephew." Heavy footfalls came down the stairs, and the color on Alexander's face immediately drained.

"Uh-uh... uncle." He gulped. "I was, uhm, I was..." He stopped stuttering as Nikolai stood before him.

The Russian had yet to even look at his nephew, focusing on the occupants of the room instead. He walked into Agostino territory, to a goddamn torture chamber, and he only brought three men. The larger two stood near the stairs, their arms crossed in silence with weaponry stocked to the hilt. I recognized the enforcer I'd assumed to be his right hand, positioned a bit closer.

Nikolai turned to look at Bella, his perusal of the girl raising the tension in us all. *"Yeshche krasiviye lichno,"* he said, his words causing her to blush.

I didn't speak Russian, however, I sure as hell was fluent in body language. And this son of a bitch was hitting on Lucky's bride. If I were anyone else, it may have amused me. But I had no tolerance for the games. Lucky shoved Bella behind his back and Al lurched forward in silent warning.

"Enough." She stepped around Lucky and extended a hand. There she was, our powerful queen, not a semblance of fear while offering a gesture of peace to the *Pakhan's* second in command. "Sorry to meet you under such circumstances." He smiled down at her open palm, and glancing at Lucky, he shook it with a smirk on his face.

"*U etoy devushki yest' yaytsa,*" he said, and the three Russians chuckled behind him.

"And they are bigger than those belonging to most men; that is, except for my husband and his men of course." She gave him a saccharine smile.

"Thank you for allowing me to be present." He extended a hand to Lucky.

I never understood the masculine need to inflict a tight grip during this social exchange, as if a knife to your carotid artery wouldn't suffice in showing who the victor would be. Both of their flexor digitorum profundus and flexor pollicis longus muscles arched aggressively as their thumbs exacted pressure. And I wanted to roll my eyes at their testosterone-induced greeting.

"I am honestly surprised you're so interested in watching your own nephew bleed out," Lucky said, pressing Bella to his side.

"It isn't something I relish in. But it is something owed." He turned his attention to Alexander, who whimpered while a dark ring permeated his jeans. "If we were in Moscow, you'd be begging me to end your life after months of torture."

"It-it wasn't me, uncle, it was father." Stricken by emotional distress, Alexander's body discharged the thick stench of perspiration, perfumed by fear.

"You stole from the *Bratva* after your father was dead!" Nikolai shouted, landing a solid punch to his nephew's zygomatic process, the bone just under the eye. "And what of Mila?" Lucky and I exchanged a glance at the mention of an unfamiliar name.

"Wh-what of her?" Alexander's feigned ignorance was obvious, even to us.

"I already know." Nikolai ground out each word.

"Alexei, that fucking traitor." Alexander's voice had elevated in pitch; perhaps the zygomatic plate hadn't been cracked after all—the whistling sound was more indicative of a nasal fracture.

"Traitor to who? You, who wanted to hurt your own sister? He is a loyal soldier of the cause. Loyal to his family. Something your father never ingrained in you." The Wolf then proceeded to inform the entire room of Alexander's diabolical intentions to steal his sister for auction. Alexei, his brother, had interceded and thwarted the attempt.

"I know the pain you have suffered, and I want nothing more than to make it right. I just ask for a piece," Nikolai declared, his entire focus directed to Bella.

It was interesting that he had chosen to address her and *not* the men in the room. The *Bratva* held the same disdain towards women that the old-school mafia did. Females were meant to cook, clean and breed—nothing more. However, Nikolai addressed her with respect and sought out her approval. Perhaps this alliance could work in our favor, thanks to Bella's esteem.

"*Moy nozh,* Adrian." He held out his hand towards his second in command. Adrian reached into his suit jacket and pulled out a folding knife. "Does this look familiar to you, nephew?"

When Alexander didn't immediately respond, I gripped the boy's chin and forced his head upward. He refused to answer but his body wracked with silent tears.

"This is the very knife your father used to kill your mother—my sister." He held it on display, allowing each of us to see the simple blade with a bright blue handle. "This blue was her favorite color, and I retrieved it from her *back* before I carried her lifeless body out of that apartment."

Nikolai stared at the offending implement for a moment, the room silent as we watched and waited for his next move.

"Mila was troubled, haunted by what she had witnessed, for quite some time. However, she was adamant about *one* very specific detail of that day." Alexander dropped his chin to his chest, openly weeping. "Yuri *and* Alexander stabbed my sister, while Alexei tried to protect Mila."

Alexander opened his mouth to speak but Nikolai backhanded him across the face. The air was thick, heavy, weighted down by the menacing bulk of the boy's betrayal. I immediately thought of Cara and all the horrors she'd been forced to suffer through. Severe trauma like we endured didn't just go away, and I knew it wouldn't for Niko-lai's niece either.

"I ask for blood in the name of my sister, and in return, I will relinquish the final blow." Nikolai dipped his head towards Lucky. "May this solidify an alliance between Moscow and New York. I will pass it along to Sergei. You have my word; we will have peace." Again, they shook hands and Lucky nodded at him in respect.

Nikolai turned quickly. And with an unparalleled precision, he attacked—inflicting four very particular wounds across his nephew's chest—before leaving the knife embedded between true rib five and six. Alexander groaned, staring down at the hilt in shock. Nikolai's eyes were filled with an aura of pure elation; he had been planning his attack for years, it seemed.

The ring of his cell phone stopped all movement in the room. "Alexei," he answered, his spine immediately straightening. "I must go. Let's meet again before I leave the city." He paid his respects to Bella and Lucky, then turned to leave the room with his men in tow.

"What did he say to you?" Lucky asked but his bride dismissed him, aiming her fiery gaze at Alexander.

"Can this be done, so we can have a honeymoon now?" she said expectantly. "No more drawn-out antics; he dies and we move on."

Glancing at one another, Al and I fell into a fit of laughter. Even Lucky was attempting to hide his grin, but the man failed epically. Bella seemed none too pleased with our revelry. And snatching the gun from Lucky's holster, she staggered towards Alexander with it raised high and to his head.

"*Gni v adu, suka.*" She smiled but it was forced. In turn, Alexander stared back at the girl with so much hate you could see the tremor in her hands.

"*Mia regina.*" Stepping around the chair, I gingerly removed the firearm from her grip and passed it to Lucky. "Take it as a wedding present from your husband."

"I love you," Lucky muttered, tucking her into his side before turning her face into his chest. The gunshot was like the hammering of a gavel. We were Alexander's judge, jury and executioner—the verdict was guilty and the son of a bitch was put to death.

With one chapter closed, we moved onto another. We headed

towards the compound in a convoy of vehicles; Al rode with me to confirm the safety of our women. Peiro texted that Octavia was underground with him. They wouldn't resurface until he got the all clear.

We pulled up to the house just as Lucky and Bella stepped out of their car. I sent a quick text to Edge, telling him to get Cara away from the city—just as a precaution. I turned to Al to ask about Sienna when a small black canister dropped into the center of our group.

"Down!" I shouted just as the flash bang went off. The pain was instantaneous and the impact throttled my chest and burned my eyes. I hit the ground and I was forced to watch—disoriented and unable to move—as men dressed in black tactical gear stormed the compound.

When a stun grenade detonated, it ignited a magnesium-based charge that released a burst of light measuring seven-million candela— in other words, it was the equivalent to setting that same number of candles aflame, all at once. At first glance, it may not have seemed significant, but imagine that single and simultaneous burst of light throttling your eyes and senses. It burned and it left you completely incapacitated. Our assailants moved quickly, cuffing our wrists and rolling us onto our stomachs with the end of their barrels pointed at our heads.

Mario and Serafina were brought out of the house, their palms raised high over their heads. Men wearing vests adorned with FBI in white letters stormed the property. Black dress shoes stepped in my line of sight and I rolled slightly on my side to look up. Dominic Moretti glared down at me—triumph embellishing his features. Glancing towards the house, he paired his gloat with a smile.

Persephone skipped out the front door. Her blonde hair blowing in the breeze as she leapt over our bodies like a game of hopscotch. Jumping into Dom's arms, she wrapped herself into his embrace and kissed him. My hearing was slowly coming back, forcing me to listen to their whispered glee, while the agents in our midst continued to call out demands that fell on literal deaf ears.

"You nearly cost me months of undercover work." John Hardwicke, Dom's partner, stood over us with his hands tucked into his vest. "If I had been unsuccessful, I would've brought down your entire organization."

Mario stepped forward but was tugged back by his cuffs. When he attempted to shake off the agent, they twisted his arm up into a submissive position. I shook with anger, waiting for someone to touch me without my permission. I was praying to *il diavolo*, asking for his approval to strike. Lucky saw my silent plea, shaking his head in warning.

"I'm glad you're okay, Bella," Dom admitted as his sister glared back at him.

"Do you know about Gio? About father?" she probed further but his only response was a nod.

"Gio is of no consequence to you any longer," John stated flatly. "He is under our custody now, as is Dominic."

"And me!" Persephone added, still clinging to the Moretti boy.

"And you." John rolled his eyes but I could see he was fighting a smile. "Take them in," he ordered his men, nodding his head to Dominic and Persephone. They were escorted to one of the vans in the driveway before climbing inside.

As quickly as they had descended upon us, the agents packed up their equipment and drove off. We all turned to look at each other, confused as to what the fuck just happened. I was at a loss; however, I was admittedly bemused by the FBI takedown of the Moretti's. As well as curious over how the fuck Persephone fit into all of it.

"Send word," Mario stated. "Lockdown is over."

Al nodded, typing out a slew of texts. "I'll confirm Sienna made it to Philly," Al muttered.

"And I need to find Tessa." Marco jumped into the conversation.

"The girl from the club? She's probably tired of your whoring ways." Al chuckled.

"No, I'm serious. I was supposed to pick her up but her place was cleared out—something's wrong."

"Marco, we don't have time for this right now. Family first," Mario commanded.

"Philly?" I interrupted, looking at the guilty expressions of my so-called *family*. "Why is Sienna in Philly?"

Mario motioned for me to follow him into his office, turning on his heel as he headed inside, while Lucky and I trailed behind him. Bella and Isabella both turned to look away as I passed, and anger settled in my gut.

"Sit down," Mario ordered, but I shook my head and remained standing. "Sienna is meeting with Romano Bianchi in Philly," he said, as if that statement alone explained everything.

"She's brokering a marriage contract," Lucky clarified, and my body rocked back like a bullet to the thoracic cavity. "She's going to marry Romano."

Sienna. Marry. Romano.

I'd heard the words but my usually adaptable cognitive faculties were slow to comprehend their meaning. For reasons I couldn't explain, I exploded in anger. Turning to the wall, I slammed my fist through the crisp white paint. The sheetrock erupted on impact and swallowed my hand whole. Something foreign and peculiar weighed down on my chest. I felt like the air had been sucked from my lungs. Pulling my hand out, I threw it back into the wall—only stopping the repetition when thick arms wrapped around my torso.

Mario was speaking but I couldn't make out what he was saying. A dark cloud had settled heavily in my head as I thrashed against Al's hold. Lucky was pressing a towel to a laceration along my wrist, the trauma having bypassed the major arteries. And as the world around me deadened, the interactions between Sienna and me over the past few weeks started to make sense.

She was saying goodbye; she was leaving and everyone knew it. Everyone but me. I stared back at each of them, disgusted by their lies, by their audacity and by their ability to appear shocked. If I didn't shrug them loose, I'd do something I'd regret.

"Sit the fuck down!" Mario commanded. I was shoved down into a chair, Al's large hands on my shoulders keeping me in place. Lucky was perched against the desk while Mario sat behind it, each of them staring at me expectantly.

"Care to explain why you're so upset?" Lucky prompted.

"As a family, we protect each other. *Only as strong as our weakest member.* How am I meant to protect this family, when you keep things from me?" I didn't appreciate their nonchalance nor their errant questions.

"That's why you're punching holes in my walls? I made a decision for one of *my* children and didn't inform you... that's all?" Mario deadpanned.

"Open your fucking eyes, dude," Al muttered from behind me.

"You love her." Lucky's added commentary reignited my anger. Shoving from my seat, I cocked my fist back. Al managed to get a hold of my right bicep and tossed it sideways before I could swing. I stumbled back to my feet, breathing fire and ready to attack the same three men I considered family.

"Go cool off and think about that," Mario ordered.

I stormed out of the office and charged through the front doors, sucking in fresh air to calm my inner turmoil. A shuffle of footsteps at my back jarred my senses, and I twisted around in preparation for a fight. I froze when I saw that it was Bella.

"I only learned this morning," she said, tears choking her, and my anger decreased by a millimeter at the sight.

"Lucky said she didn't want you to know. Everyone was ordered to secrecy." She wiped at her eyes as she spoke.

"Why?" I growled.

"You would've forced her to stay," she explained, to which I agreed. "And she would've, but not for reasons that were fair to her."

I didn't entirely understand what Bella meant. If I had learned of Sienna's impending engagement, of course I would've told her to call it off. She would've upset the family too much with her absence, and it would've created unnecessary discord. I would've figured out a way to ensure she stayed with me. *Me.* I stilled at the thought, staring at Bella in confusion.

"That face. That right there, is what she needed to see. What you needed to figure out on your own." She smiled. "I knew you were sleeping together. It was her way of saying goodbye; it was something she could hold onto. She needs to know what you feel for her, Apollo; it's the only way to make things right." I was prepared to respond, but swallowed my words when Rocco's name flashed on my cell phone screen.

"Apollo. Fuck, man. She's gone!" he shouted into the receiver.

"What? Who's gone?" I asked as Bella darted into the house, screaming for help. Mario, Lucky and Al stormed outside a minute later and I put Rocco on speaker.

"We got ambushed on the way to Philly. I don't know who they are, but they took her!" he continued. "I'm trapped in the fucking car. They flipped us and I can't get out."

"Track him!" Lucky ordered.

"She took something with her; she said to call Andersen. Oh, fuck, my leg!" There was no doubt that pain plagued his voice, but it was the underlying note of fear that made my heart race.

"My office now!" Mario ordered, everyone turning to follow his lead.

"We've got you. Someone is on their way." I hung up on Rocco

I hesitated mid-stride, staring at an incoming text from an unknown number. It took only a second for my blood to boil and my hands to shake, as I glared at the image loading on my screen. Even covered in blood, eyes filled with tears and tape across her mouth, Sienna was the most gorgeous sight. A sense of calm settled over me as my mind hyper-focused on the simple message. It was an address and a warning.

Come alone or she dies.

I didn't need anyone's help; I'd save her on my own. Then I'd fucking destroy whoever had touched her. No one fucked with what was *mine*. And with that, realization struck me like a punch to my gut... she was mine. I hadn't understood it before, but all of these years, there's always been this... *something* about her.

She was simply *mine,* and I would make sure everyone knew it.

You're mine, Sienna.

CHAPTER 31
SIENNA AGOSTINO

I needed water. At minimum, two gallons.

My head was pounding and I was so damn thirsty. I lay still for a moment, unsure if I was crossing that slim line of vomit territory or not. Every time I downed tequila, this is what happened—at my age, you'd assume I knew better by now. What did I do last night?

"I know you're awake." A familiar voice startled me, my mind churning before landing on the reality of my situation.

I took stock of my body, accounting for all my appendages. My hands were tied at my back, my ankles bound with zip ties, and I was definitely missing shoes. Shoes! I'd only worn those once and now I was *officially* pissed.

"Ow!" I rolled over onto my side, the rough concrete scratching at my skin.

The aches from the accident were setting in and I felt like someone had kicked the shit out of me. I slowly opened my eyes and took in my surroundings. I was in some sort of rundown, potentially abandoned warehouse. I could smell the water; it was close. I was still in the city —near the Hudson River.

"Hello." At the sound, I turned to face the traitorous bastard that had abducted me.

"What the fuck are you doing?" I asked with a grunt. "What do you want?" It took one dumb motherfucker to look at me with such sinister satisfaction, barring fear of what my family would do in return.

"You mean, what do *we* want?" Two men stepped out of the shadows and approached us. "Just finishing up a little vendetta with Apollo."

"You can't be serious." I chuckled humorlessly at them. "The man has no feelings, no moral compass. He won't care that you've taken me, but my family will. You've signed your own death warrant."

"You really have no clue!" Laughter echoed around me. Closing my eyes, I swallowed past the bile rising in my throat. "His actions have proven otherwise because there is *you*. The woman he can't have, yet can't leave alone. He's incapable of letting you go. He'll come for you."

"Is that what this is about? You're jealous of his loyalty to me as Lucky's sister. Jesus, you're fucking pathetic." She was a sad excuse of a sniveling whore. "Cassandra, isn't it? Are these two trying to fight for your honor? To absolve your loose pussy because Apollo wouldn't claim you?"

"Oh, Sienna. Now I get exactly what he sees in you." She squatted in front of me, pushing a piece of hair out of my face. "Witty, strong and quite beautiful. This, you, all of it will be his undoing. When he realizes just how much he actually *does* care… it'll be too late."

She lifted a hand and the two men stepped around her, looking down at me with blank stares. They had the same bone structure, eye and hair color—they were most definitely related. The taller one grabbed me under my arms, sitting me back on my ass; the other stepped around me and before I could make a smart remark, he tossed a right hook.

I wasn't as engrossed as Octavia but dirty romance novels were my guilty pleasure. In so many stories, the hero rose above pain and certain death to save his one true love! Well, those writers were full of shit because punch after punch, no one came to my rescue and the pain only increased. It was just a short time before I felt myself fading into darkness.

"Don't worry, the lacerations are minor." The proximity of Cassandra's voice startled me as she inspected my face. "You're fortunate I am in my residency, almost a full doctor." She offered me a proud smile.

"He helps pay for your education and whatever else a whore like you needs, and you want to hurt him?" She seemed intelligent, was decent to look at and yet, here she was, throwing it all away for one man. A man who was knowingly ruining us all.

"Not me. Them." She pointed at the brothers. "They offered me a decent amount of cash for information. At first, I did it for my mother. Then, I did it for me. Do you know he called your name out when we were having sex?"

"You're a sick bitch." I grunted, spitting a wad of blood at her feet.

"And the man you love is even sicker." She continued to smile down at me. "He got the message; he'll be here soon I'm sure. Then, *they* will end him." She gestured to the two men in her company.

So many things seemed so inconsequential at the moment. All of the doubt, the hurt and the games we played had stolen too much time from us. Time we could've spent in each other's arms. Time we could've spent exploring what this was between us. Instead, we were both so stubborn and so reckless we'd lost out on everything. My temples were throbbing and my stomach threatened to upheave when a wet, warm tongue ran down my cheek.

"I bet every part of you tastes so good. You rich girls know how to pamper yourselves, how to make men crave you like a drug." The older brother's lips wrapped around mine, muffling the scream caught in my throat. He pulled down my romper, baring my chest. "Protected and pure, something I will happily destroy in front of Apollo."

He shoved me backwards, laughing as my head slammed against the broken concrete. I was in agony and beyond embarrassed as my breasts were on display. Cassandra cackled along and I wanted to kick both of their asses. But I was so damn tired; sleeping sounded much better. I closed my eyes, feeling myself start to drift off, when something touched me and I jolted awake.

"Sh, now." The younger brother readjusted my clothing, covering my naked chest. "I'm so sorry. I am going to try to get you out of here."

I stared into his eyes—waiting for the mockery or false promises of hope—but there were none. He couldn't be much more than sixteen, and it was clear he wasn't as deranged as his brother. Whatever the reasoning, bringing him to this moment in time, he was obviously here out of allegiance to his brother. I understood that type of loyalty; it's what would kill me in the end.

"Car coming!" Cassandra shouted, standing at the threshold of the rundown warehouse.

"Fuck." The younger brother sighed, pinching the bridge of his nose.

"Just let me go. I'll protect you from him and from my family." I rolled onto my knees to grovel. The older brother grabbed me under my arms, pulling me to his side.

The bindings on my legs forced me to lean into him as he pinned me to his chest, a knife at my throat and a gun to my temple. As the car pulled up, my first thought threatened to spill a bubble of laughter out of me. Al was going to kick *his* ass for scratching his beloved car. The second was absolute terror as I watched *him* approach us in slow motion.

The car door slammed and everyone's spine straightened as he prowled towards us. His suit was cut perfectly to his muscular frame. The blank expression and dangerous glare added to the uncertainty of his impending murderous rampage. I was like a sheep being led to the wolf for slaughter, and I was practically panting for him to ruin me as we bathed in the blood of our enemies.

"That's far enough," my captor ordered, pausing him mid-step.

"Release her," Apollo demanded, looking me up and down. "Whoever you are, your trivial attempt to hurt Mario Agostino by taking his daughter has ended. Here and now."

"Whoever I am?" The older boy laughed, while the younger

shifted nervously on his feet. "I shouldn't be surprised that *il mietitore* doesn't remember me. I guess your list has been long."

And then I saw it.

He was just a sad little boy trying to act like a grown up with a vendetta. He was in over his head, but his eyes held the promise of vengeance. He was going to enact his plan or die trying, with his little brother at his side. I could tell Apollo noticed it too. It was in the way his muscles rippled under his suit; he was lethal and looking for his chance to strike.

Apollo stared back and forth between the boys. There was something there, a recognition, but he hadn't figured it out yet. The hands at my neck shook, causing the knife to dig a little deeper, and I had to bite my lip to silence a whine. A metallic taste filled my mouth as my teeth broke through, red spilling down my chin and finally releasing the sound. Apollo's body tensed and he took two more steps.

"Fuck that whole family. I only care about hurting *you*." The man-child grunted before slicing the blade across my skin.

Apollo's hands were shaking; his eyes were dark and feral. I could see *il mietitore* was on the cusp of taking over, threatening to destroy any one or thing in his path. Once again, he looked back and forth between the two *kids* that held me hostage, his mind churning with his attempt to place them. He opened his mouth to speak but froze, his eyes glancing behind me as the true traitor stepped from the shadows.

"Hello, lover," Cassandra crooned, walking up next to me.

"Cassandra." His tone was flat, dead. Both boys shouted for him to stop when he took yet another step forward. "I assume you have a proposition or a reason behind this death wish." It wasn't a question.

"This isn't my show. I'm just here to see your world crumble around you. I told you to go to her, but you didn't and now it's too late." The fucking bitch smirked at him.

"Cassandra, what is the meaning of this?" Another step.

The older brother laughed, the sound manic and his pupils dilated. "I wanted to hurt you, to fucking break you, and Cassandra told me how. And my-oh-my if she doesn't taste sweet." He shifted me into

Apollo's view, running his tongue down the side of my neck. I twisted in his grip, trying to get purchase and smash my head into his.

"You." Apollo started then stopped, his eyes filled with shock. "I know who you are."

My captor chuckled, tucking the gun in the back of his pants and wrapping both hands around my neck. He cut off my air and my lungs burned as panic settled into my limbs. I jerked back and bucked, trying to free myself but my body was already in agony. My fight slowed and my heart pounded against my ribcage until suddenly, the boy released his fingers and repositioned his knife—the cold metal stinging my abused flesh.

"Sienna!" Apollo shouted, forcing me to look at him as tears dampened my cheeks. "Baby."

Four letters. One word.

My heart broke as I stared into his enraged and startled eyes. Cassandra was right—she had found his one weakness. And it wasn't his loyalty to the family. I was more than that. Sometimes what we needed the most was right in front of us; we were just too blind to see it. I'd been in love with Apollo since the moment I met him, but I never thought I'd see the day I'd become his undoing.

And with that realization, I lost my fight to be strong as another settled in… I was going to die. We were too far away from the center of the city; no one was coming to rescue us. I had fought so hard to separate myself from my family… now all I wanted was to see them one last time. And I wanted Apollo to hold me, to be the last thing I saw before I died.

"I love you." I choked the words out.

His eyes flared and his jaw dropped open. Grabbing his chest, he ran his fist over his heart as if in pain. His expression softened and his honey brown eyes melted into pools of anguish and… love. He felt it. Fucking hell, I felt it. I cried harder, the pain in my heart hurting worse than my body ever could.

"Oh. My. God. It took until this moment for you to get it!" Cassandra started laughing as the boys looked at her confused. "Love, Apollo. You fucking love her."

His brows pinched as he stared at Cassandra, his eyes marred with pure horror, like he couldn't fathom such a ridiculous idea. Then he looked at me and he relaxed, a warmth inhabiting my chest. And before he could even open his mouth to speak, I understood his intentions.

"You've started a war you cannot possibly win. You've come here for me. Let her go—this is between us," he chided. "Once you release her, I will come willingly."

"You already came willingly! You're both going to die! I am going to take everything from you! Just like you took everything from us!" The boy was shouting and waving his knife around like a lunatic.

"I said let her go!" Apollo demanded. He stepped closer, forcing Cassandra back.

"My mother killed herself because of you! She popped pills to numb the pain and left me to raise my brother and mourn our father. Alone! The lies, the rumors… she let it all consume her and she left us!" The fucker was losing his cool, the knife again pressed into the pliable skin of my throat.

"I'm not sure where you've gotten your information from, or if you simply lack a capacity for cognitive thinking. But I killed him because all of those *alleged* rumors were true," Apollo's voice was flat, not a single trace of emotion.

The younger brother stepped forward. "Let the girl go. You can tell he's not lying."

"Sienna, baby, it's going to be okay." The tenderness in his voice elicited my cry of pain. "I'm so sorry." His eyes snapped back to the threat.

In the movies, the villains always hesitated, grappling with indecision; while the heroes were able to anticipate the next movement and act out in defense. But my captor didn't hesitate. My captor didn't make any big reveal. The moment Apollo stopped talking was the same moment my captor pushed his blade into my ribs. I stared down at the knife sticking out of my side in confusion. Glancing back up at Apollo, I wanted to ask him what happened.

"No!" Apollo darted forward, but the older boy moved quicker.

He pulled the knife from my torso, swiftly stabbing me several more times. Then he dropped me to the ground, pulled his gun and fired three shots as Apollo collided with him. They fell in a heap of grunts and a flurry of limbs. Twice the size of the kid, Apollo was easily getting the upper hand.

"No!" Cassandra shouted, grabbing the gun. "Get off him!"

Apollo either didn't hear her or didn't care, not faltering from his assault and continuing to pummel the prone form. The younger brother was at my side, pressing something against my ribs, the pressure making the excruciating pain so much worse that I struggled to stay conscious. His lips kept moving but I couldn't hear him. I couldn't hear anything until the first gunshot.

My neck snapped in the direction of the sound. Towering over the older boy, Apollo stared at Cassandra in anger, crimson stains pooling across the center of his perfectly white shirt. He turned to charge for her. Realizing his intent, Cassandra fired twice more and his body jerked backwards with each impact.

Six shots.

I was unsure how many had made actual contact, but that was the number it took to take him down. He was covered in blood and the color quickly drained from his face. Dropping to his knees, his eyes focused on me before he collapsed onto his stomach.

"No!" I tried calling out but the pain of my heart breaking was too much.

"Si-Sienna." His cheek flat on the concrete, he never broke eye contact. "I-I do. I... I."

"Oh, fuck. Oh, shit!" Cassandra cried, dropping the gun onto the ground.

"Shit," my captor repeated, slowly rising to his feet—his face a swollen mess as he stared down at us. "We need to dump him in the Hudson," he said to his brother as he approached Apollo's motionless form.

"No, please. Don't, don't do that. Leave him alone," I begged, turning on my side as my fight slowly dwindled.

This couldn't be it. Not for us.

Ignoring my pleas, the brothers grabbed him under his arms and dragged him towards the edge of the rocks, the water raging below. Cassandra watched in silence, her arms wrapped protectively around herself. I reached out a palm, the familiar handle of the gun fitting perfectly in my grip.

"Help him!" I ordered Cassandra. "Now!" I said, aiming the barrel center mass.

Her mouth dropped open and she raised her quivering hands, like that would protect her. This fucking bitch was dying one way or another. I could feel myself fading as the gun shook between my fingers. I was about to repeat my demands when the sound of a large splash startled both of us.

"No!" I screamed, tears rolling down my face. The brothers came running and I started pulling the trigger, long after the magazine was empty, and unsure of where I was even aiming.

"Fuck!" One of the boys shouted, but I couldn't see through the pain.

"Where's my knife?" Another voice rang out.

"Let's just dump her somewhere on the way out. Someone is coming—we can't stay here."

"Grab her." I was yanked upwards under my arms and dropped into a vehicle. The pain in my torso was almost as bad as the pain in my chest. My body was sticky. I was caked in my own blood while I continued to bleed out.

He's not dead. He's too fucking strong.

"Push her out and let's keep going." A door opened and someone shoved me from behind. Unable to protect myself, I hit the ground hard and fast.

I was alone, in a barren wasteland of bushes and weeds somewhere outside the city. And I couldn't breathe; Apollo had been the air that filled my lungs. The sky was slowly settling and soon darkness would descend. And it, that darkness, would be my new home. My light was dumped into the river, and my heart was submerged in the icy-cold depths right along with it.

"Dragotsennyy malenkiy kotenok." Looking towards the deep

voice, I stared at the most serene gray eyes; they were animalistic, like those of a wolf.

"Precious little kitten with some feisty claws." Another voice came; this one familiar.

"Stay with us, *kotenok*. Keep those beautiful eyes open." Warm arms wrapped around me, picking me up off the ground. "Alexei, grab her legs."

I faded in and out, exhaustion sweeping over me like a heavy blanket. Someone poked and prodded my side, ignoring my pleas to be left alone. Every time I felt the sweet embrace of darkness someone shook me awake, shouting at me to open my eyes. I cried and yelled, wanting to be left alone. To be left to die.

"*Da.* Lucky, we've got her." My head flopped over and gray eyes smiled down at me.

"Let me die." I repeated my inner thoughts. "They killed him. Killed my heart." I cried harder, whimpering in pain. Whether it was physical or emotional made no difference—the sting was all the same.

"Who?" The gray eyes asked me, but someone else answered.

"Apollo." I *knew* that voice.

I felt like I had drifted off for a few seconds before I was jostled awake again. Gray eyes carried me into a bright room, placing me on a soft bed as people moved all around me. The ache started to evaporate and I spit up blood, coughing to free my throat.

"Apollo!" I shouted. Turning my head, I saw my brother. "Hudson. River."

He nodded his understanding before barking orders into his phone. I breathed deeply as a calm settled over me.

"Lucky, meet my nephew—Alexei." Gray eyes spoke as I drifted closer to my darkness.

"You! You motherfucker!" my brother growled. Things shattered and people yelled, but I didn't care.

Maybe I was dead. Maybe I was medicated. Whatever the case, I felt nothing but relief. Relief from the pain, and relief knowing that Lucky wouldn't stop searching for Apollo until he was rescued. He was too strong and too damn stubborn to die. He had to be. For me.

Someone was touching my arm and it was annoying the ever-loving-shit out of me. My side hurt, and it felt like they were pulling duct tape off my skin. My eyes were like sandpaper and I couldn't open them. I could hear people moving around me, and the hushed angry whispers of my brother. My thoughts were muddled and I couldn't understand what was wrong with me.

And then it hit me like a tsunami, the pain sweeping in like a dangerous current. Once I was in its depths, there was no freeing myself from the promise of death.

"Apollo!" I croaked, blinking a few times before I looked around at my family. "No!" Overcome by my emotions, I kept screaming.

"Sienna, calm down!" My mother was leaning over me, crying and holding my head as Al gripped my arms and pinned me down.

"Do it," my father ordered Lucky and I felt a pinch to my arm.

"We're still looking, Sienna. Sleep, sis, we'll find him." Lucky tried to sound strong, but we all knew the outcome.

I spent the next who knows how long in and out of sleep. I was either exhausted or they kept feeding me sedatives. Anytime I did open my eyes, I bombarded whoever was in the room with questions on Apollo. But it was the same each time. *They were looking. Nothing yet, but they weren't giving up.*

"If you didn't want to marry me, all you had to do was tear up the contract." A deep voice startled me awake. I blinked twice before focusing. Romano was leaning over my bed.

"Getting stabbed seemed easier," I whispered.

"You wound me." He gave me a soft smile and handed me a cup of water when I started coughing. "I have a friend that served in the Seals."

Connor Williams was a decorated retired Navy Seal, who was previously in charge of search and seizure. Apparently, he didn't end a mission until he completed what he was hired to do. Air, land or water —he always succeeded. I didn't know what to say when Romano relayed this information. How could he tell me he'd find the man I clearly desired more than him? His dark eyes held me prisoner as we sat in a relaxed silence.

"I must go." Again, he smiled down at me, dropping his lips to my forehead before disappearing through the door. I was just starting to fall into a miserable sleep when Lucky walked into the room.

"This Connor, he's already got a crew running," Lucky confirmed, walking to the window and looking out at the compound's vast gardens. "They will find him, Sienna."

"Where are we on the brothers and that little bitch?" I asked. I enjoyed watching *il diavolo* take over my brother.

"First we have another situation to discuss." Lucky called for someone to come into the room.

"Wolf." My eyes opened wide as I spoke the singular word, the large body of my savior leaning over my bed.

"My reputation precedes me." He was clearly Russian, and his gray eyes were bold against his light hair. "Nikolai Volkov."

"The Russian Wolf. I thought I was dreaming when I was being rescued by a wolf." He chuckled at my confession.

"I wanted you to officially meet my nephew. Alexei, come in." He turned towards the door.

"Take a deep breath," Lucky warned, standing at the foot of my bed with his arms crossed.

"Andersen, what are you…?" My jaw went slack.

"I promise you, Sienna, it's not what you think. *You* poached *me* from Alias Marks," Andersen—Alexei—whoever said. "When I left Russia, I rebuilt myself as Andersen Farewell."

"I believe him," Lucky muttered dryly.

"I was unaware of the connection, if that helps," the Wolf confirmed.

"No, it doesn't. Alexander was your brother? All of those conversations!" I took several deep breaths, as my brother had suggested, inhaling through the sting. "You had so many opportunities to tell me!"

"What was I supposed to say, Sienna? Once I learned what my father and brother were up to, I tried to stop them. I tried to protect you."

"Get the fuck out." I closed my eyes, the ache in my side and in my heart unbearable.

"Sienna." His voice sounded defeated, but I refused to look at him.

"I said get the fuck out!" I screamed, grunting with the pain.

"Alexei, leave," the Wolf ordered. "I told your brother, and I promise you, my nephew's intentions were good."

"We'll talk later." Lucky gestured for the Russian to exit, and those gray eyes sent me a wink before leaving.

"Now where is that whore Cassandra?" I asked, Lucky's smile returning.

"You need to rest." He laughed when I stared at him expectantly. "I guess she didn't know you were still alive because the stupid bitch didn't run. Al found her at *Hush*." He cracked his knuckles.

I hated my brother when we were younger. He was the King of the castle that I wanted for myself. However, over the years, he's earned my respect as the future leader, but more importantly as an incredible brother. We were born from the same cloth and together we would set the world on fire to protect each other.

"I am going to fucking maim that bitch." I snarled. Pushing Andersen's betrayal aside, I focused on my revenge instead.

Women were curious creatures. At heart, many were good natured, harboring the best of intentions for those around us. But then there were others—cold, deceitful little bitches—who were no more than fucking bullies. And Cassandra had fucked with the wrong bitch.

I was going to enjoy ripping her apart… piece-by-fucking-piece.

EPILOGUE
SIENNA AGOSTINO

"**D**o you need a tampon and Midol, Al?" I glared at my best friend as I stepped into my clothes. "Will that stop your emotional bitching? Because no matter what you say, this is fucking happening."

"You're talking about going after someone that almost killed you. No, I won't stop my bitching! You're still fucking limping!" Al roared, pacing my bedroom like a wild animal.

I sealed my lips because he didn't know that my mind was even worse than my body appeared. Connor and his team were still scouring the Hudson for any sign of Apollo. Each second, each minute and each hour I went without news, I lost another part of myself. That was out of my hands, but taking care of something else *was* in them.

"That's why I have you with me. You won't let me down." I smiled, wincing as my stitches on my lip pulled tight. I wasn't doing a good job of pleading my case, but it didn't matter.

I limped downstairs and into the foyer before walking out the open front door. My family stared back at me—Bella and my mother watching me closely—their pain just as palpable as my own. Not a single one of us could ignore the void *his* absence created.

Several men circled around each other, speaking in harsh low tones. I slowly moved towards them, keeping my head held high and shielding my pain with anger. My dad's eyes softened, but Marco and Lucky shared murderous glares at the sight of my disheveled appearance.

Connor was the only one to offer me a smile. The few visits he'd made to give me updates were... interesting, to say the least. He had a cocky yet flirtatious personality that made me laugh. It was like he didn't know how to take himself seriously. On my worst days, he sat with me and told me stories about a red-headed spitfire named Em that he was trying to tame. But his efforts seemed futile.

Strange, strange man.

"What's up, baby sis?" The Seal's jaw was sharp and angular, and it gave him a hardened edge. But his smile was playful. "Are you ready for this?"

"Yes." I ground out my response, and he jumped right into discussing our plan.

We piled into the SUV and took off for the club. My little brother was on one side, Lucky the other, while Connor and Al sat up front. I grabbed Marco's hand and squeezed it. His blue eyes turned to me, filled with an anger and with a weight I'd never seen on him.

"He warned me and I didn't listen," Marco muttered. "Apollo. He told me I needed to be better and I didn't listen."

The sting inflicted upon hearing *his* name threatened to break my resolve. I coughed past the lump in my throat and squeezed my brother's hand again. Every member of this family was battling with the unknown status of our best friend. Of my love.

"Tessa is missing. No one has seen her, heard from her, nothing. Her apartment door was open... there were signs of a struggle." He froze for another moment. "Apollo told me people always watch for weakness, and if he noticed that Tessa had been around more than once, so would someone who wanted to hurt us."

My little brother was finally growing up, but it wasn't in the way any of us wanted. He was hurting, his position in the family affecting someone he cared for. He was a lovesick puppy more often than not, but that girl was clearly special to him. No matter how short their *relationship*—a term I used loosely—Marco cared for her.

"Fuck this. I'm not waiting anymore," I growled, sliding off the leather seat and closing the door behind me.

"Goddamn it, Sienna!" Marco growled back, before grabbing my arm to stop me. "You're staying put and I will get answers."

We entered through the backdoor of *Hush* and I was guided into an office. The room was a neutral, muted gray with a large desk in the center that was covered in loose papers. I leaned my back against it, sitting on my hands to keep them still.

"Wait here," Marco barked, locking the door behind him.

There was a round clock hanging on the wall and every second that ticked by, I shook a little more. My adrenaline and my strength were fueled by pure hatred. I couldn't think past my turmoil and I wanted *her* to feel it. *Ten-fold*. The rattling of the lock refocused my attention. Cracking my neck from side to side, I waited.

"You've got to be fucking kidding me." It seemed to be my new favorite catch-phrase. Staring at the figure that walked into the room, I was at a loss for more words. My need for retribution, and the promise of enacting it against Cassandra, somehow turned into sitting in a car on my way to get answers; it was the story I hadn't been prepared to unfold.

The long hallway inside reeked of mildew, like it had bad air circulation or something; even though it led to an open room filled with desks, shuffled paperwork and computers. Several uniformed police officers watched silently as we stopped in front of a closed door. I was ushered into a tan room with a table and two chairs.

What made me falter was the man that was handcuffed to the metal furniture. Gio Moretti stared back at me, his smile dropping as he took in my battered face. He was a tall and lean man, but now that he wasn't wearing his signature suit, I could see just how toned his arms were. He boasted thick muscles, covered in a light smattering of dark hair and threatening to shred his orange prison jumpsuit.

"Even bruised you look incredible, Sienna." He motioned for me to sit. "I'm surprised this stupid bitch got you here."

"And why exactly am I here, Gio?" I asked, genuinely confused by what was happening.

"I wanted you to hear everything from me before the story got distorted by stupid little girls." He snarled at my escort before looking back to me. "My little brother has been chasing at my coattails since before his balls dropped. Everyone loves to think I am the *idiota* of my family. But they're wrong. My father was the biggest idiot, Dominic not too far behind." Pausing, he demanded, "Give us the room."

I glanced away from his intense gaze to the armed officer, nodding at the unspoken question. Another man sat behind Gio in the corner, playing on his phone and paying us little mind. I noticed that he didn't move to leave with the others.

I wanted—no, I needed answers. He was the one that caused all of this, every bad thing that had happened. It was time I got my piece before my family took theirs.

The door opened to reveal Dominic Moretti handcuffed at the wrist, a metal chain around his waist and connecting his arms to his feet. His eyes narrowed in and focused on only one person in the room, the same individual who had escorted me here. The venomous look he imposed sent unwanted chills running down my back, and the cold room felt like it dropped ten degrees along with it.

"Seems my brother's little pet has ruined us both," Gio laughed. "Oh, sweet Sienna."

When Gio opened his mouth again, the shit that he spewed out was so shocking it almost didn't seem real. But once he started, the fucker didn't stop. It was like a river of truths and unparalleled plotting. My jaw dropped and when he finished, I had no clue what to say.

What could you say when someone told you they created an empire built off the pain of others? What could you say when they told you they gave up everything to protect *you*, destroying all they'd amassed? I didn't know what was up and what was down anymore.

"All of this was your own doing. Do you want me to offer a thank you? Because you won't get one." My brazenness only made him smile.

Dominic Moretti thought he'd shielded himself enough to keep his nose clean, but Gio had covered all of his bases. When the FBI came knocking down his door, he sent them right over to his brother. The entire male line of the Moretti family had been erased in one tactical move made by the *idiot,* eldest son.

How fucking wrong all of us had been…

"Will you watch after Bella? Your brother seems capable, but we do stupid things for love."

"Like?" I couldn't help poking the bear.

"Like damning yourself to the firing squad for a woman that merely tolerates you." He paused, the room filling with a strange emotion. "Anyway, I'll get out eventually."

"How?" I asked, to which he started laughing.

"I have my ways. And because I'm me. I didn't make it this far for some little tart in a skirt to destroy me. The evidence they have is circumstantial at best." He looked towards the door. "Did they find him?"

His sudden question snapped my focus back to him. I shook my head, my eyes filling with tears. "Fuck. Me. All this time, I was worried about Philly when it was never Romano at all, was it? Shit, I didn't see that one coming." He started laughing harder.

Leaning over the table, I allowed all of the grief and anger coursing through me to land in a solid punch to his nose. My knuckles snapped in pain and he grunted as blood poured from his nasal cavity. I stood tall, my tears now dry, as bubbling rage seeped over and obscured my limited patience.

"I hope they lock you up and throw away the key. If you ever do get out, I'll fucking destroy you if you come for me," I hissed. Turning my back on him, I walked towards the exit.

"Don't tease me, baby! That threat only makes me want to work harder to get out of here!" And I kept walking as his obnoxious laughter lessened and the door closed behind me.

"Did you get what you needed?" I asked, the moment I crossed the threshold.

"No, unfortunately. Civil liberties and all that nonsense. That was his attorney in the room with you." The supposed tart in a skirt responded with a shake of her head.

Fuck me, they couldn't legally record the confession he'd just made.

"Fucking slick bastard." I laughed, because otherwise, I'd cry.

I returned to the SUV, glancing over at our driver. His thermal shirt was rolled at the sleeves, and his olive complexion had me curious.

"*Parli Italiano?*" I asked. His mouth twitched but he remained silent.

His exposed arms allowed me to see the Italian thorn tattooed on his forearm. It had writing that wrapped around it, but I couldn't read it from that distance. I had seen it before, on someone else. But who? I couldn't remember. Something was off—though I couldn't put my finger on it—and as we pulled up to the hotel, I'd run out of time to ask.

I arrived through the main entrance and stopped to stare at the patrons milling about. The bar near the lobby was buzzing and the elevators were coming and going, everyone moving about their day. This city was my home and these people were enjoying it like I never had before. Unwilling to see the bad in the city, they thrived off being *normal.* Well, who the fuck wants to be normal?

I was goddamn Sienna Agostino and this fucking bitch was about to meet her worst fucking nightmare. You didn't take what was mine and not have a very, very painful death coming for you.

"He took care of you!" Al roared, pacing in front of the chair the girl was strapped to. For some odd reason, a sense of calm washed over me as I watched her.

Most of my family and Lucky's men were present, standing in various positions around the room. Cassandra's nose looked broken; blood trailed down her chin and onto her lap while Bella cradled her right hand to her chest. I smirked knowingly at my sister-in-law, of course she'd taken her revenge on that cunt's face.

"I-I'm sorry, okay? They made me do it! They threatened my mom!" She cried out her lies with an incredible performance, that is until she saw me.

"If I recall correctly, which of course I do, you wanted to *hit him where it hurts*. Correct? You even laughed and smiled down at my bruised and bleeding body when you said it." I stared at her, the coldness of the room rivaling my demeanor.

"I had nothing left b-but my mom! They threatened her until I acted like… like… I enjoyed the idea of hurting people." She looked to the floor, her body rattling with exaggerated sobs and the kind of tears brought on by self-pity, because she had been caught, and not because of her own actions which led to that plight.

"You're fucking dead. Say your piece, bitch, because it's the last thing you'll ever do." Removing my jacket, I cracked my neck from side to side.

I was no longer standing in a basement that smelled like bleach, rusty tools and decay. I resigned myself to the fact that I was changing inside and out, demanding justice for the man who was so cruelly taken from me. And with those thoughts, I was transported back to *that* day.

"You fucked up." He growled, biting the flawless skin on my neck —that perfect spot just under the ear. "I warned you to stop these games. Fuck. Me. You truly are ruinously beautiful... I just don't know who it is that will be ruined beyond reparation. You. Or me."

The answer was me… He ruined *me* that day. I always thought women were weak when they said they fell for a man and everything changed. It was only fair to lose a part of yourself in the game of love, if you took something of theirs at the same time. For me, for us, we both lost parts of ourselves. And Apollo, he may not have noticed it until the very end, but I took his love—the very thing he never thought existed.

"I'm going to fucking enjoy this." Then I cocked my arm back and swung.

EPILOGUE
MARIO AGOSTINO

If I were a proud man, I'd struggle with admitting that I let my family down. But in so many unbearable ways I had. I wanted my children to have everything that I had fought so hard to accomplish. I came from nothing, moved to a new country for a fresh start. I had twenty-five dollars in my pocket, holes in both my shoes, a cocky personality and a mean right hook.

I lied, cheated and stole to survive. Then, once I was able to tread above water, I used my brain and the muscles behind it to shake down the rich. I used the proceeds to build up neighborhoods for immigrants like myself. Little Italy was a dream I'd had, an image I wanted to create for my children.

In life, there were many hitches and mine happened to be my appetite for success. The skies the limit, I would fight to my death to own this city. So, I created an empire in which my children were starting to take over.

Success was arduous and came with a heavy price tag. One that I was currently paying as I watched my oldest daughter take out her grief and anguish on the face of her foe. Sienna was always my favorite. I knew parents weren't supposed to admit that, but I saw so much of myself in her. The moment she learned the kingdom was meant for a boy, she fought like hell to create her own. Which she did, flawlessly.

Whatever she decided to do, she threw herself in headfirst. Just like she did when I pushed Philly on her. It wasn't because I was so adamant that she needed to be wed—fuck the mafia stereotypes. It was because I watched her—day in and day out—fawning over a man that just couldn't comprehend what it meant to be loved and to give love.

It was no fault of his own that he'd spent his youth fighting to survive insurmountable abuse and trauma. I tried seeking help for him but every doctor told me it was too late. There was only so much "rehabilitation" a person could complete when they were damaged goods. Rehabilitation meant restoring and rebuilding, but the kid was never given the foundation nor the coping skills in order to accomplish such a feat.

I replaced his anger with the voice of broken children; the souls no one would save. He created *il mietitore* to vent his rage, to destroy those that deserved it—he was the defender of the weak.

It broke me a little more each day, watching her create new ways to get his attention. She deserved the world and *settling* for a man—one that none of us thought capable of loving her—wasn't good enough.

It wasn't until that day in my office, right before Sienna was taken, that I realized how badly I'd fucked up. He was a loyal soldier. A loyal son to me because of what I'd taught him to harness. If I would've just sat him down and talked to him about why *he* was worthy of love, then maybe this wouldn't have happened. If I hadn't pushed her to Philly, maybe he'd still be here.

I had no idea how things had gone off the tracks so quickly and so terribly. For once in my life, my decisions were haunting me—making me doubt myself and how to repair my family. We were the Agostino's, a resounding threat to anyone who dared come for us. But how did we start rebuilding ourselves to overcome our biggest downfall, our hearts.

Mine broke for my eldest daughter, her pain visibly manifested by the blood soaking her skin.

It broke for my eldest son, holding his new wife so tightly to his chest; he was petrified of losing her, just like he had his best friend.

It broke for my younger boy, who having always struggled to take this life seriously, now realized his actions had the potential to hurt someone else—that French girl he had grown fond of.

And finally, my heart broke for the most innocent of us all, the sweetest soul. I had forced Octavia away, putting her in lockdown until it was safe, because I was scared. I was scared that her heart was far too soft for the destruction I saw as imminent. Soon I would marry her off to a rising politician to get her away from all of this permanently. I'd do anything to keep her safe.

My phone started ringing, snapping me from my thoughts. It was a number I didn't recognize, so I ignored the call. I turned back to Sienna—her inner turmoil palpable while her rage was dwindling.

"She's dead, Sienna..." Bella muttered, urging Lucky to stop his sister.

Sienna had zoned out; I'd bet she didn't even realize she was holding a knife in her hand. All of this was so normal to me—to my family. And it made me sick to realize I deserved the pain they were forced to bear. And they didn't. A father shouldn't sit idly by while his daughter mauls another woman, as his family watches. But I had, and I was happy this bitch was dead. Now we just needed to bring Apollo home.

We all turned as footsteps echoed and a shadow descended into the basement. I saw Sienna pivot, her eyes filled with the hope of who it could be and quickly deflating when she realized it wasn't. Connor Williams stepped towards the family, his face an empty mask.

"We found him..." he muttered, each of us holding our breath to learn the truth, to learn if Apollo was dead or alive. My phone buzzed again—the same unknown number lighting up the screen.

"Yeah?" I growled.

"Hello, Mr. Agostino." An altered, machine-like voice greeted me. "I'm curious. Have you accounted for all of your children?"

I stared back at three out of my four offspring, annoyed this call was interrupting our news. Everything went silent when a second voice came screaming from the other end of the line. It was so loud and stricken that everyone else in the room heard it too.

"What did I do? P-Please. Why am I here? What have I done?" Octavia cried out in pure terror.

"Perhaps you aren't here because of your own actions." The man on the phone answered back. "Maybe, it's the sins of your father that have dropped you at my door."

"Don't hurt her!" I barked into the receiver.

"I was raised by simple rules, Mr. Agostino," he stated dryly. "Eye for an eye, tooth for a fucking tooth. You hurt my family... I am going to *enjoy* destroying yours."

The phone clattered, as if it were dropped, and the footsteps were walking away. Octavia started screaming all over again, except this time it wasn't from fear... her cries were pain-induced. My little girl was being hurt as retribution for something I had done.

Many of my wrongs over the years flashed through my mind. It would be impossible to pinpoint—on one hand alone—which exactly it could be. That thought, the sheer volume alone, made me sick. I looked around the room to the terror-filled faces of the people I loved and dropped to my knees, defeated by the realization that I had been the cause of all of their suffering.

I would find Octavia and offer myself in her place. I'd die happily for anyone of them. Sienna was crying harder and I couldn't tell from any of their faces if Apollo had been found alive or not. Everyone was talking—their mouths were moving—but I couldn't hear a damn thing.

White noise replaced my consciousness and I tasted blood. We were coming, Octavia. Don't fear, we were going to destroy those who were brazen enough to take you. After all, what was one more sin added to a lifetime of perpetual damnation anyway?

TO BE CONTINUED...

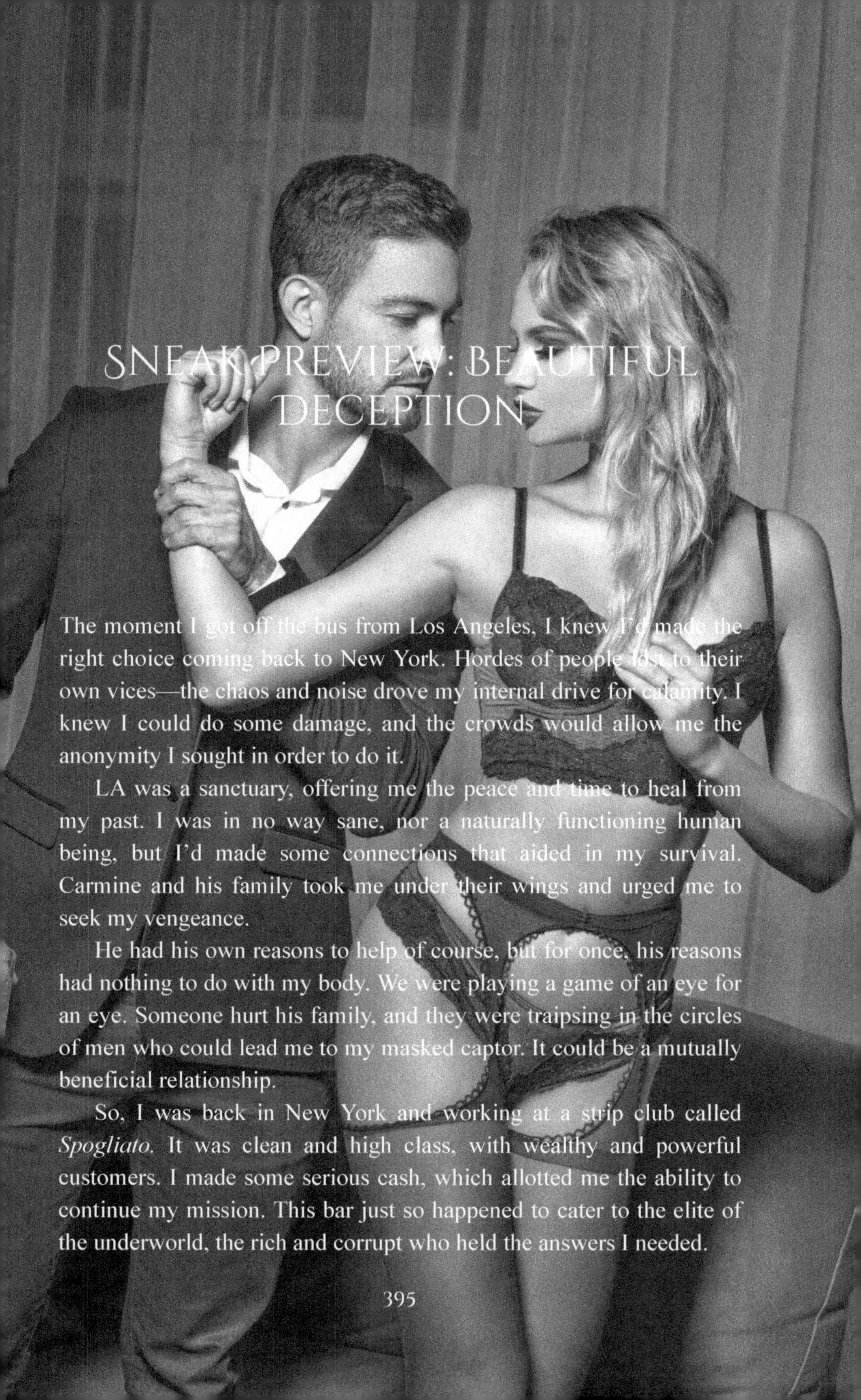

SNEAK PREVIEW: BEAUTIFUL DECEPTION

The moment I got off the bus from Los Angeles, I knew I'd made the right choice coming back to New York. Hordes of people lost to their own vices—the chaos and noise drove my internal drive for calamity. I knew I could do some damage, and the crowds would allow me the anonymity I sought in order to do it.

LA was a sanctuary, offering me the peace and time to heal from my past. I was in no way sane, nor a naturally functioning human being, but I'd made some connections that aided in my survival. Carmine and his family took me under their wings and urged me to seek my vengeance.

He had his own reasons to help of course, but for once, his reasons had nothing to do with my body. We were playing a game of an eye for an eye. Someone hurt his family, and they were traipsing in the circles of men who could lead me to my masked captor. It could be a mutually beneficial relationship.

So, I was back in New York and working at a strip club called *Spogliato*. It was clean and high class, with wealthy and powerful customers. I made some serious cash, which allotted me the ability to continue my mission. This bar just so happened to cater to the elite of the underworld, the rich and corrupt who held the answers I needed.

I chose this place because it was owned by the eldest Moretti son. I planned to use him to get a lead and take him down with the rest of the scum. I just hadn't planned on one thing: the fact that he was pure, raw sex, wrapped up in a pleasing package comparable to that of an Italian god.

Dom Moretti was the picture of control, power, and dirty, dirty sex.

His face was all hard angles, and his body was perfectly sculpted under his button-up shirts; even his suit pants pulled tight to his firm ass. He made me want to crawl on my hands and knees, begging for the smallest taste. He exuded masculinity and discipline, the type of ownership that was capable of harnessing my demons.

One taste, and he turned into an addiction I couldn't shake. His intendance helped me in all the ways I was unable to help myself. Little did I know that the chase for his hard dick would take me down the battered, broken road it did.

Because nothing in my life could ever be simple. Or kind.

The door opened and light poured into the room, forcing me to blink several times. Dom walked inside with all the swagger of a man swinging something heavy between his legs and a million dollars in his pocket—both of which he possessed. Stepping up to my cage, he dropped to a squat in front of me—a silent stare down as I waited for his command.

"Are we ready to try some freedom today?" he asked me, his voice dark and edgy, yet filled with such dominance, and my body thrummed to life.

"Yes, sir." I grinned back as his eyes filled with suspicion.

I loved to push his buttons. The thrill of my disobedience appeased my inner monster threatening to break loose. He helped me manage the ever-present darkness. Under his command, I could think normally and maintain a semblance of a functioning life—the key that locked my vault and kept the demons at bay.

Well, as normal as one could be under the thumb of a trafficker. Yeah, I was the girl on the arm of a man suspected of being the east coast's most powerful skin peddler. He would calm my demons and give me the answers I'd been hunting for.

"Get dressed." The harsh scream of the metal bar echoed in my mind.

My room had black walls with a dark red carpet and satin everything—expensive clothing and jewels completed the aesthetic. One side was the wealth he gifted me, the other was the pain and control he brandished.

"Persephone. You try the patience of a saint. Get the fuck in the car," Dom growled from the bottom of the staircase.

I may be a glutton for punishment, but even I struggled to maintain a calm heart when Dom lost his patience. Sometimes, no matter what I did, it wasn't good enough for him. The man loved two things: influence and... *his sister.* No one could compare to Mirabella Moretti—she practically hung the moon.

It was borderline disconcerting, the way he spoke of her.

The SUV was idling outside of Dom's mansion as I exited the front door. This was my home—at times my prison—and Dom refused to share me with just anyone. I was his top earner at *Spogliato,* and what he liked to bury himself deep inside of at home.

"Sit. Now." He pointed to the seat beside him.

"Do you like?" I ask, motioning down the length of my outfit.

My black pencil skirt was tight, showcasing my slender frame. I paired it with a black lace bralette, a white-gold diamond necklace, and his favorite red-soled stilettos. My blonde hair was left long down my back with a slight curl, and my makeup was simple: black eyeliner to accentuate my blue eyes.

"Business casual?" he asked, depositing his phone back into the pocket of his jacket.

My smile was my answer. I shifted slightly, letting the slit of the skirt ride up my thigh while barely covering my panty-less state. His eyes burned with hunger as he watched the movement; his calloused hand grabbed my thigh and squeezed hard enough to bruise. Gripping my chin with the other, he forced me to look into his eyes. The man before me changed in an instant—the hunger replaced with a menacing darkness.

"No panties, hm? Is this your attempt to distract me?" Dom stared into my eyes, not needing my response. "I give you a chance at freedom, and yet you push my semblance of restraint *the moment* I let you out of the house." He growled with such ferocity; my thighs slammed together to allay some of my desire.

His palm, still on my thigh, tightened with my movement. His dark brown hair made his smooth olive complexion seem more caramel in color. His honey eyes turned dark—the deepest shade possible. This was the Dom that I craved. I felt whole, not like I was falling apart at the seams.

Licking my lips, I stared back at him—brown eyes to blue— begging him to make a move... taunting him. On a growl, Dom's free hand wrapped around my neck and tugged me closer, while the other continued its impenetrable grip, awkwardly pinning me to the seat. He squeezed my throat, closing off my airways with a delicious tenacity that should cause me pain but instead heightened my desire.

"You see, my little pet, I know your game. You're thinking of all the ways you could be punished, begging me for it. But I let you out of that cage to show you it's time to harness that inner demon." He didn't ease his grip on my throat, my face turning blue as my insides reveled in the delicious torment. "You will behave, then I will deal with you at home."

He released my neck, and I gulped in copious amounts of air. I stared back at him hungrily, my body having released additional endorphins and forcing me to writhe in need. His hand on my thigh pinned me in place as I pleaded to squirm—trying to gain control of myself.

"Fuck it." He growled suddenly, maneuvering me beneath him. "You beg me to punish you when you can't control yourself. Yet, you make me lose *my* control." With softness I almost didn't believe he could possess, he wiped a stray piece of hair from my face. His hand was still on my neck—holding me down—and his knee was bent on the seat to keep my legs apart.

"I'm sorry," I muttered softly, my body melting under his strong embrace.

"Don't lie. There isn't a sorry part of that delectable little body. Not now, but there will be when we get home," he promised.

Pulling out his dick—long and heavy—his eyes turned glacial as I licked my lips. He snarled his response as he grabbed his hard length and slammed inside me. I screamed at the contact, my insides soaking wet and moving to conform to his size. No matter how many times this man fucked me (we didn't make love, or have sex even; we fucked… and hard) his girth still took me by surprise.

My pristine pencil skirt was shoved up against my stomach—and I'm pretty sure I lost a shoe—as he folded me like a pretzel, fitting awkwardly on the back seat. His large, solid frame assaulted me with thrust after angry thrust, his rage increasing my pleasure and making me teeter on the edge of bliss.

"Don't you fucking come. Not yet, Persephone." His breath came in sharp pants. My body was tempted to disobey and take the final lunge off the cliff of nirvana… but his face warned against it. "Fuck." He brought my leg higher, lifting my ass in the air as he pounded into me, my shoulders imprinting on the seat.

"Oh, fuck." My breathing sounded strange as my body contorted against his maddening assault.

"Now. Fuck. Me. Come." Our shouting as we climaxed together threatened to shatter the windows.

The insanity within my head finally reduced enough that I could breathe again. It's hard to explain, and it's never made sense to me until I met Dom. The need for chaos was always lurking under my skin, threatening to break loose, to appease my need for revenge. I couldn't harness my hold on my own sanity, and my mind often sent me to unstable places.

The door on the vault shook as all my secrets swirled inside, chaotic like rain ready to burst from a cloud.

Dom's restraint, his grip on both my metaphorical and physical leash, took that choice away. I couldn't run free without his approval. It's sick—definitely fucked up to admit—but making sense of my reality for other people wasn't my concern.

After years of seeking help, only two things have worked. One: I allowed myself the chance to seek my revenge with no manner of blood spared. Two: Dom's unique ability to harness my inner beast.

"Fuck. Me," Dom muttered, tucking himself back into his pants.

I laughed at him. "Ready so soon?" I twisted in my seat and began adjusting my own clothes.

"Look at me." He grabbed my chin, forcing my gaze to his. I blinked a few times under his scrutiny, feeling my head clear. "There she is." He smiled lightly, kissing my forehead, before he released me and reached down to hand me my discarded heel.

I took a deep breath. I'd been adrift for what felt like days. Dom had brought me to a meeting and I—well, I lost it, destroying their operation from the inside out.

I've been stuck in my own head since.

"Persephone," Dom barked, snapping me out of my reverie. "Fix yourself and let's go." I adjusted my bralette and made sure my skirt was in place before sliding out of the vehicle.

"Sir." I smirked as Dom checked me out before turning to the older gentleman.

"Mr. Moretti, nice to see you again." Dom's realtor reached out a chubby hand.

"Hello." Dom shook the proffered palm and tugged me behind him when the man went to reach for me. "Shall we?" Dom urged him forward, but I didn't miss the realtor's repugnant glances.

I couldn't help but smile at Dom's actions. I took the stage at *Spogliato* every Friday night, eight o'clock sharp. He'd watch from above the platform in his glass office as I danced for him, pushing his buttons as I crawled across the elevated flooring while allowing men a closer look. It was all a game—the push and pull between us—one neither of us would be the winner if we kept toeing this dangerous line.

The realtor wandered the large warehouse with adjoining offices, going over specs, pricing, and other monotonous details. Dom and his business partner, John, needed a larger space for their enterprise—away from prying eyes.

"Does it have private access to the water anywhere?" I attempted to confirm.

None of it sat right with me, but we all had our parts to play.

Dom continued to speak to the salesman, shaking hands before we went separate ways. I could feel the anger radiating from beside me.

We walked to the waiting SUV, his grip still wrapped around my bicep. I was holding a fist at my side; my jaw was closed tight. I stared at the concrete in front of me to avoid saying anything else. Dom yanked me onto the sidewalk, hiding us behind the idling car.

"What the fuck did I tell you?" Dom growled from within an inch of my face. "I took you out of your cage to test your training. And you, my little pet, you failed… pathetically. I told you I didn't want you involved, and you just had to, didn't you?" He was referring to my question about the water.

I could feel eyes on us. I didn't have to see anyone to know when someone was watching me. Call it a sixth sense I'd picked up when I was a child, but it was always accurate. I'd seen the car pull up across the way, driving into the Agostino owned lot. I don't know who *he* was at the moment, but he was watching silently, and it was annoying me.

"I didn't do anything wrong." My voice was strong with an undertone of annoyance.

But each word was like a slap to Dom's face as he growled in displeasure before throwing me against the car. My svelte frame bounced off the unrelenting metal—flying forward. Dom grabbed me by the neck and pinned me to the car.

"Nothing wrong." He snarled in my face, my own agitation instigating a mental shutdown. "Try, you didn't do a fucking-thing-right." He slapped me lightly across the face, snapping me back into the now.

"I'm sorry," I lied. I wasn't sorry, not in the least.

"We all have our roles in this world, Persephone. And if you don't watch your back, I'll change yours very *fucking* quickly." Dom was always quick to remind me, as if I didn't already know. Shoving me away from him, he straightened his tie in the metal's reflection. "Get in the fucking car."

I stumbled backwards as he sat inside and slammed the door. Staying close to the fence posts lining the adjacent property, I addressed our onlooker, still lurking in the shrubbery, before inviting him to the club so I could play with him.

I could sense a foreboding danger lingering under the skin of that one. Whoever he was, he was loaded with a darkness not much unlike my own. Except I let mine out to play in different, *positive* ways.

I positioned myself in the SUV, and it pulled away the moment my door closed. Dom was already on his phone, displeased with whomever was on the other end. "I have more pressing matters than to attend your luncheon. I will come see Bella once my business has concluded," Dom stated angrily to the caller.

"Dom, be there and do not be late. End of discussion." A voice boomed from the receiver.

"We had a guest," I said as soon as the call ended.

"We did, indeed," he confirmed with a sigh, tapping out a text. "Take us to Vino," he ordered the driver.

Yeah, he'd seen him too. And we didn't play well with others.

"A sexy luncheon, sir?" I licked my lips in anticipation. His phone rang, stopping him from answering me.

"Hey, unknown suspect overheard Perse and me, nothing meaningful," he said to his partner, John—I presumed. "Okay, I have to meet my father at Vino. Yeah, Bella is home." My spine straightened at the mention of the Moretti daughter and her presence back on US soil.

"Am I invited to meet the infamous sister?" I whispered, skimming my fingertips up his thigh to grab his growing erection. His hand struck out—quickly stopping my exploration—his grip tight and painful.

"I will send Persephone home with the car. Can you meet her there and lock her down for me?" he asked John, smirking at my annoyance.

"Fuck." I growled and sunk back down into my seat.

"John will meet you. Be a good girl until I get back." Dom tugged me forward for a chaste kiss, pulling away much too quickly. I grabbed his neck, yanking him back to me while trying to deepen the kiss but he halted the gesture.

"I want you," I whispered, licking his lips and enjoying his taste as it exploded on my tongue.

"My pet, aren't we insatiable today? Have I not given you enough attention?" Dom mocked me with vicious intentions.

"Never. And you could give me a little extra since you're sending me to my room like a little kid," I glowered, and his handsome face lit up in response.

"Sorry, my pet, I have things to do and no time for you to be one of them." His laughter only pissed me off more.

"I'm sure it's the first refusal of many to come," I muttered to myself, but Dom heard it, his angered expression thrusting back into my line of sight.

"What's that, pet?" He grabbed my chin roughly. "Don't fuck with me and these little jealous tantrums. Are you forgetting your role here? Do I need to send you away?" The asshole raised his phone in the air.

"Enjoy your lunch," I conceded, staring straight ahead.

"John is waiting for you at home to put you in your cage. I think this freedom today was too much for you." Then the bastard kissed me on the nose before exiting the car. "I'd say behave yourself, but I know you won't. So, Gabriel is here to ensure you make it home." He stepped aside and one of his guards clambered in.

"Seat belt," the guy spat his directive at me as Dom closed the door. When I didn't immediately jump to do his bidding, he abrasively shoved me onto the interior. Reaching across, he tugged on the belt and strapped me in.

I stared out the window, glaring at Dom through the tinted glass as he stood on the sidewalk waiting. The patriarch, Anthony Moretti—I assumed, since I've never met any of Dom's family—emerged from the limo first with his back to me. And next, I suspected, was his eldest son, Gio.

Then I saw her, the woman I'd heard about—incessantly—since Dom first took me. *Mirabella Moretti.*

She had long raven locks that stretched down her back, her body lithe and feminine as she moved in her designer dress and heels. She was gorgeous and twice as sweet—or so I'd been told.

Dom checked up on her while she was away in Italy. Apparently, he had concern over their father's plans for her future. I felt such pity for the girl, as she'd presumably be married off to someone rich to live the life of a doting housewife!

Sarcasm.

We sat there, watching Dom lovingly pull his sister into his embrace. "What the fuck are you waiting for? Go!" I yelled, my babysitter laughing at my expense.

"Jealous?" Gabriel prompted. "She is a hot little piece of ass." He gave her a vulgar appraisal before adjusting himself in his seat.

I cackled, observing how he grew uncomfortable when I didn't stop. Dom tapped the window, motioning for the driver to go, as I kept up my hysterics. He didn't look back as he followed his sister inside, no second thoughts about dismissing me.

"Crazy. Fucking. Bitch," Gabriel said, enunciating each word.

I taunted him, reminding him of all the ways Dom would torture him, should he learn of his disrespect towards Mirabella. I couldn't rein in my laughter as I watched the terrifying realization settle over his features. With no preamble, he cocked back a meaty fist—effectively busting open my lip—as he threatened me to silence.

"And now you're a dead man." My laughter continued as I held my head in my hands. I stared at him sideways from under my veil of hair, watching in jubilation as his slow mind wrapped around what happened.

"Not my fault you tried to run away," he ground out, his words dripping with acid.

"Did I, Norm?" I asked the driver, who stared back in the rearview. His head shook in response, much to Gabriel's dismay.

The car pulled up outside of Dom's mansion, and John was standing on the front porch awaiting my arrival. I may be headed inside to be locked up, but at least I wasn't counting down the hours until my death. Opening my door, John went to help me out of the car but stopped short. My brain was fuzzy, and I couldn't instruct my fingers to unbuckle my belt.

He pulled my hair from my face, as his gentle hands tucked it behind my ear. His eyes switched almost immediately—from kindness to fury—as he took in my appearance. I tried to smile but winced, swallowing back the bile rising in my throat from the force of the impact.

"Norm, do you mind taking Miss Persephone to her room? Please ensure her *cage* is appropriately locked before you leave." He helped me out of the car, handing me off to Norm's soft embrace.

"Easy now," Norm cajoled, guiding me into the house as my temples pounded.

Fucker may've given me a concussion. My stomach twisted with nausea, and my head was thrumming behind my eyes. We made it into my room—the sounds of the metal scrapping against metal alerting me to our entrance—then sweet, sweet darkness took over just as the cold flooring settled into my bones.

ALSO BY DAHLIA REIGN

<u>Agostino Crime Family Series</u>

Contracted to the Devil: Book One

Clever as the Devil: Book Two

Beautiful Deception: Book Three

And Twice as Twisted: Book Four

<u>La Reina de Escorpiones Duet</u>

Infinite Sorrow: Book One

Endless Deceit: Book Two

www.TheDahliaReign.com

About the Author

Corporate sales by day, closet romance novelist at night—Dahlia Reign has always had an unparalleled taste for dreamy alpha-men. In her youth, Dahlia had journals by the stacks that she used to jot down her innermost thoughts; subsequently, turning them into romantic stories. Now, years later and with her picturesque alpha-man at her side, she's taken the literary world by storm. Her man, her pittie and an overactive imagination mixed with her bleeding heart—she's set off to tell the world her stories. Buck up and grab a bandaid, shit's about to get heavy.

facebook.com/authordahliareign

instagram.com/authordahliareign

tiktok.com/@authordahliareign